"WHEELER IS A MASTER CREATOR OF CHARAC-TERS—A STAND-OUT PERFORMER."

—Dale Walker,
El Paso Herald-Post

"Richard Wheeler's novels of the old west transport the reader straight back to that fabled era: you intimately know the territory, the people, the times. If you haven't yet trav-elled into the past with Wheeler, do so now!"

—Marcia Muller,
author of *WHERE ECHOES LIVE*

"WHEELER NOW JOINS THE RANKS OF LARRY McMURTRY, GLENDON SWARTHOUT, TONY HIL-LERMAN AND DOROTHY JOHNSON."

—*Billings Gazette*

"From the moment I read his first novel, *WINTER GRASS*, I've been a fan of Richard Wheeler's writing. What he does better than most is consistently, book after exciting book, draw his memorable characters with bold bigger-than-life strokes. Already a master at pacing and story, Wheeler lends his magic touch to exploring the little-known dynamics of an entire era with sensitivity rarely seen in today's writing on the opening of the West."

—Terry C. Johnston,
award-winning author of
THE PLAINSMAN series

"*BADLANDS* is a wonderful classic, so vivid and pow-erful you'll be slapping the dust from your jeans. This is a novel which will delight, charm and inform. Wheeler breathes life and soul into his characters, taking the reader under their skin. If you have any interest in America and its marvelous heritage, this book is for you."

—W. Michael & Kathleen Gear,
authors of *PEOPLE OF THE EARTH*
and *PEOPLE OF THE RIVER*

By Richard S. Wheeler
from Tom Doherty Associates

BADLANDS

RICHARD S. WHEELER

TOR

A TOM DOHERTY ASSOCIATES BOOK
NEW YORK

This is a work of fiction. All the characters and events portrayed in this book are fictitious, and any resemblance to real people or events is purely coincidental.

BADLANDS

Copyright © 1992 by Richard S. Wheeler

Cover art by Darrell Sweet

A Tor Book
Published by Tom Doherty Associates, LLC
175 Fifth Avenue
New York, NY 10010

www.tor.com

Tor® is a registered trademark of Tom Doherty Associates, LLC.

ISBN: 0-812-51997-3

First edition: August 1992

Printed in the United States of America

0 9 8 7 6 5 4

To Barbara Beman Puechner,
for everything.

Acknowledgments

I am deeply indebted to two anthropologists, my friends W. Michael Gear and Kathleen O'Neal Gear, for supplying me with valuable research materials; and for their criticism and encouragement. I am also indebted to Faith Bad Bear, curator at the Museum of the Plains Indian, Cody, Wyoming, for her detailed and illuminating explanation of the relationship between Indian artifacts and their spirit owners. And also to my gifted editor, Robert Gleason, who knew how to make it work.

CHAPTER
1

Candace Jane Matilda Huxtable wished she had loosened her corset before stepping off the edge of the world. The trouble was that man Van Vliet. Every time he peered at her from the mottled ruin of his face she had the impulse to flee to her cabin and tighten it.

A corset had always been a comfort. The fine baleen whalebone stays had armored her against the world, pinched a waist that didn't need pinching, and stiffened her back into a model of British dignity. The stays, snugged into the layered linen of the corset, were faintly visible through her summery nankeen, a caution to the others who stood there on the hot bank of the Missouri River waiting for the deckhands to unload all their cargo.

Behind her, sweating deckmen eased the wagons down the wobbly stage from the deck of the *Spread Eagle* to the arid bank. The white boat rocked in the muddy water, hissing steam from its escapement and belching smoke, a live monster eager to thrash the river again with its great side paddles.

The others in the group eyed her with dismay. Professor

Wood's stare was frosty, but J. Roderick Crabtree seemed to be faintly amused. She wasn't even one of them, although her father had been. They hadn't invited her. The Smithsonian Institution hadn't funded her. And worst of all, she was an unmarried woman in a wild land where women shouldn't be.

She ignored that: she'd show them soon enough she could do field work as well as any male. She didn't expect a hearty welcome and a toast, but she'd come anyway no matter what they thought about it. Her father, Cecil Henry Huxtable—professor of natural history at Trinity College—would have smiled, given his blessing, and utterly disapproved. Knighthood had come only months before he'd died, a sudden recognition by Her Majesty. But ultimately, his reputation, his enduring honor in the history of mankind, would rest not on knighthood, but on Candace, who intended to complete his work.

Nothing had surprised Candace so far except the guide, Rufus Crowe. She'd expected a lean ruffian in fringed animal skins, a weatherbeaten, sun-blackened, scragglebearded, mean-eyed child of nature. Instead she found a slightly fleshy man in a worn tweed jacket that was leather-patched at the elbows; a man with even white teeth and curious blue eyes behind small gold-rimmed spectacles. The Indian woman beside him was obviously his concubine and seemed unable to speak a single word of English, though she plainly understood it.

Mrs. Rumley, Candace's chaperone, quickly formed her own opinion. "A degenerate," she whispered. "Behind the veneer is the brain of an ape!"

Nebraska Territory was just as it had been described to Candace by the clerks at Hudson's Bay headquarters down in London—a harsh brown land that would wither the soul of an Englishman. Its grasses were turning tan; a brass sun poked at her with malicious intent; a dry wind sucked the moisture from her flesh.

The ruin of old Fort Pierre stood up the slope—what was left of it anyway. The American army had bought it from the fur company in 1856, three years ago, and abandoned it almost at once, finding not enough fodder and wood there. Now the ruined fort, half butchered for firewood, brooded over the flat like an abandoned castle. The party could have debarked at new Fort Pierre several miles north, but had chosen not to. It would be just that many miles farther from the Badlands.

She felt grateful to the lord directors and clerks of Hudson's Bay for their advice. She brandished a sturdy cotton parasol against the hostile sun. She wore, as well, a straw hat with a wide brim and a crown entwined with silk roses in magenta and orange.

And, finally, she wore green goggles. The summer glare, the knowing men of Hudson's Bay had warned her, would blind her, drive her eyes into a tight squint until tears ran, give her headaches. So she'd tracked down a Portuguese oculist and dragged him to Great St. Mary's on Market Square, pointed to a stained-glass image of shepherds and sheep, and shown him the exact shade of green she wanted for one set, and then over to the great gothic chapel at King's College started by Henry VI, and shown him the precise blue she wanted in the other pair, a blue so azure she desired no other. In time he had produced two sets of goggles, cowled by brass and good harness leather and anchored with adjustable leather bands.

She wore the green pair now, and found that it had a benevolent effect upon these Dakota wilds, staining everything greener. Normally she wore her thick chestnut hair in a severe bun, but she couldn't do that and wear her Brighton straw or her goggles, so she'd plaited it into braids and anchored her hat with two mean hatpins she meant to use on Archimedes Van Vliet if he ever came within three feet of her person.

Slowly the sweating boatmen unloaded the rest of the dun-

nage from the *Spread Eagle*, the American Fur Company
riverboat that had carried them from St. Louis. While the
crowded boat rocked gently on the turbid river, the rivermen
led the six drays down the stage, the Smithsonian four first
and her own last. Theirs were nondescript draft animals of
some mongrel Yankee sort but they looked sturdy enough.
Hers were Clydesdales, seventeen-hand taffy-colored beasts
with Roman noses, white blazes, and feathery hair tufting
down the back of each leg. Take the Scottish horses, the
clerks had told her shrewdly. They'd fetch a fine price later
in the States, and pull the wagon as if it were a toy.

When a boatman handed the halter ropes to her, Candace peered up through her goggles at the giant green
animals, vaguely alarmed. She knew nothing about them.
She had intended to hire a man at new Fort Pierre. A
slight tilt of her parasol set them rearing backward, yanking the Manila rope from her gloved hands.

"Oh, blast!" she said, going after the ropes snaking
along the clay. But the apparition with the parasol seemed
to excite the beasts all the more, and they sidled away
from her even as she closed on them.

"You shouldn't say that word," said Mrs. Rumley.
"You're a proper lady. They use it in Billingsgate."

"Well, blast!"

"Miss Huxtable, stop," said Crowe.

She did. A moment later the Clydesdales did also, and
began plucking grass. Crowe leaned over and gathered up
the dragging halterstales, smiling. She took them gratefully.

"So good of you," she murmured while he stood there
somehow absorbing everything he could absorb about her.
"Mister Crowe," she said crisply. "I don't know how to
harness them. If you'll show me just once, I'll have it. I'll
never bother you again."

She did not miss the triumphant gleam in the eyes of
Professor Wood.

"In a moment," Crowe said. "I'm beholden to the ones that're paying me. But I'll work it out."

"I'll pay you!"

He smiled ruefully. "It's not for me to say."

A blast of steam from the ship's whistle upset the Clydesdales, which wrenched their halter ropes. But Candace hung on. The *Spread Eagle* came alive, snorting like some prehistoric dinosaur. Deckhands wrestled the stage on board while others unwound hawsers from the posts jammed into the bank. Ruffians crowded the rail as the packet drifted loose and lost ground in the current. Then its paddlewheel bit the river, and the packet pushed upstream, destined for Fort Berthold and Fort Union.

A hush settled over them. The last of civilization had vanished. Candace peered at them all, suddenly aware that she stood in a wild land of savages, drought, starvation, cold, and heat. Her sole protection was the gaggle of scholars and professors she'd thrown in with.

How distant sweet England seemed. She'd braved the terror of an Atlantic crossing on the *Great Eastern*, the new queen of the seas, 693 feet long. She'd chosen it for safety: it had been built of iron and had two paddlewheels and a screw, five stacks and six masts rigged for square sails. The thought of fire in the bowels of a wooden hull had given her fits. But the *Great Eastern* had crossed to Boston in two weeks, which Mrs. Rumley had borne with great fortitude.

From Boston they'd taken a clean Mallory Line steam coaster down to New Orleans, then a gaudy palace of a Mississippi riverboat to St. Louis in time to board the *Spread Eagle*. Not until Candace was on board and her steamer trunk stowed had she met her colleagues and learned the nature of her offense against science.

CHAPTER
2

As long as they were on the *Spread Eagle*, Cyrus Billington Wood had nurtured the forlorn hope that a miracle would happen: she'd come to her senses; or the pilot, Bailey, would talk her out of it, or young Chouteau, son of the fur company magnate, would forbid her. But it didn't happen, and eventually Professor Wood and his colleagues had adopted the perfect tactic: they'd said not a word to her—a clear signal of what lay ahead. Should she get off the boat, she'd face more of the same for an entire summer. But the frosty silence had no effect.

Wood swallowed down the disgust that boiled up his throat. It'd never do to lose his temper. He never lost his temper, though this wretched business had driven him closer to it than anything he could remember.

He was stuck with her and her chaperone. He couldn't abandon them here. She'd forced the issue simply by disembarking. That's how it'd been from the beginning, when that first letter of hers dropped onto his desk, a letter bearing a stamp with the image of Her Majesty Victoria, and canceled in Cambridge. He remembered the contents vividly. Miss Huxtable had heard that Wood planned to lead an expedition to the Badlands in 1859 under the auspices of the Smithsonian. She wished to go along, and would do it on her own purse. She wished to complete her father's work, and the Badlands, with its vertebrate fossil trove, would be the key.

Of course he'd responded at once: no, impossible, not a place for women, and there'd be the matter of propriety, a lone woman with married men. And anyway it'd do her no good. Field work was demanding, dirty, hot, and unsuitable for a woman. What's more, it'd upset Spencer Fullerton Baird of the Smithsonian, who'd agreed to underwrite the party to the sum of three thousand dollars.

Of course Wood had encased this all in the cocoon of cordiality, more for the sake of her renowned father than anything else. But he had made it abundantly clear that it was not possible, not even thinkable.

Much to his consternation, a few weeks later he had found another letter upon his desk, this one announcing her intention to come regardless. This time he got Baird himself, down in Washington City, to inform her in the strongest language that she would not be welcome; that the whole journey would be too hazardous; that the necessity of caring for a woman would gravely interfere with their field work.

She'd replied again, saying she'd come anyway.

And here she was, an odd duck spinning her parasol and peering out at them from behind green-lensed goggles. At least she had brought a chaperone, but the dumpy little woman seemed even less suited for the wilderness than Miss Huxtable. And somehow other females had come along. Such as J. Roderick Crabtree's slave, Gracie. Crabtree had promised that Gracie would look after them all, cook their meals and see to their comforts. Rufus Crowe had a woman, too, making four of that sex.

"Wood, you're taking it too seriously," said Dr. J. Roderick Crabtree. "After she skins her knuckles a few times, we'll employ her as an amanuensis."

"It's the propriety of it."

"Oh, now, we're two thousand miles from Spencer Baird," said Doctor of Philosophy Archimedes Van Vliet. "When the cat's away, the mice can play."

Professor Wood sighed unhappily.

Propriety kept a man civilized, he thought. That was why he wore a black clawhammer coat when he lectured, as well as his starched white shirt, high collar and black bow tie, none of it visible beneath his vast gray beard.

He had anticipated informality among colleagues, good talk around campfires, a certain relaxation of language. Around the Yard he'd always kept his tongue buttoned, and he had supposed it would be rather nice to say, out here two thousand miles from Boston, just what he thought of those scamps Darwin and Wallace, or his doubts about Linnaeus. But Candace Huxtable had changed all that.

There was Crowe, buckling all those harness straps to the dray, and there was Miss Huxtable, studying the matter like a freshman wanting an instant master's degree. Crowe buckled the breeching in place and then backed the brown dray toward the wagon that held their camp gear and staples. The great animal backed easily, and stood while Crowe hooked the trace chains to one of the singletrees.

That seemed to be all the woman needed. She snapped her parasol shut with a decisive clap, stuffed it into her wagon, and began dragging out a heap of harness. This she laid out on the clay and began sorting its parts. Then the woman sighed, peered about sharply at the rest of them, who pretended to look elsewhere, and lifted the collar and hames.

She was going to do the unthinkable! She was going to lower herself beneath her station and do a liveryman's labor! Wood watched, mesmerized, as she tried to slide a

collar and hames over one of her taffy-colored Clydesdales. But the horse sidled back, stretching the halter rope
that had been tied to her wagon.

"Oh, fudge," she bellowed.

"Tut, tut, tut," said Mrs. Rumley, purselipped.

"That's strong language. Do you suppose she got it from
her famous father?" asked J. Roderick Crabtree.

"We'll hear worse," said Professor Wood.

"I should hope so!" said Dr. Archimedes Van Vliet.
"Do you think she wears Amelia Bloomer's pants?"

"I'll volunteer to reconnoiter," said Dr. Crabtree.

The Huxtable woman freed the straw hat from her head,
and dropped it into her wagon. Then she tackled the harnessing again. This time she slid the collar on without a
dab of trouble, and followed with the bellyband and mar-
tingale. With an eye upon Crowe as he harnessed another
of the Smithsonian wagons, she buckled on the breeching,
and tackled the complex bridle. That proved to be too
much for her. The horse evaded the bit, and bobbed its
head.

Crowe turned his own tasks over to his squaw and helped
the Huxtable woman bridle her horse. Then he helped her
back the horse toward her wagon and hook the trace
chains.

It would be a ghastly trip, Wood thought. And more's
the pity, because he'd pinned all his hopes on it. If great
reputation eluded him this time, at age fifty-nine, he'd sink
into obscurity. The thought brought a great pain to his soul
as he watched Mrs. Rumley settle herself on the wagon
seat like a hen.

CHAPTER 3

Rufus Crowe helped the stiff British woman with the harness, admiring her determination as he worked. She would be as good as her word: she would learn it the first time, and never bother him with it again.

"There, Miss Huxtable. Have you ever driven a team?"

"I'm afraid not."

"Perhaps one of the gentlemen could help."

"I'm afraid not."

"I'll show you in a bit. There's some tricks and cautions."

"I'd be grateful."

He'd sensed the division between them almost at once, and wondered about it. He needed to know everything about each party he guided. Strife was dangerous in a wild land, especially with the Sioux so bitter about the encroachments of the whites.

"I believe we're ready, gents," he said. "We'll do a few miles today and rest. Tomorrow we'll settle down to it."

He watched closely to see what would happen. By some previous arrangement, Professor Van Vliet took the reins of one wagon, and the South Carolinian, J. Roderick Crabtree, took the lines of the other. The head of the expedition, Wood, didn't hesitate to join Van Vliet, and that confirmed Rufus's suspicion that no love was lost between Wood and Crabtree. He waited for the rest. Crabtree's slave, a wide, dour woman, didn't join her master on the wagon seat. Apparently she'd walk.

"I suppose we can leave," Rufus said. "We're going to follow an old road that runs from here to Fort Laramie, easy all the way, water all the way except for one small divide between the Teton drainage and the White River. You-all spare your horses."

Tonight he'd instruct them. He'd found that pilgrims always listened better after experiencing some of the hardships of the trail. This shouldn't be a hard trip, but greenhorns had a genius for turning the simple into the painful.

"You southern, Mister?" asked Crabtree, the Carolinian.

"Independence."

"A pity."

He nodded to his cheery little Brulé woman, and they started the parade, walking their misshapen ponies toward the confluence of the Teton and the Missouri, where they'd leave the great river behind. He-yah-zon didn't understand English, a situation that Rufus Crowe found much to his liking. He had not given her the name, which meant Toothache, but he found it appropriate. He-yah-zon cooked and kept house, such as it was, and provided him with tobacco and other pleasures, talked in streaks at meals, and left him to his dreaming, which was his principal occupation. In fact the Brulés called him Dream Man, and considered him a holy one, an impression he did not neglect to cultivate.

He peered behind him, wondering how the British woman was managing, and found that her Clydesdales had pulled her wagon smartly into line behind the others. She'd eat a lot of dust, and probably end up a lot less starchy before the day ended.

The fur company had set this up and given him a two-hundred-dollar credit at the trading posts. Scientists, they'd told him. Funded by the Smithsonian Institution in Washington City. They'd dig fossils at the Badlands while he hunted and protected them; later he'd take them to Fort Union, where a keelboat would take them south in the fall. Van Vliet was along to study the Lakota. Dr. Crabtree had made a name for himself as a cynical critic given to puncturing academic vanities in obscure journals. Crowe thought he'd enjoy Crabtree.

He nodded to He-yah-zon, knowing she'd continue to lead these pilgrims down the clay trail as plain as a turnpike, and reined his ewe-necked mare, letting his clients slide by as if he were a mayor reviewing a Fourth of July parade. They were plainly as curious about him as he was about them. As they rattled past, they eyed him politely.

"Crowe, you're not what you seem," said Crabtree as he steered past.

The guide nodded slightly. He watched the sweating black woman shuffle along, prevented by her station from sharing the seat with her master.

Wood and Van Vliet rolled past, smiling toothily at him. As they would to a freshman, he thought. He nodded, peering over his gold-rimmed half-spectacles at them.

When the Englishwoman drew up, he turned his mare and fell in with her.

"It's a splendid wagon," he said, eyeing the masterful bit of coachwork, lacquered olive with red trim and gilt, and reinforced with brass furniture. "And harness," he added.

"Mister Crowe, it's the best I could buy. Everything's

the best. They told me I'd need it. It might save my life. Were they right?''

"One can usually make do.''

''We're so far from everything. The whole world stopped at the river.''

Crowe shrugged. "It takes getting used to.'' He rode silently, knowing that she glanced furtively at him from time to time.

"How do you stay so—so pale?'' she asked suddenly.

He didn't know himself. He rarely wore a hat, yet the flesh of his face and body looked as smooth and youthful as when he'd escaped from Missouri seventeen years before. "It's because I don't work. My father wanted me to work like a mule. He had a livestock business, buying and selling, and planned to make me slave to it. So I ran off as soon as I was old enough to steal his rifle.''

She gazed at him from eyes full of doubt. "You're working now.''

"Oh, I suppose. A little bit now and then to buy shot and powder. Mostly I don't. I live with the Sioux and have no need. The women work. Toothache works.''

"Toothache?''

He pointed ahead. "He-yah-zon.''

"Oh. You've made a drudge of her, like that poor kaffir up there walking beside Mister Crabtree.''

"It's her natural lot.''

"I'd invite her to sit here if I could!''

"Why don't you?''

"Why—I just might.''

He waited for more.

"Are we in danger?''

"It's not the same as England.''

Miss Huxtable peered around. "Will we see savages?''

"I imagine.''

"Will they—harm us?''

"It's possible, if we upset them.''

"But can't you do something?"

"Sometimes."

"What'll they do?"

"I suppose you reckoned all that before you bought your fare."

"I hadn't," she said quietly. "I only wanted to work."

He waited. People often told him more if he just waited them out. He kept his mare abreast of the lurching wagon seat.

"My father died before he could finish something important. I'm going to try to finish it for him."

She steered the Clydesdales around a scatter of gray rock along a slope. "See, I'm good with the horses, wouldn't you say? My father was Cecil Henry Huxtable. He was knighted, you know. I've got to finish it. And do my own work as well."

"What'll you find at the Badlands, Miss Huxtable?"

The green goggles turned directly toward him. "I hope to find out whether he was right or wrong. It's worse than facing savages, sir."

CHAPTER
4

T he guide halted them at a rare grove of scrubby
cottonwoods after only six or seven miles.

"I imagine this is far enough the first day. Just enough to
accustom the animals. Tomorrow we'll go the distance."

Dr. J. Roderick Crabtree tugged the lines and then
stepped easily to the dry clay, springing his legs once or
twice. He wished to relieve himself but the women complicated matters. On the other hand it'd be far more complicated for them, he thought, amused.

Behind him, Wood and Van Vliet pulled up, then the
old maid from England. He watched them all benignly,
knowing he was going to enjoy the next moments. Large
questions would be settled directly. He laughed softly as
he plucked a japanned canister filled with good Havanas
from the breast pocket of his creamy linen suit—which
remained spotless because he had artfully chosen to lead
the caravan and avoid dust. He selected one of the thin
stogies, licked, pierced, and lit it, sucking ecstatically.

Silently his slave woman wandered down to the bank of

the creek and began harvesting firewood. She'd cook him
a fine meal. She was halter-broke; didn't need a whipping
and knew her place. He'd owned her for twenty years, and
she knew his wants as well as he knew what to expect of
her. In Charleston she'd been his housekeeper at his home
near the Ashley River.

Gracie returned, bent under a load of sticks, and he
watched her select a spot near the creek to cook a meal.

"It's been a hard day, eh, Gracie?"

"Your big toe must ache, master."

"Not as much as my spine. A wagon's hard upon the
backbone."

"You coulda rode me."

He wheezed joyously. Good old Gracie.

She grabbed an enameled blue teapot and dipped it into
the river. "The water in that no-account excuse for a river's some awful. I think we'll have the dogtrots."

Crowe heard her. "It's alkali. I imagine you can live
with it. Let it set a while and it'll settle. There's some call
it the Bad River, and that's a proper name."

"Baaaaad River," she said. "I hope it don't bother your
frail and fossilized constitution, master."

But J. Roderick Crabtree didn't hear her. He was sucking on his heady cigar, expelling the fragrant plume
through his waxed mustache and shiny black Vandyke,
and watching to see what would happen next. He eyed
Wood and Van Vliet furtively, and then the old maid. She
had to be in her upper twenties, but it was hard to tell
under that battle armor. He had an affinity for old maids.
They were like him, cynical about the opposite sex.

She stood there beside her matched drays, lifting the
floppy straw hat from her glossy brown hair. Then she
pulled her goggles free and settled the hat back in place,
a corset for her brains.

They all waited for something, and Crowe didn't dis-
appoint them. He unhooked Crabtree's horses, stripped

the harness off, and led them to the river. The animals nosed the water around, distrusting it, but finally pushed their muzzles in and began sucking. Then the guide picketed and hobbled them on the sparse grass upstream. He took care of the other pair of the expedition's horses, and without pause unhitched the old maid's Clydesdales and took care of them as well.

Wood looked affronted. Van Vliet had vanished downstream somewhere, out of sight of the old maid. Crowe's squaw was unloading gear from his pack mule, ignoring the rest except for an occasional glance. But Crabtree focused on Wood. The chairman would begin the waltz.

Cyrus Billington Wood ambled toward the shade of the only cottonwood tall enough to provide any, and stood there like a professor upon his podium, the limbs of the cottonwood providing a sort of heraldry behind him. He cleared his codfishy throat several times.

Ah! thought Crabtree, a true scholar and gentleman.

"My dear colleagues," Wood began. "And Miss Huxtable."

Very good, thought Crabtree, the sheep had been separated from the nanny goat. He sucked greedily on his Havana, burning off an eighth of an inch in one voluptuous draft.

"I will proceed directly to the matter at hand, so that we can go about our business. Ah . . . Yes . . . Ah, we have a most irregular situation here. Most irregular."

Van Vliet appeared from downstream, straightening his pants.

"Miss Huxtable, your presence here was not anticipated, and I confess that until the very last, I supposed it would not really happen."

The old maid stood stock-still.

"It poses certain, ah, problems, not only for the members of the expedition, but for our sponsor, the Smithsonian Institution. It is certainly, ah, irregular to have women present."

"White women," Crabtree amended, enjoying himself.

Wood did not deign to answer. "We have, of course, a situation that might excite scandal in the minds of others," he continued. "To make matters even more delicate, there is the matter of your credentials, Miss Huxtable. If you had, ah, an advanced degree, our sponsor, whose approbation we count dear, might understand, provided that it was all done in the full and innocent light of day.

"I've given much thought to the matter as we've made our first progress this afternoon. I've wanted to do what is just and fair. I'm mindful, as well, of the distinction of your late father, God bless his soul, and in deference to his memory, I've hit upon something. I should like to hire your services. Why, we need a good cook and house-keeper, a laundress, a dutiful helpmeet. We'll return to camp each day soiled and tired and hungry and thirsty, and what more noble office of womanhood is there than to have a spot of tea waiting, and clean duds, and hearty repasts? It'd enhance our work. I believe, Miss Huxtable, that this would quite perfectly resolve our difficulty, and make the matter official. As for chaperonage, we have Mrs. Rumley and these other good women with us to seal your virtue. Now, of course, I realize you have certain designs of your own, and I intend to keep you well informed, in simple layman's language, about what we uncover as we chip and drill and hammer away to bare the secrets of the ages. And thus you'll fulfill your purpose, to supply an addendum, I imagine, to the work of your esteemed father. We've no funds to pay you, of course, but I'm sure my colleagues and I will gratefully acknowledge your kind assistance when we publish our papers."

He paused, awaiting her response.

She laughed. "Professor Wood," she replied, "your proposition is enchanting. But you can cook your own blasted meals."

J. Roderick Crabtree sucked on his stogie and smiled.

CHAPTER
5

It had been, actually, a command, although the British woman refused to recognize it. Cyrus Billington Wood wondered whether he ought to take a firmer tone. He was, after all, chairman of this expedition, and the responsibility for its success rested on his shoulders. He wondered what to do. He couldn't very well abandon her—nor would she permit herself to be abandoned. She'd drive her wagon along behind the rest as if she had all the right in the world to do it.

Defiance was something he'd dealt with at Harvard. Let a student behave improperly, and there'd be a warning or two. Let him persist in his abominable ways, and he'd be out on his ear, a disgrace to his parents. But this snippy Englishwoman wasn't a student, and this barren grassland wasn't the Harvard Yard. He knew he'd need collegial support. After they had all dined he'd gather the gentlemen privately and discuss the matter.

Ah, if only she were male! He thought affably of those platoons of eager boys, ready and willing to make their mark. Ah, the hordes of them, whose smooth young faces all blurred together over the years. He remembered just a few who had wanted to do something in the awesome field he'd made his own. Those few he and Priscilla had had to tea many an afternoon. "Get the details! Look under surfaces!" he had cried. "Learn while the others are out larking! Then the world will know a true doctor of science."

Ah, if only this one were a doughty boy—why, he'd call it audacity and not impertinence. He sighed, peering furtively toward her glossy wagon. If only she would cook for them, he wouldn't have to depend on the labor of a chattel slave. Cyrus Billington Wood wished he had the courage to refuse the black woman's victuals and cook his own. It seemed wicked to take advantage of the institution he loathed and fought against.

He felt weary. Apart from a few forays into the New Hampshire hills, he'd never done field work. He knew this would be his one and only field trip, and he hoped his listless body would endure the privations. But he'd had to come: this was his last, desperate hope. If he failed, he'd leave no mark upon his field and die in gray obscurity, two dates on his headstone and nothing in between.

"I imagine I ought to say a word or two," said Crowe. "Now that we're on the way."

The summons pulled Wood out of his ruminations, and he hurried over to the guide, who stood in the shade of the cottonwood. Van Vliet drifted over, and so did Crabtree. The Huxtable woman poked her head out of the wagon and then clambered down, a billow of saffron skirts. She'd abandoned that loathsome straw hat and goggles.

"I suppose we'd call this a shakedown drive today," Crowe began, peering at each of them in turn from unblinking blue eyes. "Tomorrow we'll travel in earnest. I thought to share a few cautions with you."

Behind him his squaw busied herself around a small

fire. Cottonwood smoke, Wood discovered, had a sour smell.

"The water here's the best you'll see for some while. This water'll settle if you let it stand. It's some alkali but most people can take it. Animals can. In a few days we'll top a hogback and drop into the drainage of the White River. That water over there isn't really water—it's a kind of stiff white stuff that never does settle out. It's not alkali, it's just thick. I don't know why—no one knows. It just stays white, like milk, and slides down the throat like a dose of powdered chalk."

"It'll ruin my tea," said the Huxtable woman.

"It won't improve it none."

"Isn't there any other—a clear spring? I have a cask."

"Sometimes. In April, May, sometimes there's springs. But you can settle the white water by dropping some prickly pear lobes into it. That'll settle it overnight. Or you can pour a little alkali water into it; take a barrel along. That'll settle it. There'll be no decent water anywhere around the Badlands, and it's worse after a rain. There's a few slumps in there, places where water's caught in a hollow. Lots of cedar in those. Sometimes a pond. But it's hard to get a wagon in. We'll probably camp on the White River. You'll have to take your wagons over to the Badlands each day. There's wood along the White— here and there. But not much. Lots of juniper around some of the fossil beds. And another thing: you're going to feel heat like you never felt. A furnace. You're going to dig from dawn to maybe noon, or early afternoon if it's a cool day. That'll be the end. After that, it'll reach a hundred, hundred ten this time of year, and you'd just baste yourself like chicken on a spit."

"What about evenings?" asked Crabtree.

Crowe shrugged. "That rock, it captures the heat and holds it like a mean lover. Scorch you until maybe sunset, then it cools fast. You could get in a few licks around dusk.''

''What about firewood?'' asked Van Vliet.

''I was coming to that. From now on, we'll be camping mostly on a hotcake griddle. There's not a stick of it. Grass and yellow clay and a few prickly pear. I'd say, grab it when you can. And get yourselves every buffalo chip you can—good and dry ones. Now, there's nothing like a good chip. It's light and firm and somewhere between gray and tan, and got a soft gentle smell of sunshine to it, and a bug or two living inside. Don't get took in by the ones aren't ripe. They don't burn none. They just smoke and stink. Folks on the Platte River road, they sling a canvas under their wagon beds and stuff every stick and chip they can find into it. You might do likewise if you want a spot of coffee in the mornings. But even the chips are scarce, with the buffalo disappearing so fast.''

''We won't see any?'' asked Wood.

''They'll be on the lower grasslands along the White, if they're around—that country's hard on them, too. But there's a regular gap west of the Badlands, and they pour through there sometimes. But we'd better not take many. The Lakota, they're getting more'n a little peeved about it. Some bands starving, and the rest hunting day and night to make do. At least there's a few elk and deer still.''

''What about the aborigines?'' asked Miss Huxtable.

Crowe eyed her amiably. ''They're some trouble, Miss Huxtable. They're half-starved, cross-grained and contrary about the trespassing. They've been some put out since Gen'l Harney stung 'em in fifty-five. You look at it from inside their moccasins and you'll understand. Buffalo, they're vanishing so fast it's hard to keep fed. White folks coming out the Platte River road, slaughtering game ten miles to either side. Strangers like us, wandering around here in the heart of their country—this here is their treaty land, their home. The heart of it's from here to the Black Hills.''

''Will they—hurt us?''

The guide seemed somber. ''I'm here to prevent it. I'm a Brulé by adoption and by office. I'm a Dreamer for them.''

''What's that?''

''I share my visions with them.''

''Well make them behave themselves,'' Miss Huxtable said.

''I imagine it'll depend on whether we behave ourselves.''

That gave her pause.

''They'll want gifts—little tolls for using their grass and hunting their game. They'll want to be feasted now and then. I suppose . . . when they come asking what the bride price for you might be—I suppose you'd better smile some and not get huffy. They'll want to know who your father is so they can offer a pony or two.''

''Oh!''

Cyrus Billington Wood allowed himself some malicious pleasure. He observed the others. Crabtree sucked a noxious cigar and leered like a devil's lieutenant, which he probably was. Van Vliet peered at her through lustful eyes parted by a whiskey-reddened nose.

''I imagine, Miss Huxtable, you ought to pretend to be someone or other's wife. For the duration, of course. It'd be safer for you. The Lakota'd be less inclined to pluck you away.''

''At your service, Miss Huxtable,'' volunteered Archimedes Van Vliet.

''I'll not be party to a fraud,'' she said, whirling off in a cloud of squash-colored cotton.

''Tut, tut, tut,'' said Mrs. Rumley.

Wood watched Miss Huxtable build a fire and start a

teapot of water heating, while Mrs. Rumley unfolded a camp chair.

That's how it'd be, he thought. They'd be utterly alone. The scholars would take mess around the cookfire of the slave. The guide would eat at his own mess.

He pitied the Huxtable girl, but it was all her own doing.

CHAPTER
6

I t would be ghastly. Except for Mrs. Rumley, she'd be alone with her thoughts and feelings for months. But she'd expected that. She could bear it. She was a Huxtable, and a Briton. She had steel in her.

A scullion! That's what Professor Wood wanted her to be. A drudge doomed to the cooking pots like that poor slave woman. She didn't care if he had trouble explaining her presence to those stuffed shirts at the Smithsonian Institution. Wood resembled a hundred Cambridge dons she'd known, decent, polite, reserved, his private feelings hidden behind layer upon layer of cordiality. But she wouldn't bend.

At sunset she peered at a prospect so bleak it shivered her soul. What awful wastes! It made her homesick, and for a sad moment she dreamed of Cambridge and greenery and long gray days when the iron clouds swept in from the North Sea, and drove people to friendly hearths.

The piercing isolation made her wagon all the more precious to her. It'd been designed by J. A. Hansom. He'd presented her with a light, strong wagon fashioned from seasoned hardwoods and reinforced with brass fittings. It had a linseed-oiled Osnaburg sheet over its bows that could be drawn and laced to make a watertight little home. They'd enameled her wagon olive, several glossy coats, and gilded it. Its hickory wheel spokes were scarlet, making a saucy contrast. As her food stores at the rear of the waterproof wagon box diminished, there'd be room for her fossils.

She watched as the Americans meandered upstream, the Carolinian leaking cigar smoke, all of them enjoying a male camaraderie that excluded her.

Perfectly fine, she thought. Their departure from camp would be her opportunity. She clambered from her wagon bench to the grass, feeling her corset bite at her hips and bosom, and approached Crowe, who sat cross-legged beside his squaw.

"Miss Huxtable," he said. "Have yourself a seat."

"I'll stand, thank you," she replied, wishing she had loosened the corset.

"You and Missus Rumley like a sample?" he asked, waving a hand toward an evil-smelling stew. "It's coyote mostly. Toothache does it nicely."

"Really, Mister Crowe, I'm well provisioned. We'll open a tin of something after Mrs. Rumley has her tea and crumpets."

"I imagine you'd like some company. I don't suppose Missus Rumley suffices."

He certainly had a direct way about him, she thought. "Mrs. Rumley keeps to herself. Would I be intruding?"

"Not at all."

"Mister Crowe, I'd hoped to hire a man at Fort Pierre to help me. Do you suppose you could be of some service? Would you take a shilling a day?"

He looked baffled.

"I suppose that's too little. I don't know what they pay you. Would you take a pound a week?"

"I imagine, if the others permit me."

"Consider it done. I'll draft a letter."

"You're kind. I'd just do it anyway. Get you harnessed up, and all."

"I'll harness them as soon as I learn how."

"Then why—"

"A woman needs help sometimes."

"I imagine a friend too."

"That too." She studied the thin squaw. "Does Mrs. Crowe speak English?"

He laughed softly. "She's a pretty temporary Missus Crowe, I think. No, she speaks only Lakota."

The Indian woman knew she was being discussed. Crowe said something to her and she squinted at Candace.

"Please tell her that it is a pleasure to meet her and that I wish her happiness."

"I will," Crowe said, and translated.

The woman squinted harder, studying Candace's fitted dress with tiny buttons down its bosom, and her yards of nankeen skirts.

"You're Cecil Henry Huxtable's child."

"They told you."

"No, not a word. I've read a sight of your father's papers. He won the Copley Medal."

"You know that?"

"Winters are plumb impossible here."

He rose and led her toward one of his packsaddles. From a pannier he pulled out a *Manual of the Botany of the Northern United States*, by Asa Gray of Harvard, and the *Journal of the Linnaean Society*, published in London a year earlier.

"Mister Crowe, you surprise me."

"I like to have something to puzzle my brain during the winter."

She surveyed his shabby tweed coat, collarless white shirt, and gold-rimmed half-spectacles. "Who are you, Mister Crowe? You've not always been a guide out in these wastes."

"I don't rightly know," he said. "Maybe you have a clue."

She knew he was fencing. "I'll find you out."

He spotted the Americans strolling back through the gloaming, and swiftly shoved his literature out of sight.

"It won't do for them to know I dabble with it," he muttered. "Right now they think I'm a competent guide. If they knew what I read, they'd think I'm an idiot. You'll keep my little secret?"

"Mister Crowe, I know that university credentials don't make an educated man."

"Or an educated woman, either," he replied levelly.

He surprised her.

"Mister Crowe, we both have secrets to keep."

CHAPTER
7

Archimedes Van Vliet found the Plains oppressive, as if an anvil had been placed upon his spirits. The boundless hills stretching to hazy horizons seemed to diminish him to some speck of life in an oceanic void. The silent reaches made him itch for his rambling brick home in Brooklyn.

They toiled up the Bad River, and then up a nameless branch that held water only in a few stagnant pools; over a rocky hogback and into the drainage of the White River, all without any break in the relentless rolling prairie. The sun bleached the color out of sky and grass and soil. Only at dusk did he discover that this world had tints after all, mostly brown, tan, yellow, and umber, the colors of a baked land. After several sweaty days they raised the White River, a turbid little stream the color of milk, with an occasional scruffy cottonwood here and there along its grim banks, each a shocking emerald in a burning white world.

On the sixth day from Fort Pierre they came upon a

whole forest of cottonwoods, and Archimedes Van Vliet discovered his Golconda. There, nestled on a gentle hill thrusting into a great loop of the White River, stood an Indian burial ground. He'd never seen one but recognized it at once from his prodigious reading of ethnological papers. Instantly he turned his team off the well-worn Fort Laramie trace and steered over the parched meadow, rocking across prairie-dog mounds and holes, the wagon creaking under him.

It woke up Wood, who'd been snoozing beside him. Back on the trail Crabtree reined up, and behind him the Huxtable girl waited to see what had drawn Van Vliet away. The guide and his squaw had ridden ahead somewhere to hunt.

"There." Van Vliet pointed a finger. "I've been hunting for one."

"Yes. Well, I suppose we can spare a few hours."

Van Vliet eased his team and swaying wagon over a sharp-edged declivity, and hastened toward the shade of the nearest stunted cottonwood. The lords of the river valleys grew stunted and twisted here, barely surviving alongside a river so laden with murky white clay that it looked like skim milk. But at last he reached shade, and clambered down to the burnt grass, unwinding his six-foot-five body.

As far as he could see through the dappled light of the grove, Indian dead lay silently on scaffolds. Not a breath of air stirred. The dead slumbered in the caldron of early afternoon. A hundred, he guessed. A treasure.

Some scaffolds had been built into the crotches of living trees. But most had been erected of four posts planted in the hard clay, with crosspieces and long poles all lashed together with wet rawhide, which had dried as hard and strong as iron. Even as tall as he was, he couldn't see what lay on the scaffolds, which stood high enough to frustrate the designs of wolves and coyotes, skunks and badgers.

"It's not my field, but I confess they fascinate me," Wood said.

Van Vliet hurried off into the midst of the dead, gulping in images and impressions, an excitement building in him. Behind him he heard the squeal of front axles turning on the kingpins and knew the rest of the party would follow.

He'd never imagined an Indian cemetery could be so large. Surely nomadic people would bury their dead wherever they were, in ones and twos, here and there and anywhere. And yet this place looked to be as large as a white man's cemetery. Perhaps it was a sacred spot and the tribes came long distances to bury one of their own here. But then he grasped the obvious: here were trees for scaffolds in a land of naked prairie.

He wondered how much room they had in the wagons, and how much he could take. They'd scarcely made a dent in the stores. Still, he had to collect all he could, even if he had to hang it in a canvas hammock under the wagon box. There'd be room for it all unless those fossil hounds got nasty about it.

"Find Crowe and tell him to make camp around here somewhere," he shouted to Wood as he passed one scaffold after another. Sunlight filtered through the branches above, mottling the ground, catching motes of dust in the dead air, but he scarcely noticed the eerie serenity of the place. He wanted a rough count first; some idea of how many aborigines lay in this city of souls.

He paused beside an ancient, collapsed scaffold that had tumbled its burden to the earth. There on the clay lay an aboriginal skull, dead grasses poking through its eye sockets. And nearby, the lower jaw, intact, some teeth in place, all of it bleached white by a thousand sunny days. Ribs and vertebrae poked from a buffalo robe that had dried to a brittle gray shroud. And the rest: an ancient bow bleached to the color of the bones, and a medicine bundle.

He wanted the skull. They all wanted aboriginal skulls

back east, to measure cranial capacity and compare with the skulls of Caucasians. He had eleven of them on the shelves of his study in the rambling house on Church Avenue. And even more in his collection on loan to the Brooklyn Institute, which he had been instrumental in expanding in 1843 into a formidable library and museum. Now he would have the best American aboriginal collection in the world! That hadn't been his original goal, but somehow the years had transmuted his desire to become a great ethnologist into a desire to be a great collector.

He pried the skull loose from the resisting clay and examined it. In his notebook later he'd enter the place, time, and circumstances. This one showed no marks of trauma. Judging from the worn teeth and the sutures, he supposed the owner of this skull had died in ripe old age, his bones shrunken. Scalp and hair had long since vanished, along with the innards. He set it down and lifted the bow, finding it light and brittle. It wouldn't be worth keeping, so he pitched it aside. He lifted the medicine bundle only to have it fall apart in his hands.

Disappointing. But about him lay a whole city of the dead on scaffolds, some of them recently erected. These would yield their treasure! He knew he should be doing things in a scientific manner. He should dig out his pencil and foolscap from the wagon and sketch these sights before tampering with them. He should bring his tape and measure heights and widths and distances from one scaffold to another. He should see whether they all faced in some direction. He should give a number to each scaffold and list its contents, sketch it, note the gender of the dead . . .

But he wouldn't. That was ethnology and he'd become bored with it. An unbearable excitement aroused him like an aphrodisiac. He felt a great weakness engulf him, the sort of weakness he felt when he confronted a cool glass of good rye whiskey and a dash of cold water. He licked his parched lips under his bristling black mustache, and planned his assault.

One scaffold drew him. It looked a few months old. Each of the four forked posts had two black rings painted around it. A warrior's scaffold. The rings represented coups. At the head of the scaffold a tall pole arched over the platform. A war shield, a medicine pouch, a war club, and a lance dangled from it. Van Vliet grabbed the pole, wrestled it loose, and gently lowered his booty.

The war shield in particular excited him. This one had been fashioned from thick buffalo-bull hide and cured into a hardness that could turn lances and arrows and even musket balls. It had been stretched over a circular wooden frame about eighteen inches in diameter. A horseman's shield. Foot soldiers carried larger ones. A spread-winged bird painted with white dyes formed the insignia. It had the curved beak of a raptor. Yellow sun rays angled off the wings, and black claws clutched a broken lance. From it hung hawk feathers and weasel skins.

Van Vliet lifted this treasure as if it were gold, hunted for sun-fading, found none, and set it aside. He studied the medicine bundle, a small leather bag that would contain the warrior's private totems and fetishes. He'd open it later. The war club fascinated him. This one had been fashioned from two opposed buffalo horns bound by heavy wrappings of rawhide to a long haft. The conical horns had been honed into sharp deadly points. He set the club aside and examined the lance. It looked to be about five feet long and had an iron point, a trade item, anchored in the slitted end with rawhide. Crow feathers hung at intervals, dangling loosely. The pole had been smoothed and dyed with ocher and white stripes. Another treasure! He hefted it happily and laid it beside the rest.

He wondered how to get at the funeral bundle. The platform stood higher than his head. He finally freed one of the crossbars by cutting the rawhide that bound it there, and then lifting one whole end of the platform off the posts and easing it to earth. The funeral bundle, lashed tightly to the platform poles, didn't move. This warrior had been bound tightly within a buffalo robe, and over that had been folded an elkhide protective skin, the whole of it tightly wrapped with thong. He cut the thong anchoring the bundle to the platform.

Excited, he cut the bundle thongs one by one until he could pull the elkhide cover loose and unroll the stiff robe under it. Much to his delight, he found no maggots or decay, no foul odor. This had been a winter burial. The body had frozen and gradually desiccated. He peeled back the robe, revealing the leathery body of a Sioux male, middle-aged, virtually mummified by the dry air. He had been dressed in his best clothing, and beside him lay a dozen things the warrior would need in the spirit world. The face had been painted red, and then daubed with a dark blue V, a great honor. This one had been through the White Buffalo Ceremony. Two eagle feathers had been placed in his hair, which was bound by a red-beaded headband. He wore a softly tanned ceremonial shirt, fringed in places, and quilled with geometric designs done in red and black. His breechclout and fringed leggins had red and black geometric beadwork, artfully done. On his feet were richly quilled spirit moccasins with beaded soles, soles that would never tread on earth. Another bonanza! Oh, how all this would look on a shelf in Van Vliet's home!

Off behind him he heard people calling, but he paid no heed. This was what he'd come for; what the Smithsonian had funded him to do.

He picked up an exquisitely quilled quiver, the quilling forming red bands around the arrow cup and bow sheath. He slid out a sinew-backed bow, long and strong and without a reflexive curve. He pulled arrows out of the arrow cup and found them to be tipped with hoop-iron points, ground and hammered from traders' metal. These arrows had been fletched with hawk feathers bound by sinew to shafts of chokecherry, and dyed with red rings, the insignia of the man's war society as well as his personal mark.

Van Vliet set the quiver on the earth next to his other booty. This one's war hatchet was a trade item, but he'd pounded brass tacks into the shaft and attached a leather hand loop at its base, binding it with sinew. He turned next to the *wotawes*, the amulets and fetishes that lay in profusion beside the man's chest. He recognized one at once, a little leather turtle heavily beaded in green. This would be the umbilical amulet, and would carry within it the warrior's umbilical cord.

All these things he would study later. His task now was to collect as much as he could, as swiftly as he could. To his mound of goods he added little bags of war paint, an exquisite polished flute, a roached warbonnet, a catlinite pipe in a soft pipe bag, quilled armbands trimmed with ermine, a strike-a-light bag, green-quilled on one side, with flint and steel inside, and a dozen amulets of stone, bone, or wood, shaped into animal symbols. Gently he undid the moccasins and slid them off, admiring the blue beadwork on the soles.

He wondered how to get at the shirt and breechclout and leggins. Finally he fought down his dread and simply untied the leggins where they'd been bound to a belt at the waist, and slid them off. The breechclout came easily. But the shirt gave him trouble. He turned the mummified body over, finding it amazingly light but stiff as dry rawhide. The shirt had to be pulled off, over the head. It didn't come. He couldn't wrench the warrior's arms upward. He wanted that shirt desperately, but decided enough was enough here.

He wondered briefly who this was. He decided he wouldn't bother to bundle the body again and restore the platform. He lacked the time!

"Thanks, my friend," he said cheerfully, addressing the dead warrior. "Hope you don't mind." He'd been a large one, but the Sioux were a large people who often looked less Mongoloid than those in other tribes. The exposed body on the hot clay would swiftly turn to dust. But it wouldn't matter. This one had gone to the spirit world, what the Sioux called the Spirit Trail, the Milky Way, the Land of Many Lodges, there to play in a paradise that contained all his ancestors and everyone he'd ever known.

A moment of doubt struck him. Ought he to do all these things in a different way? As a trained scientist? Ought he to open scaffold bundles at all?

"Van Vliet!"

Professor Wood was striding through the dappled light. The weary old man paused and stared, his shrewd gaze absorbing the tumbled scaffold, the mummified body, the pile of booty. "I wonder about this," he said. "I think we ought to have a word with Crowe when he comes in. He's off somewhere looking for a deer."

"What's there to talk about, Cyrus?"

"The Lakota."

"These things are priceless. And this is just the beginning. Wait until I open a child's scaffold. Wait until I show you the dolls, if it's a girl, and the little shield and bow and arrows if it's a boy."

"How'd you get all this stuff so fast? You're taking notes, I trust."

"Well—I just wanted an advance look before I began."

Cyrus Wood contemplated that. "Archimedes," he began, "we're here for the sake of science. That requires systematic study. It requires that we don't ruin a site before—"

"It was just one," Van Vliet replied, feeling an upwelling of irritation. He itched to get rid of the man, set him to work on his rocks and fossils. "Look, old man. I've got about a hundred scaffolds to examine. I think you should just get along to the Badlands and leave a wagon here for me.''

"No," said Wood in a decisive voice that surprised Van Vliet. "We'll camp upriver a bit tonight, and you'll have all of the day to work. But I must insist that you come with us. If you don't, I'm sure we'll never see you again.''

CHAPTER 8

Candace Huxtable steered her Clydesdales over rough bottomland, following the other wagons. They were heading toward a copse of cottonwoods beside the White River, perhaps a quarter of a mile from the Sioux burial grounds. The sun had barely passed zenith, but she knew they'd camp there.

Those ahead of her drove into a pleasant glade, shaded enough to protect them from the merciless sun. She saw at once that this place had been a resort of travelers. She spotted several rock-rimmed fire pits and stone tipi rings.

"We'll camp here, Mrs. Rumley."

"I can't imagine why."

"So that Doctor Van Vliet can gather artifacts."

"It's a pity to waste artifacts on him. His mind wants improving and so do his manners."

"It's for science."

Mrs. Rumley stared. Whenever she stared, Candace felt she was being glued down.

"I'll read *Sense and Sensibility*, thank you," said the guardian of her virtue.

"Whatever you wish, Mrs. Rumley. We'll have tea later."

Mrs. Rumley had become increasingly difficult. It had never occurred to Candace, when she'd engaged the widow after a brief interview, that Mrs. Rumley would consider herself a companion only. Candace had been forced to cook or starve, tidy the wagon or leave it a mess, all under Mrs. Rumley's disapproving eye.

"Scullery work is beneath your station, Miss Huxtable," Mrs. Rumley had announced the second night out.

"Why, then, help me!"

"You must hire a scullion, Miss Huxtable."

"I'll advertise for one," Candace had muttered. Since then, nothing had changed.

She'd hoped to get to the Badlands and the fossil beds as quickly as possible but she didn't really mind this delay. It was all for the sake of science. She could catch up on her daily journal, which she'd been assiduously keeping in the hope of publishing an account of her adventure.

She halted her wagon near a majestic cottonwood that would shade her even when the sun slid far into the northwest. She wrestled the harness off the Clydesdales and buckled her fine English hobbles onto their forelegs while they nibbled on her straw hat. One finally pulled it loose and flapped it up and down. She retrieved it, and the hatpins, and let the horses graze unpicketed while she made camp. They struggled clumsily down to the riverbank and poked their great bowed noses into the milky flow, pushing the water about, barely tolerating it. About her, the others settled in as well—all but the guide and his squaw, who were hunting, and Van Vliet back among the scaffolds.

Beneath a great cottonwood Professor Wood was stripping harness, a task that Van Vliet usually performed.

Gracie was gathering firewood, and would soon start some tea for her master, who stood in his linen suit, surveying this new corner of the universe with his usual leer.

"Go fetch me some Indian bones, master. I'll make us Indian soup. That's my specialty, Indian soup with lots of pepper. Almost as good as my fricasseed Crabtree."

"I lust for mulatto stew," the awful man retorted.

Gracie hummed cheerfully while Crabtree began unharnessing his drays, obviously more concerned about their condition than Gracie's. Somehow he did this each day without sullying his suit, which mystified Candace. Her clothing had become grimy.

Candace dug around for her father's field desk, a light birch and brass affair the size of a portfolio. It contained her blank buckram-bound journals, a metal flask of India ink with a leakproof stopper, various pens, and a box of Josiah Mason steel nibs from Birmingham. She decided to take her fringed white parasol, too: the straw hat wouldn't protect her fair English flesh in that inferno.

Thus parasoled and hatted and goggled and fitted out with writing tools, she embarked toward the burial grounds, only to have Professor Wood detain her.

"Ah, Miss Huxtable. That's not a suitable place for a proper woman. I think you'd better—"

"Professor Wood! May I remind you I'm not a part of your expedition and you have absolutely no authority over me. I shall go where I choose and do what I choose." She seethed, and met his steady gaze with her own smoldering one, though he couldn't see it behind her green goggles.

The old man drew himself up. "Miss Huxtable," he said quietly. "If this were my classroom, why, I'd have you stand up, and I'd admonish you to conduct yourself in a proper way. But this isn't a classroom, is it? Of course I have absolutely no authority over you. I don't suppose God does either. You're a masterless woman. But I beg to remind you, Miss, that you attached yourself to us. And having done so, you've burdened us with your care. We can't escape protecting you and your companion. If you have your good father's civility, you'll heed our cautions."

He said it mildly, but she saw the steel in him. Chagrined, she stammered a reply. "I'm . . . sorry I affronted you," she said. "I wish to see the burial place; that's all."

He stared grimly. "I can't prevent it. I don't believe it's a sight for your eyes." He turned back to his work, and she marched resolutely toward the cottonwood forest.

She remembered her long, wintry childhood on the River Cam, and her early discovery that colleges, universities, libraries, and scholarship were all the exclusive domains of males—at least in England. The ancient colleges of Cambridge were, every one, schools for boys, staffed by mumbling men. The few girls she'd met, daughters of professors, had been confined to housekeeping drudgery like her mother. But she'd been a saucy girl, and had often slipped into the gloomy arenas and lecture rooms, sitting unobtrusively at the very back of those cold chambers. She'd been caught, of course, but usually the professors had let her stay: she was good old Huxtable's girl, and just being a bit spicy, was all.

She'd listened solemnly, wherever she'd been tolerated or unobserved in the halls of academe, sopping up whole universes she'd never imagined, geometry and Latin. Thus was she educated on the sly, her own father and mother all unsuspecting, the chancellors of Trinity and Pembroke and King's and Corpus Christi and Queen's and Magdalene blithely unaware of the budding scientist in their midst—even if she never took an examination.

She passed through broken woods, twirling her white parasol to make the fringes fly, and came upon the burial place, which straddled a gentle hill rising above the White River. It didn't seem somber at all. The platforms rested well over her head, and she could see nothing of their burdens. A few were lashed to cottonwood trees that swayed with the breezes. Around these trees the aborigines had piled thorny brush, apparently to keep beasts from eating the dead.

But then she spotted an ancient, bleached scaffold that had collapsed, and around its base a heap of human bones and the gray remains of skins and fur. Death brushed softly past her. Off a way she spotted Van Vliet wrestling feverishly with something. She might as well see what, she thought.

She thrust her chin forward, stiffened her spine within the fortress walls of her merciless corset, and marched toward the American.

She found Van Vliet in the process of collapsing a scaffold by yanking two of the uprights apart so that one of the crossbars would drop and spill the platform poles. He was having a devil of a time of it. She spotted a scaffold he'd robbed a few yards away and wandered in that direction, but he yelled at her.

"Miss Huxtable, I wouldn't want you to see things you'd rather not see," he said, sweat rivering from his brow.

"I can manage, thank you." She proceeded to the site and at once regretted it. A mummified aborigine, wearing only a shirt, lay upon the ground like dried-up Roman statuary. And nearby lay a pile of Van Vliet's loot.

"Very well, Doctor Van Vliet. I'm now educated." She said it flippantly, but within her heart she quaked.

"It's no English churchyard, is it?" he said.

She hastened from that pillaged grave back to where he was working.

"I think this'll be a woman," he said. "No lance, no shield hanging over it."

He gave one post a final shove, and the crossbar sprang loose. The platform slowly sagged down, almost as if it were being lowered by spirits. A dusty, brittle bundle remained lashed to the deranged poles. Van Vliet cut the lashings and lifted it off. It seemed terribly light in his hands, she thought, and then realized that of course it would be: a human body without liquids would weigh very little.

Fascinated, she watched him sever the rawhide thongs and peel an ancient buffalo robe back, bit by bit, until the frightful remains lay exposed to the glare of the sun. This one—an ancient woman, judging from her long hair— hadn't mummified; it had largely decomposed, leaving bone and black masses of something under decayed clothing, carpeted with the fine husks of maggots, which shattered into tiny flakes as he worked. This had been a summer burial. Blowflies had crawled in and laid thousands of eggs, which had become larvae growing within their thin husks, and then maggots eating the rotting flesh. Those old husks clustered everywhere and the opened bundle exuded a strange bitter smell.

"Ah!" he cried, snatching up an exquisitely quilled tubular pouch and opening it. "Perfect! An awl pouch! Her pride and joy!" He brushed maggot husks off of it.

She stared at him, dismayed. "Doctor Van Vliet, have you no respect for the dead?"

"Not a bit. She's an aborigine. A Lakota."

"I should care very much if those were my bones," she said, but he didn't seem to hear her. He'd discovered the woman's sewing kit and a little doeskin doll, a hide scraper with red and black dots incised into its handle, and her *wotawes*, amulets and fetishes, and danced about, holding them up to the sun.

"I would indeed," she said. "I think they would too. She's someone's mother, you know. She laughed and cried once; brought children into the world. Sewed clothes for them with those awls you're holding."

"Ah, how right you are. But science can't afford sentiment."

"My feelings exactly, Doctor Van Vliet. I think you'll

add nothing to ethnology if you have no sense of the mortal whose tools you hold.''

He didn't reply. He'd discovered that the dead woman's moccasins had survived without being stained by the decay, and was plucking them off, scattering maggot husks. They came easily, everything within and around them disintegrating into rubble. These had been quilled blue and trimmed with rabbit, but had no beads on them. This woman had been poor. Candace wondered if Van Vliet had discerned that. He shook them out and tossed them onto his growing pile.

After plundering that scaffold he hurried on to the next, leaving the wounded grave obscenely open.

''Aren't you going to return them? Put them back?''

''No time! No time!''

She knew she wasn't watching a scientist at work; he was a grave-robber as ghoulish as any who dug into a cemetery. He'd perfected his scaffold-collapsing, and this time he easily shoved the forked posts apart until the crosspiece fell, exposing another bundled body. He cut the thongs and yanked the brittle buffalo robe back, exposing a ghastly skeleton—all that was left of an old man. The artifacts had been stained by the foulness, but some were intact.

''Ah, look at this!'' he cried, plucking up a handsome quiver filled with arrows, and a sheathed bow. The quiver had been dyed in brown, black, and cream geometric patterns, and its doeskin was fringed at its base. He pulled the bow out, finding it perfectly supple. ''Bone-backed! A rare one!'' he said, and thrust it at her. ''That's ramshorn from a mountain sheep,'' he said. ''It's an art some of them had. But the old boy probably traded for it. Lakota didn't make them much.''

He extracted other treasure from the stiff folds of the robe: a war club with a grooved stone head wedged into a split haft and anchored with sinew and decked with brass tacks in circlets around the haft; a red catlinite ceremonial axhead, smoothly shaped; a necklace of bear's claws with a large trade bead between each claw; a cedar flute incised in a spiral pattern; a fringed and green-dyed strike-a-light bag with an oval steel Hudson's Bay striker and flint within; a knife sheath glistening with seed beads, and within it a Green River knife; a long pipe with a catlinite head in a bag of velvety leather, probably unborn buffalo; a half dozen fetishes, including a turtle image and a piece of deer antler; and a porcupine-tail hairbrush.

Then he turned to the skeleton itself, picking up a bone breastplate trimmed with large blue beads, and an armband.

Candace watched the pillage, fascinated in spite of the deepening sadness that stole through her. The whole assault on that scaffold had taken barely ten minutes. Van Vliet gathered his booty in a heap while eyeing the field desk she toted.

"If that's a field desk, you can do me a favor," he said. "And help me keep this business a science. We've got to keep the old chaps happy at the Smithsonian. If you will, draw a map of the place, each scaffold a little rectangle. Then note the contents. Do an inventory. Label that one over there—see the skull?—that's site one, old man, scaffold decomposed, bones on the earth and disturbed. And over there's site two, warrior, do an inventory, eh? And the squaw was site three. This is four. Inventory, that's what I need, and a quick description of the, ah, remains. And anything unusual."

"I'm not your amanuensis," she said, knowing she had spoken too harshly.

"I need you."

"I'm not trained in your work . . . But if you wish to dictate your findings I could write them. Only if you do it properly, piece by piece." It seemed a great concession.

He laughed cheerfully. "I didn't know you had such a command of anthropology."

She stared at him, unbudging. "I know a little about my father's work. That's all."

"Well, I'll make notes later. Look at all this!"

He waved a hand toward the scores of scaffolds that had not yet yielded their secrets. She knew he'd break into most of them by sundown at the rate he was going, and leave a desecration in his wake like the ruin of a hundred virgins. She wondered how the Sioux would react.

"I think you should restore the scaffolds."

"Why? They all come tumbling down over the years. Come now, Miss Huxtable. These are nomadic aborigines. They've the memory of children. A week after they send one off to the spirit lands, they forget him. You see, you're thinking like a proper Englishwoman, not a child of nature who sees death and decay every day."

"I think the dead are loved and remembered," she said stubbornly. "And you should put them back up—for our safety."

He sighed. "Now there's the difference between a trained anthropologist and a—person. We can't let sentiment interfere with our observations."

"You're not observing."

"Of course I am. By this evening I'll have the greatest Plains collection, Lakota collection, on earth. It'll take me months to clean and study what I've got here and write it all up. You could help, you know. Ah, get into something looser and come help me work. You're a bright girl; you'll get the hang of it." He eyed her from an amused, beet-red face.

A girl, was she! She'd thought of herself as an old maid, and by most standards that's what she was and what she intended to be. A very proper one too. The breath of scandal would never reach her, though she knew that an occasional curious fool would wonder about her reclusive ways. It delighted her that he knew she was corseted and proper. Let him always remember that. "No, thank you, Doctor Van Vliet. I think I'll leave it all to you."

"Well, at least tell Wood to send a wagon over. I'll fill it up! And tell him to bring a nip. It's hot here."

She'd seen enough, and it had upset her in ways she couldn't fathom. Wordlessly she left him there and hastened through a wall of choking hot air to the campsite, wanting to talk to that mild guide she had come to trust.

CHAPTER 9

Puzzled, Rufus Crowe worked his way back on the river trace, wondering what had happened to his party. He peered over the neck of his mustang at the well-worn trace, and saw no sign of wagon-wheel tracks. They simply hadn't come this far.

He and He-Yah-Zon had made no meat, though they'd beaten the brush along the White River for miles hoping to scare up a mule deer. They'd not even seen a pronghorn through the searing white afternoon. It seemed so much harder to find meat these days. The buffalo herds had diminished, though sometimes he still spotted whole valleys black with them.

The trading had done it, he thought. Traders wanted good robes; the Indians wanted all the things they saw on the shelves—knives, rifles, axes, hatchets, hoop iron for arrow points, blankets, steel needles and thread, bolts of calico, iron cooking pots, and all the rest. Yes, white men had slaughtered buffalo wholesale along the Platte road to California. But that scarcely accounted for this swift, frightening decline in the herds of the sacred *tatonka*, as his friends called them.

For as long as he could remember the great herds had been seventy or eighty percent bulls because all the Plains tribes relished the softer meat of the cows. Crowe had spoken more than once about it in the councils, only to have the Sichangu headmen stare at him as if he were daft. If only they'd limit their hunts to bulls, the herds would explode again. He sighed, knowing how close they all were to starvation because of tribal tradition and their immutable belief that the herds were limitless, a perpetual gift of Wakan Tanka.

Just when Crowe was beginning to worry about his clients he spotted their campsite a half mile off the trail in some cottonwoods beside the river. Pearly smoke lifted from the place, caught in the horizontal rays of a dying sun. He veered toward the wagons while curiosity gnawed at him.

Uneasily he remembered that in that grove lay a great Lakota burial ground, much revered by the People for its abundant trees. Of course the scientists were studying it! Measuring it, writing it all down in their journals, extracting a knowledge of Lakota burial customs from the scores of scaffolds, their rendezvous ahead with their guide quite forgotten.

He had wandered through it once, with a bright curiosity that never had been satiated by his long exile in the wilderness. He was curious about everything, including Indian burial customs. Books had been his undoing as a boy. Books and journals had sustained him as an adult. Each riverboat season, he had haunted the forts along the Missouri offering finely tanned robes for books and journals of any sort. These he read through the long winters in the lodges while the Lakota peered respectfully at him and knew he was making magic. Some of his adopted Brulés even called him *wakan*, or one endowed with holy insights, and had given him a shirt fringed with hair locks as a badge of office. And thus he'd been invited to help decide the most important issues.

What he knew of the natural sciences he resolutely hid from these scientists, except for Miss Huxtable. She was like him, far better educated than the world would ever surmise. When he'd first glimpsed her on the Missouri River bank, he'd seen something surpassingly lovely in her—but far above his vagabond station. He knew, sadly, that he would never win more than a distant smile from her.

"Ah, there you are, Crowe," Professor Wood said. "No meat, eh? Maybe at dusk you'll have some luck. We stopped early. Hope you don't mind."

"Where's the other wagon?" Crowe asked.

"Doctor Van Vliet wanted to examine that burial ground—that's his field, you know. He's collecting over there right now. I suppose he'll show up when darkness shuts him down."

Crowe wanted to say that the things there were *wakan*, sacred, and not Van Vliet's to pick up, but he merely smiled. "I'll go over."

Miss Huxtable was staring at him. "Mister Crowe, please look at what Dr. Van Vliet is doing."

"Of course, Miss Huxtable." He discerned a sharpness in her voice that spoke loudly to him. She stood apart, as usual, boiling something in a pot at her own fire.

He turned his weary pony eastward, and He-Yah-Zon followed behind. As they approached the great burial yard she lagged back, hesitant to offend the wheeling columns of spirits that soared like bird-flocks about the holy place.

They found Van Vliet in the center of carnage, loading the wagon with mountains of spirit-journey things. At every hand stood the ruins of scaffolds, collapsed poles sprawled on the earth, pillaged body bundles opened, the skeletons strewn like so many buffalo carcasses after a great hunt. Twelve skulls, some with hair still attached, lay in a line at Van Vliet's feet.

"Aieeee!" cried He-Yah-Zon.

Rufus Crowe sat his horse speechless, the enormity of it driving words and thoughts from his brain. He watched in shock as Van Vliet hurried to beat the night. When Van Vliet plucked up a fringed elkskin shirt quilled with yellow and brown patterns across the chest, Rufus's soul froze.

"*Tu la! Tu la!*" Toothache screamed.

"What's that all about, Crowe?"

"She said shame on you."

The Lakota woman screamed, yanked the neck of her mare around, and fled into the gloom, kicking her pony hard.

"That's her father's shirt you've got in your hands, Doctor Van Vliet."

CHAPTER
10

Candace watched Archimedes Van Vliet steer the groaning wagon into camp just after dusk. He looked triumphant. The wagon had been festooned with Sioux paraphernalia, spears and coup sticks and shields hanging like pennants from bows, the sides of its box, and the fold-down rear boot. Beside him rode Rufus Crowe, looking stern. He led a packhorse. His squaw wasn't with him.

Trouble, she thought.

Professor Wood and Dr. Crabtree rushed to the halted wagon to examine the booty, exclaiming at it all while the rest followed.

"Van Vliet! It's a bonanza!" said Wood.

"Hmm, hmmm," buzzed Crabtree. "Stone-age gimcracks and whizbangs! Furniture for stone-age heavens! Cradles for neolithic brats!"

"Gents, this is the finest aboriginal collection ever gathered into the hands of a white man," Van Vliet announced. "I must have twenty of everything. I assure you, even if we find nothing else worthwhile, this expedition's a success. It'll take a year just to clean and classify everything. Why, there's things I've never seen and can't identify!''

"Extraordinary!" said Wood.

Crabtree sucked on his cigar until the end glowed orange, and smiled, his observant gaze flicking from one treasure to another, probably calculating pounds and pence, Candace thought.

"Haunts," muttered Gracie. "I see more than I can count flyin' around there. Spooks. They're gonna be with us now."

Crabtree heard her and chuckled. "Gracie, you're looking at wood, bone, leather, metal, cloth, and feathers."

"I'm lookin' at stuff flyin' around like owls and bats."

"You're superstitious."

"They's one buzzin' you like a vampire."

Crabtree exhaled a plume of cigar smoke in assorted directions and smirked.

Rufus Crowe slid wearily off his Indian pony, peered about as if undecided about something, and then approached Candace. "May I share your fire?" he asked. He was not smiling.

"Certainly. We'd welcome the company. I have a thousand questions to ask—"

"I'll answer most of them in a moment."

He didn't unsaddle his horse, but he did loosen the saddle cinch and picket the horse on good grass near her wagon, close to her Clydesdales.

"Well, tell me this: are we in danger?"

He nodded, his gaze locking with hers for a moment. She felt intuitively that some sort of understanding had passed between them. He unburdened his packhorse also, and picketed it nearby. His motions were studied, deliberate, as if he were waiting for something. She sensed what it was: the passing of the first blush of excitement

about all that booty, the passing of Van Vliet's infectious
enthusiasms as he showed them one piece after another: a
beaded cradleboard, a war shirt, a dyed umbilical totem,
a feather-decked war shield.

"Mister Crowe," she said, "I thrust myself upon this
expedition, being perfectly cheeky about it. And all I did
was sign my death warrant."

"I hope not, Miss Huxtable. You're not a part of it.
And you're a woman, which'll help some."

"I won't put up with impertinence from savages," said
Mrs. Rumley.

"I'm not reassured," Candace said.

"I wouldn't want you to be."

"What if we were to drive back to Fort Pierre and hail
the first boat?"

"It's too late."

A chill slid through her. "But—can't something be
done? Can't these things be put back? And the bundles
returned and the scaffolds put up again?"

A gentleness suffused his face. "You tell me."

He was right, of course.

"Can't you bargain with the Sioux? Can't we pay
them?"

"I'll try that, too, I imagine."

"What would they want in trade? I'll give anything in
my wagon."

Crowe turned silent.

"I know what!" said Gracie, who'd been listening.
"They take Doctor Van Vliet and slit his throat—after they
torment him a few days. That'll be the trade."

Candace could see from the look on Crowe's face that
the black slave had come close to the mark.

Crowe pulled out a small briar pipe from somewhere in
his baggy tweed jacket, and deliberately tamped sweet-
smelling tobacco into it. "I might help. I'm a Dreamer

among them.'' He clenched the unlit pipe between his teeth.

''Mister Crowe, I'm quite afraid. You can't imagine how hard it is to confess it. We British—''

''You're the wise one among us.''

He wasn't soothing her a bit, she thought. He hadn't denied any of the imaginings of her fevered mind.

When full dark had settled and the American scientists had examined much of the booty, the last of it in the wavering light of the fires, Crowe stepped toward them.

''A word, gentlemen.''

Candace wondered again at his elegance.

They turned at last to their guide, and he waited a moment more, obviously wanting their full attention.

''The Lakota equip their dead with the things they need for their spirit journey,'' he began. ''Always the best, always the things the dead cherished most. Often they kill his best horse to carry him through the spirit lands.''

The scientists listened amiably.

''But it's a long trip along the Spirit Trail to the Land of Many Lodges. Each spirit has to pass by an old woman, Hihankara, the Owl Maker, and show that he's been tattooed on the wrist or the forehead. Or the chin sometimes. If the marks aren't there, she pushes the ghost off the trail and it falls to earth. Here.'' He waved an arm around. ''If it comes back, it wanders around here forever.''

''Ahhh,'' said Gracie in a low voice.

''If it passes Owl Maker, it goes on past Tate, the wind, and is judged by Skan, the sky. And if it reaches the Land of Many Lodges, it lives in paradise with friends and relatives and all the needful things of nature.''

He waited a moment or two.

''You take away the things they need for their journey, and you take away their hope of paradise. I imagine that'd upset their relatives here on earth. Like my woman, Toothache. She saw her father's shirt in Doctor Van Vliet's hand, hollered some, and took off to her people—and mine.''

That's where she'd gone! He had certainly caught their attention, Candace thought.

"I imagine you'll be seeing some mighty upset sons and daughters and brothers and sisters coming along pretty soon.''

"Excuse me, Crowe," said Professor Wood. "But the sun and wind and rain topple the scaffolds, ruin the implements, and yet the tribesmen don't seem to mind.''

"The sun and the wind come from where they're going. They don't mind that. But they do mind anyone not a part of their natural world snatching the things the spirits need on their journey.''

"What are you driving at?" asked Wood.

"I imagine they'd agitate some for putting us to death. Certainly putting Doctor Van Vliet to death.''

"Remedies, man," snapped Crabtree. "Don't bore us with diagnoses. Give us your cures.''

"You ought to put it all back. Bundle it up. Put the scaffolds up tomorrow.''

"No, no, no," shouted Van Vliet.

Crowe waited, looking as mild as always.

"This is a king's treasure! A collection beyond price! There's little risk in it. I've been studying the Plains aborigines for years. They're children. They'll be vexed a day or two and forget it the first moment they see some buffalo. We'll give them a feast. We've some gewgaws. Even a spare rifle or two for trading. I brought a whole trunk of stuff to trade to the aborigines for things I want. We'll give them a few ribbons or pots or a butcher knife, and it'll be fine.''

"For your safety—put it back.''

"I can't. It's—dismantled. It can't be done.''

"Surely, Archimedes, you took notes, made an inventory of each site," Wood said.

"The sites aren't important, Cyrus. The cleaning and sorting and identifying are important, and that's what I'll spend the rest of my time out here doing." He turned to his skeptical colleagues. "We'll give them some trinkets and that'll soothe them, I'm sure. I've studied them for years."

Wood turned to the guide. "This expedition's already a great success. Crowe, go to them and tell them we'll dicker, make amends, and all that."

"You should give it back," said Mrs. Rumley. "The whole lot isn't worth one good English grandfather clock."

"Professor Wood, it'd be worth my life to go to them now."

"Haunts," said Gracie. "We take that stuff with us and a mess o' spirits come along devilin' us. We won't go a day without something awful happenin'."

"Gracie, mind yourself," said Crabtree.

"Master, your long hair make a pretty good scalplock."

So would mine, Candace thought. She wondered if she'd ever sleep through a night again.

CHAPTER 11

Candace drew the wagon cover closed, and quaked in the dark, knowing that a thin layer of cloth would not keep her safe. She sat on her tiny bunk, an arm's length from Mrs. Rumley, who exuded eau de cologne. Every creak of a tree or gentle flap of the cover shot a bolt of terror through Candace. She tried to focus her fractured thoughts, but she couldn't: they floated incoherently through her head.

Dark had descended and the camp lay still. When she peered out of the wagon she could just make out the others, sleeping or pretending to. The Americans had agreed they would let Van Vliet keep the artifacts—but if trouble came, they'd give everything back.

She stared into the thin light of the stars, discerning almost nothing. As she sat there, she grew aware of how grimy she was. And now her soul felt unclean as well, Van Vliet's dirt upon it.

The White River ran only a few yards away, screened in places by chokecherry brush and willows. She yearned

to wash there, but feared to step into the night. She dug
around in the blackness until she found her ball of English
lavender soap. Then she wrestled with the long parade of
tiny buttons down the bodice of her dress, and pulled it
free. Maybe she could wash it as well as herself. She
released the cord that clamped her corset tight, and felt
her body rejoice. She'd always worn a Huxtable Company
corset. For more than a century her Huxtable ancestors
had manufactured corsets for proper Englishwomen, and
it had given her family a pleasant competence. Her uncle
Colin ran the company. The thought of him drew her
mouth into a prim pucker. He was dying corsets scarlet
and black and adding French lace around the hems, as if
the corsets were meant to be *seen*. Still, the business had
never prospered more, and his shameless corsets had been
the rage of London.

Hers was more modest. It had been sewn from un-
bleached linen and buckram and was practically indestruc-
tible. Its stays had been shaped from fine, flexible baleen,
the jaw plates of baleen whales. The baleen had been
cured, cut into long strips, and sewn by skilled tailors into
parallel pockets between the buckram lining and the linen
exterior.

Now, freed of its restraints, she felt suddenly vulnera-
ble, a soft female in a hard world. She ought to wash the
corset too. She felt a mad passion to wash and scour every
stitch she'd worn, as if the scouring would float away the
troubles that had engulfed her.

She donned her blue wrapper and slid into the night.
She winced her way in cloth slippers toward the gurgling
river, keeping a sharp eye on those slumbering forms in
deep star-shadow under the other wagons. The dome of
heaven above her vibrated with life, supplying her with
enough light to make her way to a gravelly spit well away
from their camp, where she could kneel and wash.

The strange tepid water cleaned her but left a film on

her flesh like chalk. Her hair would be dulled. Still, when she'd finished she felt better. She peered around fearfully, then washed her corset, chemise, and petticoat, wondering if the cloth would be stained. At last she slid into her wrapper and carried her unmentionables back to her wagon.

"Miss Huxtable." The low voice rose out of the blackness. It was Rufus Crowe's.

She startled violently. He loomed near her wagon, a compact form in the night. "You peeked!"

"No. If I were peekin' I wouldn't be talking here. I waited here. Could we talk some?"

She stared uncertainly, not trusting. And yet he, above all, was the one she needed to talk to. "Turn your back and wait."

She draped her wet clothing over the seat, clambered into the wagon, snapped the door flap tight, and groped around for dry things, wondering why Mrs. Rumley wasn't guarding her virtue. She settled for a dry petticoat and chemise, and then pulled the wrapper over her again.

"Don't think you can take liberties with me," she whispered as she climbed out.

He didn't say anything, and led her straight out of the glade to open prairie. The hot earth still shot heat through her thin slippers.

"Here's as good as any," he said, settling into the bunchgrass about two hundred yards from the cottonwood grove. "We don't have to whisper."

"What do you want?"

"I thought you might want to ask me some questions. You're wondering what to do. Maybe I can help."

She studied him contemplatively. He'd settled to the ground and was waiting. "What're the Sioux going to do?"

"Listen to Toothache; talk it over; come visiting to see

for themselves. I don't know what they'll do to Doctor Van Vliet.''

"Would they hurt him?''

"They could. More likely, because I'm guiding, they'll warn him not to take anything from a scaffold, and let it go at that—this time. Of course they'll take back what he took.''

"Are the rest of us in danger?''

"You're never clear of danger from the Sioux.''

She thought about that, not liking it. ''Mister Crowe, should we—should I—drive back to Fort Pierre?''

"How badly do you want to do your work here?''

She sighed. ''I've come across an ocean and a continent for this, Mister Crowe. Is that answer enough?''

He didn't reply at first. Then, ''I hope you don't turn around. I think it'll smooth out, and you'll have a fine summer.''

"I'm not sure it'll stay smoothed out, Mister Crowe. That man's going to get into trouble again and again.''

"Well, I imagine Professor Wood'll have something to say about it. He's the chairman.''

"You know, Mister Crowe, I never gave a thought to the character of those who'd be my colleagues here. It was a great mistake on my part. All I could think of was getting in with them, by hook or crook.''

"I notice they don't exactly welcome you, Miss Huxtable.''

She smiled at him. ''I'll do my own work and not worry about it. When summer's over I'll have my fossils, and that's what I came for.''

"I sure do admire you. I'd like to help you, Miss Huxtable. I can find fossils. I've seen a heap of them around. I've sent some down the river for old Chouteau. I'd like you—you and your companion—to eat with us. Long as you're not welcome to eat with the rest.''

"I'd enjoy it, but I'm afraid Mrs. Rumley—''

"—won't sit at table with a savage. Watch us chewin' buffalo with our fingers." He laughed softly.

His amusement flustered her. "Really, when I interviewed her I didn't imagine—" She sighed. "You're kind to offer to help me. But I believe I can manage alone."

"I'd like you to teach me. I'd like to talk. Around here I don't get to talk to white people. I don't talk about fossils and science with Toothache."

"Teach you?"

"Tell me about your father."

"What?"

"Your father."

"What about him?"

"He published an abstract of his forthcoming work in the *Journal of the Linnaean Society*, didn't he? Two years ago. I enjoyed the hypothesis, but I think new research will overtake it."

"How on earth do you know about that?"

"I read."

"You—want to talk about that? Now?"

"I do. His theory, that the species specialize as they adapt to adversity over eons of time—I think that'll stand up. But I'm not so sure about the rest of it—his belief that God created an archetype of each creature and nature modified it a thousand ways. Now I imagine you're here to look for—"

"Mister Crowe, you amaze me."

"I was hoping to get this employment so I could talk to some real paleontologists. I never met a one until now. All I know is what comes up the river on the boat. I subscribe to some journals. I didn't realize that those doctors yonder wouldn't want to talk with me—but I sure want to talk with you. And learn. I'd do anything you need done."

His offer and his request troubled her. "I'd better think about this. It was kind of you to help me decide . . ."

"I want to help you, Miss Huxtable. I can help find the fossils."

"I'm sorry, Mister Crowe. It'd take a learned person to do that."

"I'm willing to learn."

"I wouldn't have time for that, sir. And you'll be busy, I'm sure."

"Well, can I watch?"

"Is this what you brought me out here to ask?"

"No. I wanted to talk about your father's ideas. He's got one leg in Genesis and one leg in science. I think you do too."

A tendril of pleasure curled through her thoughts. "Well, that's true. My father's hypothesis that the Creator fashioned the archetypes is the foundation of his thinking. God put them on earth; nature and adversity modified them over millions of years. Really, Mister Crowe, his book's about specialization, and about how it all came to be. He's done more in that field than any other; he's studied hundreds of turtles, not just by type, but by environment and specialization. And lizards—do you know how many kinds of lizards there are? Do you know how the chameleon survives? He was working on the mammals when he died. If I can finish it—"

"—it'd be a great book."

"My fair copy is over a thousand pages, and he complained he couldn't get all his information into one volume. There's been so little written about the specializations of species and what caused them. Even if he's wrong about divine archetypes and Wallace and Darwin are right—Cecil Henry Huxtable will still be a great name in the natural sciences."

"I've been thinking along those lines myself."

He was discomforting her. "I think it's time for me to retire."

"You come here from love, or duty?"

"How can I answer something like that? Mister Crowe—you're most kind. But really, you're not trained to discuss—"

"Are you? Your academic credentials don't seem to be honored by the learned doctors over yonder."

"I didn't come here to discuss my credentials."

"I imagine you're well schooled as that whole lot."

"You have no way of knowing that. A layman like you . . ."

A resignation seemed to settle in him. "I'm grateful for your time."

Rufus Crowe had piqued her. She peered at him, seeing almost nothing but sensing a bond. She sat in the warm night, feeling less afraid.

"You think I'll be safe?"

"No, that's not really what I'm saying. I imagine that if you want something awful bad, you'll go ahead. If not, you'll get cautious and retreat."

"I intend to stay."

"I take it you sort of invited yourself."

She nodded. "Worse. They said no and I came anyway."

"I get the sense of it."

"I have no academic credentials."

"There's a lot of learned fools around."

"When I was a girl I sat in the back of the lecture halls. No one minded very much. Or if they did, they were too English to complain about it. I read everything that I could. But none of that counts, you know."

"Maybe you're here for more, Miss Huxtable. You'd like to prove your own worth to them."

"Mister Crowe: you don't understand. No matter what I do or achieve, they won't recognize it."

"Maybe you'd like to try anyway."

"More than I can tell you. Do you know what I dream of? I want to do better than the whole lot of them! Not just because I'm a woman. I want to make a great contribution. As a person."

"I notice you go to some lengths not to be taken as a woman."

Candace bristled at the impertinence. "Mister Crowe, my gender is not important to me, and perhaps that's reflected in my conduct."

"No matter what you do or say, or how you dress, or how many pairs of goggles you wear, you'll never say a word or take a step without my knowing you're a woman."

She digested that, not liking it. "I think we should go back now. Thank you for helping me."

She rose. He didn't.

"You think I'm causing you trouble you don't want. I'm sorry. I see you as a friend I can talk to. I got just a smatterin' of learning. You got fine credentials even if you can't say it. I just was hoping you didn't mind some old mountain boy trying out dumb ideas on you."

"Your ideas aren't dumb. And you're not a boy, Mister Crowe."

"Miss Huxtable, where you come from, everyone from a street-sweeper to a nobleman's got a station. I've got no station. I'm right off the station list. So if I say anything you don't like, don't pay it any heed. You go on back to Cambridge and be the first woman professor. They'll call you an eccentric old girl."

She laughed, pleasantly insulted.

He turned solemn. "Miss Huxtable, I want you to know something. You're not alone here. I'm going to look after you. I'm going to see to it that no one harms you, my Lakota people or—anyone else. I'm going to be the man you didn't get to hire. You go sleep now, and don't worry your head about a thing."

She stood, comforted and thrown off balance at the same time.

CHAPTER
12

The early dawns in these northern prairies amazed Gracie. She didn't know why the sun decided to rise at four in the morning here. The sun told her when to rise and when to sleep. That's how life went for a slave. With the first gray light she rolled out of her ragged blanket and began collecting cottonwood sticks for the morning fire.

Deftly she carved some tinder from the fuzzy interior of cottonwood bark and added some tiny filaments of wood she peeled from a bone-dry stick with her butcher knife. She scratched a sulphur match and soon had a blaze. She trudged down to the river and filled her blackened coffeepot with milky water, then returned and rested it on an iron grille over the fire. While the water heated she ground roasted coffee beans in her master's mill and poured the grounds into the water.

From the master's wagon she extracted a heavy bag of cornmeal, a crock of lard, a sack of ground salt, and her griddle, and began to mix the johnnycakes. She was required to feed all the scientists. The Englishwoman fed herself and her companion. She wondered what the guide would do now that his wife had left. Gracie envied a woman who could run away and not be chased with bloodhounds and men with whips.

None of the others had risen, but they would when they smelled her coffee. They would wolf down her johnnycakes and only Professor Wood would thank her. He always did. It amused the master and annoyed her. He'd get her into trouble if he kept doing that. Then, while she scoured the tin plates and forks in the river, they would harness the teams and break camp. And if she didn't finish on time, her master would fume and threaten her with a beating while they all lounged around watching. The Englishwoman had once started to help, but Gracie had shooed her off angrily. Those English didn't know anything! Her master knew how to make life miserable.

Not that she couldn't make his life miserable too, she thought as she whipped the johnnycake batter and extracted two flies and a white mealworm from it. She'd known him a long time. She was forty and he fifty. He'd bought her immediately after he'd become a physician and a man of leisure in Charleston. She scarcely remembered her first master, a red-faced, red-tempered tobacco planter. She'd never known her father, but she remembered her mother, Belle, gaunt and field-broken.

Crabtree had taken her to his big brick house in 1832 and showed her the kitchen, the iron stove, the pantry, the well outside, the two parlor stoves that burned coal, and the little room off the kitchen where she'd have a pallet. "You'll keep house," he said. "I shall be quite particular. No dust. Fresh linens once a week. Flowers in the vases at all possible times. And never, never put your miserable digits on anything in my study. If you misbehave I shall be impossible to live with." She'd nodded, big-eyed and fearful, not knowing what half his words meant. The study, she found out, was buried in books and rocks and stone bones.

As the years passed, he talked to her more. "A fool, that Wood," he'd tell her as she dusted. "Hasn't got the brains of a gnat. I'll have to tear the man's work apart in the next issue of the *American Philosophical Society Journal*."

She'd learned fast enough that her master privately mocked everyone who studied rocks and bones and fossils and monstrous beasts. That's why he came here: he wanted to make fools of them all, including the Englishwoman and her dead father. Out here his friendship with Wood was warm and touching. She chortled secretly: the old Crab didn't fool her for an instant. J. Roderick Crabtree reminded her of a big red-necked vulture, always sharpening his beak on a dead tree.

He'd never touched her, and she was grateful. Many masters did. He liked to flirt with white women in fancy parlors, and was always dashing off for afternoon Madeira in his creamy linen suit that she constantly cleaned and pressed. She'd become aware that he feared women, even including her. It amazed her that the man would cower behind his wheezy humor whenever he visited with women. She sometimes made use of her insight. She could get away with things if she didn't press too hard.

Her own existence had settled into a stupefying loneliness and despair, broken only by her daily forays into the markets to buy food. There, furtively, she had a moment to gossip with other domestic slaves. But she could do nothing to assuage those yearnings she'd felt when she was younger for a man and her own babies and a lot of friends. She tried not to think about such things because they made her weep through empty nights, only to awaken red-eyed, to begin another hopeless day.

Her sadness had thickened over the years. She had no future, present, or past. She had no reason to live, and often wished she could die. This trip had been especially hard. The stiff boots he'd bought her had chafed blisters into her toes and heels, and her lumbering walk beside the wagon had been a scorching torture that didn't end when they had stopped for the day, because she had to begin a meal at once. At night she nursed her ruined feet in the river, divining that the white water had miraculous healing powers. But neither it nor the lard she rubbed into the wounds relieved her, so her limp deepened each day. He might have let her sit on the opened tailgate; that would have been suitable for a slave. But he'd made her walk, and she knew why. It amused him to see the abolitionist Professor Wood in a silent fury about it.

The others rose at last. She wondered briefly whether they would try to repair the damage to the burial ground or go ahead. But it didn't matter. Curiosity was a luxury for those who had some control over their destinies. She had none, and their decisions ultimately meant nothing . . . unless . . . A furtive thought flickered through her mind. Maybe the Indians would take her away! A thousand miles from any white men.

The thought surprised her. She'd become so comfortable with J. Roderick Crabtree that such an idea seemed disloyal. Bit by bit she'd cleared tiny corners of liberty in her life with him. Small things, like taking an extra hour to do the marketing.

"This coffee's awful, Gracie," said her master.

"It's too white," she retorted.

He laughed nastily. After twenty-seven years they knew each other.

She didn't wait long to learn what would happen that day.

"We're going ahead with the artifacts, Crowe," Wood announced briskly. "As Doctor Van Vliet says, what's done can't be undone. We don't think the aborigines will attack us. Doctor Van Vliet assures us they'll come see what we're up to, protest, and all that. And we'll tell them it's all for the sake of the Mystery of the Universe. You'll translate, of course.''

''I imagine Doctor Van Vliet has them figured out,'' Crowe said tartly.

Gracie scrubbed tin plates and sighed. The Indians would come, and that pleased her.

CHAPTER
13

It took them three more days to reach the Badlands. Each day they rattled along a worn trace, with the White River burning on their left and grasslands stretching to hazy horizons in all directions. Rarely did they pass a tree, and when they did the event was so welcome that they often paused under it, as if to greet a long-lost friend. When they encountered patches of prickly pear, one or another of them would hack off some lobes and drop them into the water casks to clear the milky water. It seemed to work.

The sun was bleaching the bunchgrasses into a tan carpet. Occasionally Rufus Crowe would pause and point to some plant or other near the trail.

"That there, with the narrow spiky leaves, is a prairie turnip. It makes a fine food," he said. "This here, with the sword leaves and the stalk, is soapweed. Its roots make a good soap for your hair. The leaves make good mats."

Professor Wood listened attentively, knowing that their guide was giving them the means to survive. He learned that chokecherries were edible; that the hips of the wild rose made a good emergency food; that the prickly pears, still showing yellow blooms, were edible after their thorns were burned off, and also a source of emergency moisture. They could be fed to livestock too.

At dawn on the second day Crowe pointed toward a white streak off to the west. ''That's the Badlands. It's an eroded wall is all, with higher prairie on the north, and the White River valley to the south. Some of the wall rises up above the higher prairies, but mostly the drop is two or three hundred feet.''

A great joy washed through Cyrus Billington Wood. There it was! The thing he'd crossed half a continent to see! It shimmered on the horizon, a magnet for any pale-ontologist. He felt somehow younger and buoyant.

''Not much firewood between here and there,'' the guide added. They all stared across a kingdom of grass where any other plants or trees were exiles and interlopers.

That afternoon the furnace heat of July wearied the horses beyond endurance, and Crowe called a halt. There would be no shade except for the tiny patches under the wagons, and they all crawled into those little havens, finding the moving air better than the oppressive shade within. The waiting seemed unbearable to Wood, and as he lay under the wagon, peering at a cloudless sky turned white with heat, he imagined himself chipping out fossil after fossil, unknown creatures, several of which would be named in Latin for him. He would add a hundred extinct species to the known fauna of the past, and complete the most exhaustive taxonomy of prehistoric vertebrates ever achieved.

Rufus Crowe started them off again late in the afternoon. The sun still seared, but it would be harmless by the time the drays wearied again. They passed a lonely cottonwood on the bank of the White, and the Huxtable woman steered her wagon over to pluck it. The others didn't stop. Wood saw her snap off dead lower branches and drop them onto the floorboard of her wagon seat. Crowe had called those dry lower sticks squaw wood, and Wood thought it was an apt term. She fell a half mile back, but after a while she caught up, snapping the lines over the croups of her big Clydesdales.

All that second day Wood squinted anxiously at the horizons, taking alarm at every heat-shimmer and trick of the air. But no Sioux came. He fervently hoped that Van Vliet was right; that it'd all blow over; that he wouldn't end up on the prairie prickling with arrows, his scalp dangling from some warrior's lance. He wondered what sort of madness had driven him here; what sort of permissiveness had let him condone Van Vliet's private pillaging under the inviolate banner of science. He had not been fooled by the sweaty man who rode beside him on the hot wagon seat.

The result of all his alert squinting was simply to make his eyes ache. He lamented that he'd not had goggles made up, like those of the Huxtable girl.

He pitied poor Gracie, limping along beside that despicable Crabtree, who seemed not to notice her suffering. Wood watched the slave woman stumble along, never complaining, pausing only to wipe her brow, rub her ankles, or hike her skirt and shake it to fan air to her soaked body.

At last he could bear it no more and the next time they paused to let the horses blow, he hailed her over.

"Miss Gracie, you're most welcome to sit here with Doctor Van Vliet and me. Rest your feet."

She backed away, as if he'd loosed a viper upon her. "You don't know! Don't get me into trouble."

"But surely Professor Crabtree—"

"No! Leave me be!"

Bewildered, Wood watched her limp back to the other wagon and collapse in its shade for a moment. And on the

seat above, dapper in his creamy linen suit and a straw
planter's hat, Crabtree observed it all with obvious glee.
Wood silently vowed that from now on, somehow, he'd
find ways to ease Gracie's burdens.

Crowe halted them in the twilight of a searing day,
choosing a flat meadow within a great oxbow of the
White. Wood realized at once that it had defensive possi-
bilities, with the treacherous river on three sides. But he
saw nary a tree in any direction; not even any rabbit brush
or chokecherry in crevasses along the placid river. He
yearned suddenly for a spot of tea, and rued the moment
when he'd whipped his drays along instead of plucking up
wood the way the Huxtable woman had.

No tea tonight. No cooked meal from Gracie. No coffee
in the morning. Suddenly he needed tea; hot, tart, transparent China tea that would slide happily down his parched
throat. Tea! He wanted a whole porcelain pot of it, steeped
from the leaves in a silver strainer, poured into fine china
cups and saucers, with a bit of lemon and sugar added!

Crowe unhitched the drays and led them down a sharp
slope to the river, testing the soft clay flats to see whether
the horses would bog in them, and then letting the animals
nose and lick the water they hated.

The Huxtable woman clambered down, stretched, wandered down to the river, where she stepped delicately out
upon the dried clay flats, and stiffly lowered her corseted
self to splash white water on her face.

Cyrus Wood felt vexed by the Huxtable woman. He
knew the reason perfectly well, and felt ashamed of it. But
there wasn't a thing he could do. He'd never, never stoop
to begging to share her fire. Not ever! And so he watched
sulkily as she clambered back up the bank and cut her
squaw wood with her camp ax. In a few minutes she had
a fine blaze going, and clear water from her small cask
heating over it. He glowered at her, the weeds of petulance
blooming within him.

She clambered into her wagon and emerged with an enameled tea caddy and some implements, including, to his astonishment, a bone-china cup and saucer. The water came to a boil in the last of a lavender twilight, and she lifted the metal pot by its bail, protecting her hand with a glove, and poured steaming water into her china cup, adding a charged tea strainer and letting it steep. She looked utterly beautiful in the wavering firelight, which fractured off the sheen of her chestnut hair. Then Crowe joined her and filled his tin cup with tea.

Wood stared at them bitterly. The two had gotten chummy lately. She'd stolen the expedition's guide.

"Gentlemen, would you care for some tea?" she asked.

"No, not ever!" cried Wood. "I don't need a drop!"

"That'd hit the spot," said Crabtree. He ambled toward her fire, while Wood stood rigid, like a mooring post buried in the clay. But when Van Vliet surrendered, so did Wood, and they made their hasty way to the blaze.

But Candace Huxtable didn't serve them. She carried a cup of it to Gracie, who had hung back, anchored to the grass by bondage. Only after serving Gracie did she serve the rest, a wry smile illumining her lovely oval face.

CHAPTER
14

The White River trail angled toward the blinding cliffs of the Badlands until Candace could see the violent erosion that had carved the bluffs into bizarre canyons divided by crenelated towers and fluted columns, labyrinths that twisted deep into the higher prairie to the north.

Closer at hand rose outlying islands, some of them eroded into toadstools with harder rock for a cap. The Badlands had been formed relatively recently. They were sculpted mostly from mudstone that hadn't consolidated well and dissolved easily in water. But here and there thin sandstone and limestone layers had resisted erosion. That's how it had segmented into fantastic forms. It all shimmered in the afternoon heat, sinister claws and spikes of rock, vertical walls, violent crannies and crumbling towers and chasms.

Her spirits sagged. What had seemed possible when she'd planned it back in Cambridge now seemed impossible. She could scarcely imagine herself crawling over such precipices and crumbling towers, scaling vertical walls, hunting for elusive fossils in their rock matrix. She'd made a mistake. Candace Huxtable had only a sneaked education, full of holes. The realization wrenched her soul. She would have been better off waiting for the fossils to be shipped east and interpreted by skilled paleontologists.

Even as the sinister cliffs defined themselves into impassable mazes, she questioned her abilities. This wasn't work for women. It was barely work for men. But then exhilaration surprised her. The few others who had come to this remote place had made mad harvests of creatures unknown, unnamed, and terrible, and had described the Badlands as the greatest mammalian and vertebrate fossil beds known to science. How could she go wrong?

She stared at that forbidding wall and began to love it. She loved the boundless sun-whited sky; she loved the harsh prospects she beheld. She loved the fierce dry air, the choking dust and bad water, the merciless land that bit and scratched, forgave no mistakes, and offered few rewards. She loved the liberty. No English hedgerow, no tradition, could stop her. She would dig and discover and observe and measure and hypothesize. She would grow like a rank weed. She'd roll on the wind like a tumbleweed and count each hurt as the education of a corseted soul.

Candace smiled. The others had shared her fire the previous night but her kindness had won her no friends. She'd awakened to frosty silence. One thing was different, though: Dr. Crabtree had dropped the tailgate of his wagon and had allowed poor Gracie to sit there. The woman had swayed on that merciless board all morning, but Candace was sure it had been better than walking.

A bit later Crowe halted the party. She tugged on the lines of her Clydesdales and stepped down to the burning clay.

"I imagine this is as close as we'll get," he said. "From here on, the river angles away."

She stared, dismayed. The nearest part of the Badlands wall seemed to be three or four miles off. She saw no comforting copse of cottonwoods on the river; only an occasional sentinel tree, which could supply enough dry wood for a meal or two and no shade to speak of.

"Are you sure we must camp here?" asked Wood.

"I imagine there's some slumps up there. My Brulé people talk of them. Places where cliffs tumbled and blocked off the drainage. Little old holes with ponds and marshes and a lot of juniper and some cottonwoods too. But I'd better warn you, I don't know if a wagon can get in there."

Professor Wood didn't like it. "This is too far away. We'd spend most of our time coming and going."

"I imagine."

"Aren't there any options?"

"I imagine you could fill your casks and drive as close to the Badlands as you can go."

"Is there grass for the horses there?"

"We can find out."

Candace was all for driving toward the sinister lands, but found herself without a voice. If she opened her mouth it'd only drive them to do something else.

"Will the aborigines spot the wheel tracks?"

Rufus Crowe peered at the man over his gold-rimmed half-glasses. "I don't imagine you'll be escaping the attention of the Brulés. They're a sight smarter than you think."

"Is the water in those slumps potable?"

"Same as the rest. Bad."

"Is there firewood?"

"There's juniper wood and cottonwood and water in some of those pockets."

Dr. Wood addressed the rest. "Gentlemen?"

"Let's go," said Van Vliet. "I need shade to sort my things."

He also wanted to hide from Sioux, Candace surmised. He was hoping their tracks would be dusted over or be rained on before the aborigines tracked them.

Dr. Crabtree started the parade again, steering his wagon off the river trace and driving toward the distant cliffs, bouncing over rough ground, the wheels of his wagon hissing over dust, banging against stray rock. Wood and Van Vliet followed in the second wagon. Candace turned her Clydesdales, glad she was at the rear. Crowe took the lead, steering them around gullies, across flats, up and down precipitous little slopes, sometimes meandering two miles to go one mile toward the looming bluffs.

Her horses sweated, their withers turned black, and she worried, knowing they were moving ever farther from water.

By midafternoon they'd reached the clawed feet of the badlands, and Rufus Crowe called a halt.

"I'm going to ride as high as I can and look for some green," he said. "I imagine you can rest your beasts."

They watched him ride into a labyrinth and vanish. Suddenly she felt less secure. The rock around her seethed with malign heat. This land didn't want her here!

She clambered down and lay in the miserable pencil of shade under her wagon. Mrs. Rumley remained inside, enjoying a headache, which always filled her with religion. Nothing around Candace lived. She saw not an ant crawling over the cream clay, and not a blade of green grass. The heat pinioned her to the earth and burned her as she sat. She felt it burn the pinched flesh under her corset until she was desperate to untie it. Each whalebone stay held her like a Commandment.

She had expected that Crowe's reconnoitering would consume the day, but in a little while—an hour, she guessed—he returned.

"I found a place. I had to tie up my horse and walk, but it's right here."

"Can we take the wagons all the way?"

"No, but we can take them to about three hundred yards of it."

They clambered into their wagons without further questioning. Rufus Crowe led them confidently toward the east, and then into a rapidly narrowing defile with eroded walls and a relatively smooth bottom, planed by torrents of water. The defile curled until the south wall cast umber shade almost across the gulch. Minutes later Candace was driving her great horses between crumbling walls that vaulted upward so steeply that the sky narrowed into a blue band. Not a breath of air coursed this sinister bottom, and the horses oozed sweat even though the sun didn't touch them.

Their guide stopped at last at a ledge that halted further passage.

"Fix your teams and we'll walk the rest of the way."

Reluctantly Candace hobbled her miserable white-caked horses and followed the others as they clambered up a steep drainage. Each step sucked her breath away, but when they reached the crest of this tumble of wind-blurred rock, she beheld a dished green valley, thick with somber juniper and a patch of brighter cottonwoods. And there, beside the cottonwoods, she spotted a marsh with cattails, and the glint of water.

CHAPTER
15

They'd found an Eden in the midst of hell. Rufus Crowe thought that heaven must be a well-watered cool place, and hell simply a place without a drink. Spread before them was forty or fifty acres of green, all of it owing to the collapse of canyon walls that damned the prairie rains and snows in the little basin. They wandered through their demi-paradise, finding the little marsh alive with bright birds and wary turtles, abundant grasses to support their horses, and ample wood and shade from the cottonwoods and junipers. The water was like all the rest, milky with the dissolved muds of the soft rock. But those prickly pear lobes would settle it.

"I imagine you could pack your duffel here."

"Will the empty wagons be safe down there?" Wood asked.

"Not entirely. The Brulés would respect them because they're my people. But not the other Sioux—or other tribes."

"What might happen to them?"

"Oh, you'd lose every piece of metal, including the iron tires. And some of the hardwood too, like the spokes—they'd make nice handles for clubs and hatchets and all."

"How can we carry it?"

"I've got a packsaddle; you've got harness. I can rig canvas bundles to your harness and haul it."

That was what they did. Through the boiling afternoon they loaded canvas-wrapped bundles on the four harness horses that would accept them, and led them single file up the narrow trail to a shaded campsite near the sultry pond. Two of the harness horses reared and fought when the bundles were anchored to the hames, and these were simply turned loose in the basin. The Englishwoman's Clydesdales turned out to be the most useful, patiently carrying load after load.

Dr. J. Roderick Crabtree watched it all, never lifted a finger, and meandered while his slave lifted and toted and sweated like a mule. Van Vliet and Wood helped the slave, but the Englishwoman had been left to her own devices.

Rufus Crowe approached the sweat-drenched woman, who was wrestling with canvas too heavy for her to lift.

"I imagine you could use some help."

"Oh, would you? The blasted canvas defeats me."

She was attempting to erect a large wall tent using a rope tied between cottonwoods as a ridgepole.

"I don't think that'll do," Crowe said.

He found some dead saplings, cut and trimmed them, and built her a solid tent frame with pole rafters. Then he spread the canvas over it, rolling up the walls a foot or so off the ground to permit air to circulate.

She stared at it dubiously.

"You'll lose some privacy," he said. "I suggest you try it this way before pegging the canvas to earth and suffering."

"Mrs. Rumley won't permit it."

"You'll want the air."

She started to object. "How will I bathe and—" She stopped and smiled. "Thank you."

"There's privacy at night."

"There's not much darkness this time of year." She eyed the others, erecting their tents about fifty yards away. "I'll find a way. Perhaps while the rest are digging . . . This'll keep me cool. Thank you, Mister Crowe. You're always most kind."

Her frank gaze met his and held there. He wrestled away the submerged emotions he didn't want to acknowledge, and smiled gently. "You're some woman."

"I have a lot of work to do."

Dismissed. He knew he'd crossed some sort of line into forbidden country, and retreated hastily, with one last lingering glance toward the grimy, angular, corset-stiffened woman of high station whose feisty courage and chiseled beauty had kindled a terrible longing in his lonely soul. He wanted her, but he might as well want to claim the moon.

He wandered, ax in hand, toward the rest. They'd followed his lead and erected durable frames of saplings lashed to trees and covered with wagon sheets. One of these was nothing but a canvas roof and single wall, open on three sides. There, Archimedes Van Vliet had collected his loot and would sit in cool comfort cleaning and preserving everything, making notes and sketches. He and Wood were draping the second sheet over a pole structure that would give them a large tent, while Gracie, sweat rivering from her black temples, toted crates and hogsheads and bundles into the rising shelter.

Wood stopped, slumping wearily. "I worry about those wagons down there, my good man."

"I imagine you should."

"What'll we do if they're stolen or scavenged?"

"I've always said living here is a risk."

"But the fossils—we've got to get them back."

"There's always a way to make do. Travois, for instance."

That didn't stop Wood's worrying. "What if they steal the horses too?"

Rufus sighed. "Professor Wood, there's no heaven on this earth. Not even here in this little hideyhole."

"Heaven's for white men," muttered Gracie.

He had no response to that. She slaved within a hell not of her making, a hell so terrible that even a chance to sit on the grass and remove her cheap shoes and rub her blistered feet was a sliver of paradise.

By dusk they'd built a solid summer camp, stored their goods, and collected firewood. The trail-weary horses grazed freely, hemmed in by rock walls, with nothing to tempt them away. Except for the bare wagons in the canyon below, everything seemed secure. But Rufus Crowe knew it was an illusion.

The illusion was broken even before they sat down to their first supper of cornmeal cakes, wearily fried by Gracie. In the quiet lavender air, six Brulé Teton Sioux rode in, one by one, and behind them Toothache.

Van Vliet scrambled toward his gear, heaped next to the burial loot.

"Don't," said Rufus sternly. Van Vliet had a Colt Navy revolver in a holster there.

Van Vliet ignored him.

Catlike, Rufus pounced, wrested the weapon from Van Vliet's hands, and shoved the shocked paleontologist away.

"Crowe, I'll—"

"Don't."

The rest stood uneasily. The Englishwomen looked terrified. Wood couldn't even unfold his body to its full height, as if he were awaiting the cut of the scalping knife. Gracie clucked and muttered and pretended the visitors weren't there. Only that devil J. Roderick Crabtree stood erect, his creamy suit bright in the lavender light, his black eyes studying the visitors eagerly, his cigar at a jaunty angle.

Crowe stood. Here, riding into the light of Gracie's fire, was a chief of the Sichangus, Little Thunder, bitter toward whites after his terrible beating by General Harney; young Spotted Tail, a powerful headman and probably a future chief of the Burnt Thigh people; Short Bull, not yet twenty, following the path of the medicine man, or Dreamer; and three others Crowe knew, all headmen. This kind of party had something important in mind.

"Tell them to mind their manners," said Mrs. Rumley. "Or I shall report them to the magistrates."

CHAPTER
16

G racie bustled over her cookfire, pretending not to notice the visitors. But she missed nothing. They wore breechclouts and moccasins. Three wore headbands to pin their loose black hair. Two had eagle feathers tucked into their hair. One wore his hair in red-wrapped braids.

They rode barebacked and controlled their ponies with loops of leather tied to the jaws. Over their shoulders they carried quivers and bow sheaths but none had a weapon or shield or war club in hand. Gracie guessed they had come to talk—at least for the moment.

Their leader lifted a hand and addressed Crowe: *"Ho-ko-lah."*

"Hello, friend," Rufus Crowe replied. *"Ho-ko-lah."* He welcomed them one by one, plainly expressing his delight. Crowe reached Toothache at last and said something that made her laugh lightly.

The guide peered around him, assuring himself that the whites understood this visit would be peaceful. Cheerfully, Gracie noted the dread that etched their faces, es-

pecially the pasty face of Professor Van Vliet. She only
wished that her master, who alone looked jaunty and un-
afraid, would be as terrified as the other white men.

"*Hew-wo,*" Crowe said.

The Sioux filed closer, cautiously surveying their hosts.
They seemed curious about everything, their gazes roving
from man to man, resting long on Miss Huxtable, who
stood stiffly, her chin high, and Mrs. Rumley, whose gaze
subdued them, and finally upon Gracie. She felt their pen-
etrating stares and ignored them.

They'd never seen a black woman, she thought. Well,
let them look! She abandoned her stirring and met their
gazes, liking these men. They had brown flesh, not far
from the color of hers. They frightened white men. Toothache grinned malevolently at the whites from atop her little dun pony, and Gracie ventured a smile at her.

"Little Thunder!" exclaimed Crowe, for the benefit of
the white men. One by one the headmen slid off their
ponies and serenely embraced the guide. The stocky chief
had a powerful build and a plain face dominated by a
formidable nose. That he radiated a stern authority was
not lost on Gracie or the whites.

The headmen walked freely about the encampment,
peering at the shelters, pausing silently before the loot
from the robbed graves, then turning again to Gracie. They
pointed at her and muttered in their strange tongue while
Rufus Crowe replied in the same tongue.

"Miss Gracie," Crowe said. "You're something they've
never seen and they want to know why you paint yourself
for victory. They paint up black when they come home
from a battle they've won, or they've got some horses they
stole."

"You tell them to mind their manners."

"I'll tell 'em it's not paint," he said, and began to
speak in that odd gutteral tongue again. At last he turned

to her. "They want to wash you with water to see if it's paint."

"You tell them to mind."

"They want to trade for you."

Gracie instantly turned silent. A false word would bring the master's cruelties down on her.

"Crowe, they don't have the price," said Crabtree cheerfully. "I paid two thousand for the girl. Worth five now."

"You got a bargain," she muttered too low for him to hear.

For one wild moment Gracie wished she'd be abducted. It might be terrible to live with the savages but it would be less terrible than all she'd ever known. She felt the intent gaze of a stocky agate-eyed middle-aged warrior, who wore a little leather bag decorated with beads upon his chest. She knew intuitively that he was sizing her up—for something.

"Mister Crowe," said Wood, "invite them to share our meal."

More damn cooking, Gracie thought, eyeing her batter. The red devils would snatch up everything she cooked.

Little Thunder said something.

"He wants to smoke the pipe here," said Crowe. "You set yourselves around and follow what I do."

He settled himself to the earth, and the other white men did the same. Archimedes Van Vliet looked like a trapped rabbit, eyeing the tattletale Toothache as if she were his death warrant. The Englishwomen hung back, and Gracie thought she should too. She added more cornmeal and stirred furiously, making a great racket with her metal spoon.

From a pair of beaded pouches dangling from the withers of his pony Little Thunder extracted a long pipe with a bowl of red stone and a twist of tobacco. Solemnly he tamped tobacco into the bowl, but even as he labored his gaze lingered upon one white man after another. He gazed for some time upon Miss Huxtable, who stood pale and rigid nearby, and finally met Gracie's own delighted eyes. He smiled slightly and muttered something to Crowe.

"Miss Gracie, please bring him a live coal on a cotton-wood leaf or a bit of bark," said Crowe.

She did as she had been commanded, dreading to be scalped. The chief accepted the offering amiably. He picked up the coal with his fingers, dropped it onto the charge of tobacco, and sucked. Then he stood solemnly and studied the emerging stars. He spoke softly, offering his pipe in each cardinal direction, lifting it toward the sky.

"He's asking the blessings of the four winds, and the Great Spirit, Wakan Tanka, and Mother Earth," Crowe explained. "This is a peaceful gathering and he's declaring it to all our ears."

Little Thunder sat down, puffed, and passed the calumet to the Sioux on his right, who puffed solemnly and passed it along to the next, who puffed and passed it to Professor Wood.

"Go ahead, professor. It seals the peace," said Crowe.

The pipe made the rounds without incident, although Crabtree elaborately wiped saliva off first. Little Thunder received it and knocked the dottle out. Then he rose.

The chief addressed the scientists, his words sharp like a flag snapping in a hard breeze, while Crowe softly translated.

"Little Thunder says you're here as my guests, and thus guests of the Brulés, on lands the white people gave the Sioux forever. He says as long as I'm watching over you, you're welcome because I'm a friend of his people.

"But he says he's feeling low because you're in trouble with the spirits in lots of ways, and your lives are in danger."

Professor Wood responded. "Tell him, please, Mister

Crowe, that we're pleased to be here and we've some gifts for our kind hosts. If this is the moment, of course.''

"I'll tell him, but it's not the moment for gifts." He translated. The chief listened intently, and continued.

"Chief Little Thunder says the white men, the *wasicu*, are doomed to terrible things because the spirits will devil you. Already the spirits have gathered here and make this place evil with their hovering about. His heart is sad for you.

"He's saying you mustn't dig the ancient bones out of the rock. The grandfathers of the Lakota people have always known about the bones, and know how they got into the rock. The grandfathers have passed it down from generation to generation. He says these here rock bones are from fearsome big serpents that burrowed into the earth because they were being hunted by the Great Spirit, Wakan Tanka. He killed them all with bolts of lightning, deep in the rock, and now their bones are pure evil and ought not to be touched by any mortal.''

"And what'll happen if we pry them up, eh?" asked Crabtree.

"All manner of misfortune will befall you."

Gracie believed the chief, and secretly began her vigil. It'd be worth dying just to see all that evil happen.

"Please tell him," said Professor Wood, "that the bones are harmless relics of ancient beasts that roamed long before man existed. We've come to learn about them because we gather all knowledge."

"*Wechatahpe,*" said the chief.

"What was that?" asked Wood.

"Death," said Crowe.

An odd tingle coursed through Gracie.

CHAPTER
17

Death had fluttered by Archimedes Van Vliet on butterfly wings. The anguish that had ballooned in him on sighting the visitors gradually leaked away, especially when the Brulé headmen sat down for a smoke. He'd studied all the Sioux ceremonies and religious rituals, and knew what the peace pipe meant.

Crowe's catlike pounce had probably saved his life, though Van Vliet could barely bring himself to admit it. It amazed him that a mild-looking guide could move so fast. By the time Van Vliet had sat down for the peace pipe ritual, the tension in him had wilted away, and he was able to listen to the formidable-looking chief—who wasn't the sort of chap he'd like to encounter in a Brooklyn alley at night.

The chief was talking about tabooed fossils, but Van Vliet knew there'd be more on the platter soon. He listened attentively as Crowe translated, the shards of his anthropological training once again measuring and packaging and string-tying the culture of the Lakota Sioux. He noticed the other headmen and the young medicine men glancing toward the women with frank curiosity and a collector's eye that Van Vliet knew well. Before the day ended, the women might find themselves possessed by the aborigines. It amused him slightly. Especially the possible fate of Miss Huxtable.

"Mister Crowe," Wood said in a professorial tone, "tell them these ancient beasts walked the earth before human beings existed. The Great Spirit hadn't made people yet. Tell them that no bad spirits hover over the bones; they are rock now, and will help us learn about that ancient world and its animals."

"Hard to put that into Sioux, but I'll try."

The headmen listened somberly, disagreement engraving their faces. Darkness had descended, and only Gracie's cookfire illumined the council. The Sioux listened attentively, as Van Vliet knew they would. The Plains Indians debated questions with great care, in no rush to come to an agreement or compromise.

"Tell them," said J. Roderick Crabtree, "that if we see any monster spirits around, we'll slay them."

Crowe stared. "The matter is a serious one with them, Doctor Crabtree." He said something to Little Thunder.

The chief started in again, not waiting for Crowe to translate. But the chief's powerful arm and pointed finger told Van Vliet that the scaffold collection was on the chief's mind.

"Well, he's gotten around to discussing what he's mainly here for," Crowe said. "He's saying the whites, the *wasicu*, are a strange people, taking the scared things from the *nagi*, the spirits who are traveling—things they loved most on earth and need in the hereafter. Plenty important to the spirits traveling up the pathway to the land of the stars. Because the stuff's been taken, all their grandfathers and grandmothers can't get where they're going. They're wandering around like lost souls, making this place bad."

Van Vliet listened attentively. He didn't mind all this.

"Little Thunder's saying that if I weren't his Brulé brother you'd be—in a lot of trouble. But I am, and he's saying that if the white *wicasa*—that's as close as he can get to saying a learned man, wise man—will give the sacred things back to the spirits—the *nagi*—he thinks they'll be able to continue their journeys to Paradise." Crowe directed all this straight at Van Vliet.

Van Vliet nodded.

"He's saying too that if you don't give the stuff back to the *nagi*—they'll turn fearsome bad and haunt you wherever you go and devil your life."

Van Vliet nodded and waited, a faint sweat building on his temples. Everything depended upon what the aborigines planned to do with the collection.

"He's saying that they'll stay tonight and feast with us. In the morning they'll build new scaffolds, big ones with many poles to hold all the stuff. Then they'll put all the belongings of the grandfathers and grandmothers on them and make some prayers and go through the *wacekiyapi*— the funeral ceremony—to give the belongings back to the dead."

Van Vliet nodded. The ceremony would be interesting.

"Little Thunder wants to know if you're agreeing. He doesn't hear anything from you."

"Let them go ahead."

"He wants more than that. He wants the belongings to stay put forever."

Van Vliet discovered an intensity in the chief's gaze that he couldn't meet, and found himself peering round and about. Anything for science, he thought. "I don't have any choice."

"No, I imagine you don't."

"Couldn't I dicker? Wouldn't the spirits like something better? A good knife or two?"

Van Vliet had his answer in a moment: "No, the things that belong to the spirits are *wakan*—sacred."

So it came down to that. Sometimes hard choices were needful. It'd pass. He'd look the same in the looking glass when he lathered and scraped each morning. "Very well," he said. He smiled at the chief.

"Archimedes—you do understand," said Wood.

"Yes!" he snapped.

"Perhaps you can trade for other things. You brought things just for that."

"I'll do that."

"It'd cost our lives to rescue your collection."

The chief's gaze bored into Van Vliet, almost as if the man could read his mind. The young medicine man leaned over and whispered something to the chief, which alarmed Van Vliet. Did these aborigines have the power to peer into a man's inner sanctum?

The chief addressed Van Vliet and the guide translated. "Tomorrow you'll be a part of the funeral, grieve the dead, cut your arms and bleed."

"Do I have a choice?"

"No."

An idea filtered through Van Vliet's paralyzed mind. "I'm going to make him a gift," he said. "A present for them all."

"Doctor Van Vliet—a Sioux knows a—a bribe when he sees one. Some gifts they enjoy . . . others . . . arouse their . . . disfavor."

"No, no, if I give them gifts, they'll return the favor—if all my research bears me out."

Crowe pondered that, finally saying something to Little Thunder, whose face was questioning.

Gifts also create obligations, Van Vliet thought as he rose, fumbled through the dark, found his trunk of trade goods, and extracted a butcher knife and five metal awls.

Solemnly he handed them out. The recipients studied them—and him.

"Little Thunder says they'll give these to the spirits tomorrow."

Van Vliet wished he could sip some of his rye.

CHAPTER
18

Strange dreams flirted with Candace all night, making the hours crawl by in fits and starts. The presence of the Sioux in the camp disturbed her. The moment she drifted off, images of the Sioux drifted through her mind. They were handsome in their own way and radiated power and strength and mastery of their world. She had gone to bed fully clothed, her only concession being to loosen the ties of her corset and remove her high-button shoes.

Candace dreamed that the Sioux who'd eyed her early in the evening was very close, inches away, his expression amiable, his intentions plain. A strange yearning possessed her. She awakened in a panic, felt cross, and wished they'd all leave at dawn. She settled grimly into her Witney blanket.

She hadn't rested a bit when the gray dawn overtook the night, but she felt grateful to be free of those threatening phantasms. She discovered a sweetness in the new day. The sun was her protector; it made the world reasonable and correct, the way Mrs. Rumley did. Her companion had already taken to her camp chair.

"You look rested, Mrs. Rumley."

"Well, of course! We had the kaffirs to protect us from wolves and those degenerate Americans."

The Sioux didn't arise until the sun had climbed above the craggy escarpment to the east. Each quietly found a place where he could bathe himself in the sun's orange light, and there meditated or prayed. One lifted his arms toward the sky.

Then, silently, they borrowed Crowe's camp ax and hewed cottonwood posts, each with a fork at the top. She had expected them to cut four, but they cut eight, and she realized they were making two scaffolds. Dr. Van Vliet offered to help, but they brusquely turned him away.

While some cut cottonwood poles, others patiently dug postholes in the clay with their hatchets. They finished both scaffolds before the sun rose very high.

"Why are they making two?" she asked Rufus Crowe.

"One for the grandfathers, one for the grandmothers."

As if to confirm this, the Brulé headmen began sorting through Van Vliet's collection, dividing men's and women's items, and setting aside those things, mostly the amulets, the *wotawes*, whose ownership they couldn't determine. Candace glanced at Van Vliet and found him watching intently.

"Is there a reason for separating them?"

"Their custom is to keep the sexes separated. There's only one dance—a courting dance—where both sexes join in. All the rest are danced by one or the other. Their lodges have an invisible line through them; women live on one side, men on the other. Their social life's divided: men stay with men; women stay with women. That holds for their children." He eyed her thoughtfully. "It goes beyond separation, too. The other sex is the enemy."

She sensed he didn't want to elaborate. Obviously the

aboriginal males had various taboos that worked against women. She thought of all-male Cambridge, and supposed there really wasn't much difference. Maybe all males were aborigines.

Little by little the Brulés loaded one scaffold with bows and arrows and quivers, war clubs and shields and lances. They loaded the other with sewing kits, awl kits, quilled and beaded dresses, cradleboards, and dolls. They set the skulls around the posts of both scaffolds and hung amulets in a beaded bag from one of the posts of the men's scaffold. If any of them had recognized the property of their parents or grandparents, they didn't reveal it.

No one had eaten. Gracie hadn't started a meal and neither had Candace. The chief motioned to Van Vliet, who came at once, a model of academic civility and blandness all too familiar to her. She knew what academic cordiality could paper over.

"I imagine Little Thunder'll begin the honors now. They'll hold a funeral to give all the stuff back to their loved ones."

She wondered if Crowe believed in any of it. She scoffed at the idea of spirits floating about. The heat was building into a hot bright day again, without a ghost in sight. If there were ghosts in the world, they were more likely to haunt gloomy English ruins and dark country inns. Impulsively she plucked up some lilac-colored flowers, and some yellow salsify from the field near the marsh, and carried them toward the women's scaffold. She hesitated, wondering if she was doing something that offended the Brulés. But none of them stopped her. She reached up, slid her bouquet up onto the platform, and smiled hesitantly at the Brulés. They watched her expressionlessly, and she feared she'd done something awful.

"You're on safe ground," Crowe said quietly. "Any private gesture carries weight."

The Brulés had settled in a circle below the scaffolds with Van Vliet in their midst.

"What will they do?" she asked.

"It'll be some sort of funeral—the *wacekiyapi* ceremony. Only this isn't exactly a funeral."

The youngest among the Brulés stood, and began an oration.

"That's Short Bull. He's giving the stuff back to the *nagi* of the grandfathers and grandmothers, and telling them how faithful his brothers are, watching over the graves and wishing the spirits success on their long walk up the path."

Short Bull paraded around both scaffolds and sat down, his song done. The others did the same, circling the scaffolds while singing some sort of song. Rufus Crowe named them: "That's Looks Backwards, mighty warrior and head of the Sotka Yuha society, powerful man. And the next is Running Antelope, a man with twelve coups—war honors. The other there with the scar is Sleeping Bear, a headman, and after him's Badger, a mighty rich warrior with lots of horses and wives. And you know the chief."

After they'd sung their songs, they settled on the ground near Dr. Van Vliet. Little Thunder summoned Crowe, apparently to translate. The guide settled himself within the circle.

The guide began translating. "Short Bull here, the Dreamer, says it's customary to honor the grandfathers and grandmothers. He says that now the *nagi*—the spirits—can take what's theirs. The things have all been reburied, and no one's ever going to touch them again. They're *wakan*—sacred—and the skulls at the base of the scaffolds are a warning forever that it's death to touch the sacred things."

Van Vliet blinked.

Young Short Bull began to address Van Vliet directly.

"He's welcoming you, since you're a *wicasa*—that's the

closest word they have for an educated man. He says you're welcome to come to the Lakota lands because you're with me. They welcome learning and wisdom too. He thinks that digging up fossil bones is a bad business but that's your way, and they'll accept it as long as you take your bones with you, or rebury them after you're done with them.

"He says your opening those funeral scaffolds was a bad mistake and offended the grandfathers and grandmothers, but you don't know Lakota ways and you're forgiven. But don't ever touch the medicine things again. He says the Lakota are mighty friendly and a good people. They're pleased you like their things so much; their art and skills are finer than all the other peoples'. They're going to send some of their people over with things you can trade for— all the things on the scaffolds from bows and arrows and shields to cradleboards. You give them something in return, maybe they can trade at the trading posts. He asks— are you willing to trade?"

Van Vliet nodded. "I don't have much, but of course I will."

Crowe translated that, and the Brulés seemed pleased.

"They hope you enjoy your stay here, and always honor the ways of the Lakota. He asks if you will."

Van Vliet glanced at the scaffolds, sighed, and smiled. "Of course."

Candace had an uneasy feeling that the man wasn't taking his vow seriously. The Brulés scowled at the man, reading him as she did.

"That's it, then. They're asking me and Toothache to keep an eye on the scaffolds. I said we would for sure."

The headmen stood, along with Dr. Van Vliet, and each clasped Van Vliet's hands to seal the agreement.

CHAPTER
19

Archimedes Van Vliet felt no relief as he watched the six Brulé headmen ride out of the Badlands basin. They'd taken his collection from him and he'd have a devilish time getting it back. He had to do something fast: every item he'd collected from the burial bundles would die a little each day in the brutal sun and wind. The leather would stiffen; the quilling would bleach white; the bows and arrows would lose their luster. Everything made of bone and skin would decay.

The worst of it was that it rested there free for the taking. No lock or strongbox protected it. Yet he could touch none of it without alerting the watchdogs, Crowe and his squaw. They'd been hired to help the march of science, but there they were, a wall between himself and the greatest collection of artifacts he'd ever seen.

The things he'd brought along for trading wouldn't buy a hundredth of that collection. He didn't know how, but he knew his collection would be in his wagon when he left the Badlands. He eyed Crowe dourly. The man was smart and it wouldn't be easy to snatch back the collection under his nose.

Around him the camp resumed its morning chores. In a while the fossil hunters would begin their preliminary surveys, looking for the strata that would yield the legendary bones they'd read about.

"I imagine you're disappointed," said Crowe.

"You didn't help any."

"I was just as upset about opening all those burial bundles as they were. But it's over. I imagine you might put all this into a fine piece for the *Journal of the American Philosophical Society*."

Van Vliet wondered where Crowe got these smatterings of knowledge. "I don't know that there's anything to write."

"I think there is. Your description of Sioux burial belief and the role played by these here items, and what the Brulés did to rebury them, would command some attention among your fellow ethnologists."

Crowe irked him. Self-taught idiots thought they knew more than they did. He hadn't realized back at Fort Pierre that they'd be saddled with a guide who had delusions of grandeur.

"What would happen if I took the collection with me? I might, you know."

"Don't even think it if you value your life—and the lives of your colleagues. And Miss Huxtable's life."

"But it'll die up there. It's dying under that sun right now. It won't last six months. Then it'll be gone—irretrievably lost to the world."

"Lost to your shelves in Brooklyn, I imagine."

The guide's bright gaze never wavered.

"And who's going to tell the Brulés? You or your squaw?"

"I imagine they'll keep a closer watch than you'll ever know or see."

"Well, there's my trip! We've hardly started and my summer's ruined. What am I supposed to do now while they all dig bones? Sit and—?" He was going to say sit and drink.

"Well, if you've a mind for it, your daily journal would be a treasure to take east. Surely you've some new insights into the ways of the Lakota."

"More insights than you're aware of. Look, Crowe, you stick to guiding and hunting. I don't need your advice."

Crowe nodded peaceably and wandered off.

Crowe had a point: if Van Vliet kept a proper journal and became an authority on Lakota and Plains Indian burial customs and beliefs about death, he'd be celebrated at Philadelphia and Boston banquets; he'd lecture in London and Oxford; he'd be invited to contribute to every learned journal on this continent and abroad.

But he wouldn't. That half-educated yokel had gotten to him.

"Ah, Van Vliet, old boy," Wood said, the bland collegial mask firmly in place. Van Vliet anticipated yet another warning.

"It's a fine day for you bone-hunters," Van Vliet replied.

"Ah, yes, we'll all have a go at it. Even the woman, I suppose. We'll have to keep an eye on her. Rattlesnakes, you know. First one she sees'll put her in a swoon." He laughed softly at his male camaraderie. "Did you see the Brulés looking at her? She'll have a dickens of a time if one comes a-courting."

"I wouldn't worry, Doctor Wood. Rattlesnakes don't bite each other. And she'll scare away any aborigine that comes close enough to notice her whalebone."

Wood laughed appreciatively.

Van Vliet waited. No professor he'd ever known had ever approached a sensitive matter directly, and old pulp-fleshed Wood was no exception. When Wood intended to broach the Topic, he'd cough and the male affability would drain from his gray face.

Which happened the next moment.

Wood stood straighter, coughed delicately into his vast beard, turned serious, and eyed his colleague intently. "We ought to go over a few things in regard to—this visit from the aborigines," Wood began.

Furiously Van Vliet cut him off. "Don't tell me. I already know. Our lives depend on obeying these savage lords in their savage kingdom."

"Well, ah, yes, but I was going to say it at considerably greater length. I suppose I would have been a bit prolix. Yes. As long as you understand we're guests here, and we're privileged to do our work undisturbed."

"*Your* work, not mine. My trip's ruined. And it's that guide's fault more than anything. Here we are at the mercy of a Lakota agent. Lakota spy."

"My dear Van Vliet, without him we couldn't even be here. The Sioux've been making an awful fuss lately."

"All right. I've heard you. Go hunt bones. I've got to figure out what to do with a lost summer."

Wood seemed taken aback. "I must say, Doctor Van Vliet—"

"Don't say anything!"

"Well, this is most abrupt."

"That's right!"

Seething, Van Vliet stared down the chairman of the expedition until the man walked off. Van Vliet stalked back to the lean-to where he'd heaped his personal belongings, and dug among them until he found the oaken rundlet of good whiskey he'd brought. He needed something to sluice away whatever was knotting his shoulder blades. He heard the comforting slosh within. From his kit he extracted his bung starter and banged the bung into the cask, releasing a fine whiff of sour mash. Then he screwed in the brass faucet and set the rundlet on its side,

making sure nothing dripped. He raided Gracie's mess,
extracting a tin cup from her dishwater, and added a splash
of the pond water, wondering how white mud mixed with
bourbon.

A moment later he settled in the shade of the wagon
sheet, and found out.

CHAPTER
20

Dr. J. Roderick Crabtree abandoned his creamy linen suit in favor of a loose white cotton shirt and white trousers, good work clothes in extreme heat, as any Southerner knew. But he retained his flat-crowned straw hat, and envied the Huxtable girl's goggles. He had no remedy in his elaborate equipage for the sunlight stabbing at his eyes. He carried a large canvas bag with shoulder straps, which contained a canteen, magnifying glass, compass, two chisels of different sizes, a geologist's hammer with a pick end, jackknife, surgical pick, brush, journal book and pencil, tape measure, a japanned tin of Havanas, matches, a vial of lanolin against chapping, white pigskin gloves, a small cushion for comfort, and a few rags.

"Well, Doctor Crabtree, shall we begin?" said Wood. "An exciting moment in the annals of science, eh?"

"Intoxicating," said Crabtree, eyeing Van Vliet lounging under the wagon sheet nearby.

"Well, what do you say we pair up and get a feel for the place, look at strata, get oriented, eh?"

"That accomplishes half as much."

"Half as much?"

"Half. It you go east and I go west, we'll cover twice as much ground."

"But I . . ." Wood paused. "I thought I'd get my bearings, eh? Sharpen my wits against yours when we look at strata."

"Why, Professor Wood, no one is more eminent in the field than you. I'm perfectly sure that you'd put a philistine like me to shame with your eagle eye and sharp chisel."

"Well, it's been a while since I've been out."

"Oh, Professor, you'll make such a monkey of me I'd be rather embarrassed. I'm just an Old Boy from the South. You're a Hahvahd man." Crabtree smiled meanly.

"Well, thank you. Perhaps I could manage it. I fear getting lost in all those labyrinths."

"Water runs downhill, Professor."

"Yes, of course. Just head downslope in those canyons and I'll come out on the lower prairies. But it's all such a maze, and this park isn't visible from below."

"Blaze a trail, Professor."

"Shall we compare notes at the dinner hour? I'm taking a pad and a pencil."

"Mine aren't decipherable."

"Yes, of course. Well, good hunting, Doctor."

That had gone easily enough. Crabtree watched the man lumber east in his black high-topped shoes, brown corduroy pants, white shirt, and black silk-backed waistcoat. He carried a pigskin satchel not unlike Crabtree's own physician's bag.

Candace Huxtable had watched all this solemnly, her expression hidden behind her goggles. She too carried a commodious bag over her shoulder, and was armed with her parasol as well as her wide-brimmed hat.

"May the best woman win," she said.

Crabtree beamed. He rather liked the old maid, but

didn't want her messing around with his fossils. "Where are you going?" he asked. "We have to keep an eye on you, you know."

"No, you don't. To the nearest river sediments."

That put her yards ahead of old Wood, he thought. "But do you know what to look for?"

"I've never done a stitch of field work. Maybe that's my advantage. I will have the eye of a seamstress."

"I'm sure you can ruin your father's reputation without assistance. But if you need help, you may count on me."

"I'd rather count on Miss Gracie."

She walked off stiffly, the spike of her parasol stabbing at the sun. She wore cool white cotton this day, a shapeless loose dress. She was heading for the path leading down to the lower prairie.

He watched her go, tempted to follow along and flirt with her just for spice. But he had his own agenda, foremost on which was proving that her father's theory of creation involving God's archetypes was rubbish. That poor old maid would be hunting for something she didn't want to find, a fossil of a transitional beast. He pitied her. Loyalty was so unscientific. Why had old Cecil Henry taken Genesis so literally? Everything pointed in another direction. Even St. Paul had called part of Genesis an allegory, but all the world's fools, including Cecil Henry Huxtable, had forgotten that.

Crabtree hiked north toward a promontory that would give him a splendid view of most of the Badlands, something he wanted to do before poking around in blind labyrinths. His practiced eye could identify strata even from a distance. What did the Huxtable woman and old Wood know about geology? Streambed deposits, erosion, deltas? The rise and fall of land masses? He'd taught himself geology, and followed through with field work. He knew he had the advantage over the rest, even though he lacked a degree in natural sciences. His medical training would help; and he'd mastered some zoology besides. Above all, he was the only good anatomist in the party. The others might find bones, but they wouldn't have much of an idea how they went together or even what family of vertebrates they belonged to.

Ah, Charles Darwin, he thought, the future is yours. Crabtree had read Darwin's abstract only months before, and knew at once that the Englishman had conquered the mysterious past; that the world was infinitely old, so old that the billions of days over the millions of years had wrought changes in creatures as they struggled against their environments; that life had to be a web; that the ancient forms of organs that showed up and vanished in the growing human fetus were vestiges of a past unthinkably ancient; that Darwin's forthcoming book would divide natural science, leaving behind people like Wood and Huxtable.

He puffed his way up steep slopes strewn with rubble, feeling sweat under his white shirt. The cool morning had been eaten away by the aborigines. But at last he eased out upon a crumbling mudstone promontory and surveyed a brilliantly lit world divided in two by a fantastic eroded wall. As far as he could see, the wall advanced and retreated, its white claws reaching out into the lower prairies, which in turn stretched to the dim line of the White River far away. It might be an awful labyrinth close at hand, but no one could get lost for long: an uphill climb would deposit him on the upper prairies; downhill would take him to the lower ones and the distant river. Here and there in the middle of the eroded country he found dense green groves of cedars, and sometimes the brighter green of cottonwoods growing where a slide had blocked the drainage, as it had in their large camping area.

He detected streaks of red strata between tan ones, all of them horizontal. Closer at hand he detected several nodular areas eroded into rounded lumps. These excited him. The scanty literature had indicated they were rich in fossils, including some bones of giants that had yet to be named or classified or wired together into a comprehensible skeleton.

He stared a while longer at country undulating like a snake in the heated air, and decided to tackle the several strata of nodules in the nearest formation to the west. From these tombs, he expected he might reap a better harvest than poor old Van Vliet had collected from his human burial grounds. It would be a place to start, and maybe the place where a Charleston physician turned bone-hunter would become the foremost paleontologist in the United States, and the foremost debunker of scientific boneheads in the world. He decided he'd exchange notes and information with the Huxtable woman and old Wood after all. Sharks need meat.

CHAPTER
21

Cyrus Billington Wood was on his own and not very happy about it. Behind him lay a lifetime of study and a mountain of fossil vertebrates that burdened innumerable shelves in Boston. Behind him, almost completed, lay a great taxonomic text describing and categorizing every extinct vertebrate he had ever read about or seen the bones of. The work would win no Copley Medal but would add to the sum of human knowledge. Someone had to organize the deluge of information about prehistoric eras, and he had chosen to do it. The college had kindly turned over a basement to his labor, and there his stone collection had grown.

He'd never galvanize the scientific community the way young Darwin and Wallace had. He performed the drudge work, putting together names, drawings, descriptions, and a few paragraphs about their significance. By the time most of the stone bones arrived in his little corner of the world, they had been tentatively classified. Once in a great while Wood might note something that suggested a new class or subclass or family or genus. Then he would produce a paper for a learned journal and would enjoy mild acclaim as a yeoman in his field. But it didn't amount to much, and the name of Cyrus Billington Wood didn't tower over the names of others, the way the name of Richard Owen did in England. Owen had invented the name "dinosaur," or terrible lizard, after studying some bones of an Iguanodon and other giant lizards taken from the Mesozoic rock of southern England. Now he loomed higher than any other paleontologist.

Now, as Wood trudged out to the fertile rock, he lusted to attach his Latinized name, *Woodii*, to his discoveries. Attached to species, his name and reputation would last forever!

He decided to begin at the bottom. At the base of the Badlands wall he'd find the oldest of these exposed Oligocene strata, and maybe late Cretaceous, if the literature on this place proved accurate. The rock laid between the two periods had been eroded away. He'd read every scrap of literature that had been published about the White River fossils.

Painfully he eased his way down narrow crevasses, skidding down sharp slopes, clambering over giant steps that scraped his soft hands. The buff-colored walls rose higher and higher above him until they choked out the sky. He twisted an ankle and felt it throb within his sturdy high-topped boots. A dun ledge offered a slanting seat and he rested there, his old heart hammering. The pain radiated upward through his calf and thigh. Oh, to be young and scramble over these precipices like a mountain goat!

At least he sat in deep brown shadow, the sky nothing but a narrow streak of impossibly bright azure above. Crabtree would have the advantage over him, he thought. A man of only fifty hadn't lost the vigor of youth the way he had. But he had the advantage over that British woman, who would be so inexperienced that she'd miss a fossil even if it poked her in the nose. He pulled a white linen handkerchief from a pocket and mopped his face. Then he studied the rock around him: he was sitting on the top of a nodular layer. Above him rose smooth mudstone, carved by the mad genius of the weather. The concretions that formed the nodules were layered between thin sandstone of warmer color, and had been described as fossilbearing in the work of Hayden and others. He studied every nook and cranny of that place, finding nothing. Ah, for a tooth or a femur!

He tested his ankle and proceeded downward, limping slightly. He paused frequently, not only to rest and slow his pulse, but to study the walls patiently. He counted patience one of his virtues, and he supposed the younger people lacked it and would therefore miss valuable finds. The gray claystone stratum interested him. He extracted his geologist's pickhammer and attacked it, finding it soft and friable. No one had found a fossil in this—so far. It looked promising, the sediment of giant rivers where beasts would have lived and died. But no giant bones poked out at him.

Wearily he lumbered down the twisting, sinister gulch until it joined with a broad watercourse that debouched on sunny grasslands a few hundred yards away. The floor. The lowest rock was harder and black, a uniform shale that had a yellowish cast to it here and there. Hayden had called it Fort Pierre shale, identifying it as Upper Cretaceous. He studied it closely, ambling along the shady wall. It rested thick and featureless, like seabed.

He walked the remaining distance to the plain, blinked at its brightness, and began his long hot hike back to the camp, feeling vaguely cheated. The reality of this place hit him hard.

He found the wagon tracks and hoofprints and followed them into the yawning canyon ahead, feeling he was on a great thoroughfare after crawling over obscure alleys. He followed the tracks up the side canyon to the wagons, hoping the Sioux hadn't disturbed them. He found nothing amiss. Charitably, he examined the Huxtable wagon too. It had been parked so close to the canyon wall he would have to squeeze himself through to check the offside wheels and box.

He edged through a narrow spot beside the front wheel, and there an odd irregularity in the gray cliff wall caught his eye. Pinned as he was, he couldn't properly bend over to study it. So he completed his passage between wagon and cliff and then crawled in on all fours, feeling most unprofessional, until he was directly under the wagon box.

There it was, a foot off the floor of the canyon, poking out of the wall. His pulse quickened. He beheld a row of giant teeth and a faintly visible bulge of bone in which they were socketed. He pulled his brush out of his bag and whisked away the loose debris. Excited, he eased his pickhammer out and chipped away a bit of the friable stone until more of the massive jaw lay exposed. A New Species *Woodii*, he told himself, laughing at his little conceit. He already knew from the flat grinding teeth that this beast ate vegetable matter. He saw no fangs, no canines.

He studied the mandible and knew he had to move the wagon. He moved backward like a crab, emerged between the outside wheels, and stood, panting. Then he put a shoulder to the front of the wagon box and pushed mightily. It didn't budge. After exhausting himself, he gave up, anger boiling through him. He would have to get help from his colleagues or Miss Huxtable. And that meant revealing his secret. Would that woman ruin his expedition in yet another way?

CHAPTER
22

The gothic walls of the canyon that Candace penetrated reminded her vaguely of Great St. Mary's, but this wasn't Market Square, and she was thousands of miles from Cambridge. Her long preparation and voyage, and especially her weeks of bold travel to this wildest corner of the unknown continent, had changed that forever. She would be a female eccentric, a species well known in England. It'd be a better life than the slavery of wifehood and mothering. She owned her share of the Huxtable Company, and it would guarantee her liberty. Determination drove her forward. She walked through an unmapped and unknown wilderness. It frightened her, not because the aborigines or wild animals might harm her, but simply because she might get lost.

She lusted for the largest fossil here. She imagined herself unearthing something as spectacular as an Iguanodon but knew it wouldn't happen. These fossil beds had been laid down much later than the Late Cretaceous, the last period of the dinosaurs—except the bottommost stratum, the Fort Pierre shale, which was marine in nature and unlikely to produce the terrible lizards.

She eyed the canyon speculatively. The westerly wall offered shade; the easterly one burned in the late-afternoon sun. She chose the shaded side. She eyed the various strata, all of which lay more or less level and undisturbed. She realized she had to confine herself to the bottom layers because she had no ladder. She decided to ignore the higher walls she couldn't reach, and systematically examine everything from the canyon floor to a height of ten feet or so. If she found a fossil that high, she'd try to persuade Rufus Crowe to build her a ladder.

She advanced her survey block by block, from invisible line to invisible line, and found nothing. She studied the strata meticulously, the way a good seamstress hunts for the crooked stitch. Nothing. She worked her way up-canyon bit by bit. The dark bottom stratum thinned and began to pinch out as the canyon floor rose. And just there she spotted a faint whorl in the rock. She stooped to see better, but her corset stabbed at her back and breasts and wouldn't let her examine something barely six inches off the canyon floor.

She settled down on her knees, feeling the rock bite them, and leaned stiffly forward, excitement building in her. She pulled a brush from her shoulder bag and wiped it briskly across the oddity, dusting away a layer of grit. Something there had once lived. Now it was rock—a shell of some sort, though her side view of it gave her little insight. She found regular indentations in what looked like the side of a cylinder. She pulled out her chisel and hammer, cursing her corset, which resisted her every move.

"Blast!" she said. Never in her young life had a Huxtable corset annoyed her. Maybe she could get Crowe to dig out whatever lay there.

She tapped her chisel delicately into the rock above the fossil, and the chisel bounced back at her. She banged harder, this time making a tiny indentation. Awkwardly she settled herself next to the wall and began tapping in earnest, each percussion shooting pain through her where whalebone dug into her flesh. She stared dourly at the little gouge in the rock, realizing that she was in for it. This mollusk would be harder to extract than she'd imagined.

She began to sweat, even in the deep shade of the cliff wall. Her buttock hurt and she wished she'd brought a cushion. Her dress got in the way, and she envied those who could wear trousers. Maybe she'd sew some before long.

"Blast!" she exclaimed, and clambered to her feet because her body howled at her. She felt a moment of despair and fought it back. She knew what she had to do, but the thought had a subversive quality about it, something quick and closeted and whispered. She glared unhappily about her. The canyon coiled in both directions, blocking her view. Above its sawtoothed walls lay patches of open sky. She checked them alertly, looking for Peeping Toms.

Satisfied, more or less, that no eyes were upon her, she unbottoned the bodice of her dress and lifted it off, ready to be outraged if anyone saw her in her chemise, petticoat, and corset. But no one did. She untied the corset and slid it into her shoulder bag, feeling delicious air eddy through her chemise and cool her lithe body. It seemed unbearably pleasant, and she suppressed an instinct to remove her chemise too. She whirled, letting all that dry air soothe her flesh. Then, reluctantly, she lowered her loose white dress over her, and buttoned it clear to the neck.

"Now then, to work," she said, feeling almost giddy with relief.

After that the work went better. Her slim body leaped to the task, and she chiseled out a furrow above the fossil, then down each side and finally underneath. She wondered how deep to go, and settled on two inches or so. Her arms weren't used to this and wearied frequently. While she rested she tried to come to grips with the realities she'd encountered this day. There'd be nothing romantic about breaking up rock all summer. It would be tiresome—in fact, exhausting—and often discouraging.

Even as the umber shadows crept up the far wall and finally plunged the canyon into gloom, she chiseled and rested, wanting to extract the fossil before she headed back to camp. A mollusk didn't answer her dreams, but it was a start. Above her, sunlight blazed off of the serrated rock at the top.

Unexpectedly the rock she was cutting broke loose under a chisel blow. She examined the piece and discovered she'd left part of the fossil behind. She tapped the freed piece gently, knocking away the matrix rock until the whole top of it cleaved away, exposing the fossil, a spiral shell about three inches across, perfectly preserved but for the bit she'd left in the cliff. She knew what it was, and that pleased her. All those furtive years of reading scientific papers and studying drawings had prepared her. She had in her hand an ammonite, a mollusk of the cephalopod variety, an extinct species that had vanished with the Mesozoic seas. So this floor layer was old after all! Much, much older than the strata above!

Suddenly she felt a kinship with two American geologists who'd been here before and had already done the stratigraphy of the American West, brilliantly cutting loose from European stratigraphy even while correlating the Old and New World strata through comparisons of invertebrate fossils. That had been the work of Ferdinand Vandeveer Hayden and Fielding Bradford Meek. Hayden had wandered through this vast country alone in the mid-fifties, sponsored by learned societies and the Chouteaus of St. Louis, locating sites and collecting fossils, staying in touch with Meek, who had told him what to look for.

But their greatest contribution had been a stratigraphic

model of the West. They'd found five layers of Cretaceous horizon and had named them locally—the Fort Pierre Group, the Fort Benton Group. Because of them, Candace felt instantly at home. The Pierre layer was sixty or seventy million years old. The lighter gray layer above it, the Chadron, was Oligocene, and only thirty or thirty-five million years old, the gap in between caused by more than thirty million years of erosion during an uplift.

She rubbed the lustrous fossil, cleaning bits of matrix out with a pick and chipping away matrix from the bottom. But the light was fading and she had to hurry back. Lovingly she settled the fossil in the nest of her bag and set off. Too late she remembered she wasn't wearing her corset. She considered the matter. It would be improper to walk into camp under the gaze of those men without it. And yet . . . it'd be almost dark by the time she got there. She'd risk it.

She found the wagon tracks, followed them up the gloomy canyon, passed the wagons, and clambered up the steep path. At a glance she saw that everyone had returned; she was the last.

"I was just getting worried," said Crowe.

"I can take care of myself, thank you."

He looked hurt, and she was sorry she'd snapped at him.

Mrs. Rumley closed her book and fastened her gaze upon Candace.

The others watched her as she passed, pretending to hide their curiosity. They all itched to learn about her day but would never admit it! She supposed they'd all exchanged their discoveries with each other.

A fresh deer carcass hung from a cottonwood limb, and Gracie and Toothache were cooking a whole loin over a fire. Suddenly Candace felt ravenous.

Van Vliet still sat under the wagon sheet stretched above him.

"Well," said Professor Wood, "did you enjoy the pretty scenery?"

She fumed. He wouldn't give her any credit. "I found something," she said, and pulled the fossil out.

Wood examined it closely. "Why, young lady, I can solve your mystery for you. This is an ammonite. An extinct cephalopod, a type of mollusk. A little like a snail, you know." He smiled gently. "You must have taken this from the floor stratum, the Pierre shale. That's Late Cretaceous."

She nodded unhappily.

"You'll want to keep a little journal, I imagine. I can help you with the spelling. It's a-m-m-o-n-i—"

"I can spell."

Wood gazed at her kindly. "Why, yes, of course. You have a copy of your father's work with you. If you need help, why—"

"Thank you."

"The proper thing is to make careful note of the place you took it. You really should get the rest, you know. A pity it broke. Be sure to describe the matrix and the stratum. Now when you return east, there's a few who can help you classify this—who knows? Maybe it's new. I know a chap at the College of New Jersey at Princeton—"

"I'll have it identified in England, thank you."

"If you'd like, I'll mention it in the *Smithsonian Contributions to Knowledge* along with our other finds."

"I'll do my own papers, thank you."

"Ah, you may find it difficult to find a—your qualifications, you know."

"That'll be my dilemma, won't it?"

"Well, yes." His voice turned hearty. "Our first fossil! And you, of all people, got it! On behalf of Doctor Crabtree and Doctor Van Vliet, I wish to congratulate you. A most talented young lady."

Wood passed the fossil to Crabtree, who rubbed it sensuously with his thumb and leered at her. "God must have gotten tired of ammonites after a few million years," he said.

She nodded, waiting for more. He peered at her from watery black eyes, faint amusement on his face.

"After all, if God created each species, then he also killed off the extinct ones. He got weary of ammonites and tried something else. Think of all the species he's created and uncreated. What a pity he didn't care for dinosaurs after a hundred million years. Do you suppose he'll get tired of us?"

She reddened. "You'll certainly tempt him."

Crabtree laughed. "He must be a mean God, wiping out thousands of species on a whim. I would have been kinder to dinosaurs, myself."

"Doctor Crabtree, you're having fun at my father's expense," she said quietly. "My father was a devout Anglican all his days, and scarcely a sabbath passed when he wasn't to be found at Great Saint Mary's, our Cambridge University church, rejoicing in the comforts of Almighty God. He was a devout Christian man and a scientist. He didn't take the six-day creation story of Genesis literally, but considered it a poetical account of creation—an allegory. But he did believe there's a Creator who created this mysterious and beautiful world and all the creatures upon it. He had no trouble at all reconciling that belief in a divine archetype with his understanding of the variation of species wrought by their adaptations to a harsh environment.

"Perhaps Mister Darwin will demolish his theory; we'll see when Darwin's book appears. If transmutation exists, there ought to be thousands upon thousands of transitional creatures, part one thing, part another, willy-nilly, with the more complex in the higher strata—a fossil continuum. But there isn't a known fossil bed in the world that has yielded that sort of thing. Instead there are huge jumps and plenty of nothing in between.

"Maybe Mister Darwin will have the basic theory right but a lot of mechanisms wrong. Maybe in a century or two science itself will lead scientists straight back to a Creator—to God. In any case, Cecil Henry Huxtable's forthcoming book—which I will finish—will stand on its own as the most exhaustive study of specialization and adaptation within species ever written. Meanwhile, sir, it would become you not to mock a man's religion or his hypotheses drawn from observation, or confuse his careful research with his beliefs."

Doctor Crabtree thrust the ammonite back to her as if it were a live snake, and sucked on his cigar. The malicious gleam in his eye didn't fade but neither did he say anything further.

She headed for her tent. She felt less a part of this expedition than ever, isolated because she was a woman. Her spirits sagged. She hungered for a hot bath but knew she'd have to make do with a scrub out of a bucket of heated water, as usual. She'd share the evening's meal with Mrs. Rumley, or Crowe and his Sioux lady.

Crowe quietly followed her through the twilight. "Toothache's got some hot water heating for you."

"That would be welcome. Thank you."

"She's got some deer about cooked up. By the time you finish washing, it'll be ready."

"I'll be a moment, Mister Crowe."

"I'd like to hear your story—how you came to find the fossil."

She smiled. "I'll tell it to you."

He brought her the water, and in the dark privacy of her little shelter she shed her dress and scrubbed herself luxuriously, using her English lavender soap. Her hair fell in sticky strings but it could wait. She extracted her corset, laced it tight, and then slid her muslin dress—scarcely soiled at all, she noted—over her head.

They ate silently. The deer meat tasted delicious. She wolfed down steaming slices of it, finishing her feast last.

"I imagine you're more a scholar than they are—but they haven't got the notion in 'em yet," Crowe said.

She shook her head. "I'll never be a scholar, Mister Crowe. Cambridge doesn't matriculate my sex. But I'll tell you about my fossil if you'd like."

"I would."

"Well, I walked west to the canyon between the second and third headland from here, and worked up it slowly. After studying the canyon walls for hours, I found this tiny thing poking out, just a few inches from my feet."

"Maybe it'll be a new species and they'll name it for you."

"Mr. Crowe, I'd refuse. I'm not here for that. I just want to learn how things fit together."

"I'd like to help, Candace—ah, Miss Huxtable."

"Don't be familiar, young man," said Mrs. Rumley. "Her station requires respect."

"I'd help you dig when I can."

"Name your price, and don't try to cheat a poor young woman," said Mrs. Rumley.

"I have no price, Mrs. Rumley. I admire Miss Huxtable and want to help."

"Beware the bold seducer, Miss Huxtable."

"I'd love to have your help, Mister Crowe," Candace said.

CHAPTER
23

Archimedes Van Vliet met the new day sullenly. His head buzzed. He supposed he had to do something to salvage his summer. He glared at the rest, who were preparing for the day, and wished them all the bad luck in the world. He felt especially annoyed by Crowe and his squaw, whose presence kept him from recovering his collection.

Mournfully he stared at the scaffolds laden with his treasure, disintegrating in the sun. He'd get no help or comfort from that old fogey Wood; and that snake Crabtree couldn't care less.

He knew what he ought to do; what a proper ethnologist would do. He ought to begin a comprehensive journal. Go back to the burial grounds and describe each scaffold and what was in it. He should record everything about the Brulé headmen who had come to the camp, including their fear of the fossils. And if that didn't fill the summer, he ought to explore the whole area for other signs of Sioux life; campsites, other burial sites, other artifacts.

He'd come equipped to hike and camp while the fossil-diggers toiled. He'd have enough material for a dozen scholarly papers.

But he couldn't. Those two burial scaffolds laden with museum treasure tied him to the camp. Everything up there was *his*, and he'd get it back somehow.

The slave summoned them to a breakfast of Dutch-oven biscuits and slabs of deer haunch. He washed it down with scalding coffee to chase away the dull ache in his skull.

The others seemed eager to begin the day, but Van Vliet looked ahead only to another bout of drinking under the awning he'd rigged from the wagon sheet. He needed a drink badly; the tension seething through his body tortured him. He'd have one just as soon as the paleontologists cleared out. He watched Crabtree hike toward the upper bluffs. That strange Huxtable woman started off, toting her work bag, wearing her straw hat and goggles and a baggy white dress again, looking like a female missionary. Mrs. Rumley settled in her chair. The Iron Matron, that's what she was.

"Doctor Van Vliet," said Wood, "may I have a private word with you?"

Van Vliet nodded. The old granny was going to lecture him about his responsibilities to the expedition. Van Vliet followed the professor out of earshot of Crowe and his woman.

"Say," the professor said, "I could use your help for a few minutes. I've a little task that takes more muscle than I have."

"What?" Van Vliet asked, barely civil.

"Help me move a wagon a rod or so, eh? It's Miss Huxtable's. I think I've found a little something in the cliff behind it, but I couldn't budge it. I'd like to keep it quiet until I see what I've got. It'll just take five minutes."

Van Vliet nodded, air escaping his bottled-up lungs in an explosive rush. "You might have asked Crowe."

"I might, but the man has his duties. You're idle, after all."

"Idle! Idle! I was going to begin my journals."

Wood nodded, ignoring the petulant tone, and led Van Vliet out of the little basin and down the steep path to the canyon below. "Good of you, good of you," he muttered. "Most collegial."

"I'm going to be the camp step-and-fetch-it," Van Vliet said between clenched teeth.

Wood eyed him mildly. "No, no. A scholar of your standing won't suffer that. I wish we could hire some aborigine boys."

"You know how the Sioux would feel about that."

They arrived at the wagons, and Wood led him to the enameled one. "I could have gotten the drays, I suppose," he said apologetically. "But it seemed a lot of work just to move a wagon a bit."

It took only a moment to roll the wagon downslope.

"That it?" Van Vliet asked.

Wood beamed. "Let me show you," he said, glancing up and down the canyon. "But don't breathe a word, eh?"

He pointed at something wheel-hub high poking out of the gray mudstone, and Van Vliet beheld a row of fossil teeth and the smooth surface of mandible.

"What is it?"

"I have no idea. It's a herbivore, though. Meat-eaters have spiky teeth, usually curved back."

"Is this a big animal?"

"Enormous."

"Convenient to find it here, close to camp and next to the wagons." Van Vliet had to fight back his envy. Wood would get to keep his booty.

Wood was nerving himself to say something, and at last succeeded. "Say, Doctor—if you have time, I could use some help with this." Wood's eyes glowed with the excitement of his discovery. He rubbed the exposed jaw with his hands, as tenderly as he'd caress his wife's chin. Van Vliet doubted that the professor had caressed any other part of his wife for decades.

Van Vliet swallowed back his anger. The soft old professor had a giant fossil to dig out, and Van Vliet was convenient. "I have my own scholarly work, professor. Sorry."

Wood looked crestfallen. "It's quite a task."

"That's mudstone. You'll chisel it out in no time, I'm sure. Look, Professor, I have papers to write. I plan to take some excursions, too—"

It hit him then, a way to get what he wanted and do it right under everyone's nose.

"In fact, I'll be using a wagon and drays for a few days. I'm going back to the burial grounds and take notes on each site, eh? I must do it while my memory's fresh."

Wood looked doubtful. "Professor, you won't disturb—"

"What's there to disturb? I'll stop at each scaffold, do an inventory from memory, and take notes." Van Vliet smiled at the old fool. "I value my scalp as much as you value yours."

"Very well. But let Crowe know. When will you be back?"

"Two or three weeks."

Wood smiled. "I guess that's what you're here for, Doctor Van Vliet."

"Truer words were never spoken," Van Vliet said, and left the old man to his hammering. He raced back to camp filled with joy. Swiftly he gathered his personal gear, dismantled the lean-to, and toted it all down the steep path to the wagons, where he loaded a wagon. His heavy whiskey cask gave him trouble, but eventually he installed that too. He wrestled the sheet over the hickory bows and tied it down, then went after two drays in the meadow. He harnessed them swiftly and led them down to the wagon, and knew he was ready.

Wood peered up from his labor. He'd cut a small trench in the soft clay rock, and had expanded the visible part of the fossil.

"Well, Archimedes, you'll be over there alone. I'll have Crowe check up on you now and then."

"No, no, I'll be fine. I'll have a covered wagon, water, firewood, tins of food, and all. Don't send Crowe."

Wood nodded. "This is a beast unknown to me. Do you suppose it could be a prehistoric rhinoceros? Look here." He pointed to a lump projecting from the cliff wall ten or twelve feet distant. "That's more of it. Oh, I'll have news to make us dance by the time you return!"

The man looked ecstatic.

Van Vliet turned the team in a tight curve while the wagon wheels shuddered and squeaked, and then rolled out of the Badlands. When he reached the old trace along the White River, he whipped the team into a smart trot and headed east, feeling giddy.

Everywhere in that boneyard were ruined items he'd cast aside, of no value in a collection, although ethnologists might make something of them. Sun, wind, rain, or the foul interiors of the burial bundles had done their work. Now he intended to grab every faded and fouled and desiccated item. When he returned to camp he'd substitute them all, bit by bit, in the dead of the night, for those lovely museum pieces up on the scaffolds. No one—least of all that Brulé squaw—would know the difference. And also by night he'd slip his collection out of camp and cache it, wrapped carefully in the tarpaulins and canvas sacks he'd brought for that purpose.

Archimedes Van Vliet laughed until he felt intoxicated.

CHAPTER
24

All that hot day Candace prowled her canyon. Odd, she thought, how she felt it was her own, a place where the rest shouldn't trespass. She supposed the others felt the same way about the areas they were probing. She examined the walls, segment by segment, and found nothing but tan clay broken by nodules. She dirtied her dress scrambling over shelves and up debris-strewn side canyons until vertical walls blocked her.

She was hunting for the bones of Oligocene ruminants called oreodonts. She knew from the literature that they were abundant here; and she knew that they, more than any other mammal, might provide her with new insights into specialization and variation. The known fossils suggested creatures rather like a pig with peculiar mountain-shaped molars indicating that they chewed their cud. They ranged widely in size, from little fox-sized animals to five-foot ones. They'd been around many millions of years, but had vanished only three million years ago. After studying the one in the British Museum, and corresponding at length with Dr. Joseph Leidy of Philadelphia, who was the foremost expert on North American vertebrates, she had decided to come here and study them herself.

The midday heat built as the high sun drove back the shade, and she opened her parasol. But as the hours passed her frustration mounted. She saw no other living thing in these twisted crevasses which blocked out most of the sky and offered nothing but primordial silence.

That silence deepened as the day wore on, heightening her hearing so that the smallest whisper, the tiniest cascade of dust falling seemed ominous. She imagined that those clay walls could collapse on her at any moment, burying her under tons of debris.

She dug in her shoulder bag for something to eat and drink, and realized that in her haste to conquer her canyon she'd brought nothing. She'd endure. The English were good at that. She walked and rested, studied every promising irregularity for some gleam of tooth or curved bone. Nothing. The minutes crawled by. Time had slowed down to torment her. She admitted to herself she felt bored. She tried to make a game of it. Hide and go seek, ferret out the clues. She found nothing.

By midafternoon she'd had enough for that day. She'd become dizzy with thirst and knew she had to drink soon. She must never again fail to carry her flask. Wearily, resenting that she had to quit before the day was over, she trudged up the familiar canyon that led toward the meadow.

And there, to her astonishment, she discovered Professor Wood near the wagons, sweat beading his brow. He was hammering at the cliff wall only a few feet from her wagon. She hastened to him, ignoring her raging thirst, and discovered that the professor was excavating an enormous mandible and skull.

He saw her and slowly stood, in obvious pain. "I'm too old for this."

"Why, you've found something!"

"Something, yes. I haven't the faintest idea what."

"It's huge."

"There's more of it poking out over there."

She followed his pointed hand and spotted a rounded bone protruding from the gray clay. His gray old face lit with joy.

"Do you think it's all connected—from here to there?"

"From the size of this jaw, I think so."

"Why, Doctor Wood, this is a major find!"

He smiled gently, something beatific in his eyes. "If I ever get it out," he said. "I was about to quit, even though I—shouldn't. But I must be sensible about my body."

He reached for his canteen and uncorked it, then paused. "I don't suppose you're thirsty?"

She took it greedily and drank the warm water with relief, finally forcing herself to leave some for him. "I forgot my flask."

"I see," he said, and drank.

"It's only midafternoon."

"I wish I had Crabtree's body. I'd dig at this all day, every day. I've had to stop every little bit. Maybe I'll be tougher by the end of summer . . . but then it'll be too late."

He looked wistfully at her, a question building in his eyes. She knew what was coming and cut it off. Help the man who'd thwarted and frustrated her from the beginning? Whose rank prejudices and condescension had stabbed her for months? Never.

"I think I know what you found," she announced coldly.

He smiled faintly. "Well, Miss Huxtable, your guess is as good as any. We'll have it identified back east, of course. Or maybe Crabtree can do it. He's an anatomist of note."

He was patronizing her again but she ignored it. "This looks very like the jaw written up in that 1846 paper written by Hiram Prout of St. Louis. His sketch looks like this jaw."

Wood looked bewildered. "I don't remember reading—"

A certain exultation built in her. "Prout called it a titanothere. It's extinct. Nothing even close to it now. If that's what it is, you'll uncover bony horns rising from the nose. A little like a rhinoceros, but really very different."

"Ah, a titanothere?" Wood looked puzzled. "Ah, yes. Eocene. Oligocene, eh? No one's ever seen a whole one."

"Maybe you'll give us one," she said, sharing his excitement.

"Why, Miss Huxtable, I hope you're right."

"That's just a guess, you know. I have no field work behind me."

"Well, an interesting guess. I confess I don't recollect Prout's paper. We teachers—you know how the academic grind is."

"Odd that you should find it here. We all parked our wagons without even guessing it."

"I moved yours a bit. Say, you'll keep this quiet from Crabtree, won't you?"

"But surely he'll come through here—"

Wood waved an authoritative hand. "Certainly. I mean, as long as possible. I want to have some of it out and identified. I just can't bear—I just can't bear asking him what it is."

"I think you know now. See that long jaw and how it curves up at right angles?"

He sighed, looking oddly dejected for a man who'd discovered the fossil of a monster.

"Well, I'll be off now," she said. "I'm done in. I didn't find a thing today."

She hurried away, not wanting him to ask the question that had been building in him. The last yards weren't so difficult, thanks to the rest and water. She found the camp somnolent. The Brulé woman had vanished; Gracie snoozed through a hot afternoon, finding time to relax while her master was off somewhere, and Mrs. Rumley sat stiff in her chair.

"Doctor Crabtree is degenerate," Mrs. Rumley said. "I won't have him examining me."

"Thank you for telling me, Mrs. Rumley."

Candace hurried to the water keg. The water within looked white. She drank greedily anyway, and then hastened to her tent. She opened a tin of stewed tomatoes and spooned it up in a most uncivilized manner. She flopped onto her pallet, enjoying the freedom of not wearing her corset. She had carried it all day in her shoulder bag just in case.

She lay quietly, knowing what she must do and hating it. Wood didn't deserve a thing. And yet, some gentle, civilized, decent part of her, the decency of the English, she imagined, insisted that she do what she must. She gave herself a few minutes of luxurious rest and then snatched her bag and headed down the difficult trail to the wagons. There she beheld Professor Wood slumped in the shade beside his discovery, too weary to continue, too excited to quit for the day.

"Would you like a hand?" she asked. "I've a good touch with the mallet and chisel. Together we could get this out, don't you suppose?"

"Well—" he said, reluctantly.

"Well, the thing won't come out by itself."

She settled at the place where he'd been cutting and started in, banging away with powerful strokes, making the mudstone fly.

"This is rather good of you," he said. "I shall mention it in my paper."

She banged harder, responding only to the call of duty.

CHAPTER
25

Rufus Crowe knew he shouldn't neglect his hunting. They depended on him for meat. He'd found no buffalo, and had resorted to the occasional mule deer he could shoot when it watered on the White River at dusk. But the hunting seemed tedious compared to what lay buried in those twisted chasms of the Badlands.

That lazy afternoon he succumbed to temptation and turned his saddle horse and packhorse into one of the mazes of rock well west of the campgrounds. He'd hunt fossils himself. He knew, from reading footprints in the dust, where Miss Huxtable was working. He sensed he'd alarm her if he bulled his way up that drainage. She cherished her privacy: he'd learned that from sharing meals with her for several days. He yearned to call her Candace, but hadn't nerved himself to be so familiar again. He had to remind himself who he was. No humble half-educated squaw man living among the Sioux would ever interest the daughter of a Cambridge don. He understood that but it didn't allay the dreams that sneaked into his mind.

He could do something else, something schoolboyish that would fill him with both joy and pain. He could find fossils for her and give them to her as if they were nose-gays. He would never be more than a rustic in the eyes of beautiful Miss Huxtable, but he could give her treasures. The day might come when she had the most and best tucked into her handsome wagon.

He turned his ugly pony into a canyon west of hers and rode easily past the darker strata, which he knew would yield fewer mammals. He paused when the canyon floor reached the lower of the two nodular zones, an area that looked like river cobbles cemented together. On horseback he could survey a lot of ground and not even feel it. He had fine distant vision, made keen by a lifetime in the wilderness. And he had his little gold-rimmed glasses for closer work.

He kicked his horse along a few steps, studied the eroded wall, then poked the animal again, his day suddenly becoming fascinating and exciting. A sense of the chase pervaded him; this hunt delighted him far more than stalking a mule deer. It took only ten minutes to spot an odd row of bumps protruding from the dun canyon wall. He dismounted and poked around the place with his belt knife, uncovering fossil vertebrae of a medium-sized animal. An easy find! He knew he must mark the place. In country where every notch and cliff resembled the rest, he had to mark it or lose it. He found a gray-weathered limb of juniper and whittled the exterior away, exposing blond wood that could be spotted. This he hammered into the sloping cliff. At its base he also built a small cairn of rock. Something for Miss Huxtable!

Satisfied that he could find it again, he mounted his pony and proceeded upward. Scarcely twenty yards away he found another fossil, this time a partly exposed skull poking up from its tan matrix of mudstone. He rubbed the gritty debris away until he could see the teeth. He saw no canines or fangs, and supposed that this would be a grazing animal of some sort. He whittled another stake. The same cairn would do for both.

Joyously he continued his treasure hunt. Gold coins wouldn't have excited him as much as these bones. He imagined Miss Huxtable's delight as he showed her these treasures; imagined her eyes lit with pleasure. He imagined what he'd say: Miss Huxtable, I'll help you pry these out if you're interested. And she'd beam at him from behind her green goggles, which covered eyes he found beautiful beyond description. He'd dig for her, clear to China if she wanted him to, even if it cut into his duties.

Pleased with himself and the whole sweet world, he proceeded up the canyon, his eye keener than an eagle's. Before the sun slid far into the northwest, he had located five more sites, including two that had larger bones in them. What a gift to lay at the feet of the lady. The thought filled him with sudden shyness.

He headed back to camp and discovered Professor Wood and Miss Huxtable at the wagons, working in deep shadow, hammering at something in the cliff wall. Amazed, he rode close and beheld the emerging form of a giant skull with great bony prongs rising from its nose.

He dismounted, tied his saddle and packhorse to a wagon wheel—realizing that one wagon had vanished—and studied the dig. Professor Wood beamed at him, his joy uncontained. Candace was doing the cutting, and looked exhausted. Her hair flew in all directions; her face was grimed with dust; her virginal white dress—which had awakened fantasies in Rufus—had absorbed a lot of gray grit.

"What do you think!" Wood demanded.

"It's quite a discovery."

"You know what it is, Crowe?"

"You're the bone collector."

"It's a titanothere."

"I believe I've read of them. Extinct. Biggest mammals to roam around here—except maybe mastodons. So far, there's been only a skull and a leg and a few ribs dug up."

"Read about them? You?" Wood sounded incredulous.

"I read a paper about a skull found here once. And other things in the *Journal of the American Philosophical Society.*"

Candace peered up at him and smiled. She wasn't wearing her sun goggles, and in her weariness she looked lovelier than ever to him. He wondered why she was helping Wood, after all the scorn Wood had heaped on her. But to wonder was to know: this woman would do what scientific inquiry required, and her generous spirit would not resist.

"We're just winding up, Mister Crowe," she said. "I'll go up to the camp directly."

"I've something to talk about—oh, never mind," he said. His finds would mean nothing to her compared to this. "I guess I'd better get to work."

He untied his horses and climbed up, suddenly morose. "Who's got a wagon?"

"Oh, Doctor Van Vliet, Crowe. He'll be gone for a fortnight or so."

Crowe sat his horse, wanting more, and Wood obliged.

"He went back to the burial grounds to take notes. He said he'd do a journal entry for each site, with an inventory."

Crowe wrestled back to the response that leaped to his mind, but Professor Wood was a jump ahead of him.

"Mister Crowe, I cautioned him, of course, and he replied that he valued his life and the lives of us all, and would do nothing that might offend the aborigines. He seemed happy to be doing something worthwhile after his disappointment."

"He's alone?"

"Yes. He insisted he'd be just fine and not to check up

on him. He'll just sketch and write and pass the time quietly.''

''He didn't want anyone checking? That's not the way folks work out here. We check each other every day.''

''Well, you know Van Vliet.'' Wood smiled in that way that academics thought was ingratiating.

''I imagine.''

He turned his horse toward the steep trail up to the slump, while Miss Huxtable gathered her tools and Wood lingered, running a wrinkled old hand over the exposed skullbone.

Crowe unsaddled his horses and led them to the tiny pond—which was shrinking day by day, he noticed. It would probably vanish in a few weeks. He thought of the shining-gold gifts he had planned to give Miss Huxtable—more like tarnished copper now. He had no claim on Candace Huxtable and he never would. His fantasies and hopes were nothing but a chimera. He would return to Toothache, his painful, cheery, funny, nagging Brulé companion for the last year, and push Miss Huxtable out of his mind.

Strengthened by his resolution, he returned to the camp, finding everyone there but Van Vliet. Crabtree had returned, looking as dapper as when he'd left at dawn. Black kettles steamed over Gracie's fire. Toothache was roasting deer loin over hers.

''I say, Miss Huxtable, would you and Mrs. Rumley join us for supper?'' asked Wood as the Englishwoman emerged, well scrubbed, from her tent.

''I—believe we'll eat at our own fire, thank you.''

''Very well,'' said Wood. ''You're always welcome, you know. Your labor is much appreciated.''

''I suppose my labor is.''

Rufus Crowe felt a surge of joy. And the joy multiplied when Miss Huxtable fixed him in her direct gaze and smiled. "Mr. Crowe, tell me about your day. I hope you don't mind if I share your fire again."

"I'm turning into a moonstruck boy."

"I suppose you'll explain that soon enough."

"I imagine I like this bone-hunting. I'll tell you about it after the vittles."

CHAPTER
26

High upon a sunny promontory overlooking the Badlands, Dr. J. Roderick Crabtree added the final touches to his map. He admired his creation. The general outlines of the portion of the Badlands within his view stared up at him from his sketchpad.

He knew he was a true scientist—the only true scientist on this expedition—and he proceeded step by step, without unseemly haste. In this case, it meant a map that would enable him to pinpoint the exact locale of each discovery. The next step would be to study the strata, compare his work to Hayden's, and then make extensive notes on the stratigraphy of the area. With careful study, the strata would reveal to him the most likely fossil beds. He would look in particular for riverbed sediments. Creatures had lived and died along the riverbeds, and their bodies were silted over there, preserved through the ages when the silts became rock.

Let the rest race around like children hunting Easter eggs. They'd find a few toys before he did, just as the

Huxtable girl had found an ammonite in the stratum near the floor of these formations, her first time out. The luck of the amateur, of course. Her find would be of little help to science unless she made a map and kept a journal— which she didn't. The British knew how to produce dabblers and philistines and amateurs.

This would be Crabtree's expedition. That's how it would be called in the histories. Old Wood was an academic pigeonholer who should be shuffling Latin names into boxes instead of undertaking the serious business of field work. As for the alleged ethnologist Van Vliet, why, he was nothing more than a body-snatcher and grave-robber wearing the fig leaf of science over his tumescent desires.

Crabtree chortled quietly and stretched in the hot air, enjoying the boundless view in all directions, north to hazy horizons on the upper prairie, south to the White River and beyond. A faint breeze filtered through his white cottons while he studied his shimmering kingdom. He had no competition here; all this was his own, though the rest wouldn't know it until they read his elegant papers.

The next step was to probe down any one of the gulches that formed the dendritic erosion pattern of the Badlands wall. He chose a gully at random and swiftly dropped below the rim of the world, following a tortured channel so narrow he had to turn sideways on occasion to pass through. It dropped precariously, once about six feet, which he negotiated easily, enjoying his youthful advantage over old Wood, and his male advantage over Huxtable with all her grimy skirts.

He paused a hundred yards down, discovering a sharp change in the strata. He'd been passing for a vertical hundred feet or so through a nodular formation with rounded concretions in a matrix of brown mudstone. But now he came upon a gray stratum of volcanic ash with a dense texture radically different from the horizontal sedimentary deposits. He measured the ash stratum at twelve feet and made a note of it. The ash had probably drifted westward from gigantic eruptions in the Yellowstone area long ago.

He enjoyed the shade and rested there. The day had grown hot and breathless. Here am I, he thought, in a gully so narrow I can touch both walls with my hands; a gulch that blocks the sky except for a thin blue strip. The smallest convulsion of nature could seal me in this tomb.

It amused him. There'd be no convulsion of nature. Its laws were knowable and increasingly understood. No longer would mankind ascribe the mysterious events of nature to spirits or demons or angels or God. Someday most of the processes of the universe would be known and explainable through chemistry or physics. And then religion would vanish. He prided himself on having an open mind; one that would entertain any thought no matter how radical or obnoxious; one that might poke holes in the sacred. He knew one thing: no God or Creator or Maker floated around unseen. The whole universe had evolved in natural ways according to laws yet to be discovered but devoid of conscious design. He had arrived at absolute atheism. His mind stood free, and that gave him a thousandfold advantage over the others.

Rested, and quite pleased with his progress, he skidded and tumbled his way down the gully until he struck a new stratum, this one tan and full of nodules again. Something caught his eye at once: flat, independent pieces of channel sandstone, the mark of a river. A fossil-bearing bed in all likelihood. He took measurements and made notes and continued downward. The gulch debouched into a larger one that carried water from several branches similar to the one he'd followed. But this larger gulch, so steep he had to cling to a wall to steady his descent, pierced through featureless mudstone.

He took measurements and notes once again, pleased with his care. Farther down, in yet another and larger canyon, he hit another nodular layer marked with reddish strata as horizontal and regular as an architect's design. Here he found channel sandstone again. This would be a first-rate fossil bed. He made proper note of it, his back to the shady western wall of a broad coulee.

As the afternoon waned he pierced into a layer of gray claystone with limestone lenses, tremendous deposits of black or dark silt from somewhere, with good fossil potential. Just before this canyon debouched upon the lower prairies, he struck dark shale along the bottom few inches of the wall, and knew he had arrived at seabed. He knew also that the Huxtable girl had clawed her ammonite from this.

Pleased with the day's survey, he hiked carefully toward camp, toting his portfolio, his restless mind chewing on all he'd seen, sorting out ages and epochs and periods. He sprang up the canyon where the wagons had been parked, feeling less weary now than when he'd started shortly after dawn. He noted the absence of a wagon—and more. Someone had been clawing at the cliffside. He meandered in that direction and beheld an exposed side of a giant skull and mandible. Astonished, he studied the monster, noting the grinding teeth of a herbivore, the long hinged jaw, and the telltale rise of a bony protruberance from the snout. The topmost neck vertebra had been exposed, indicating that this could be a fairly complete skeleton. The light had dimmed but his keen eyes didn't miss the bone projecting from the cliff wall a dozen feet away.

A titanothere lying on its left side. Maybe the first complete skeleton. But it would be an awesome and dangerous task to get the whole thing. Those vertebrae would lie seven feet into that cliff. He peered upward at the inclined wall vaulting a hundred feet or so up, and knew at once that the overburden couldn't easily be pried away.

So! Old Wood might get a footnote in some history of paleontology after all! That's all the old boy wanted, a

footnote somewhere, in agate type at the bottom of some
dreary page. Crabtree chortled. He knew he could read
the secrets of a skeleton far better than most; that his own
paper on the find would be more valuable than Wood's.
He examined the massive skull again. From an earlier skull
and a few bones, a tentative size had been assigned to
adult titanotheres: thirteen or fourteen feet long; eight or
nine feet high; four feet across the pelvis. This one might
be larger. He could see that this animal could open its
jaws very wide. Later he'd get an exact measurement. It
had a small brain for a beast so large. When those nasal
horns were uncovered, he'd be able to guess at how they
were used from their shape and wear and the scrape marks
on them.

Old Wood! Surely this didn't belong to the girl, off digging seashells and parading the canyons under her parasol
as if this were Piccadilly Circus. Laughing, he sprang up
the path into camp, expecting to see Wood strutting around
in full feather, like a male peacock during the mating.
Maybe he'd pluck a feather or two.

CHAPTER
27

When dawn was more a promise than a reality, Candace met Rufus Crowe and together they left the hushed camp. She wanted to see the fossil sites discovered by the shy man striding beside her. They walked down to the lower prairie and then westward through motionless cool air. He steered her unerringly toward a distant mouth of rock as the sky grayed.

"This time is the most dangerous on the prairies," he said. "A bunch of warriors need about this much light to see their targets."

"Are we safe?"

"With my Brulés, yes. At least if Doctor Van Vliet keeps a lid on that teakettle. There's other bands, you know. Minniconjou and Oglala come through. Sometimes Cheyenne or Pawnee. We all have to take our chances."

They reached the mouth of a canyon and entered it as light quickened on its western palisade. The rainbow magic wrought by dawn delighted her. When the light lay horizontal, as it did now, the prairies and bluffs turned lavender and salmon and squash-colored, and the lower skies as green as the sea.

"Here," he said. A cairn lay at the foot of a slope; a stake poked from a steep grade.

She gathered her stained skirt and began an unladylike ascent of the incline. He offered her a hand and steadied her as they climbed. His friendly hand felt good in hers.

A line of bumps poked from the buff clay, vertebrae of some creature larger than a wolf. She knelt over the find, uncertain what she was seeing, looking for a skull. This would be all hers to dig.

"It's beautiful! How can I ever thank you?"

"I have my thanks already just looking at your face."

She smiled, a faint worry nagging her. She hadn't worn her corset. She stood to let her bodice fall loosely about her once again. "I don't know what it is, but I'll find out. Perhaps Doctor Crabtree will help me."

They meandered from site to site, and Candace studied each with growing joy.

"I could help you dig them out. Find time for that."

"I'd like that if it doesn't take you from your duties, Mister Crowe."

"I want to. A man finds time to do what he wants no matter how busy he is. I plain want to."

"Why?"

He smiled at her hesitantly, his gaze direct. "I admire you. You've been kinder to the rest than they've been to you, and that counts with me. And besides, I just plain want to do it for you without a string of reasons for it. I live by impulse and feeling."

"I'd welcome the help."

"I've an awl and a knife and hatchet, but no chisels."

"I brought two spare chisels I'll lend you—but guard them with your life."

"Miss Huxtable, I'll be the most careful digger you ever did see."

She sighed. "I really must help Professor Wood."

Crowe seemed disappointed. "He's not helping you any."

"That makes what I'm doing all the nicer, doesn't it."

"You didn't come all the way here on your own purse just to help some glory-hunter."

In truth, she'd said the same thing to herself. But the professor was an old man. He'd made a great discovery, and for the sake of science she would perform her duty. For the sake of simple kindness too.

"Thanks to you, Mister Crowe, I won't have to hunt for sites when I'm free. And you'll be digging for me—for which I am grateful. But what a pity it'd be if Professor Wood could take only the skull and a bone or two back with him. We'd all ache, wouldn't we?"

On their way back they found Professor Wood chipping away at the mudstone. He looked up testily.

"Where've you been, eh? I thought you'd abandoned me."

"Mister Crowe was showing me some fossils he found. They're very promising sites."

Wood peered at him. "This expedition doesn't need amateur fossil collectors, Mister Crowe. It needs daily care of our horses, meat for half a dozen hungry people, fresh water, a comfortable camp, a translator . . ."

Rufus Crowe nodded serenely.

"I'll eat and be with you directly," Candace told the professor, irritated by Wood's assumption that she had signed on as a permanent laborer.

At the camp, Toothache had left them coffee and slabs of deer loin. Candace ate hastily, gathered her tools, and went to work. She found Wood staring into space.

"Ah! There you are!" he said. "I'm not quite up to it."

"We'll take turns," Candace offered as she settled herself beside the skull. She attacked the overburden concealing the neck vertebrae, but after a half hour her arms felt like lead, her shoulders ached, her back hurt. She realized this could eat up much of her summer.

"I need to rest," she said. "I'm going up to camp for some coffee."

"Well, if you must. Science is a demanding taskmaster, Miss Huxtable. I tell my students, if they wish to enter its sacred precincts, they must be prepared to set aside every personal comfort."

She handed the hammer and chisels to him. Sulkily he took them and crawled to the notch in the wall. Candace climbed wearily to the camp and stretched out on her pallet, grateful for the respite. After a half hour she rejoined Wood. She found him frowning at the narrow streak of blue above, lost in his own reveries. He'd done nothing.

She plunged in again, venting a deepening anger as she peeled away overburden from the long fossil. She grew hot and sticky as the day heated up, but still she clawed away the friable rock until her whole body hurt. Then she set her tools down and stood up, feeling her back kink.

"I suppose it's my turn," he said. "I was hoping you'd get a little more done before the nooning."

She'd come to a decision.

"Professor Wood," she said. "I've decided to help you in the afternoons and devote my mornings to my own digging."

"Why, Miss Huxtable! Oh! That would be most unfortunate. Have you no loyalty to science?" He eyed her sadly. "This is the most important fossil discovery in years. Maybe ever. It ranks with the Iguanodon."

She didn't feel like arguing with the man, but found herself replying anyway. "Are you suggesting that my work won't be important too?"

"Why . . . Miss Huxtable, I fear your summer will be wasted if you do that instead of helping with this."

She stood her ground, feeling a rocky courage burgeon

in her. "Professor Wood: I'm here at my own expense to perform research related to specialization of species. I'll help you after it gets too hot to work out in the sun at my diggings. It's cool here in the shade."

"Very well," he said dolefully. "I can't stop you. I had intended to write a word of gratitude in the notes of my papers."

"A word of gratitude!" She laughed wildly. "As if I'm a chore girl! Maybe I'm not what you think."

"I don't follow your reasoning," he replied stiffly. "You do owe us a bit, you know. We've taken on the burden of caring for you and Mrs. Rumley, bringing meat to you, seeing to your safety."

"You do as much for Gracie," Candace retorted, and wandered back to camp, a knot of pain in her chest.

CHAPTER
28

F ear was not something that Archimedes Van Vliet
had imbibed much of in his life. But the farther he
drove away from the protection of Rufus Crowe, the more
the scorched prairie turned ominous, as if demons lurked
in every crease of land ready to pounce on him.

He was rattling along a road that was open to whites by
treaty, but that didn't comfort him. Aborigines would do
anything they chose, treaties or not.

He reached back into the lurching wagon for a tin mug
and drew a slug of whiskey from the cask. He added a
dash of milky water from a crock. With a little whiskey-
courage he'd handle trouble better if it came. All that fierce
day he sipped White River water laced with whiskey and
sweated it away faster than he sipped, while his wagon
bounced and swayed.

The spirits cleared his head and made his mind dance.
What had seemed so simple when he drove his wagon out
of the Badlands had become increasingly complex now
that he put his mind to it. From now on, he planned to be

a cat burglar, a phantom. Anyone wandering into the burial grounds would see only a big, bulb-nosed ethnologist taking notes and making sketches. No one would ever see Van Vliet performing his complicated night business. His colleagues wouldn't know what he'd done, or what was in his wagon, until after they'd all left the Badlands and were heading home.

Late in the third day he raised the burial grounds, shimmering peacefully within the curve of the White. He tugged the lines, halting his sweaty drays, and stared at the place from some distance, wary of trouble. The wind had died. He saw nothing but cottonwoods standing silent. All was still, yet his dread would not leave him.

He turned the resisting horses toward the boneyard. He'd have his collection, even at the devil's own price. The wagon creaked and groaned like the wail of widows, making his imagination leap and startle.

When he finally plunged into the glades and sun-dappled parks that contained the dead, he recoiled at the sight of his own marauding. When he'd first seen this place it had lain serene and orderly. Now at every hand lay the ruins of scaffolds. Human skulls and bones, ancient robes, blankets, and heaps of things too far gone to be named littered the dust. He'd turned a sacred Sioux place into a dump.

He poured a generous slug of spirits to replace all that he'd sweated away, added the white mud, and sipped again, summoning peace. Then he drove his wagon to a shady glen and made camp.

His next task was to find a cache for the stuff he picked up. He found a thicket close to the river where some chokecherry bristled like a fortress. He whittled away an opening into a leafy cavern close to the ground that would contain everything he collected. Only someone deliberately looking for something would ever notice it.

Satisfied, he turned at last to the great burial fields. He meandered lazily through them, hunting not so much for the ruined artifacts he would soon gather as for things he'd missed before. He found none. His frantic, ruthless quest had been so thorough that nothing worth owning remained—except for whatever was in the tree scaffolds. He counted eighteen of them lurking above him in the hissing leaves, none of them opened, each with its treasures. His heart soared. Those first! He would open them all before he did anything else!

He needed to devise a ladder. He retreated to his wagon, dug out an ax, and headed for the riverbank, where some box elder saplings thrived. He cut and limbed several, and notched them for the crosspieces, sweating out the juices of his long ride as he worked. It would have to be a strong ladder to carry the weight of his six-foot, five-inch frame, and a tall one to reach scaffolds that hung ten feet above the ground. He realized he had nothing to anchor the steps to the poles. He puzzled it out in his mind and finally hit upon his answer. He raced through the burial grounds until he found what he needed: a fairly new buffalo robe in good condition. This he cut into strips with his knife, sawing at the tough leather until he had plenty of heavy thong. He soaked it in the river until it swelled, and then used it to tie each rung into place. Tomorrow, after the leather had dried and shrunk, he'd have a sturdy ladder. And then he'd go on a treasure hunt.

He knew what he wanted most: he wanted to find a little girl's grave. In it he might find a tiny doll's cradleboard, exquisitely quilled, with a little deerhide doll tucked in its pocket. He'd give his eyeteeth for an artifact like that. They'd been described by traders but no collector of Indian artifacts had one as yet.

His back howled at him so he straightened up—and discovered he was not alone. Fifty yards away stood a dozen Indians with a horse bearing a travois. Even at that distance he knew they weren't the ones who had visited the Badlands camp. Some of these were women. They all were gawking at the ghastly desolation around them—and at him.

He stared back wildly. His rifle was in the wagon, a long way off. Not that a rifle would help him anyway. He stood and waited, wondering if he'd see the sun set.

CHAPTER
29

Van Vliet studied the funeral party: seven men, three women, and a boy and girl. A woman in her middle years had cut short the hair on one side of her face, the traditional mourning gesture. Van Vliet glanced at her hand and discovered a red stump where a finger had been, the other mourning gesture of widows. A man had died. He had been brought here by parents and his warrior-society brothers, who had cut mourning gashes in their upper arms. Before the burial was done the horse would die: they'd slit its throat next to the scaffold so that it could carry its master through the spirit worlds.

The aborigines peered about them, absorbing the chaos and desecration, muttering and pointing as they studied sliced-open burial bundles askew on the clay. They didn't approach and he realized, slowly, that they were as terrified of him as he was of them. Perhaps they believed he was Iya, chief of all evil, the cyclone demon; or maybe Iktomi, the Trickster, son of Rock. He understood their dread. Nothing but an evil cyclone would tear a burial ground to shreds.

The old man gathered his courage and plodded forward, his rheumy black eyes fixed upon Van Vliet. The old man wore his white-shot hair in braids held in place with a red headband. His seamed flesh had caved in around his bones, yet he still looked powerful enough to kill with a blow. He gazed at the ladder and at the burial scaffold in the cottonwood above, then lifted an ancient arm and pointed at ruined scaffolds, one by one. *"Wi a ka,"* he said. *"Ece. Tuwe kakesa?"*

Van Vliet understood nothing.

"He conon so?"

Van Vliet instinctively shook his head.

"He camon we?"

"Look, old man, I can't speak Lakota. Do you know English? French? Dutch?"

The man stared blankly. Then, slowly, he formed signs with his swollen, arthritic fingers. But Van Vliet couldn't read them or speak the hand-language of the Plains.

Suddenly inspired, Van Vliet pointed to himself and said "Iya, Iya." The chief of all evil. The act mesmerized the old man. "Iya!" Van Vliet yelled, his hoarse voice carrying to the others. "Iya!" He forced himself to laugh, letting it boom out of him and roll across the bonefield. He followed that with an eerie wail that echoed through dead air and out upon the prairies. He would be Iya to them, and they'd run like rabbits. He hadn't become an ethnologist for nothing!

But the old man didn't run. Instead he padded toward Van Vliet's distant camp, where the white sheet of the wagon poked through leaves. Van Vliet followed him cautiously. The Sioux grandfather entered the camp, peered into the wagon, and poked around in the gear that Van Vliet had unloaded.

"Wasicu," the old man said.

White man. Van Vliet knew that word, and knew he hadn't turned himself into Iya, chief of all evil, after all. The terror he'd somehow gulped down slid back into his belly again and burned a hole in his chest. He wondered if he could befriend the man.

Impulsively Van Vliet dug into his trunk of trade items, plucked a twist of tobacco, and handed it to the old man. But the old man leaped back as if Van Vliet had handed him a burning brand. The tobacco fell to the earth and lay there like a dog's stool. The old man stared at him again, then wheeled away, padding along as lithely as a young man. Van Vliet hoped it might be over, but it wasn't. The old one summoned the warriors but kept back the widow, the old woman, the other woman, and the children. The husky Sioux males closed toward him looking like the executioners at a beheading. Van Vliet gulped and controlled a need to void. A fleeting regret pierced through him: was his collection worth this?

The Sioux men formed a half-circle around him as if he were an elk. They were impressive, tall, powerfully built men, some carrying battle scars that snaked hideously across flesh the color of clover honey. They motioned him back to the camp, where they fanned out and hunted through everything, opening his trunks, poking about in his wagon, and probing the underbrush. They were obviously trying to discover what he'd taken. They'd find nothing!

They were thorough, covering ground throughout the burial area and along the riverbank. Van Vliet smiled at them, knowing he'd won. Each scaffold and bundle had been pillaged, and yet Van Vliet hadn't a single item of Sioux manufacture in his possession. They gathered together and talked among themselves. When they pointed at Van Vliet's hobbled drays, he realized they were debating whether to steal them. Some seemed to be opposed, maybe because of the treaty which gave white men permission to follow this road without being molested.

But Van Vliet was wrong. The debate ceased suddenly. The Sioux men spread through the ruined scaffolds until they found one that could easily be put back together. This they did. They raised a tilted post, restored the crossbar, and lashed the platform poles in place. Then they gently freed the long bundle from the travois and lifted it to the scaffold while the women and children wailed. Van Vliet, feeling cockier every moment, was beginning to enjoy this: how many white men had ever witnessed a Sioux burial?

The dead man's *Akicita*, or warrior-society, brothers planted a longer pole at the head of the scaffold. From it they reverently hung the dead man's shield, a beauty with hawk feathers dangling from it, his lance decked with crow feathers, and finally his medicine pouch. They all stood quietly then. Van Vliet knew that next they would kill the warrior's favorite horse.

But that didn't happen. Instead, the warriors haltered Van Vliet's powerful drays, unhobbled them, and brought them to the scaffold.

"But those are mine!"

They peered at him blandly. His words had less power than a moth's wings.

The older and most formidable of the dead man's *Akicita* brothers led a draft horse to the scaffold, sang a song to it, and cut its throat with one glinting slash of his belt knife. The horse spouted crimson blood, wheezed, and slowly capsized. Its knees shook; its hocks weakened. It stumbled and righted itself with terrible effort. But then at last it rolled into the earth as gracefully as a doe settling into grass.

Van Vliet gaped in horror.

The grandfather said something to him: *"Iho lena eanyanka yo."*

They left as quietly as they had come, taking Van Vliet's remaining dray with them. One of the Sioux men lifted the weary grandfather and then the old grandmother onto the big draft horse. Then they wended their way out of the burial grounds, carefully avoiding the carnage in the grass as if it were never to be touched. They turned westward on the river road, leading the horse with the empty travois, leaving Archimedes Van Vliet in his boneyard with no way to carry his spoils away.

CHAPTER
30

J. Roderick Crabtree eased out upon a promontory that divided two drainages, and slowly surveyed the corrugated canyon walls below him with his powerful field glasses. He'd long since made a system of it, pausing at any promising irregularity that popped into his lenses. He had spotted nothing of consequence except a patterned dome that probably was a fossil turtle. He noted it in his journal and let it pass: he was after larger game. Wood's blundering luck was annoying, but Crabtree decided not to think about it. Let the old fool dig out his titanothere all summer.

A brisk breeze this sunny morning kept him cool and dry, but by afternoon the heat would blister him. His straw planter's hat and white clothes would keep him comfortable for a while. He liked this dry climate better than steamy Charleston, where the smallest exertion raised an oily sweat most of the year.

This day, he knew, he'd stake out some fossils. He'd done some fine background work, with stratigraphics and the map and copious notes on formations. He felt altogether cheery, glad to be in the world's most famous fossil beds.

After peering at the eastern wall of the drainage he swung his feet around and began glassing the west, a maze of formidable crevasses, serrated ridges, and shadowy holes. A wooden stake whizzed across his lens, and when he swung his glass back for a closer look he discovered a whitish fossil bone poking up nearby. Below, at the floor, stood a small rock cairn. Whose work was it? He continued his sweep of the westward drainage and discovered more stakes and fossils and cairns. Not Wood's, certainly. The dotty old boy hung around his titanothere as if it were the buried treasure of Jean Laffite.

Miss Huxtable's, then. It surprised him. He glassed down-canyon and discovered her sitting on a gentle slope carefully chipping away mudstone from an exposed vertebra. She wore her straw hat and goggles. She'd rolled up the sleeves of her white dress, and unbuttoned the top of her bodice. Beside her rested her folded parasol and a wicker basket. He watched her work, admiring her slender form and her obvious skill with chisel and hammer. Of all the known fossil beds on earth, he thought, this one was the best for a woman to work. The matrix rock was little more than compacted clay, and it peeled away without shattering the fossilized bone itself, unlike other sites where hard rock would fracture the fossil when it cracked.

He enjoyed her lithe beauty and wondered about her. She'd shed her fortresslike corset, much to his delight. She obviously detested him, in part because he loved to play Mephistopheles, and in part because he owned Gracie and used her hard. And also, he guessed, because a certain mockery pervaded everything he said. Back in Charleston the ladies all thought him a great tease and a flirt. Actually, his manner was a way of fending off their empty-brained conversation.

But Miss Huxtable was different. He'd spotted a formidable education in her, though she took pains to hide it. Old Wood had imagined she'd gotten lucky when she had identified his titanothere from an exposed mandible. But any bright daughter of Cecil Henry Huxtable would have had unusual opportunities—and would probably have made the most of them. He suspected she might be the best-read natural scientist here, even if she hadn't so much as a bachelor's degree in darning socks. He chuckled.

He studied her some more, enjoying the oval of her face, the clean jawline, lovely chestnut hair, and slim shoulders as it all bobbed in his powerful glasses. He really needed a telescope on a tripod to keep her from flying every which way in his view. She'd be the envy of Charleston society with a face and form like that, though the manhood of Charleston would be puzzled and repelled by her stern manner. In the several weeks he'd been in her company, he'd never seen her flirt. Not so much as a coy laugh or a batted eyelash. She had all the female wiles of a Carmelite nun.

Which intrigued him. If he could ever piece those corsets, visible and invisible, that encased her, she might be the very woman he'd dreamed of, a companion of the mind as well as all the fruits and desserts and pastries.

He'd visit her. His fossil-hunting could wait a few hours. And in any case, whatever she'd discovered would be valuable, giving him some idea of the strata to examine. He slid his glasses into his field kit and moved backward like a crab over the precarious tumult of rock, sending down cascades of grit. He found a promising gulch leading to her canyon and followed it until the sky narrowed. When he stared upward it was like peering at heaven from the bottom of an open grave.

A while later he emerged upon a broader canyon, and passed the first of several cairns and staked fossil sites. He hurried along, his curiosity growing with each step, until at last he spotted her well above him, sitting on a slanted shelf of rock, studying her handiwork.

"Why, Doctor Crabtree," she said with no welcome in her voice. Her hands suddenly busied themselves buttoning the top of her bodice until she was sheathed in white clear to her pretty neck.

"You've had some luck."

"That's a good word for it. Mister Crowe showed them to me."

"Ah, I'm envious. We employ the guide to find us meat, and instead he finds you fossils."

"You may own Gracie, Doctor Crabtree, but you don't own Rufus Crowe."

Crabtree laughed easily. "What have you found there, Miss Huxtable?"

"I believe it's an oreodont. This is the lower nodular layer with channel sandstone, and one's been found here before."

"I'm puzzled, Miss Huxtable. What's an oreodont?"

She peered at him but he couldn't see her eyes behind those walls of green. Her pursed lips gave her away. "You're toying with me, Doctor. I'll permit myself to be toyed with if you'll mind your blasted business. They're typically three or four feet long, an extinct form of ruminating pig, some with short tusks. There seem to be several types. Does that satisfy you?"

"Oh, not really. Perhaps I'd better have a look." He said it in a way he knew was maddening to her. Without waiting for her response, he scrambled up the treacherous slope and settled himself at her side, studying the emerging backbone. "Perhaps you're wrong."

She peered at the fossil. "I believe I'm right. When I get the thing out I'll know. My work will deal with variation of oreodont species. I examined one in England. I've been in touch with Doctor Leidy. They ranged over this part of North America for thirty-five million years or so—and vanished rather recently. Doctor Leidy has several—Hayden sent them—and believes one could find many more here. Thirty-five million years is a long time—time enough for all sorts of varieties to appear.

"One of his, *Leptauchenia*, is radically different from the one he has from this stratum, *Merycoidodon*. I'm here to find out why and how. If possible, find other oreodont species here. It may not be as—as dramatic—as dinosaurs, sir, but it'll make a large contribution. And a fine paper."

"I'll help you. I help ladies in distress."

"Doctor Crabtree, you may wish to continue your work."

"I'll lend you my expert knowledge of anatomy."

"There must be a thousand canyons like this, Doctor. As many as you wish. But this one's mine."

He chuckled happily. "It is? By patent or the Queen's decree, I suppose. Science is a process of sharing facts. Scientists are all bound to each other in unholy wedlock."

"I'm going to collect alone. If I don't, the records will say that these were collected by Doctor J. Roderick Crabtree and Professor Cyrus Billington Wood with the assistance of a Miss Huxtable. You may take your chisel elsewhere."

He liked the heat in her face and the caliber of her mind. He wondered again how she'd fit among the ladies of Charleston.

CHAPTER
31

Buffalo. The sight of them always gladdened the heart of Rufus Crowe. He reined his pony to a halt and studied a herd that numbered perhaps twenty-five, and looked to be largely bulls except for a cow and calf, and perhaps a pair of heifers. He couldn't tell at this distance.

Crowe slid his Sharps rifle from its well-oiled saddle sheath, and checked the primer. The air lay so still he couldn't tell whether his scent was drifting toward the herd or not. Buffalo had a keen sense of smell and could hear well, but didn't see as well as other beasts.

He dismounted slowly, deciding to abandon his horse and stalk in a crouch along the bank of the White River, which wouldn't help much. He tugged the horse down to the river, where it balked at the sucking quicksand, and tied it to driftwood. Then he crept upriver. When he came within a hundred yards of the nearest buffalo, they smelled him and watched, faint snorts alerting them all. He continued to creep, taking advantage of a good cutbank, until he was within fifty yards of several, including the cow and calf. Then he lifted his head slowly above a grassy mound, settled the barrel of his Sharps on crossed shooting sticks, and chose his target. Not the cow, as succulent as she might be. He would do that much for his Brulé brothers and sisters. He chose a young bull standing broadside seventy-five yards away, aimed at the heart-lung spot just back of its shoulders, and fired. The bull shook its head, began to leak blood through its mouth, and sagged to earth knees first without taking a step.

The rest trotted away, tails arched high. He let them go. The meat of this buffalo would rot before they could eat it all. He reloaded, released his horse, and walked to his buffalo. It lay dead but twitching as muscles spasmed. He watched it warily. Dead buffalo had a way of springing up and goring the unwary. A horde of green-bellied flies swarmed around its mouth.

Satisfied at last, he approached, kicked it and got no response, and settled down to the sweaty work. He would take the tongue, a great delicacy. That would be all he could carry. But he and Toothache would come back for the rest of it with other horses and a travois. He yanked the bull's head up to stretch the neck, and then sawed it apart until he could cut the massive tongue loose from its roots. He felt a freshet of cool air and peered around. Off to the west he saw towering cumulus clouds building over the pencil line of the distant Black Hills. But here the lower prairies shimmered in morning heat under bleached skies, and the acrid smell of buffalo laced the air. The dead eye of the beast reproached him.

He rode rapidly back to the camp an hour away, up the gulch past Professor Wood, who sat beside his bones, obviously wishing someone else would chisel them free. He found He-yah-zon collecting dead wood from the surrounding junipers. She pointed to the cloudbank approaching from the west, and he knew she was putting dry firewood under cover. When she saw the tongue he carried in his lap she smiled—buffalo always elicited a smile from his woman—and hurried toward the ponies nearby.

While she gathered what she needed, he rode over to Gracie and laid the tongue before her.

"Buffalo. We'll get the rest," he said. "It might rain and you'll want to get wood down here and keep it dry."

"Why should I get wood? Why should I cook tongue? Maybe I won't." She sounded cross. "All you do is make more work. Maybe it'll rain and I won't have to." She eyed the heavens prayerfully. "I'm not a slave for one master no more; I'm a slave to a mess of you. I'm up to my eyeballs with slave-cooking. I'll cook until I die, and be glad you don't eat me for supper that night."

"I imagine you'll relish the tongue. It's a sweet meat."

"You may as well eat my tongue than poor old black buffalo."

"Your tongue's not fit to eat, Miss Gracie."

She placed her hands on her ample hips and glared at him. "I'm just another beast o' burden, master."

"I hope the tent sheds water," said Mrs. Rumley, who was listening.

He-yah-zon arrived on a pony, leading another. They left camp, skidded down the steep trail past Professor Wood, who was dozing with his back against the bones, and paused at the throat of the gulch to attach a travois she'd left there. Then they rode toward a towering wall of clouds, a sort of Badlands of the sky.

A half dozen crows surrendered proprietary rights to the dead bull when Crowe and Toothache rode up. She grunted, not liking to butcher a bull. Their horses sidestepped away from the iron smell of blood caught in the eddies of cool air whirling around the grasslands now. Crowe tied their reins to the bull's hock. He sawed down the gullet from throat to belly while Toothache cut around the limbs and skinned back hide bit by bit. She wanted the hide even if it had only summer hair and wouldn't bring much at a trading window. He helped her, which she accepted testily because he was doing time-honored women's work and she thought his help demeaned him.

They'd scarcely tugged the resisting hide loose from the upper side of the bull when the heavens darkened ominously. Across the whole west and north black-bellied clouds shot blue rain, while above they growled and flashed within their towering columns. For a brief time the work went more easily because the icy air eddying out of the sky cooled them.

The rain arrived on a clap of thunder, just as Crowe and his woman were wrestling the carcass over to pull the hide off the nether side. In moments the spray pierced his old tweed jacket and chilled his chest and legs. But both of them kept on, even while water rivered from their hair and sopped their clothing and turned the brown horses black. A bolt of lightning stabbed a bankside tree a hundred yards away, and the following crack of thunder battered them. She stared at him fearfully, but he continued the long labor. They had no place to hide.

The next crack shattered the air nearby and panicked the horses, which yanked loose and careened away with broken reins flapping. Toothache trotted after them while Rufus scraped out the guts and began quartering the small bull, using a hatchet rather than his knife. By the time the woman had caught the frantic horses and picketed them again, he'd hacked a rear quarter loose. He dragged it to the travois, grateful that the deluge had made the ground slippery, and anchored it on the crosspoles. The rain shifted to hail that swept in like charges of grapeshot. It stung him. But the deluge sluiced away the hot blood and made his labor cleaner and easier. He hacked the second haunch free while his woman sliced down to the bossribs, the tender hump meat that most Western men swore tasted better than prime beef. He skidded the haunch into place beside the first while the travois poles bowed under the weight. He didn't know whether the pony would make it back to camp, or how they'd wrestle the meat up that final grade. The clay beneath his feet had turned to grease, and every step would be treacherous.

The rest of the bull would have to wait for the next trip. They started eastward, slogging and skidding over greasy gumbo that threatened to topple even the sure-footed ponies. Crowe felt numbed to his bones, and he could tell from the determined clench of her jaw that Toothache was chilled. The horses labored in muck that balled under their hoofs, and he felt the mud cling to his boots like something alive from under the earth trying to suck him into it.

As they struggled closer to the Badlands wall a rumble from the bowels of the earth overrode the hiss of the rain. He realized he was hearing the roar of torrents boiling down every canyon and branch of the Badlands. From each of the great gulches a silvery sheet of water flooded onto the lower prairies. The Badlands had been transformed into a black wall dripping pewter-gray water, and he could scarcely recognize the familiar promontories and gulches. They passed the mouth of the canyon in which Candace had been working, and he noted the frothy stream racing out of it. The Badlands didn't lack for protective overhangs, but he could remember none around the site she was digging.

The horses started to play out before they reached the canyon trail up to their camp. The runoff ran deep and threatened to tip the travois and capsize the horses.

"Take them as far as the wagons," he told her. "I've got to ride back. The white woman."

She nodded scornfully.

He watched her struggle upslope through pastern-high water, leading her burdened mare. The pony bearing the travois followed. He knew she'd make it and the others would help drag the meat into camp. After letting his horse blow, he turned it back toward the lower prairie. It fought him, wheeling toward the camp.

"Here now, we'd better look after Miss Huxtable."

He kicked the angry horse out onto the flat and westward into a lessening drizzle, wondering what he'd find.

CHAPTER
32

The storm had caught Candace unaware. One moment she was chipping with her chisel in hot sun; the next, great clouds billowed across the narrow strip of sky between the canyon walls. Light and warmth failed in the space of a minute. The rain pelted hard, as if shot from the sling of an angry god, smacking her thin cotton dress and rattling off her straw hat and stinging her neck below the bun of her hair. She collected her tools and tucked them into her shoulder bag, intending to hike back to camp. She opened her cotton parasol only to have water spray through and hail pummel the thin fabric until it sagged. She'd only ruin it if she kept it open.

The storm snarled above her, the clouds flashing and cracking, and she remembered the Sioux legend about the bones: Wakan Tanka was angered by the ancient creatures, and drove them into the ground with the lightning bolts. Was this Sioux God angry with her for baring the bones? She peered about frantically for a refuge and saw none. She stood on a sloping shelf high above the canyon floor.

The wall about her vaulted upward a hundred feet; the path to the canyon floor dropped so steeply she could barely negotiate it even when it was bone-dry.

Her summery dress mopped up water and weighed a ton and clung to her, robbing her of body heat. Even on that slanting shelf she stood in an inch of rivering waters that whirled around the exposed fossil and cleaned away the debris. She feared it would suck the bones away too. It collected on the canyon floor, covering it, roiling south toward the lower prairie. She heard a dull roar and knew that water churned through every little gully, mingling with other rivulets, joining in the larger branches, and tumbling into this gulch on its way toward the White River.

She had to find an overhang somewhere and that meant getting off the shelf. She took one step and landed in a heap, her feet sailing out from under her on clay that had turned to grease. Her hip hurt; her elbow bled.

"Ow!" she bawled, struggling to get up. Standing had become an art. She feared she'd careen down the steep incline to the canyon floor. Mud hung like lead ballast on her. She scrambled to her feet at last and peered fearfully at the terrible slope, thirty feet or so of rough incline that would batter her if she lost her footing. The canyon ran water, but it didn't seem high.

She had no place to go. She sensed she'd feel warmer if she could pull her icy dress off, so she undid the twenty bone buttons of the bodice and then lifted the soggy skirt over her head and tugged until she'd freed herself. She set it in a heap. Her sopping chemise and petticoat pasted themselves to her too, but she felt warmer without the dress. She was planning to tackle the slope when she heard a rhythmic spashing and saw Crowe on a dripping horse plowing up the gulch toward her.

She watched helplessly as the water-blackened horse splashed toward her through muddy water over its pasterns. The guide, as soaked as she, paused and stared up at her. She realized suddenly that her wet chemise clung translucently to her breasts; that her petticoat hung transparently about her hips. And she had no refuge from that unwavering solemn gaze.

"Well, turn your face away, blast you!"

"Miss Huxtable, I can't."

"What do you mean, you can't?"

"Miss Huxtable, I'm—I'm sorry. I'm here to help you if you need it." His eyes never left her.

"I don't. And if you're a gentleman you'll turn away."

He bowed his head and stared into the water swirling around the legs of his horse. Something subdued and gentle rose from him, tugging at her.

"It was good of you to check on me. But please leave. I'm almost naked."

His eyes lifted to her again, and she saw a yearning in them that irritated her. "Mister Crowe!" she cried. She held her arms over her chemise, hiding her breasts.

"Mister Crowe, I won't tolerate this familiarity. If you think something will come of this—you're quite mistaken."

"Some things I can't help."

"Of course you can. You've made your own choices. You chose to come here and—and consort with savage women."

He nodded gently. "I'm not courting you. I know what you think of me and what I'm called back east. But I'm here to help. You're cold to the bone and need a way down off that ledge, and a dry place."

The promise of a dry spot under some overhang was more compelling than his gentle tone. "All right, blast you, get me out."

A faint joy lit his rain-washed face. "Do you have a geologist's hammer with a pick on it?" he asked gently.

"Yes."

"I think you can use that to back yourself down the slope. I'll climb as high as I can and catch you."

She pulled her pickhammer from her shoulder bag and tentatively smacked it into the soaked mudstone. It caught and held, even when she tugged on it. She turned and smiled at him, caring less about what he saw.

Wordlessly she eased down the slope on her hands and knees, checking her sliding with a sharp rap of the pick point of her hammer. It seemed to work. But half way down she remembered she'd forgotten her dress.

"Blast!" she muttered, and attempted to climb back up to fetch it. But that didn't work.

"Your dress," he said. "I'll get it after you're safe."

She eased down another ten feet, but then lost control and skidded. He caught her in powerful arms and held her for a moment. And then he lifted her up to his saddle as if she were weightless.

She meant to snap at him, but instead wondered at the steady strength of his hands as he caught her. She settled herself meekly in the sopping leather, her petticoats hiked much too high. Wordlessly he took her pickhammer and clawed his way up the slope with the agility of a mountain goat, defying the greasy surface. He returned with her dress and handed it to her, a look of pleasure in his soft eyes.

"Thank you, Mister Crowe," she said.

He nodded and led the horse up the canyon, walking through foamy water. She began to shiver and couldn't stop.

"You're going the wrong way. Please take me to camp directly." She could not stop the convulsing of her body, or the numbness creeping into her. She'd never been so cold, even in Cambridge in January.

"You're in danger if you're shivering like that. There's good shelter above. Under sandstone ledges. Hard shale below. I've got to get you dry."

"Go back to camp!" She clenched her teeth to keep them from chattering.

He didn't. He slogged up the canyon and followed a branch toward a looming dark overhang so high that she didn't need to dismount. They escaped the rain suddenly. Her flesh rejoiced. The ground underfoot was bone-dry. He lifted her off the saddle. She stood numbly, feeling the cold air steal what little warmth remained in her.

"Here," he said, peeling off his grubby tweed jacket. "It's soaked, but wet wool holds the heat some." He draped it over her shoulders. It felt heavy and clammy.

"Please walk," he said. "Make heat."

"I'm too tired."

"Please, Miss Huxtable. You're in more trouble than you know."

She tried, feeling water sluice around in her high-topped shoes, hating every step. He peered at her, something somber in his gaze.

"I'm going to have to be more familiar."

She wondered what that meant. An odd weariness engulfed her.

He loosened the girth of his saddle and lifted it off. He pulled an ancient, sweat-caked gray blanket from under it and unfolded it. "I'll take my coat, and you wrap yourself in this."

But he confused her. Everything seemed confused. She stared, doing nothing.

"That's what I feared," he said. He pulled his coat off her shoulders and wrapped the partly dry blanket around her. She felt too tired to care. He helped her sit down with her back to the cliff wall, sat beside her, and drew her into his arms. He felt warm and the blanket caught heat, especially when he pressed it tight around her. Warmth crept into her at last.

"Mister Crowe, don't take liberties," she mumbled, and slid into a gentle fog.

"I love you, Miss Huxtable," she heard him say from a distant shore. "And I wouldn't take liberties ever."

CHAPTER
33

The nausea of defeat gripped Archimedes Van Vliet. He stared at the retreating funeral party, itching to whip them all. They'd stranded him, butchered one of his draft horses and stolen the other. Now his wagon stood useless. He lacked the means to carry his collection away. A vast indignation swelled in him. The whole earth ought to be cleansed of these barbarous people; what did they do but impede the progress of better men? When he got home, he'd write some scorching letters to Washington City, telling them to get on with it, stop dithering and open up the West.

He glared at the dead horse sprawled beneath the burial platform. In a day or two it'd stink, ruining the whole area. Maybe the coyotes and wolves would clean its bones before the air turned too rank. He wondered why the savages had killed the big draft horse. Probably because it was larger than any they'd seen or owned, a better mount for the soul to ride on the spirit road.

He poked disconsolately around his camp. They'd taken

nothing. His tins and sacks of food were safe under the wagon cover and his tools hadn't been touched. He would have to abandon everything here and walk the forty hot miles to the Badlands, taking only what he could carry. But if he did, he'd never again see anything he left behind.

The pain of indecision grew so intense that he retreated to his cask and drew four fingers of spirits from it, adding a splash of the foul water. The first sip seared his throat and promised calm. He continued to sip until he could think quietly. He hated the thought of trudging up the White River for two days, only to announce to his colleagues that he'd lost everything.

He poured another stiff drink and meandered through the ruined boneyard. He should leave at once, but he couldn't bring himself to do that. If he stayed here long enough they'd come for him, probably with the other wagon. And if he stayed, he could continue to collect. Heartened, he meandered through the cottonwood groves, studying the virgin scaffolds nestled in them, the lust building in him once again. He did a careful count: twenty-two untouched bundles up there, more than he'd realized.

He swallowed a fiery dose of spirits, drawing courage from the heat in his belly. He knew that if the Sioux caught him, they'd kill him this time. Not even the protection of Crowe would save him if they caught him red-handed.

He stared into his own soul, knowing his weakness. He could no more stop collecting than he could stop drinking. He watched his hands tremble, knowing how his fingers itched to get busy, to lift the ladder, to saw open the first bundle, to feel his pulse climb as he plucked out one treasure after another.

He lifted the heavy ladder and wrestled it into a limb that held the scaffold above. He glanced at the tree-dappled meadow, looking for anyone who might stop him, and saw no one. He climbed up, testing each rung cautiously, unsure of his handiwork and aware of his 220 pounds. The ladder groaned but held. This bundle was thin and desiccated; the platform had been here for years. He drew it to him and it came weightlessly. With his Barlow knife he sliced the binding thong and carefully peeled back the crumbling elkskin cover and buffalo robe under it. He found an old man, chestnut-colored and completely mummified. He wore only a plain buckskin shirt and leggins and worn moccasins, all without decoration. A pauper, probably. Van Vliet poked around for amulets and found none. Nothing. Who was he? A Sioux? A medicine man who'd renounced all possessions? A chief who'd given everything away? It didn't matter. It made no sense to waste his time on pauper graves. Annoyed, he backed down the ladder and dragged it to the next cottonwood, which supported two scaffolds.

He struck gold at the next scaffold. He cut the brittle bundle open in the shivering shade of a thousand cottonwood leaves, and peeled an exquisite black buffalo robe back until he beheld a middle-aged woman completely mummified, the brown flesh drawn tight over her bones. He studied the woman. She'd been buried in her finest ceremonial dress, with green and yellow quilling on its bodice. He tugged the robe away from her feet and found them encased in new moccasins that had never touched earth, beaded in green and yellow geometric designs and lined with rabbit fur. Excited, he peeled the robe entirely away so he could work. This one had grieved shortly before her own death: her hair had been shorn on one side, and the index and middle finger of her left hand had been severed at the outer joints.

A squirrel chattered angrily. Wildly he peered through the benevolent leaves and saw no one. Safe. He found everything he'd hoped for: an awl case with steel trade awls in it; a soft strike-a-light bag made of unborn buffalo-calf hide; a leather disk on her chest, suspended from her neck with a bone-bead necklace. A yellow-breasted bird had been delicately painted on the medicine disk. He lifted it and found that it was thick, and probably contained her sacred totems between its front and rear covering. Around a desiccated finger hung two antler rings, one of them scrimshawed finely. And that was just the beginning. Tucked around her were beaded paint bags, a sewing kit, wood and bone amulets, a bone whistle, a porcupine-tail hairbrush with a fringed buckskin-wrapped handle, and a horsehair bridle.

Treasures! Swiftly he stripped away the rings and pocketed them. He wrestled the necklace over the mummified head and eased the medicine disk to the grass below. He tossed the bags and amulets and bone things to earth. He loosened the thongs of the high winter moccasins and eased them off the brittle and unyielding feet, grateful that he didn't have to saw off the feet themselves. He admired the moccasins a moment, knowing the care and craft that had gone into their creation. This pair had hawk bells attached so that the woman could jingle her way along the spirit trail.

Above all, he wanted that blouse of whited, fringed doeskin. It had been tanned to velvety perfection and quilled joyously, with exuberant bursts of yellow, the labor of a happy artisan. But how to take it? It had to be pulled over her head. He had to lift her arms up. They lay at her side, rigid in their final position. He tugged gently but the shoulder joint didn't yield. He yanked hard, but the right arm was locked in place. Finally, pinning the woman with one hand and jerking her arm with the other, he twisted it upward. Things snapped and cracked within, but eventually he got one arm in place, and then he tugged and jerked her left arm until it too poked straight over her head. Even then it was not easy to tug the old, dry blouse off without damaging it. But bit by bit he eased it over her head and up her arms until at last he had his treasure.

Beneath, the woman's dry flesh had sunk around her

bones. She was small and fragile, the color of rust. He removed her fringed skirt easily—it too was a treasure, because of the bright quillwork around its hemline. Done. She'd have to pass through the spirit lands without her clothing. He laughed at the thought, and loathed himself at the same time. He took one last look at the pillaged bundle and the desiccated body with its arms akimbo, but found nothing more to take.

He stepped carefully down his rickety ladder. *I will do anything,* he thought as he collected his booty from the swaying grass and carried it back to the covered wagon. *And pay any price,* he added as he packed them in an empty trunk and buckled the lid down. He peered about, suddenly fearful that he had been spied upon. *The guilty flee when no man pursueth,* he thought, remembering a Biblical verse. A great thirst had built up in him.

CHAPTER
34

She had stopped trembling, and that was a good sign. She wasn't asleep, but was nestled subdued in his arms, absorbing his warmth. Rufus remembered a dozen summer storms that had drenched him with forty-degree water and pelted him with ice, leaving him so numbed he fought for life. This storm had been like that.

He held her patiently, watching the rain die and the gray skies break apart, leaving glassy pools like shattered mirrors. Finally the July sun plowed through the tan canyon and made it sweat. Heat rose as swiftly as it had fled. Candace witnessed all this silently, like a woman who'd watched a burglary. She withdrew from his embrace and sat against the cliff wall, still primly huddled in the gray saddle blanket, which she tucked under her chin.

She studied him, and he pretended not to notice. "Thank you. I'm all right now." Her voice seemed as soft as blue velvet.

"You look better. I knew you were mighty chilled." He was grateful that she'd steered the conversation to neutral ground. His confession of love embarrassed him now. He'd lost his head. He arose, chased the stiffness from his joints, and stepped out from under the dripping overhang. He picked up her cotton dress and wrung it out, then spread it carefully over a steaming slope where the sun would pummel the transparency from it, turn it thick and opaque and safe again.

"What time is it?"

"I imagine it's midafternoon."

"I promised I'd help Professor Wood."

"I imagine he understands why you're late. I don't suppose he's chipping away."

She smiled at Rufus, and for a moment their gazes locked. He saw no walls within her eyes; only curiosity. He felt that tidal wave of need crashing on his beaches again. It came to him every time she noticed him. He felt hopeless standing in the rising tide.

"I do wish I could do my own work. I have so blasted much of it. The sites you found for me—they're more valuable than you know, Mister Crowe. Most of them are oreodont fossils. And that's what I wanted to find more than anything else. You see, there are oreodonts in the lower strata, and also above, separated by millions of years. According to the literature I've examined, two very different ones have been taken from here—and that's what I'm studying. Specialization." She smiled at him.

It sounded like praise from heaven to Rufus Crowe.

"If you're going to help Professor Wood, I'm going to help you. I know where more are. In that upper layer full of round rocks."

"You do?" He heard excitement color her voice, like the songs of the heavenly host.

"I'll show you. You go help Wood. I'll root out ten or fifteen oreodonts."

She laughed, the music of the spheres. "Mister Crowe, it isn't just the fossil that counts. It's the place. The stratum. Nearby fossils, especially of plants. It's whether it's a riverbank site. It's the coprolites in that stratum."

"What are coprolites?"

"Fossilized feces, mostly from predators, meat-eaters that preyed on the oreodonts. Those are important; they'll help me."

"You show me some. I can hunt sign. I know bear sign and buffalo sign and elk sign, and moose, but I'm a little rusty on coprolite sign."

She laughed. "I haven't seen any so far. Mister Crowe, maybe you should help Cyrus Wood and just abandon me to my work."

"You're prettier."

She pouted. He'd said the wrong thing.

She looked at her dress. "I'll put that on now. Perhaps you'll wait down the canyon?"

"I'll turn my back. You toss the blanket at me and I'll saddle this old pony while you're busy."

She eyed him distrustfully, but nodded. A few minutes later they splashed down the soggy canyon, she bedraggled in her muddy dress, he in his shabby old tweed, steaming in the sudden heat. She seemed more distant than ever, someone miles above him even though they swung easily along side by side, their hands sometimes touching.

He'd never been in love before. He'd never supposed he had a sentimental thought in his head. A maddening need overwhelmed him. Shyly, he glanced at her, admiring her thin nose and chiseled jaw, her slender neck and lithe figure. And even more did he love the way she attacked life. She sensed his glances and dug into her shoulder bag, extracting her goggles. She slid them over her stringy hair, drawing a curtain between them. But just walking beside her was reward enough for a hundred years.

They struggled across the lower prairie, fighting gumbo with every step, and penetrated the gully that would take them to camp. He noted that Toothache's travois was empty; she'd gotten the meat back, probably with help. When they reached the wagons they found Professor Wood beside his titanothere, admiring the rain-washed bone. Wood perched on a stool that kept him well above the slop.

"See what the rain did! It cleaned the site!"

"It looks just the way I left it," Candace said.

"Yes, well, it poured before I could do much. I suppose we'll have to redouble our effort now to make up the lost time."

She scooped up a chisel and pried away the water-softened claystone matrix without even using a hammer. In moments she'd freed the top of a vertebra. Triumphantly, she handed the weapon to him. "The rain's softened the mudstone. It should be easy now."

"Yes, yes, of course. A blessing, the rain. I must make hay before the sun shines." He chuckled at his joke.

They left him staring dreamily at his treasure and wiping steam from his spectacles. They struggled up the last of the path, which had turned to grease, and entered the slump to the music of water dripping off the whole Badlands wall. The pond had swollen, and looked like a pool of milk.

Gracie had collected rainwater and done her master's laundry, which hung whitely from a line. The two haunches of buffalo hung from a cottonwood more than leaping-wolf high. Toothache squatted before a smoky fire, nursing it.

Miss Huxtable turned to Crowe before they reached her tent. "I won't ever forget this."

He wondered how he ought to take that.

"I intend to acknowledge you in my papers."

"I was afraid of that."

"Oh, blast!" she cried, a peal of delight erupting from

her. She clasped his hand and squeezed it. Astonished, he kissed her gently on her cheek. She smiled.

"Tut, tut, tut," said Mrs. Rumley.

Across the camp, the dapper J. Roderick Crawford puffed a cigar and stared. But Rufus Crowe didn't mind.

CHAPTER
35

Near the top of the Badlands wall, J. Roderick Crabtree had at last found something worth digging. It was a fairly complete skeleton about the size of a cow. This fantastic beast had tusks like a pig and enormous flaring bones at either side of the head. Bossribs projected upward from the vertebrae. He'd uncovered enough to know that he'd discovered something for which there was no name, and probably no family, genus, or species. It tickled him. He'd keep it a deep secret. Something like this was worth a dozen failed expeditions. His only problem had been the hard sandstone, which required brutal, daylong toil. But the creature was worth it. He'd give the world a monster.

He'd spent that day freeing that fantastic skull and jawbone, and had learned from the grinding and cutting teeth and tusks that this monster was probably omnivorous. The tusks showed signs of injury—deep scrapes and gouges, whether from digging roots or fighting he couldn't say. The great bony plates radiating from the skull and jawbone had to be armor of some sort, valuable for ramming prey or enemies.

He had spent the last penny of his energy hammering sandstone long before the sun began to plummet in the northwest, but he kept on tapping, loosening pieces, releasing the treasure in the rock. He was no Wood. He'd have his beast in hand before the Harvard professor had the head of the titanothere in the wagon.

Just about at quitting time he sensed he wasn't alone, and turned, expecting to see the guide or maybe the Huxtable woman. Instead he found himself staring at two aborigines whose nocked arrows pointed at his chest. Both warriors were painted, one with a fantastic ocher mask slicing his face in two. Both were stocky and powerful. Above, looking like fangs along the lip of the Badlands wall, were forty or fifty more, all of them studying him; all of them painted for war.

His stomach slowly turned over. He felt the hot wetness of his own urine, and it appalled him as much as his impending death. Never in his life had his body betrayed him. He thought he would die; that J. Roderick Crabtree and his monster would vanish from the mind of mankind; that his young life would stop like a broken clock. He set down his mallet and chisel, expecting execution.

One of them ran a finger over the partly excavated skull, and then yanked it back as if he had been burned.

"Hew-wo," said the other, and gestured to Crabtree.

Crabtree followed, on legs that wobbled, up the gulch and out onto the upper prairie. The mounted warriors crowded around him, exclaiming at his white clothes, straw hat, trim beard. He felt death lurking in those war clubs, battle-axes, feather-decked lances, sinew-backed bows, trade muskets, and sheathed knives.

A young headman—one with a notched eagle feather tucked into his hair at the rear—ended the commotion with a word, and motioned to Crabtree to head toward the camp below, which they could see from this lofty lip of the prairie. He stumbled down a steep trail between rising columns of mudstone, clambered over a three-foot ledge, and twisted his way downward. The horsemen followed, even over the ledge. His back prickled with the awareness of a dozen arrow points aimed at him. They emerged upon the slump at its westernmost extremity, and were greeted by the nervous snorting of the two Clydesdales. Instantly the aborigines rode toward the giant draft horses, fascinated. In moments they'd captured both of the taffy-colored giants, and stood around them exclaiming, pointing at the feathered legs, the massive hoofs, the huge Roman-nosed heads with blazes running down them. The great horses stood half again as high as the thirteen- and fourteen-hand mustangs they rode.

Across the meadow the camp stirred. Wood vanished into juniper brush. Candace stood frozen. Mrs. Rumley fixed the visitors with an imperious eye. But the guide and his squaw were loping toward him, shouting something at the visitors in Lakota. So his captors were Sioux. He might yet see the sun set. The squaw's face was wreathed with joy, and she began jabbering with the visitors, and soon Crowe was shaking hands as well.

At last Crowe turned to Crabtree: ''These here are Hunkpapa off to take some Pawnee scalps and horses. My woman's a cousin of one. I've got some explaining to do. They don't like your bone-collecting none.''

Crowe turned to the Hunkpapa warriors who'd gathered around him, talking with authority and punctuating his words with a clap of hands. Once in a while he pointed toward Crabtree or the others, who'd nerved themselves to approach. The mild, soft-spoken Rufus Crowe had somehow transformed himself, and his tone of voice took on a stridency that suggested he had authority among them. The warriors who'd captured the Clydesdales released them sullenly, and Crabtree sensed that Crowe had gained control.

Gracie approached, and instantly created another sensation among the warriors. Crowe pointed at her and talked some more, and pointed at Crabtree too. Slavery was something the Plains tribes understood. They had slaves of their own. Some of the curious warriors crowded around Gracie, examining her hands and arms, rubbing them.

"Mind your manners," she said amiably. She looked happy. Wood, who had nerved himself out of hiding, looked tense. So did Miss Huxtable.

The Hunkpapa discovered the two large scaffolds, and wanted to know all about them. Crowe obliged, and Crabtree heard the name Van Vliet mentioned. He knew that Crowe would tell the story without guile. Toothache had her own version to tell when it came to the scaffolds, and they all listened to her as well.

Crowe turned to Crabtree: "They're going that way—past the burial grounds—tomorrow. I hope Doctor Van Vliet's been behaving himself like he said he would."

"What if he hasn't?"

"I can't guarantee his safety."

Crabtree shook his head. Van Vliet would commit suicide if it would add to his collection. "Somebody better warn Archimedes tonight," he muttered.

"I ought to introduce you. This here is Pizi, or Gall. He's the war chief for this here filibuster." Crabtree beheld a powerful young man in his twenties, with thick cruel lips, disdain in his eyes, and murder in his nostrils. He wore his hair divided into wrapped braids. "And this young man's Tatanka Yotanka, Sitting Buffalo Bull. It'll do to call him Sitting Bull. He's a Dreamer, a medicine man like me, coming along to steer 'em straight against the mighty Pawnee. He's powerful and full of ambitions." The Dreamer had burning coals for eyes set in a diamond-shaped face.

The Hunkpapa meandered through camp, knotting around Candace Huxtable, who didn't take it calmly; tiptoeing around the formidable Mrs. Rumley, and eyeing Cyrus Wood with dismissing gazes. Toothache wandered with them, obviously gossiping and saying cruel things about them all.

"I imagine they're staying for supper."

"Gracie, start roasting one of those haunches," Crabtree said.

She glared at him. "I could roast me medium rare, master. Taste better. Or you. You'd taste worse, even well done and cooked brown. My land, cooking for a mess of wild Injuns."

Crabtree cracked his whip hand in his other palm, a gesture that always set Gracie scurrying off without another word. He watched her add to the fire and then wrestle the huge haunch down from the thick limb that supported it. By herself, she dragged it to her fire. She began sawing it into pieces, slicing meat as if she were murdering someone. He noted it. Several Sioux gathered around her. She smiled at them. He noted that too.

Candace Huxtable stood her ground, her face drawn, her pose unyielding as warriors crowded around her, poking and pinching. Crabtree noted that she was wearing her armor again; she'd started that after the rain. A pity too, hiding a figure so lissome under all that. The Hunkpapa had discovered it, and were insolently running fingers along the slight ridges of whalebone. She said not a word but her eyes blazed at them.

Wood fared worse. Crabtree watched the gray professor double over, slowly straightened himself, and careen toward the juniper thickets, looking so green he seemed to be in the throes of dyspepsia or heart failure. Crabtree followed, concerned, his medical instincts rising within him. He shadowed Wood as the stricken man swung around a low juniper, fell to hands and knees, and vomited up everything in his belly with wrenching, gasping eruptions that spewed over his beard. When it was over, he clutched the earth and sobbed.

Crabtree knelt beside him and put an arm around the trembling man's shoulder. "Cyrus. Come to the tent and I'll give you a little paregoric to settle your stomach."

The professor quieted under Crabtree's grip, and finally sat up, his gray cheeks tear-streaked. "God bless you. I'm too old and set in my ways," he said. "Field work's for the young. And the brave. I can't endure the sight of what I am."

"Cyrus—look." Crabtree pointed at the damp stain along the inside of his left leg. "We can't always be what we want to be. Our bodies betray us."

"You too?"

"I was frightened witless."

"I thought—I'm a long way from Harvard Yard, Crab."

"We're safe enough, it seems. That's what we hired Crowe for. Say, Cyrus. I've found something up above. Something I can't identify, but it seems to be a giant boar of some sort. An omnivore at any rate. I wonder if you'd come up after the Hunkpapa leave and give me your opinion."

"You want my opinion? I'm no anatomist, Crab."

"You're a taxonomist, and maybe that's the discipline I need. I don't know what I have."

Cyrus Billington Wood managed a smile. "I'll do that, Crab. The moment they leave."

CHAPTER 36

F illed with a rich calm wrought by the paregoric, Professor Wood ventured back into camp. At every hand, Hunkpapa warriors meandered through the place, boys and men among them curious about the way white men lived. A crowd of them peered into Miss Huxtable's tent while Mrs. Rumley tutted. Others had drifted out to the pasture to amaze themselves with the sight of the Clydesdales as well as the expedition's two draft horses. Others stood before the scaffolds with Van Vliet's artifacts upon them, heatedly debating. Some watched Gracie build a cookfire. The headmen surrounded Rufus Crowe and were questioning him earnestly, no doubt about the true purposes of this foray into Lakota territory. Wood hoped that Crowe could supply a satisfactory explanation—especially about Van Vliet's purposes here.

Crowe saw him and broke free from the headmen.

"Professor, I imagine these people would like to see your titanothere, ask you a few questions. I told them about it."

"I couldn't do that, Mister Crowe. How could it be translated? What if they damage it?"

"I can explain, one way or another. I think it'd be wise. They're as curious about you as any ethnologist is about them. You're a mystery to them."

"I really don't see how—"

"You just be yourself, a professor. Your task is to do some teaching. I'll do the rest."

Wood knew he couldn't escape it. "Very well. But I fear my explanations won't appeal to them. I'll get us into trouble."

"I'll do what I can. I've interpreted the world of white men for them for many years."

Unhappily, Wood clambered down the steep grade to the canyon where the titanothere slumped in its rock cage. Behind him, Crowe gathered the warriors and led them to the digging. Slowly they gathered around the half-exposed titanothere skull and mandible, amazement in their faces. A few reached down to touch the amazing horn bones erupting from the nose of the skull. Others pointed and muttered. But most of them carefully concealed every thought, and stared at the strange skull as impassively as one would stare at a stump. The young medicine man, Sitting Bull, gazed evenly at the skull, saying nothing. The war chief, Gall, stood arrogantly to one side, as if to announce his scorn of all this.

"Professor, they want to know what this is and how it got here in rock."

"I'm helpless, Mister Crowe. Their aboriginal concepts won't permit me—"

"Just talk."

Wood drew himself up, and suddenly he was no longer standing in a wild place in the federal territory of Nebraska, but at his lectern, with some acned boys ready to devour his every word.

"Well," he began. "This creature roamed the world

long ago—longer than anyone can imagine. Long before mortals existed. There probably were many like it. This land wasn't dry the way it is now, but lush and wet. This creature ate vegetable matter, not meat, and a body that size required a lot of it, a lot more than today's dry climate could grow."

He listened to Crowe translate. The Hunkpapa listened solemnly, absorbing whatever Crowe was saying to them. Wood doubted that it was very close to his own words.

"They want to know how you know that."

"From the teeth. The teeth of plant-eaters are made to grind." He pointed at the molar-like teeth at the rear of the jaw. "We'll know more when we can see the feet. The bones will tell us whether the animal lived in swamps, whether it lived on dry land. From the feet we'll know something about the climate they lived in."

"They want to know why you're digging it out."

"We—scholars—wish to learn all there is to learn about the world around us. And to discover the secrets of the past."

"They want to know if you're afraid of releasing the spirits."

"No. I know of no spirit hovering here. But knowledge shines like sunshine, and ignorance is like nighttime for us."

Crowe translanted that and soon had another question: "How did it get here? They can't imagine how bones got here in rock."

Wood nodded. "Once this was a floodplain of a great river, probably flowing out of the Black Hills to the west. When this animal died it wasn't inside the earth, but on the surface, just as we are, probably near a stream. Its body was swiftly covered with silt, perhaps in a spring flood. Soon it was buried in silt that kept the air from reaching the bones. The rest rotted away or was eaten, but the bones remained under the silt."

Crowe translated and soon the guide had another question. "He wants to know why the bones didn't rot too. Bones in the earth rot, he says."

"Tell him he's right; bones can decay. But what he's seeing here"—Wood pointed at the fossil skull—"isn't the original bone. It's rock. Little by little the waters replaced the calcium in the bone with other minerals until the original bone disappeared and something just like it remained in the hardening silt—which slowly became rock."

Crowe took some time with that, hunting for Lakota words or parallel ideas. Wood spotted Crabtree and Miss Huxtable in his audience, and hoped they'd take over. All this taxed him.

"This one wants to know how silt became rock. Did Wakan Tanka do it?"

"No, natural forces turned it into shale. As the rivers deposited more silt, it buried the fossil deeper and deeper. Water, pressure, heat, and chemical reactions did the rest."

"Sitting Bull, here, says it's not so. That the Lakota story is the true one. He's a Dreamer and he knows."

Wood nodded. It had come to the impasse he'd anticipated.

The young Dreamer began his own oration, his tone forceful and obviously contemptuous.

"What is he saying, Mister Crowe?"

"He's saying that the bones are the handiwork of Iktomi, the Trickster, who put them there, deep in rock, to fool these white men. But no Lakota should be fooled. I should add that Iktomi's a sort of fallen god, like Lucifer, one of the evil powers. The Sioux have several of that sort. He's saying this here's a bad place for the Hunkpapa, and they're likely to lose their war medicine if they stay here. He's saying they got to get their ponies and leave, or maybe the Pawnee'll whip them."

The warriors retreated up the path, collected their ponies and spare warhorses, and rode solemnly past Wood, Crowe, and the rest, to the lower prairie, heading for the White River. Wood watched them go, glad of it but afraid that he'd somehow stirred up trouble. Within a few minutes, the last sound of passage faded and Wood and the others found themselves alone. They stood in eerie silence in the deep shadow of late afternoon.

"It's not like them to skip a meal," said Crowe. "That boy, Sitting Bull, he's got a mighty big voice with them."

"I wish it were bigger," said Crabtree.

CHAPTER
37

F or days, Archimedes Van Vliet cleaned, polished, and sorted his artifacts. He stalked the burial ground gleaning the things he'd missed. He walked to other cottonwood groves along the White, looking for the occasional tree burial, and found a few. He spent a week numbering each item and recording it in his ledger. But pleasure eluded him, and nightmares plagued him. He sensed menace lurking in some nameless, faceless form.

He awoke one July night with a start, and sat up in his wagon, sweating heavily even in the coolness. He yanked his blanket aside and let the chill air rebuke the sweat and terror. Greed. He had named his phantom. He arose stiffly and peered out of the covered wagon into the burial grounds. The aborigines imagined lost or homeless spirits darted around in them, rather as white men imagined ghosts in a cemetery. Some things, he thought, were common among all cultures. He spotted no spirits, visible or invisible.

Greed was his demon. It could kill him. That message

had carved itself into his brain. He had to conquer it now, once and for all, or die; he had to pack a kit and make his feet walk westward up the White.

He felt a moment of sheer disgust with himself. He hadn't become the person he'd dreamed of, a respected anthropologist doing valuable studies of the native Americans for the sake of knowledge. No. Somewhere along the way the disciplined scholar had decayed into a graverobber, a ghoul. The shame of it swept through him.

Chastened by the whips of conscience, he dressed and began to gather some things to take along on his long walk to redemption. He had trouble finding things in the fading dark, but at last he had a knapsack ready. He stared at the useless wagon, thought longingly of what he'd collected from the first tree scaffolds, and forced himself into the burial grounds. The gray haze of predawn illumined the scaffolds nesting in their tree-beds above him as he resolutely headed for the Fort Laramie road.

He reached the far edge of the burial grounds, feeling them tug at him like a hungry lover. He reached the Laramie road at about first light, the moment when he could see back to the mass of cottonwoods. That's when his nerve failed him. He needed two fingers of spirits. Desolated, he retreated to the wagon, and quickly poured two fingers of whiskey. His vices held him in their grip. He sweated anew, more from the terror that seeped into him than from the harsh spirits that burned his throat and spread hotly through his belly.

He unpacked his kit the way a prisoner organizes his few belongings in his jail cell after the door has slammed shut. He envied the world's disciplined people, the ones like Crabtree who controlled the demons inside them. He envied old Wood, who'd lived in simple academic virtue, the master of his own ship even if that ship hadn't ventured very far. He envied the Huxtable woman, so crisp and in command, as if she had nothing inside her to fight, nothing that might defeat and shame her.

He ignored breakfast but poured another dose of spirits, needing their traitorous comforts. Then, even before the sun had rolled up from under the earth, he spread his most prized possessions out before him. One was a remarkable elkskin scalp shirt with twenty-seven human scalps dangling from it, including one brown-haired one. Another was a cradleboard studded with brass tacks. Now, along with the treasures on the scaffolds in the Badlands, he had enough to endow two or three museums, even after keeping the choicest for himself. The curators at the Smithsonian would stumble all over themselves to catalogue and display what he would bestow on them. They'd name a room after him. The thought almost banished the dread that had been breaking out of him like bad sweat.

All morning he examined the artifacts that held him prisoner. After a whiskey nooning he removed the rest of his booty from its riverbank cache and stowed it in the landlocked schooner. It was evidence against himself, he thought.

Through the afternoon he worked on his other task, collecting the ruined items he'd discarded weeks before during his one-day rampage through the Sioux cemetery. In hellish midday heat he wandered around the ruined scaffolds, plucking up desiccated shields, foul-looking clothes, faded and broken bows, rotten trade-cloth shirts, and all the rest. All of it was corrupt or so dry it crumbled in his hand; or so sun-bleached or rain-leached its luster and color had vanished. He hadn't missed a thing worth keeping. That gave him pleasure, this affirmation of a quick, decisive eye for the valuable.

By late afternoon he'd gathered up a mountain of the rubbish, along with some fine skulls for Eastern doctors to play with. He toted it all to his camp, armload after armload, wondering how to take it back to the Badlands.

A way of putting it all to good use was forming in his mind. He had to find two or three horses, any horses that could pull travois.

That's when he discovered the aborigines. They stood at the edge of his camp, forming a great circle. Coppery bodies, bare except for moccasins and breechclouts and a few ornaments. None of them said a word. He heard, faintly, the snort of horses some distance away. He felt his heart slide into a running gait, and knew he must calm himself. He arose, poured a four-finger shot into his tin cup, and added the splash. It went down hot. He had named the demon, and now the demon would kill. He sighed, wishing he had walked away that morning; knowing he never could. His rifle lay inert, well out of reach, among his supplies. He realized he had committed suicide that morning.

Like wraiths they emerged from shadows and padded toward him as silently as light slid up a western slope at dawn, or shadow retreated at noon. A lot of death, more than he could count offhand. And there'd be more death holding the horses somewhere outside the sacred grounds. He finished off the cup, feeling the fire numb his innards, hoping it'd numb his brains. They slid toward him, all of them carrying battle gear, clubs, lances, bows. And yet he saw no drawn bow or nocked arrow, or lowered lance.

He arose shakily. "Ah, company," he croaked. "Have a drink."

None of them did. They crowded closer. He fathomed they were Sioux; he'd seen enough to recognize the general body type: tall, stocky men, heavily muscled, less Asian-looking than most other tribes. These were ocher, white, black, and vermilion paint; a few wore lacerations and ridged scars and puckers where no puckered flesh should be. They had war plans, and he took that for a good sign.

"Lakota," he said. "Welcome."

No one replied. They continued to study him as if he were a new species for their collections. One, a young man with a diamond-shaped face hewn from burled maple, had demon eyes that saw straight through him. Another of them, a heavy-boned young man with cruel lips, nodded. Several older warriors approached him, narrowing his breathing room like a tightening noose.

"Ah, hold it there. Let's talk, eh?"

A sour sweat bloomed all over him, dampening his shirt in moments. His circle of life diminished to ten feet.

"I'm sorry," he croaked. "It got away from me. I'm really a scientist just gathering information about you. I have a weakness, you know."

They closed the rest of the way, and laid hands on him; not roughly, but in a manner that turned him into a prisoner instantly. He feared brutality, the slash of knives, the smack of fists, torment of burning brands, but experienced nothing like that. Instead they led him to the burial grounds, where he beheld several more of them resurrecting a scaffold. These warriors had straightened the posts, restored a crossbar, and were sliding the poles onto it to make a platform.

It dawned on him that this scaffold would be for Doctor of Science Archimedes Van Vliet.

CHAPTER
38

The Huxtable corset pinched Candace's waist, and fought her every move as she worked, but she knew she'd never be without it again. It armored her against the yearnings of her unruly female nature. Stiffly, as if in a plaster cast, she whittled mudstone away from her fossil bones, making determined progress each day.

She had become an old hand at it all, learning the most economical ways to chip away the matrix rock. She labored until her muscles ached and then labored further, hoping the pain would go away. It never did. Even under her battered straw hat she had burned red wherever her flesh had known sun.

When he could, Rufus Crowe worked on a fossil a few hundred yards up-canyon and in a more recent stratum. His was another oreodont, but its rear parts had vanished, probably eaten by bone-crunching predators of that age. She'd asked him merely to strip away the overburden until the fossil lay exposed in its matrix. She'd do the rest. She needed to examine its surroundings before extracting it. His work excited her: the oreodont he was exposing was significantly different from hers. They both had forty-four teeth but the canines of his had developed into short tusks. She meant to find out how and why that specialization had happened.

Except for one morning when a sharp shower forced her to retreat to camp, she usually worked well into the hottest part of each day. Then she walked to the cool, shaded gulch and the north-facing cliffside where Professor Wood's titanothere slumbered in its rock bed. One could work comfortably in that shade through the heat of the afternoon.

"Ah, there you are," Wood said one day. She detected reproach in the tone, but so modulated by academic blandness she barely caught it. "The work goes so slowly."

"Well, what did you get done?" She was voicing a question that politeness forbade. The longer she'd labored on his project, the more it became obvious to her that he intended to have her dig out the entire skeleton of a creature the size of an elephant.

"Why, I got out my surgical tools and cleaned the eye socket. See there." He pointed at a shining ring of skull-bone.

He was doing laboratory work. His field task was to extract the giant and pack it in ways that would preserve it during its long trip east. And to examine the stratum from which it was plucked for fossils that could help to date it. But instead he'd lolled around, worked twenty minutes with medical tools, and then slid back into his dreaming.

"That's not what is needed." She was committing lèse-majesté and knew it.

"Why, my dear Miss Huxtable, I don't believe you've the credentials to be saying that."

"I think you're shirking."

He blinked. He peered about, not meeting her relentless gaze. "I must remind myself you're not my student," he said, speaking the Aesopian tongue of the Harvard Yard. His meaning loomed harsher than his words. It didn't deter her.

"You're expecting me to dig that thing out; to move ten or fifteen tons of rock; to chisel under these giant bones, loosen them and load them. You know you are."

His jaw worked and his head reared back until he peered down his patrician nose at her. "Your tone is unbecoming."

"You don't deny it."

"I do deny it. I'm here to supervise."

She laughed. "Blast, that's it exactly. You've not done a lick of work. You don't intend to. You're here to supervise."

"I'm not a young man, Miss. You don't expect a man of my age to be swinging pickaxes. That's for the young and healthy. My lifelong discipline is scholarship."

"Then why did you come here? To watch others dig?"

"This inquisition is quite improper and we really must shake hands and pull together. I assure you of my goodwill."

"You can show me your goodwill by cutting into that cliff."

"Now, now, Miss Huxtable. I regret this little contretemps. Let's proceed, eh?"

"I'm not sure I wish to. I work hard at my own site. My muscles hurt but I don't stop. I get thirsty in that sun, and that tepid water doesn't help. But I carry on, and I've an oreodont, ninety percent complete, ready to remove."

He sighed. "It's all admirable, Miss Huxtable, but what a waste. For the sake of science, we really should tackle this titanothere. Come now, don't you feel the excitement of a discovery like this! I do. I can just see this magnificent specimen towering in the Museum of Natural History, or the Smithsonian, with our names engraved on a plate beside it."

"It should be my name, not yours."

"Why, I found it." He looked affronted. "I have papers to write. Studies of every bone. It'll take me years."

She debated it, filled with doubt and pain. Should she sacrifice her entire summer, her long trip across the ocean, her own studies, her father's work and reputation, for this? Maybe she should. It'd be unspeakable, a crime, to leave a prize like this in the ground at the end of summer. He was right: the giant fossil could scarcely be more valuable. Paleontologists thus far had only a hint of this monster from a few stray bones. Every natural scientist in the world would point a finger at her, shake his head, and tell the rest that this sort of selfishness marked the dilettante. It'd close doors. It'd evoke malignant gossip.

If only she could see him worn down at the end of each day, his old body hurting with the trying. If only he joined her while she hammered, he opening up the rear of the fossil while she worked on the front. If only he would laugh, tell her he didn't think he could swing the pick again, and keep on swinging it. If only he'd just pick up a chisel and begin to hammer!

She knew what she had to do, even if her choice stirred up the whole academic world. She hated the choice, but she would live with the consequences.

"Professor Wood. I'd help if I saw you trying."

"What are you saying, Miss Huxtable?"

"I have no intention of freeing this giant fossil by myself. I have my own studies to pursue, upon which I have spent thousands of pounds."

"You're abandoning science for your own little project?"

"No, I'm not abandoning science. I'll not be a victim of your blasted laziness."

He gaped. "You're quite rude."

"I'm worse than that. I'm truthful."

CHAPTER
39

A daydream gripped the imagination of Cyrus Billington Wood so intensely that he lost contact with the world around him. He slouched against his giant fossil, deep in the shade of the Badlands gulch, but his mind had flown an ocean away.

He saw his great titanothere cleaned and polished and wired together, occupying a place of honor in the Museum of Natural History. And beside it a bronze plaque proclaimed that this sole example of a hitherto unknown subspecies was named after its discoverer, Professor Cyrus Billington Wood. Next he imagined himself sitting in his dreary office at Harvard and finding upon his desk a letter from England informing him that he had won the Copley Medal, which would be presented to him at a meeting at Somerset House of the Royal Society in London. And would he do the society the honor of attending?

The Royal Society! The most esteemed scientific organization in all the world. Why, Isaac Newton had once been its president! Wood imagined himself in a black cut-

away with a starched white collar and a black cravat, on a
dais along with all the great men of science. At his elbow
would be none other than the great Richard Owen. And
alongside, the geologist Charles Lyell; and John Henslow,
Adam Sedgwick, George Peacock, and William Whewell.
And also Thomas Wollaston, Sir Joseph Hooker, Charles
Darwin, Thomas Huxley, and Alfred Russel Wallace.

And of course it would be Owen speaking, Owen pro-
posing a toast to the Queen and then to Wood. They'd
hang the medal on him, a glinting medallion suspended
by a silk ribbon, and he'd hear the enthusiastic applause,
which would swell into a standing ovation—and something
within his old academic soul would melt with joy.

He peered at the fossil skull, of which only the top
portion had been excavated, along with the neck vertebrae. He studied the looming rock that formed the canyon
wall and entombed his fossil. And he sighed. Excavating
that monster by himself would be like writing an encyclo-
pedia single-handedly in six weeks. He shuddered. Time
was fleeing. In six weeks, early in September, they would
have to drive north toward Fort Union, where the fur company had agreed to hold a keelboat and crew for them until
October 15. After that the weather would close in on the
two-month downriver trip to St. Louis.

He arose, feeling his old carcass unfold stiffly. He would
have to bring this matter to the collegial attention of Crabtree.

Majestically, with the measured tread of the righteous,
he clambered up to the grassy hollow and the camp, and
saw Gracie at her toil there. A plan took shape in the forge
of his mind, heated by the bellows of emergency. He
marched up the steep incline to the upper prairie and proceeded westward. Then he clambered as fast as dignity
permitted down a frightful chute and into a gulch where
Dr. J. Roderick Crabtree labored bare-chested with chisel

and mallet, freeing the forelegs of a curious boarlike monster. The man's dishabille disconcerted Professor Wood.

"Doctor Crabtree, may I have a word?"

Crabtree grinned, set down his tools, and lifted a flask of milky water, guzzling an ocean of it.

"An emergency. Let me guess. It's not a titanothere. It's a plaster of paris hoax."

Wood blinked, knowing he would endure collegial ribbing if that would help. "It's about the woman."

"Ah! She's rejected your suit."

"Ah! Hch. She's too bluestocking for my tastes. No, Crab. I fear she's derelict in her duty."

Crabtree eyed him skeptically, saying nothing.

"Her duty to science, to decency."

"She's quit working for you."

"Tut, now. She wasn't working for me; she was making a contribution to science. She's announced that her oreodonts will require her full-time attention henceforth. She'll not participate in excavating the titanothere. And she impugned my character twice. Can you imagine it?"

"No, I can't imagine it," said Crabtree, the lift of his lips belying him. "What did she impugn?"

"My industry."

"And how did she impugn it?"

"Why, she ignored a lifetime of scholarship and toil, and instead told me she would no longer assist, allegedly because I wasn't meeting some sort of standard. Of course I told her I'm not young and don't manage well in the field, but it didn't stop her reckless decision. Do you suppose we could require her labor?"

"Certainly. But that doesn't mean she'll oblige. It's her pounds and pence that brought her here, Cyrus."

"I feared you'd say that. I thought we might tell her to leave camp unless she performs necessary services."

"Ah, Wood, she's not a slave, and there's the pity. You need a slave." Crabtree had started to grin noxiously.

"Well, that brings up the other matter. In principle, you know, I detest the abominable institution. But emergencies suspend things, eh?"

"Gracie."

"Yes, if you would."

"One thing you should know about a slave, Wood. Sometimes not even a whip will force a slave into doing something she doesn't like. She's frightened witless by stone bones of monsters in the ground."

"But you could command her."

"Well, well, look at you," Crabtree chortled. "The great friend of Harriet Beecher Stowe."

Wood endured the mockery with dignity. Opposing slavery was one thing; an emergency use of a slave was quite another. Why, he'd feasted on Gracie's slave cooking for weeks now, and it didn't alter his convictions.

"I have a fine, braided whip with a leaded tassel on it in my kit, Wood. For disciplinary purposes. It's difficult, sometimes, to make a slave do what you require. Especially if the slave is terrified of what you want. I'll lend you the whip. Tell her I lent her to you."

Crabtree beamed at him. The Charlestonian had become insufferable.

"You won't issue the command?"

Crabtree shook his head and lifted his mallet and chisel. "She's all yours, Abolitionist Wood."

"Perhaps I can induce her, for a small wage—"

Crabtree clamped a hand over Wood's arm. "Never pay a slave, Wood. Pay me. I'll charge you fifty cents a day." The menace in Crabtree's gaze settled the matter in Wood's mind.

Wood made his weary way back to camp, feeling more and more despondent. He discovered Gracie scrubbing roots of some sort beside her black kettle. Timorously, he sidled up to her. She glared from beneath the yellow bandanna that clamped her hair to her glistening dark brow.

"Miss Gracie, would you help me with my fossil?"

"You asking or telling?"

"I'm asking for help, Miss Gracie."

"You sure you're asking? What's the master say?"

"I'm asking. He . . . said I could have you."

"You're telling. Mister Wood, when a white man asks some old slave, it ain't asking."

"I'm asking. I wouldn't think of violating your choice."

She laughed, cynically, and stood up, her hands on her ample hips. "Yeah, I could go dig your old fossil. I'll do that if you'll take care of all this." The sweep of her arm indicated the whole camp. "I tell you what. I'll go dig them bones. You stay here and cook the meals. You wash the dishes. You go find the firewood and cut it and haul it. You keep a pot o'' coffee on for you tired scientists. You haul the water about three times a day and hunt down them prickly pear pads to settle the white stuff outa it, and watch out for stickers, they get you. You keep a washpot heated up and do the master's clothes each day, and hang 'em up to dry. He like 'em white, pure white, so you gotta scrub good. You can hang up his bedroll, and clean his tent too. You can gather greens and dig roots that Tooth-ache showed me. You do that and I'll go scratch your rock."

"I shouldn't have asked, Miss Gracie. You're certainly busy."

"You sure this is asking, not telling? I get told most of the time." Sweat ran freely down her cheeks and neck, dampening her baggy cotton dress.

"I, ah, appreciate what you do each day to keep camp. I hadn't quite realized—"

"No, no one realizes. We're invisible, like haunts."

"Well, now I see."

She plucked another bulbous root up and began to wash it.

"Servants are a problem," said Mrs. Rumley. "I had a woman who wouldn't wash windows. I had to let her go."

Ten minutes later he reached his titanothere skull, ran a loving hand over it, pulled out his dental pick, and began cleaning its teeth.

CHAPTER
40

A sickness engulfed Archimedes Van Vliet. He felt his legs turn rubbery, his stomach flop. His pulse catapulted. Wildly he thrashed, trying to free himself from the iron grips of several Sioux warriors, but he could not overmaster them. He struggled anyway, sobbing, gasping, feeling the booze leak from his pores. But he was as helpless as a thrumming fly in a spider's web.

They dragged him to the base of the scaffold. He begged God, he beseeched the angels and archangels, he pleaded and sobbed, he cast wild prayers upward, he cried, but they didn't free him. Instead, two warriors with rolls of rawhide thong bound his trembling legs at the ankles. He felt the thong bite his flesh. Then they bound his hands before him, wrapping the tough cord around and around his wrists until he scarcely felt connected to his fingers.

None of them spoke. They lowered him to the grass. He peered up at them, bronzed savages against the azure sky, the last thing he would ever see. One of them knelt at his head. That one clutched a great handful of his hair, and Van Vliet felt the bite of a knife. He was being scalped.

"Ah, God," he sobbed.

The knife bit into his skullbone in a small circle, raising pain in him like a torch flame. Then he felt an awful yank that almost popped his skull loose from his neck, felt a ripping, and a curious nakedness. The warrior held up Van Vliet's hair and said something. Van Vliet stared in horror at a three-inch patch of his brown hair and flesh—a ritual scalping to doom his spirit to wandering this place for ever.

Pain crept down his head and drilled into his brain.

"I'll give everything back! I'm sorry!"

One of them brought an ancient burial robe, brittle from years on a scaffold, a robe Van Vliet himself had cut loose. They lifted him by his shoulders and feet and settled him on the robe and rolled it over him. They left his face free; they would let him think about his crimes for a while, hogtied and facing the sky. Two of them ran tough cord around the ancient robe, wrapping him in a murderous package, clamping down his arms, his legs, his feet. Then several of them lifted him up to the platform. Its poles corrugated his back. He faced the glaring sky, bound so tightly that he could scarcely move. His head sailed into space.

He could see nothing of them now. He dared not struggle lest they wrap more cord around him. His heart pounded his ribs and his pulse skidded through him like hammer blows. A fly crawled over his naked skull, tormenting him.

Nothing happened. He listened sharply, his senses keen. He didn't know whether they watched or had left. He thought he heard the muffled sound of unshod hooves. He saw a crow fly over him, and discovered a new terror. Raptors would land on him while he still lived and pluck out his eyes and eat his cheeks and nose.

He felt his own sour whiskey-sweat. The shroud had swiftly become a furnace that would bleed him of his juices until his heart pumped sludge. He had to think, find some way out. His mind had become razor-edged, slicing through desperate ideas.

He understood the whole thing. This had been a war party, and they'd do nothing to turn their medicine bad. Everything about him was taboo. Probably those who had touched him would bathe in sweetgrass smoke, a ritual cleansing.

He forced himself to lie still, against all instinct to fight his bonds, until he could endure it no more. Tentatively he lifted his knees and found he could move a little. He jackknifed his legs over and over, jamming his knees up, making room within his shroud. He tried to raise his arms and found them hopelessly pinioned. But he kept at it, stretching the cords that held the brittle old buffalo robe, giving himself a precious half inch of leeway.

But the effort was taking a terrible toll in sweat. He'd be dehydrated and dead long before he writhed himself loose. He could writhe himself right off the scaffold and fall seven feet to earth.

He lay still, his mind reeling from one thing to another. Time leaked by more slowly than a turtle crawled. At last he slid into a merciful stupor, his mind whirling through green hills, through visions of his parents, through an orchard laden with rosy apples, ever more distant from the burial grounds along the White River.

When next he grew aware of where he was, he discovered darkness around him. The air felt cooler. But his thirst had become unbearable. Water! He'd give anything to lift a flask of ordinary water to his fevered lips. He wanted to plunge into cool water, splash in it, smacking his jaws over gulps of it. His tongue had grown thick. His head ached from the lack of it. His throat felt like hot iron.

He experienced blinding flashes, white lacing his universe, and ascribed them to dementia. Everything wrong with him now was rooted in thirst, and he could think of nothing else. "Give me water," he begged a merciless God. But the thunder that rumbled around the flashes finally pierced to his intelligence. With the arrival of a real storm came the desperate hope of rain.

"Hurry!" he croaked.

It did come, tentatively at first, on the sharp eddies of cold air from above; spraying enticingly across his face, tormenting because it popped here and there, missing his mouth, smacking his forehead, thumping on the dusty old robe that buried him. He snapped at the drops like a rabid dog, his teeth clapping on stray missiles. He licked one off the tip of his bulbous nose. Frantic, he stretched his mouth open until his jaw ached, trying to funnel every drop. He caught only a few.

A sheet of rain swept in on a gust that rattled his shroud, but it wasn't enough. He couldn't lick it or eat it fast enough. But the patter turned into a rhythmic downpour, slowly soaking his buffalo robe until it lay heavy, chilling him, the rain trickling through cracks in the robe onto his flesh. The rain popped and hissed and finally roared, making his robe resound with its percussion. The heavens above him snarled and raged and rebuked him, casting lightning at him, reducing him to a gnat on the toe of an angry God.

A tiny stream collected along a wrinkle over his chest and trickled down to the edge of the robe, pouring over his neck. Desperately he tried to shrug the robe higher, squeeze down so that the flow would wash into his opened mouth. His efforts brought the flow only to his chin, missing his mouth by a precious inch. He rammed his arms upward, lifting the ancient leather over his chest, and at last some water splashed into his mouth. He gulped it down. It was worth more than all the world's artifacts. Bit by bit he drank, praying the storm would continue. He swallowed greedily, mouthful after mouthful. Maybe a quart. His body revived and he felt solace in his flesh. But all too soon the summer storm slackened and wandered away, leaving his thirst partially slaked. He lay quietly in the sopping cold dark, wondering what to do next. When the water-soaked rawhide that held him began to dry, it'd shrink. He had only a few hours.

CHAPTER
41

Each day, Rufus Crowe hurried through his duties so that he could dig fossils. Soon after dawn he checked the horses. He usually had trouble finding them because copses of dark juniper hid them and they had gotten coy. But he hadn't forgotten the hungry look in the eyes of the Hunkpapa as they studied Miss Huxtable's giant Clydesdales. A horse like that would make a king of its owner.

He kept an eye on the dwindling grass in the little basin, and on the shrinking pond. Before the storm, he'd been on the brink of moving camp, but the runoff had enlarged the pond and rejuvenated the grass. Maybe they could last a few more weeks. The place certainly was convenient, pinning in the horses without fences and keeping out thieves.

But hunting consumed most of his time. The expedition depended heavily upon the meat he brought in. Toothache had shown Gracie what was edible among the flowers, and as a result they'd eaten young prairie turnips several times, adding greens to their diets. But the need for more meat never ceased. He hunted pronghorn early mornings on the upper prairie, and mule deer on the lower prairie each evening, often shooting them when they came to water at the White River around dusk.

He'd become concerned about Van Vliet. But when he'd proposed to Wood that he ride over there to check, Wood had insisted that the guide stay close at hand. Crowe suspected that Wood didn't want the expedition to be without a translator.

"My good man, Doctor Van Vliet is young and healthy. Quite able to go about his work without troubling the Sioux. He's got the whole summer to catalogue his discoveries while we dig here," Wood had said.

Crowe silently disagreed.

But at least Wood's command left Crowe with more time to do what he wanted. Often, he rode his battered pony up the rugged gorge where Candace Huxtable labored. He loved to chisel the fossils loose. But more than that, he loved to linger beside Miss Huxtable, the two of them alone.

The more he saw of her, especially in those moments when she pulled her goggles loose and peered at him with solemn, gentle eyes, or lifted her straw hat and pulled a wisp of damp chestnut hair back from her smooth forehead, the more he knew she was not only ravishing; she was a sublime spirit. Whenever he clambered off his pony to sit beside her a while, he turned shy and stumbled over his own tongue, and felt an odd despair mingled with joy. She had absorbed all this kindly, but with a careful distancing that subtly let him understand that a badlands had been fixed between them.

She never ceased to call him Mr. Crowe. And ever since the great deluge, she had never ceased to immure herself in the durance vile of her whalebone. It had cost her; he knew that. He loved her so much that he regretted ever seeing her lithe form under the drenched translucent cotton. He had never forgotten that moment—and neither had she. It had transfixed him, flooded him with hunger, filled him with a great tenderness. But now he wished it had never happened, so that this Englishwoman could work unfettered by the armor that shielded her from the dart and lance of his needful eyes.

"Why, Mister Crowe," she said one morning, "You came just at the right moment. I'm going to lift pieces out, and if any stick, I want you to cut them free."

"I imagine I can."

The oreodont's skull came easily and so did a length of neck vertebrae still encased in mudstone. But when she lifted the partially crushed ribcage it didn't budge.

"Here, let me," he said, eyeing the mudstone-filled chest cavity. "That's heavy."

She had chiseled a trench deep under the ribs but not far enough. When he lifted, it scarcely budged. But he twisted it slightly and opened space for her to chisel the two ribs underneath that were still trapped. He watched her work while crouching, her slim body tortured by her corset, her once-white dress grimed brown. She had the loveliest back and shoulders ever given to woman, and when she stretched her arms, the dress drew taut around her and melted him to wax. Her lips had compressed into a determined line, and her hair had broken loose, tumbling over her shoulders like a caress. She had to set her straw bonnet aside to reach where she needed to. He felt the tap of her hammer through his hands as he held the heavy lump.

"Blast!" she exclaimed. "I'm tired."

She clambered back and waited for him to lower the pinned fossil. He continued to gaze so raptly that he forgot, and only when he registered the dismay in her face did he let go.

She brushed her unruly hair back. It stuck to her wet forehead. "Mister Crowe, I'm flattered that you admire me—you reveal every thought in your head, you know. But you must consider me exactly as you would consider a man. I'm here for science."

Then, as if she sensed her tone had been too sharp, she smiled at him. "You've done so much; I couldn't accomplish this without your kindness. I want you to know . . ."

"I'm sorry," he said, crestfallen.

"Don't be. I'm sure you understand."

"I guess I do. But Miss Huxtable, I plain—love you. I admire you. You're the first woman I ever could talk to. I know I'm the last one on earth you'd ever care about. I suppose you'll go back to England and find yourself a proper dainty Englishman. But I just can't hide—"

"Shhh!" She smiled at him, but it was the smile of a mother for a son. "We won't talk about this. We'll bury this and never say another word. Mister Crowe, let's be friends."

"I thought I was."

She laughed easily. "I hope I have time to dig eight or ten oreodonts from both the lower and upper strata. That'd be a fine summer's work. I can clean and study them later in England."

He nodded, aware that the topic had shifted and she was asking him to shift too. "Miss Huxtable, I keep wondering why you need fossils at all. Your father was working on specialization within a genus. I imagine the world's full of living creatures that differ. Why've you come all the way for fossils?"

"My father's work wouldn't be worth as much without the fossil evidence. You see, it'd be like a daguerreotype taken in one moment of geologic time; this and that species, such and such variations, all frozen in a portrait. He's done that. But it isn't enough to make his case, and that's why I'm here. Only with a fossil record—over ages of time—can we trace the changes, bit by bit, that lead to specialization so that, say, one oreodont might eat grass, and another prefer shrubs."

"You think it was God that started it and maybe designed the species, an ant one day, a caterpillar another, an ape or two on Saturdays?"

"My father did. His views were close to Richard Owen's. Owen believes in archetypes, you know. The original of the species, the Platonic idea of the species, perhaps placed there by divine means. Geology seems to support him. The transitions from one form of life to another are abrupt from one stratum to another. It's as if a Divine Finger touched clay and made a new creature once in a while. And the case for transmutation—the idea that one species went through intermediate stages to become something higher—isn't much supported by the fossil evidence. There's the Archegosaurus, of course. Richard Owen thinks it's a transitional creature between a fish and an air-breathing amphibian, a transmutated fish."

She studied him, as if wondering whether to continue. "But both Owen and my father have supported the idea of specialization caused by environmental factors. We know so little. Why some species haven't changed at all; why some clams are the same as they were in the Paleozoic. And how do species change? What does it? No one knows."

"I imagine it's mixing religion, taken on faith, with science, based on observation and proofs."

"It's a struggle, isn't it? My father believed all his life. He died mumbling a prayer. He always thought science and religion would be reconciled. I think they will too, but maybe in two or three hundred years. Maybe when the last secrets are revealed, in scientific fields we can't even imagine, all the strands of science will lead back to a divine mind." She paused. "To answer your question: I do. It's hard to imagine a universe so wondrous as an accident. There. I've confessed. What about you?"

"I'm not so sure it's a beautiful world. I've seen wolves butcher a buffalo calf; seen 'em pounce on a fawn and pull down an old bull too. It's mostly war I see."

"That's true. Sometimes I wish God were a vegetarian."

"Vegetarians fight—for food, for turf, for mates. You ever see a couple of bull elk fighting for a cow? That's war and they kill."

"It's not a world I would have made."

"I imagine if we mortals were only herbivores, we wouldn't be mortals."

She gazed at him, startled. "Why do you say that, Mister Crowe?"

"If we didn't have a taste for meat, we'd be crawling on all fours. We'd have hooves and maybe tails. We'd not have fingers and an opposing thumb. We'd not have much of a brain. It takes cunning to kill prey or make tools to kill prey. I figure we're like we are because we're meat-eaters."

"We don't have to keep on eating meat, you know."

"Yes, we do. I think we'd stop being human if we quit. I don't really think that killing animals to eat's evil, Miss Huxtable. I've seen men sicken without meat; sicken without greens, too, and if meat's something we need, I'm for it. The Lakota are buffalo-eaters, and a lot healthier than the white men I know. As for suffering, what carnivores do is put an end to a lot of it. Lots of prey is sick and old and hurt, and a wolf or a catamount puts an end to it.

"I'm inclined to let nature be nature. Whether I got the way I am because God made man, or whether I got here because millions of years of little changes bent an ape into *Homo sapiens*, I still have a nature, and it's a meat-eating nature. I remember the Bible saying all food's good. I wish it'd said steaks are better."

She smiled, and sat quietly a moment, thoughts crossing her face like cloud shadows.

"You obviously accept Darwin's ideas about the transmutation of one line into another. Where did you get that? It's terribly radical, you know."

"Every year, when the fur company steamer stops at Fort Pierre, it drops off a bundle for me. I pay for them with a score of buffalo robes my ladies fix up for me. I got the bundle at old Pierre when I met you."

"Here? You have natural history journals here?"

"I haven't had time to read much yet. I do that winters."

"You keep surprising me, Mister Crowe." She studied him. "Did you say ladies?"

"I did. Four or five, all told. Five, including He-yah-zon."

She seemed flustered. "Not all at once, I trust." Something prim had infiltrated her voice.

"Miss Huxtable, the Plains Indians have got different notions about how things are between a man and a woman. And about divorce. They're apt to switch around a lot. If a man comes to his lodge and finds his stuff sitting outside the door, he's been divorced."

"Oh! The poor children."

"Ah, it's not a problem. The child belongs to his mother's clan. Everyone in sight's a cousin or father or mother or uncle or grandparent to a child."

"Did, ah, you divorce them?"

"Mostly my ladies divorced me. First they're excited about hitching up with a *wasicu*, and think they'll get rich because the white men bring in the cloth and kettles and all. But they get tired of it fast enough, and want to have them a real warrior, a big proud Sioux with a lot of coups and a few battle scars."

"It seems—loose."

"Well, it's not like some Puritan meeting. The Cheyenne are pretty strict, at least about a maiden before marriage. Crows are a lot looser."

She seemed flustered. "Are you—married?"

"Well, it's not quite like that. A Lakota man and woman just take up with each other."

"You're very experienced," she said, an edge on her voice.

"I don't know anything about white women. Not a lick."

"I think we should go back to work, Mister Crowe."

They did, and in a half hour they had extracted each

piece of the oreodont skeleton and eased the parts into
burlap bags.

"My first! All that's left is to get it to my wagon. Would
you help with that, Mister Crowe?"

"I imagine we can hang those bags from the saddle."

He knotted the two bags together and hung them from
the saddle seat, while she watched joyously, her face
bright. "There. We can walk back."

She stood glowing, as if all the joy in the universe had
poured into her and radiated outward, blessing every blade
of grass it shone upon. He had never seen her like that.

"Thank you, Mister Crowe," she said softly. For a long
galvanic moment she stood there, and then she stepped to
him, embraced him gently, and pressed her lips to his cheek.

"I look at you," he whispered, "and I listen to your
musical voice, and I know you're the most perfect of God's
creations in all the universe."

His arms drew her to him, and for a moment she was
willing. But then, before his heart began to sing, she gently
pushed him away, her cheeks flushed. She seemed as disconcerted as he.

"Mister Crowe . . ." She stood on that high hot shelf,
peering into a whitewashed sky, and he caught the pulse
in her long, slim throat.

She averted her face. He could see only the fortress wall
of her back. "Mister Crowe, let's take this blasted fossil
to my wagon before I turn into one."

CHAPTER
42

The more J. Roderick Crabtree excavated the strange beast he had found, the more he worried about taking it east. The expedition had only the two Murphy wagons with which to haul Van Vliet's stuff, Wood's giant, and his own. He didn't doubt that Miss Huxtable would fill her wagon and decline to haul anyone else's material.

When Crabtree realized just how large the armored skull was, he began to probe the eroded mudstone seven or eight feet away, allowing for the probability that the beast's backbone had arched at death. After poking through overburden for several inches, he hit pelvic bone and recognized it at once. He chipped away enough of the soft matrix to find lower vertebrae and much smaller bossribs, and the top of a large femur. Whatever it was, this creature measured every bit as large as a cow, but with a more massive head. These bones and their matrix might be all that could be stowed in one of the wagons.

He faced a formidable task. Not only did he have to free the whole skeleton, but he had to haul the pieces down to the wagons. Some of them would weigh a couple of hundred pounds. He paused, rubbed the aching small of his back, and wiped sweat from his brow. A glance at the low sun told him it was quitting time. He'd put in a long day, forcing his weary body beyond its normal limits. His findings had been spectacular: he'd have a fairly complete skeleton.

A quick survey had affirmed that these bony plates swelling from skull and mandible had been repeatedly gouged, cracked, and healed. This monster had either been violent and pugnacious, or had constantly needed to defend itself from even more aggressive animals. He patted the ugly head affectionately. The thing had almost no brain cavity, which tickled Crabtree all the more. He'd probably found a dumb giant pig. Maybe *Sus Giganticus Van Vlietum*. The thought filled him with cheer. Archimedes would feel honored, which made it all the better.

He collected his tools and his kit, and trudged wearily to camp. Another day and another washload for Gracie. Each morning he headed into the field wearing pristine white. Each night he returned in mudstone brown, usually with a few new rents in his cottons, which she miraculously mended before day's end.

He found her at her cookfire, her brown face glistening as she salted a deer loin. The juniper-wood fire hissed and spat as grease dripped into it, and acrid smoke layered in the dead air.

"Did Professor Wood speak to you?"

"He did."

"What did he say?"

"He ask me to go dig them bones."

"And?"

She peered up at him with fear etching her worn face. "I said, you asking or telling? And he says, I'm asking, and I says yes if he takes care of the camp and your stuff, and he says no thanks and goes back to his bones."

"He doesn't know how to make you do anything. What if I tell you to go dig bones for him?"

She peered up at him, resignation in her yellow eyes. "You're the boss."

"That's right. But I don't want you to dig his bones. If he asks again, say no."

She stared at him, bewildered. "You sure change your mind."

"It's my privilege, Gracie. If you owned me it'd be your privilege."

"You wouldn't be worth owning."

Pleased, he trotted down the steep path toward the lower prairie and Wood's fossil. He found the professor leaning over the titanothere skull, excavating with a surgical pick.

"Ah! Crab. Look at this. I've got three of the beast's teeth looking like new."

Wood had indeed scraped away the matrix material and had polished the stone molars until they shone. "Very good, Wood. By the end of summer you'll have all his teeth polished."

Wood looked ashamed, and puttered about, collecting little tools the way a jeweler gathers his tiny screwdrivers. "I think I'd be good at cleaning fossils," he said. "It's a natural trait."

"How are you going to get this out?"

"Well, I haven't quite come to it."

Crabtree peered up at the retreating slope, heavily channeled where rivulets had sawed it. "Look, Cyrus, you've got to remove the overburden. The slope's about forty-five degrees. You can't notch in, except maybe a foot or two. The whole thing'll come down on you if you cut too deep. It's a plain pickax job. Break it up on top and shovel it away. Work down. There must be twenty tons, maybe thirty, that have to go."

"I know."

"You can't escape it. Tomorrow, you'll have to swing

the pick. A few weeks of that should get you down to the fossil. It'll be quite a task. It's likely to be fifteen feet long if it's got a tail.''

''I know.''

''I gather you asked Gracie.''

''She was busy, Crab. I couldn't pull her away—''

''You should never ask a slave. It weakens my position. It's dangerous.''

''Well, I pitied the poor woman—''

''Don't pity a slave. She's a mule. Just think of her as a mule.''

''Crab, do you think everyone could help me for a few weeks? You and Archimedes when he gets back, Miss Gracie, and Crowe?''

The old professor looked like a beggar, hat in hand. Crabtree smiled. ''Cyrus, have you thought about how you'll get this thing back east?''

''I confess I haven't gotten to that. Wagon it to the river, I suppose.''

''Well, I'm a little concerned. Our two Murphys and four drays can't haul it all. The ribs alone are likely to weigh a ton and the skull—well, who knows?''

''I suppose we could make several trips, Crab. This is it; this is the one great discovery of this expedition.''

Crabtree didn't argue it, though he was tempted. ''Well, remember that Archimedes'll have some things to go; I'm sure of that even if the Sioux howl for his scalp. I'll have my stuff. Of course Miss Huxtable will fill her wagon as full as she can. And there's all our gear.''

Wood looked even grayer than usual. ''You're telling me I should abandon this.''

''Not at all, Cyrus. Mark the place. Cover the skull. Come back with a larger work force and more wagons next year. You'll need block and tackle, half a dozen men, plenty of wagon bed.''

''And more money than a professor has ever seen in a

lifetime." Wood looked forlorn. "I'll be too old next year, Crab. Sixty years."

Somehow, Crabtree believed him. It wouldn't be age but despair that pinned him to Harvard next year. That and lack of funds. But that was Wood's dilemma. His own was to take his giant boar back east. "Well, Wood, when I get back I'll write Baird and absolutely insist that they fund you to come get this."

"It may not be here. Robbers could find it. A storm could wash that skull away—"

"Oh, pshaw, Cyrus. The aborigines are scared to death of it, and no white men know of it, and if you pack material around it, it can't weather."

"I'll never see it again," Wood whispered.

"There's things that can't be helped, Cyrus. We don't have the men to dig through all that rock. It's hard luck but who can change it? Oh, if everyone here, including Miss Huxtable, were to pitch in, and if we had the use of her wagon, and if we got Crowe and his squaw to haul our personal truck on travois, we might get it out. But the truth is, we didn't come prepared for a fossil this size."

"We've two wagons."

"Maybe there's not a whole skeleton in there, Cyrus. Maybe you haven't got what you think you do."

"It's missing only a right rear foot."

"That's a large assumption. You can't exactly see through rock."

"It was a dream," said Wood. "The only one I ever had."

CHAPTER
43

Archimedes Van Vliet considered his options. Tomorrow, not long after dawn, the heat would build and the sun would murder him as he lay helpless on the scaffold. He contemplated rolling himself off. It would be a seven-foot plunge and he could not soften the fall with his hands or legs. On the ground he'd face another terror, predators that could eat his flesh, rip away his face while he lay helpless.

The White River ran almost a hundred yards distant. If he somehow managed to roll himself there, he faced yet another terror—drowning. Once he rolled into the water, like a log, he'd have no way to keep his face clear; no arms or feet to keep him from whirling. And yet, when he thought about it, he knew that was his sole hope.

Pain radiated from his naked skull, giving him a throbbing headache. The bindings on his wrists were so tight he couldn't feel his hands.

"I'm greedy," he muttered. "Greedy for life more than all the rest. Maybe Greed will rescue me."

The Sioux war party had meted out perfect justice, he thought. If he chose to rob the dead, let him wander the burial ground forever. He understood them perfectly, and admired the Sioux medicine man who had condemned him. Odd, how he felt a brotherly affection for his executioners, his Lakota brothers! They'd sing a song about him around some campfire and his legend would grow.

Filled with dread, he convulsed his body toward the edge of the scaffold until he felt no support under his feet. Slowly, he swung himself around, always constrained by the tube that imprisoned him. At last he lay crosswise, his legs projecting into space. His heart hammered. The whole business of turning ninety degrees had exhausted him.

He wriggled some more, felt himself gain a few inches, frantic with the fear of plunging head first. When at last he teetered on the edge, it was not as he wished, legs directly below him, but at a bad angle. Any more rolling and he'd go over. It would have to be that angle or nothing. He gulped air and jackknifed himself over, feeling himself drop almost flat. His legs struck first, and then his shoulder, shooting pain into his chest before his head banged something hard.

He lay panting on the rough ground, feeling something—bones maybe—jabbing him. He moved his shoulder. It hurt. He rested, fearful of a wolf or bear. It struck him that he didn't know in which direction he lay, and might roll away from the river.

He wished he could find some sharp edge of bone or rock to abrade the cords binding his legs, and he peered about looking for something like that. But all he could see in the dim starlight was grass poking up around him. When his pulse had settled he tried a tentative roll in the direction he hoped would take him to water. Much to his surprise, he found it was not difficult. A slight flex of the knees rotated him half a turn; another flex completed the turn. He completed a dozen rolls before resting. He felt grass and rock poke him through rents in the brittle old robe, and hoped that the robe would continue to disintegrate as he made his way.

He proceeded by tens. Once he rolled into a cottonwood and had to retreat and twist himself slightly toward the south. He got his direction from the North Star and the Big Dipper. Several times he heard the whisper of animals. But he couldn't see them. He hoped they were more curious than hungry. Then a creature loomed over him, its foul breath on Van Vliet's face.

Van Vliet roared, an eerie shriek followed by a butting movement of his head. The animal vanished—for the moment. Van Vliet sobbed, feeling utterly helpless. He rolled again, twenty more times, until his racing pulse warned him to rest. He'd lost track of where he was: the cottonwoods above, blotting out stars, frustrated him. A slight slope, however, gave him a clue to the direction of the river. The earth under him dropped so swiftly that he feared rolling like a sawn log into the river. But as the robe around him shredded, he found he could jackknife his legs and keep from spinning out of control. Rocks and sticks abraded and lacerated his legs, but he ignored that, grateful for another iota of control.

He knew he had come close when the grass turned thick and moist, but he didn't hear the faint burble of water. Then he rolled into a wall of brush, and knew he faced trouble. The White was guarded in some places by brush; in other places it ran between banks with no vegetation other than grass. He'd hit a barrier and would have to roll upslope, turn himself ninety degrees, and work along the bank until he found an open area. But first, he thought, he'd try to roll straight through. He gathered his strength and whipped himself into the wall, feeling it fight his progress, hearing it snap and hiss at him, and finally catapult him backward.

Still, he'd come close. His strength had eroded. His

limbs trembled. He pressed his eyes shut and gulped air into his laboring lungs. Then he tried again.

This time he rolled deep into the barrier, felt stalks yield under him, felt them sag as his momentum petered out; felt them hold him suspended, a prisoner—and then felt himself slowly tumble through. He hit cool water with an astonishing splash, rolled face down and whirled lazily. He felt bottom only a foot or so under the surface, and found himself waiting, waiting, waiting for the turn that would bring his face up to air.

In a panic, he thrashed, helpless, his body convulsing within its prison. He swallowed water, coughed, ate air, felt himself drifting and then grounding, his head sliding up a gravelly slope while water poured over the rest of him.

He sobbed, coughing, gasping, and finally shuddering. But the tepid water ebbed past, soaking his robe, cooling his body. He had reached his limit and didn't care where he was; he only wanted to breathe. He fought away the blackness and finally surrendered to it, tumbling into a private world, unaware of the passage of time, or the steady throb of water gurgling through his tattered robe and washing the rawhide thongs that held him.

A gray light brought him to his wits. He peered around, startled, unsure of how he had arrived there, feeling chilled to the marrow. The thong clamping his wrists yielded as he tugged his arms. He tried his legs, and discovered that the softened thongs gave them some freedom. Steadily he tugged his wrists apart, gaining tiny increments of liberty as the sopping rawhide loosened. Then at last he pulled his right wrist free. Rejoicing, he waved his freed arm around under the pinioning leather, poking, stabbing, and finally ripping the ancient, soaked buffalo robe apart.

A few minutes later he stood on the bank in the soft light, free. His only thought was to get to his wagon and collapse on his bedroll. He pushed through brush, took the hillside one step at a time as the sky lightened into blue, and stumbled to camp. He tumbled into the wagon, fell onto his blankets, and slid toward oblivion.

But sleep didn't come. With limbs of stone he clambered into the dawn and found his tin cup exactly where he'd left it beside his cask. He drew four fingers, added a splash of milky water, and sipped greedily. Peace radiated from his belly into his brain. He stood slowly, and carried his bedroll down to the river. He found a place where he could hide, a strip of grass walled by brush, and surrendered himself to oblivion.

CHAPTER
44

For the next few days Cyrus Billington Wood wandered dreamily about, alighting like a bee at Crabtree's diggings and meandering out to watch Miss Huxtable unearth another oreodont. But most of all he lounged in the shade beside his titanothere skull. They'd become friends, he and his titanothere. Crabtree, Wood noted, slaved in hot sun, drenched in his own sweat. Likewise, Miss Huxtable labored through the heat, beads of sweat on her brow, her white cotton dress stained with dirt and perspiration. He knew Crowe was helping her, but he could hardly fault the guide. Crowe had performed his camp duties meticulously.

In private moments Wood examined his aging carcass, noting his sagging white belly, the slumping of unused muscle from his ribs, the expansion of his waist. He noted as well his increasingly tricky bladder, his backaches, his occasional migraines, and vision that required separate gold-rimmed spectacles for close work and for distant observation. Nor did his occasional need for a purgative escape him. He knew his heart didn't beat as steadily as it once had. It raced frantically whenever he exerted himself. No. He would not dig up the titanothere.

He'd return to the dark confines of Harvard, and labor once again to pound natural history into the heads of feckless boys, under oceanic Boston skies. Back to the comfortable ruts. Soon Priscilla would be placing tea and toast and marmalade before him each morning, filling his dresser with darned stockings, freshly ironed shirts.

He'd head back to the gloomy halls and finish out his years in obscurity, rattling out his lectures in an increasingly scratchy voice until one day they would make him professor emeritus. One day he would dodder about his house, unknown and unwanted, a flyspeck on the rolls of science. Each day he'd take the air, aided by a cane, and greet his former colleagues heartily as they hurried to the library or the next class. They'd inquire after his health and dash away to pursue their own glory, and teach the next generation of boneheads just as he had done for four decades.

The thought of all that raised a curious lump in his throat, and turned defeat into something worse, something like shame. He was seeing a life lost, a life lived too timidly. All the dreams, the Copley Medal, the glowing praise from Richard Owen, the shining bones of the titanothere thrilling those who wandered into the Museum of Natural History—all that had vanished along with the firm flesh of his arms and chest, and the decay of his will.

He rubbed the snout of his friend the titanothere, imagining how it had roamed the marshes, terrorizing anything that crossed its path, its pronged nasal horns a weapon as formidable as a battering ram. It had been a lord of the Oligocene. But he was no lord of the Quaternary. Anything but. He'd leave this one behind, like a sweetheart in a foreign port. In a few weeks he'd say good-bye, never to see this beauty again.

That night he couldn't sleep. His mind whirled loosely

through heresies and follies. He pulled away his bedroll and lay in the stillness, the tang of canvas in his nostrils. He rolled out and clambered to his bare feet, intending only to satisfy the demands of his perfidious bladder. He found himself dressing, not really knowing why. In a few moments of groping about, he'd pulled on a shirt, trousers, boots, and a moth-eaten cardigan that had fended off the damp chill of his office for years. A nearly full moon opened the world, making it easy for him to negotiate the familiar trail from the slump down to his titanothere. He didn't pause there, though. He trudged to the lower prairie, where the moon whitened a land without fences, where a mortal could walk to the end of the earth. Above him loomed the clawed wall of the Badlands, mysterious and seductive, where thousands of the world's finest fossils slumbered now, just as they had through aching eons of sun and rain and wind and never-ending change.

He felt oddly free, and a little feisty in the moon-washed night. Nothing stirred except his mind, which cast loops and snares at misty ideas, and caught nothing. The chalky world might have been the landscape of either heaven or hell, depending on how he felt. Maybe he'd permit himself some moon-madness. Were the old legends true? Did people turn mad in the light of the full moon? Did ghosts fly and animals howl?

If he were a young man, with a young heart and a young mind, what would he do here in fossil paradise? Here in paleontologists' heaven? He'd dig! He'd sweat the way Crabtree sweated, feel his muscles hurt and heal and hurt again; chip and bang like Miss Huxtable, overcoming the disabilities of skirts and modesty to do what she would. Yes, he'd dig! A naturalist might come to a paradise like this once in a lifetime. He was here! A thousand miles from houses and streets and schools!

He pressed his hands against his spongy belly. He clasped the small of his back at the place that had tormented him for years. He studied his arthritic hands, lumpy and blue in the wash of the moon. He breathed in the high Plains air, and exhaled it, feeling his lungs labor. This living corpse that was the vessel of his spirit was no more a tool to unearth a titanothere than was a teaspoon.

But his moon-madness lay upon him, and he considered the pleasure of trying. Not of winning. He didn't even consider the possibility of hauling tons of rock east. But just trying. He didn't understand his madness. Surely his rock-ribbed Puritan ancestors from New Hampshire wouldn't understand either.

The fantastic wall seemed mysterious and beautiful as he studied it. He peered up its ghostly canyons, faintly hearing the wild, archaic grunts and squeals of bizarre creatures lying within its bosom. The moonlight lanced straight to earth like knife blades, somehow awakening the strange spirits of other times, furtive and primal and wicked. And none was so terrible as the titanothere.

In the morning, when the moon had surrendered to the sun, after coffee and some of Gracie's johnnycakes, he'd get the pickax and maul and begin to humble the rock sealing his titanothere. He'd clap rock like a demented man. He'd made dents in the slope. Crabtree would come and smirk, and shake his head. Miss Huxtable would lift a delicate hand to her face to conceal a skeptical smile. But he'd do it until his body turned into India rubber and he raised awful blisters on the heels of his hands. And he knew that within a half hour after he started he'd wish he'd never surrendered to such folly.

CHAPTER 45

Professor Wood had supposed his muscles would begin to ache in a few minutes, but that wasn't what happened. He clambered up the grade above his titanothere, feeling the thump of his heart, and banged the mudstone with his pickax. It cut into the soft rock, scattering chips. He raised the pick with wobbly arms and struck again. For several minutes he banged away, loosening less rock than would fill a bushel basket.

And then his body rebelled. What smote him first was a nausea that clamped his belly and pushed upward into his aching chest. And then a violent trembling of his arms and a loss of grip. He could scarcely clutch the pickax. Desperately he drove the pick down again only to have it skew sideways, barely missing his boot. He settled to earth on the steep slope, wheezing and sobbing, feeling tremors convulse his arms and shiver his chest.

And yet, within ten minutes his body had recovered its precarious equilibrium, and he tackled his work again. By the time his old carcass betrayed him again he'd loosened a foot or so of the soft stone in a yard-wide patch, and sent it rattling down to the floor of the canyon. But now his arm muscles and back muscles began to protest, and he added dizziness to his nausea and tremors. He felt sick.

And yet glad. It didn't seem much, but there, in the brittle clay above his titanothere, lay a pocket. He pulled a handkerchief from his trousers and mopped his face even though he hadn't raised a sweat. He waited for his body to recover, but now it took much longer. He couldn't lift his arms without triggering spasms that shook and twisted his whole frame.

He reckoned a half hour had slipped away before he could try again. He felt grateful that no one had come by to witness his folly. Miss Huxtable had swung down the canyon before Wood had set to work, and Crowe was long gone on a hunt. Wood dribbled water from a flask into his mouth, though he wasn't thirsty, and rose again, his body betraying him with every step.

He thought that he needed a military cast of mind. He would tackle the work with the same single-minded purpose of a sapper laying explosives under an enemy fortress. Like the sapper, he might die. And yet that didn't matter so much as his haunting fear of not trying at all. He staggered to his feet, feeling every tendon of his legs curse him, and began his dentistry again, whacking and banging, spraying rock until he couldn't lift the pick. He set it down slowly, afraid it'd slip from his unruly fingers. He felt his gorge rise, and slid down on all fours to empty his belly. But he experienced only dry heaves, and then he collapsed onto the steep slope and lay inert and frightfully sick.

Some while later he'd rallied to the point where he could clamber down to the floor of the gulch. He stood there, disappointed in himself, yet noting that a little rock had indeed accumulated at the foot of the slope. He needed an hour in his bedroll, and lumbered slowly up to the camp. Gracie's coffeepot hung over hot juniper coals. He yearned for some but knew he couldn't even lift the pot.

"I saw nothing new on my Nature Walk," said Mrs. Rumley.

"Perhaps you should look harder. Study ants."

"There are no ants."

"Perhaps you could help me dig."

She fixed him with her gluey gaze. "You are dreadfully mistaken about me," she announced. "I don't do that."

Mournfully he staggered to his bedroll and stretched out in it, grateful for the respite. An hour later he felt ready to try again. An iron will had blossomed in him. He made his way down to his excavation, and clambered slowly up the slope to his tools. This time he paced himself, a half minute or so between strokes. It went a little better, though his entire body screamed at him.

Late in the morning he'd reached the end. It wasn't the pain, but loss of muscle control. Frustrated, sobbing, he quaked to the earth and lay on the steep slope, his heart fluttering like a caged bird within the claws of his chest. But even as he lay fearing death, he felt a certain pride. Beside him, gouged from living rock, was a dish-shaped depression that hadn't been there at dawn. He estimated that he'd moved one percent of what needed moving.

It took him ten minutes to clamber up the five-minute trail to camp, and then he shuffled straight toward his tent.

"You all right?" Gracie asked.

"Never better," he replied, surprised at his own answer.

"You look so red I'm thinking you're not well."

"A little water's all I need. Could, ah, you pour some?"

She eyed him suspiciously but dipped a tin mess cup into the cask and handed it to him. He grasped and dropped it. She leaned over and filled it again. "You're not all right. I better get the doctor."

"No, please don't. I'd rather keep this quiet."

She handed the refilled cup to him tentatively, and this time he clasped it with his right hand while clamping his right wrist with his left hand to slow the tremors. He lifted the wobbling cup to his lips and got half of the cool water into his mouth but lost the rest.

"I'll be better when I rest. Thank you, Miss Gracie."

"Don't thank me. I do nothing because I want. I do what I'm told and that don't earn no thanks."

"Miss Gracie. Don't be cross with me. I wish to God I could help you—"

"Don't help me. Don't help no slave."

She sounded so petulant that he didn't debate the matter further. It filled him with so much sadness and indignation that he almost forgot his body. He shambled to his shelter and collapsed. His body would have its revenge now.

He realized that achievement was something that could never be taken from him. He possessed it no matter how misguided or humble. That little dent in the slope would be written in the record of his life, no matter that Crabtree would mock him or Van Vliet shake his head. The dent couldn't be stolen, and he cherished it the way a butcher might number the slaughter of his thousandth cow, or a train conductor pleasure himself in his five hundredth run. And so he lay content even as he ached.

Time slid by him, and late in the afternoon he found Dr. J. Roderick Crabtree looming over him.

"Gracie told me," he said. "You've earned the wages of sin." A certain mockery lifted his lips. "I went down there and had a look." As he talked, he sat down beside Wood and took his pulse and felt his forehead.

"I'll be all right."

"Not if you're intent upon committing suicide."

"My body will harden. I'm going to continue."

Crabtree settled back, frowning. "I'm going to give you a little laudanum. Enough to put you to sleep. In the morning you'll forget this nonsense."

"No laudanum. I'm going back and punish myself some more."

"Cyrus, suppose by heroic effort you free your titano- there. How do you intend to take it east? If you leave it here exposed, it'll decay. Who knows when the next qualified man can get to it? It'd be a crime against science, to use a phrase you're familiar with."

"I'll find a way, Crab."

"Look, science is a cooperative enterprise, not a competition. The next man'll be happy to have the site you've located, and you'll share the discovery."

"I'm not doing it for that, Crab. I'm doing it to prove I can. It's for me."

"Bang on some other rock, Cyrus. Don't spoil the site. Better yet, don't bang at all. You're dangerously exhausted."

Wood struggled to sit up. "I don't want to die, but I'll risk it." He stood, feeling pain punch him, and limped away, not wanting to discuss the matter further. He headed for his dig once again, feeling Crabtree's amused leer at his back.

CHAPTER
46

A whole summery day eluded Archimedes Van Vliet's sensibility, and when at last the howl of his body restored him to the world, the sun was plummeting toward the northwestern horizon. He slaked his thirst with tepid water from the cask, but he could do nothing about the odd ache of the naked skull. Even the slanting rays of the subdued sun irritated his skullbone. He found his beaver-felt hat and settled it gently over his head, instantly feeling its protection against the sun, air, and vicious flies.

He walked to the scaffold that had supported him, and found at once the thing he was looking for, lying like a dead mouse in the grass. His scalp. They had not taken it. He had known they wouldn't. Everything about him had been tabooed. He picked up his own hair and examined the severed part of him. The ritual scalping had involved only a three-inch oblong patch of his scalp—enough to doom his spirit to wander the earth, homeless, forever. He wondered whether Crabtree could somehow sew it back on his head, anchoring it to the living scalp. Maybe it'd last a few years and protect the bone, which was so sensitive a breeze made it ache. Tenderly he pocketed it. It would make conversation in Brooklyn.

His thirst still raged, so he poured two fingers of whiskey into his tin mess cup, dashed water into it, eased his back into the comfortable roots of a giant cottonwood, and sipped. The whiskey would clear his mind the way snuff cleared the sinuses, and he'd plan his next moves.

The wagon was as useless without horses as a ship without a sail. The next party of aborigines would dismantle it, taking every scrap of iron from the tires to the kingpin, along with the wagon sheet and anything else that caught their fancy. He would have to walk back to the Badlands and get the other pair of drays and hope the wagon survived his absence. His colleagues would be unhappy but he would take the horses anyway. He could ride one horse and lead the other, then drive his wagonload to the Badlands.

As night settled around him his world shrank until he could see only a few starlit feet in any direction. His mind turned inward. Doctor of Philosophy Archimedes Van Vliet did not shrink from the landscape of his soul as it was revealed to him. The candor with which he examined his nature was, he knew, his only strength.

The half-scalped and half-intoxicated and half-consumed man sitting under the cottonwood tree was far removed from the comfortably fixed young Van Vliet who had dreamed of becoming a renowned ethnologist making great contributions to the infant sciences of man and society. The young student never saw the worm already gnawing at his soul.

The man under the cottonwood pitied the old Van Vliet, the scalped and hurting Van Vliet, prisoner of greed and lust. Nothing could change him. Once he had thought attention to the merciful God might heal him. And that had resulted in his last flurry of churchgoing, until he had found he was bored and wanting a nip as the pew bit his bones. Money had concealed his drinking behind damask curtains; money had veiled his long, slippery fall from a serious scholar into a predator, even as he endowed museums with artifacts, donated collections, and became known as a great pioneer of ethnology.

He knew he hadn't the slightest care about the success or safety of his colleagues. If he had to steal the remaining horses and a wagon to take his collection east, he'd do it. If it meant that Wood and Crabtree might have to abandon important finds, it didn't matter. He'd steal the Huxtable woman's wagon and Clydesdales if he had to. He had no choice. A prisoner of greed lacked the luxury of caring about other mortals.

If his plans endangered the whole expedition, he couldn't help that either. He would take the artifacts regardless of the mood of the Sioux. The safety of Miss Huxtable, Mrs. Rumley, old Wood, Crabtree, or even Crowe, could not be the concern of an enslaved man.

The next morning he dragged the heavy wagon sheet into a chokecherry thicket and bundled his best pieces in it, taking care to hide it from the casual eye. He filled his canteen with whiskey and then hid the cask high in an odd hollow of a cottonwood. He packed his knapsack with some tins of biscuits and hid the remainder of his chow. He tucked away the rest of his things here and there, in knotholes and forks and thickets, until only the naked wagon remained. He followed the White River road west, never far from its vile water. His felt slouch hat protected his aching skull and shaded his squinting eyes. His occasional sip of whiskey renewed his courage. An occasional piece of hardtack or a tinned biscuit sustained him.

On the evening of the third day he reached the Badlands, tired but unmolested, and found his way up the gloomy canyon that would take him to the grassy slump. He passed the excavation at the wagons but found no one there, and climbed into the meadow, steering toward the woodsmoke at its west end.

Gracie was washing the dinner plates. "Why, Mister Van Vliet," she said,. "You gave me a start, creeping up like some old devil."

A head poked from the tent. "Archimedes!" said J. Roderick Crabtree. "You're back!"

They emerged from their shelters, Miss Huxtable, Mrs. Rumley, Wood, and finally Rufus Crowe and his squaw, all of them beaming with pleasure.

Crowe looked Van Vliet over, his gaze upon the knapsack. "Well, Doctor, I'll help you unharness the horses and pasture them."

"There aren't any horses," said Van Vliet, enjoying himself after all.

The guide said nothing. Van Vliet found it disconcerting.

"A burial party sacrificed one and stole the other."

"Sacrificed?"

"They admired the draft horses, and chose one to send to the spirit land along with the warrior they were burying."

"The horses!" exclaimed Crabtree.

Crowe frowned. "That's unusual. It's not like them to steal your horses and kill one—unless you were doing something that bothered them."

It was time for candor, Van Vliet thought. He intended to take his artifacts east and they may as well face it. He'd tell them some of it, but not his plan to exchange ruined artifacts for the ones on the scaffolds here. "I was collecting from the tree scaffolds I'd missed."

Wood frowned. "Archimedes, that was reckless."

"I came here to collect Indian artifacts and that's what I intend to do. I'm going back with the other draft horses to get the Murphy wagon and everything I gathered from the tree sites."

"You're endangering the lives of everyone here," Crowe said.

"The aborigines need not know about it. They know only about the ones on those two scaffolds there."

"The Lakota have a way of knowing everything that happens here."

Cyrus Billington Wood straightened himself and addressed Van Vliet. "As chairman of this expedition, I have certain duties and one of them is to ensure the safety of all of us. I'm afraid I must prevent it, Archimedes. I'm terribly sorry."

"What're we going to do for horses? I've a fossil to take east," said Crabtree. "It'll fill one wagon. We need the other for our gear. I must say, Van Vliet, we're in a pickle."

Miss Huxtable remained silent, not offering her wagon.

Van Vliet watched the tempers build around him. He didn't intend to argue. He knew academics. They could fight for weeks and months and years using words as bullets, but they'd stand by meekly if he simply did what he wished to do without consulting them. "I'll take the draft horses and bring back the other wagon and my gear."

"You promised you wouldn't collect," Wood accused. "You said you'd go back to make notes and sketch your sites."

Van Vliet ignored him and turned to the guide. "Crowe, can you bargain for travois horses? I've some trade items—cloth, knives, some powder and lead."

"I imagine." The guide seemed less indignant than the others, perhaps because he saw more options than they did. "I didn't quite get the story about how you lost your horses. I need to know every little detail."

"A burial party, several warriors, an old couple, some younger women and children, arrived with a dead warrior wrapped in a robe on a travois. They looked around, not liking what they saw''—he smiled—''and found me and my camp and horses. I couldn't understand them, of course, but they argued about me and finally took the horses. The one they had intended to sacrifice they kept— and slit the throat of my draft horse. I suppose the larger horse was a larger companion for the dead.''

''I need to know whether they blamed you for the ruin of their burial grounds.''

''Oh, yes. They looked it over. They wandered into my camp. They saw no, artifacts because I'd hidden them. But they knew I'd been collecting.''

''I don't suppose you know which Sioux band.''

''I've no idea.''

''It doesn't matter. That kind of news travels like prairie fire. Most of the Lakota nation'll know of it by now. I must say, we're in a touchy spot. I've got some talking to do, and some gift-giving. Those trade things'll help. I doubt that I can get horses, not if they're feeling bad about your . . . collecting. While you were away, some Hunk-papa—a war party—stopped here. Did they visit you, too?''

''Oh, yes.'' He did not lift his hat.

''What happened?''

''They went off to war.''

The guide waited for more, but Van Vliet had said all he intended to say.

Professor Wood turned to the guide. ''Mister Crowe, is there any reason we should recover that wagon?''

''Not unless we can come up with two horses for it.''

''Would they have any at Fort Pierre?''

''They keep a horse and light wagon. But I know they won't let us have the horse. Especially if we're in trouble with the Sioux. They'll do nothing to drive away their trade.''

"Mister Crowe, we're in your hands. I'll follow your recommendation."

"Well, I imagine Doctor Van Vliet and I should ride over there on my saddle horses, and take a packhorse with us to fetch his gear. I want to see the place and get some idea of how the stick floats."

That wasn't what Van Vliet wanted to hear. He bit off a protest and smiled.

"Very well," said Professor Wood. "I'd like you to do that in the morning." He spoke with a crisp authority that seemed to conclude the matter.

"But how are we going to get our fossils out?" asked Crabtree.

Professor Wood smiled. "That was the question I asked you a few days ago, Crab. Now the shoe's on the other foot. It appears that only Miss Huxtable will be able to take her collection with her." A certain malicious pleasure lit his eyes.

"Could her Clydesdales pull the second wagon tandem?" Crabtree asked.

"I don't think so, not clear to Fort Union."

"We could change our plans and go back to Pierre."

Candace Huxtable stopped the speculation. "I'll have several tons of fossils and rock in my wagon, plus all my supplies. I'm sorry, gentlemen."

"Very well, then," said Wood. "We'll do what Mister Crowe recommends. You'll be off in the morning on horseback to get your gear. Please hurry. I'm a bit on edge when we have no translator here."

Van Vliet had expected something like that, and knew what he would do. They weren't going to like it but he had no intention of abandoning the greatest collection of Indian artifacts ever assembled. He nodded at them all and meandered to the cookfire, where Gracie glared at him and handed him a bowl of tepid antelope stew.

"I don't know about you, Gracie, but I don't mind being a slave," he said. "All my decisions are made for me."

"He owns my body but he don't own my mind, so maybe I ain't so slaved as you."

They understood each other. He smiled and ate.

He avoided the tent where Crabtree sat writing in his journal by the light of a coal-oil lamp and Wood lay in his bedroll. He could feel the emanations of anger, polite academic emanations of course, radiating from that quarter. He made a show of unrolling a blanket extracted from his knapsack and then wandered into the dusk. He needed to find the horses and a halter and a bridle. He found the tack hanging from a cottonwood limb, plucked the two items from the rest, and laid them at the foot of the cottonwood. He found the horses grazing between some juniper thickets in the northeast quarter of the meadow. He hoped they'd stay there. He approached the two expedition drays, letting them become familiar with him again. He'd take them if he could, but if he couldn't he'd take Huxtable's Clydesdales.

Satisfied, he drifted back to the camp, noting that Crabtree had extinguished his lamp. Van Vliet slid into his blanket near the others and waited for time to pass and the moon to rise. When that happened he quietly slid out of his blanket and padded toward the meadow. He found the drays in the area where they'd been earlier. One proved skittish so he tried the other, and soon had it haltered. He led it away and the other followed, just as he'd hoped. In minutes he had a bridle in its mouth. He found a rock for a step, and swung onto the broad bare back of the bridled one. Then he steered it down the trail to the lower prairie, leading the other horse.

An hour later he cut the White River road, a black rut in the silver light, and headed east, debating whether to come back with the wagon full of artifacts or head toward Fort Pierre with only the small collection from the tree scaffolds. Greed won, as he knew it would. He elected to return to the Badlands, rob the two scaffolds there, and switch the ruined things just as he'd planned. It never had been a debate. Greed would always win.

CHAPTER 47

Gone. Cyrus Billington Wood stared helplessly at the horse herd, which now consisted of the guide's saddle horses and packhorses—and Miss Huxtable's Clydesdales. Archimedes had vanished with the expedition's two remaining draft horses. Crowe made one last tour through the juniper thickets and returned.

"He's gone, all right. I imagine he left with the moon, which rose after midnight."

"Well, follow him and get them!" demanded Crabtree. "I've a summer's work to take east!"

"I think he's got a halter and a bridle. Rode one horse and led the other."

"Well, go after him!"

Crabtree was obviously incensed. Professor Wood felt heartsick. Worse than that, he was utterly at a loss about what to do.

"I'm not sure that's a good idea," said Crowe.

"What's the matter with you?"

The guide spoke softly. "You're asking me to bring him

back by force because we all know he won't come just
with the asking. You're asking me to put a firearm upon
him and compel him. And if he refuses, what am I to do?
Shoot Doctor Van Vliet—or the horses?"

"Perhaps we ought to listen to Mister Crowe's ideas,
Crab," said Professor Wood unhappily. "I would certainly oppose using force of arms upon a colleague."

They waited for Crowe, who seemed pensive. "Doctor
Van Vliet might pack up what he's got there, drive to Fort
Pierre, and try to go downriver in any passing keelboat.
He might send the horses and wagon back by hiring some-
one to drive them here.

"I imagine he won't, though. If I understand Doctor
Van Vliet correctly, I'd wager that he'll come back. He's
a man that wants it all—including that stuff up there." He
waved at the scaffolds. "He'd risk your disapproval—if he
could take that too."

He measured his words. "It might not be too bad if he
did keep on going to Fort Pierre. You know why. He's
going to take what's here, too, and that might get us all in
trouble with the Lakota—worse trouble than you can imagine. Maybe this is good."

Doctor Crabtree obviously wasn't mollified. "That's
gutless. We need both wagons. I want you to trade for
horses."

"Crab, we need draft horses, not Indian ponies," Wood
said.

"Our guide can break ponies to harness. We have a few
weeks. We need the wagon team Van Vliet stole—and we
need to have Crowe trade for horses and train them to the
other wagon."

"Well, Doctor Crabtree, I'll lend you a saddle horse
and you can fetch Doctor Van Vliet back by force of arms.
I beg your forgiveness, but I'm not inclined to do it."

Wood had heard enough. "I'll not have a distinguished
scientist and partner in this expedition dragged here at

gunpoint, no matter what he's done. We'd never hear the end of it.''

Crowe smiled, his innocent face alight. "I think that makes sense. I imagine we'll see Van Vliet in a few days—unless the Sioux molest him. They could. He's alone, and he'll have a wagonload of stuff.''

"That still doesn't solve our dilemma,'' Crabtree persisted. "How will I get the work of a whole summer east?''

"My dear Crabtree, you didn't concern yourself about *my* summer's work a few days ago," Wood replied acidly.

Crabtree snorted. "What work?''

The work, Wood knew, that was now torturing every cranny of his body and making him so sick he wondered each hour how he could continue.

"There's always ways," said Crowe. "Travois and travois ponies.''

Cyrus Billington Wood straightened his aching body, his mind made up. "Thank you, Mister Crowe. I'll ask that you negotiate for ponies with any aborigines you can find. We've a few trade items as part of the expedition's resources—two rifles, power and lead, knives and awls, and some cloth. You may use them as you see fit.''

Surprisingly, Crabtree smiled. "We'd be better off shooting Van Vliet. If he comes back with that load of contraband, I'll do it," he said, and wandered off.

"Miss Huxtable, have you any opinion about this?'' Wood asked democratically.

"I didn't know women's opinions count among you," she retorted, with a certain glimmer of amusement.

"Your Clydesdales speak louder than words," said the guide. "They're all hoping you'll donate one to them and use the other for yourself.''

Miss Huxtable laughed and turned away.

Professor Wood stood quietly, letting the pain engulf him again. In the heat of the crisis he'd forgotten it for a few moments, but now it struck him like the smack of whips. He'd hoped that if he toiled a few days, his muscles would firm up and the pain would diminish. It hadn't happened.

"Oh Lord," he groaned, "help me do what I have to. For no reason at all."

And with that he trudged painfully down the path from camp into the cool canyon to begin tormenting himself again.

Miss Huxtable caught up with him en route to her own diggings. "I wish I could help," she said earnestly. "I must say that cheeky man hasn't helped your expedition any."

"You shouldn't refer to Doctor Van Vliet that way, young lady. He's a great ethnologist."

"Oh, he's the cheekiest rotter I've ever seen. He could put us all into a tight corner."

Wood didn't argue it. "What would you do differently?" he asked pointedly. "Tell me. If it preserves our professional dignity I'll consider it."

"If he comes back, I'd confiscate the rest of his loot—by force if necessary—and toss it up on the scaffolds with the rest. Then I'd give him a saddle horse and suggest that he make for wherever we're going. Fort Union. Well ahead of us."

"He'd only sneak back and steal a wagon again."

"You can remove wheels and keep them in your tent under guard."

"Maybe you've something there, young lady."

They reached his diggings. "Professor Wood," she said gently. "You're working very hard. I admire you. I know it's painful for you." With that she leaned toward him and kissed him on his woolly cheek. Then she hiked down the canyon. Wood rubbed his cheek where her lips had touched him, filled with wonder. His eyes misted, but he fought back the sentimentality at once. Utterly improper. Utterly improper! Old Cecil's daughter wasn't a bad sort, he thought. Not bad. Gave the expedition a little salt and pepper.

He clambered up to his excavation, reliving her kiss as pain stabbed his body. He peered with unwonted pride at the shallow pit he had gouged. It ran approximately the length of the titanothere, and at its upper end he had lowered the overburden by more than two feet. He had done it through unspeakable torment, having to wait minutes between each swing of the pick or scoop of the shovel because he couldn't make his muscles bend to his will. He had done it while his head rang and his lungs wheezed and his heart wobbled on its hinges in his chest. He had done it while his blistered hands could barely hold the pickax, and the tremors in his biceps destroyed his control of the swing. Now the fruit of his labor was visible and impressive, a miracle.

That morning he attacked the mudstone with special ardor while his mind wrestled with his difficulties. No wagons. No horses. Nothing to be done but wait. It would be up to Rufus Crowe to get them out along with their gear and their fossils. He banged ferociously, ripping huge hunks of overburden loose, knowing that this day he would achieve more than he had thought possible. He'd go back to camp weeping with pain, strangely joyous and wondering why he assaulted a fossil he couldn't take east. Her kiss and compliment had done it.

CHAPTER
48

A heavy August heat lay over the plains, and each new day was born hot and dry. Candace found it debilitating. Nonetheless, each morning she dutifully trudged out to her canyon and dug until the caldron of the sun grew unbearable. Heat blasted down on her, ricocheting off the canyon walls, sucking moisture out of her and melting her will to wax. But she had come too far to surrender, and continued gamely, wiping sweat away from her damp curls, feeling it soak into her stained dress.

She yearned for a bath. The grubby camp life had abused her flesh and clothing alike. Even though she dutifully scrubbed her things in the milky water, nothing came clean, including her body and hair. She felt not just dirty but ugly, like some creature that had rolled in grime. Her corset had become a torture to her.

Rufus Crowe had been forced to abandon her because of new duties. The small pond shared by people and horses and myriad wild things had grown rank, until they feared disease if they continued to drink from it. So Crowe had

begun making trips to the White River with a packhorse
carrying two twenty-gallon casks, an eight-mile round trip
that consumed half his days. What's more, the hunting had
gone bad. The heat had driven animals to shade. He spent
long hours, day and night, stalking elusive antelope and
mule deer, rarely seeing any. His Sioux woman, Toothache, had filled in a little with roots and berries from the
lower prairie, but a stew of roots didn't satisfy after a
grueling day out upon the scorching rock.

Candace had emergency rations: hardtack, biscuits,
things in tins, but not enough to last the summer. She'd
become as dependent upon Crowe's hunting as the rest.
He vanished long before dawn to hunt, reappeared in the
morning for his water haul, and then hunted through the
hot afternoons into twilight—looking haggard and hot.
He'd even quit wearing his battered tweed jacket. She'd
sweated through the days, missing his company as she
extracted her fourth oreodont, another of the ones he had
found.

Whenever they'd rested, they'd chattered amiably about
fossils, Indians, and the American West. She'd become
terribly fond of him. They had shared their histories and
dreams. He'd listened gravely and shyly, adoration never
leaving his soft eyes.

This early August day the heat redoubled itself until the
earth became a forge. The sun hammered her upon an
anvil of rock. Her battered straw hat defended her, and
her goggles at least kept her from squinting until she had
a headache. She worked desultorily and finally stopped.
Something in her will eroded. Crowe was gone, and
wouldn't show up. She wiped greasy sweat from her brow
and slid down to the floor of the canyon. There she unbuttoned her sticky bodice and unlaced the corset and
yanked it free. The sweat pinned beneath it at once began
to evaporate and cool her feverish flesh.

"Ah!" she exclaimed, as she buttoned her dress again,

leaving it open at the neck. At once her young body felt lithe and at ease. She'd muscled up a great deal in her weeks of digging, and now she could clamber over the serrated chasms of the Badlands like a mountain goat, hopping easily from chasm to ridge.

She attacked the oreodont's backbone with renewed vigor in spite of the blast of the sun, muttering and grunting as she smacked her chisel into the matrix, digging the usual trench around the fossil that would permit her to undermine it and lift it out of its eons-old tomb. She found nothing exotic or romantic in the daily drudgery, but each small triumph exhilarated her.

She was hunting down specialization as assiduously as a butterfly collector netted his prey, and she had found it, especially in the feet and in the teeth, eye sockets, nostrils, and jaws. Each of her oreodonts, taken from different strata, had been a separate species.

"I imagine you're having a good day," came the voice immediately above her.

She whirled and saw him standing there, smiling. Her hand flew to her unfastened bodice and she clutched it closed, while voicing her pleasure. She reddened slightly and didn't know what to do. Buttoning would be too obvious. She opted to stand straight and let matters take care of themselves.

"Why, you're here," she said, disconcerted.

"I thought I'd check. You're a candidate for sunstroke if you keep chiseling hot rock in this heat."

"I hadn't thought about it . . . It's good of you to check."

"Miss Huxtable, there're times when it's not wise to be digging. I think you'd better find some shade until late afternoon."

"I can't bear to be idle."

He weighed that. "I imagine I better stay, then. Hunting's no good with all the creatures holed up."

"Mister Crowe, I'll stop whenever I feel symptoms. I'm quite able to care for myself." She said it sternly, more because she was aware of her unbuttoned bodice than because she believed what she was saying. In fact, his concern touched her.

"You're so red in the face I'd say you're in trouble now." He motioned for her to follow, and reluctantly she did. He retrieved his horse and led her up-canyon, turning into a branch that proved to be shady and cooler. He stopped under a concave cliff capped by channel sandstone.

He lifted his flask and handed it to her: "Good water. I got it at a clear seep off to the west."

She drank the tepid water gratefully. It had none of the slippery sediment that she'd suffered for weeks.

"No game," she said.

"I can't find even a cottontail."

"Will this last? This heat and the poor hunting?"

"I'm afraid so. August is the worst."

"I won't be able to work afternoons?"

"And late mornings."

"What about the others?"

"Doctor Crabtree's a physician and knows the signs. Professor Wood's mostly in shade, though I worry about him too. He's a transformed man with some devil or other licking at his soul."

"I can't bear to be idle, Mister Crowe. Perhaps I could help him if he's working in shade."

"I suggest you rest, Miss Huxtable. Right here, each afternoon."

She smiled. "You're very kind."

"I'd like to find you here each afternoon and talk."

She felt her pulse lift as much from panic as from yearning. She realized at once that this cool refuge under a towering wall was an utterly private place in the middle of a maze. A private place for—what? Something galvanic slid through her body, some anticipation she dreaded and wanted all at once, until her mind boiled with confusion.

"Mister Crowe—Mister Crowe—" she faltered. "I don't think this is a good idea."

"The sun's a worse one."

"This is a private place."

"I understand. Miss Huxtable, I've got my own life and my own woman. I'm wrestling with things."

"I know. But you mustn't. We mustn't make mistakes."

"Miss Huxtable, I'm not much, just a wandering man as far from civilization as I can get. But I—I care mightily for you. I can't express it very well, and I'm foolish . . ."

"Yes, foolish," she muttered through a constricted throat. "We mustn't be."

Solemnly he poured some water into a bandanna and mopped her face, wiping away sweat until her forehead and cheeks and neck felt cool. Then he lifted her right hand and mopped it clean, and then her left. Then he poured more of the sweet water and wiped his own smooth face clean.

"Don't, Mister Crowe."

He stood, walked up the gulch, and stripped a vagrant sage plant of its silvery green leaves, and returned, mashing the leaves in his hands. He rubbed her face and hands with the fragrant leaves, and then his own, until she felt newly minted, and not even her stringy hair or sweat-damped dress could rob her of the song that was rising in her soul.

"Please, Mister Crowe. It'd ruin everything—between us."

Then at last, after the long ablutions, he gathered her into his arms and kissed her. She felt herself melting into him, her lithe body forming into his own hard one, and knew all this was the most foolish thing she'd ever done, and she didn't want to stop because it seemed holy. Something utterly wild, as fenceless as these vast lands, as reckless as the Western sky, consumed her. She had never experienced anything like this mysterious and irresistible yearning that confiscated her senses.

"Don't," she protested, but he ignored her.

She felt herself at an abyss, and suddenly wrestled free, pushing him away, her heart hammering wildly. "I can't! Don't you see? I can't!"

He released her.

She collapsed into the cool earth and wept bitterly, her whole being racked with great sobs, riven by her desire and the compass setting of her life.

CHAPTER
49

Archimedes Van Vliet made his way back to the burial grounds unharmed. His nervous scanning of horizons yielded no sign of Sioux. He didn't know what he'd do if they swooped down on him, but he supposed he might survive.

He felt the pangs of guilt because he had snatched the last horses from his colleagues. But he told himself that his needs were larger than theirs; their rock bones would last, while his collection was perishable and had to be protected at once.

The broad draft horse he rode split his legs apart and made every mile a torment, but he didn't mind. This harness horse and the one he led would pull his loaded wagon to Fort Union and the keelboat waiting there.

Let them all rage. It wouldn't matter. They might try to reclaim the horses and wagon but he could deal with it. Wood could scarcely wrestle a fly from a dinner plate, and the slight Crabtree would think twice before tackling a six-foot-five Dutchman. Besides, they were all wrapped up in

professional courtesy, and wouldn't do anything rash.
Manners and morals, he knew, were the refuges of the
weak.

Thus heartening himself, he trotted his horses through
a hot day, watering them at the White River, and covered
the forty miles well before dusk. As he approached the
gloomy confines of the burial ground a curious foreboding
filled him; it was as if a thousand outraged spirits of dead
aborigines hovered over the place, warning him not to
enter. He puzzled over it: he had opened hundreds of burial
bundles and not felt anything forbidding or supernatural,
but now his flesh crawled.

He paused at the outermost precincts and studied the
parks beyond, a scatter of ruined scaffolds, bones, and
wreckage. He saw nothing, neither hostile tribesmen nor
angry spirits, though his head buzzed like snake rattles.
Even the horse he rode became nervous, bobbing its great
head, shying at nothing. And the gelding he dragged behind him halted, almost jerking him off his riding horse.

"Move!" he roared, as much at the horses as at the
unseen legions fluttering ominously around him, the evidence of them as thin as angels' wings but affecting him
and his great horses as much as lashing whips.

They moved, however grudgingly, and he rode into the
dark fields of the burial grounds, past mortal skulls and
ribs and grinning jaws poking from desiccated buffalo
robes. He grinned back, supposing the bones were enjoying a great joke.

The spirits danced along the rim of his soul, and he
conjured one out of the dusk, a great rawboned warrior in
a breechclout. *Why have you taken my honors from me? I
walk along the path to the stars past the old hag and the
trickster, and no one knows what I did for the People, or
who my counselors are.* The leonine warrior stared at Van
Vliet, and then dissolved into the borderline of light. That
one seemed all too real.

He steered his nervous horses through the whispering gloom toward his camp, past the slaughtered horse-brother of those he rode and led, still rank and noxious in the heat, past collapsed scaffolds, and then past one scaffold that rested trim and intact in the branches of a weeping and desolate cottonwood. He paused, the hair on the nape of his neck rising. He had collected from that one, scattering its poles and tumbling its robe-wrapped burden to earth, where he had sliced it open and extracted a prize war shirt. But there it stood, each pole in place, newly bound with thong; the burial bundle tightly wrapped, as pristine as a newborn. He tugged on the rein and stared. Then he steered the horse closer and peered upward into sinister writhing leaves. This was real. He peered sharply about and saw no one.

He proceeded toward his campsite, feeling as if the door between this world and the next stood ajar, permitting illicit intercourse of flesh and spirit. His first glimpse of his lair reassured him: the wagon stood unharmed, its iron tires and fittings intact, its naked hickory bows poking upward. His second glance undid all the relief wrought by the first. There stood two figures, one a woman and the other a boy, both Sioux. The woman's sleek black hair had been shorn on one side, and an unhealed stub of index finger spoke of the self-torture of a widow. She had Indian features and slate eyes; he could see that in the remaining light. She wore blue cotton adorned with seed beads.

The solemn youth was slim as a whip, with glinting black eyes that never blinked. His hands clasped a bow with a nocked arrow, which pointed at Van Vliet with an awful authority. The presence of doom sent a chill through him. The adolescent boy could drive that feathered messenger of death into his chest faster than he could unsheath his Navy Colt, cock it, and explode powder.

"We thought you would return," the woman said in

English. "I am Watching Owl. This is my son, Makes Coyote Bark. He saw in a dream that you would return."

"Uh, you speak English."

"My father was a *wasicu*. A trader. For eighteen winters I lived with him. I know his words. Then he gave me to Ota Kte."

"Ah, I am pleased to meet you. Perhaps the boy will set his bow aside—"

"No. We wish to have the war shirt of Ota Kte. And his *wotawes* and flute and war paints. These things we will return to his spirit, *nagi*."

"What war shirt? Madam, I am quite baffled—"

"The one you took from his body by twisting his arms up and pulling it off."

"I have no clue—"

"The boy's arrow will persuade you."

"But madam—" He remembered the shirt vividly. It was the finest of its kind. It had been made of whited antelope hide, soft as velvet, quilled with a geometric design of blue and orange, fringed at the hem, with a band of azure and yellow beadwork around it. And it bore an incredible fourteen scalps, artfully dangled from the chest and arms and shoulders. One was a white man's, with long blond hair. The shirt was priceless, one of the greatest of his prizes.

"Get it."

"I have no knowledge of it."

"Then die." She said something to the boy, who drew his bowstring back.

"If you kill me you'll never find it."

"We will find it. We haven't looked."

"Then kill me!" Van Vliet cried. He couldn't surrender a war shirt like that.

She eyed him contemplatively. "I will look. He will keep his arrow aimed at your heart."

The boy stood before Van Vliet, his bow half-drawn, its lethal iron-tipped arrow aimed at him.

"Let go of the horse and get off," she said.

Reluctantly Van Vliet released his lead rope, and slid off the other horse. She artfully snatched bridle and rein, staying well clear of him and her son's arrow. Then she led away the horses. The horses!

"Sit."

He did, irked at all this. "You'll never find it!"

The pointed arrow followed him down.

"That scaffold—it's yours!"

"It is the scaffold of Ota Kte. We will give him his things back, for the journey of his *nagi* to the Land of Many Lodges."

Van Vliet had the eerie feeling that the image that had formed in his mind earlier, the rawboned warrior who spoke to him, was that of this woman's husband.

She said something to the boy, and he bent his Osage orange bow to its limit, until the muscles of his arms rippled.

"I'll find it!" Van Vliet cried.

"Stand. Turn your back. Drop the belt that holds your revolver."

Sweating, Van Vliet did as he was told, moving his arms slowly, quaking with the dread of an arrow through his back and into his heart. The belt slid to the grass.

Lithely she snatched it away. "Show us," she said.

Grimly, Van Vliet hiked to the thicket of chokecherry where he'd hollowed out a nest for his canvas-wrapped treasure. He pointed at it. She waved him away, muttered something to the hard-eyed boy, and then slowly dragged out Van Vliet's entire lode of museum-quality pieces. She clawed back the canvas while he watched in a rage. In moments she had unearthed the precious shirt, held it up and scrutinized it, and then began the harder task of sorting out her man's medicine bundle and amulets and to-

tems. The boy's arrow never wavered. By the time dusk
settled she had recovered what she wanted. Reverently she
held a small leather natal turtle in her hand, a medicine
bundle that had hung from the chest of Ota Kte, some
leather paint pouches, some amulets made of seashells that
had been traded inland, spirit moccasins with blue beaded
soles, and two notched eagle feathers.

"Why did you take this?"

"He has no need for it."

"Ah!" she hissed. "No need. Why are whites buried
with a cross in their hands? Why are they dressed in their
best clothes?"

"Madam, there's no comparison. There's no religious
necessity—"

"Don't lie to me. Why did you take this?"

"Because I want to show them to people in the city
where I live."

"Show them? Why that?"

"Because. I wish to give them to museums."

"What is that?"

"A place where things are collected and shown. It gives
us knowledge of all people. People like you."

"It gives you no knowledge. Things. Things! I know
from my father what the *wasicu* want. Things." She
pointed back toward the camp. "Go!"

"Am I free now?"

"No. I will put these beside the burial robe of my man
and say many prayers and do the *Hanblecheyapi*, the cry-
ing for a vision. Maybe I will see your death."

Frost formed around his heart. "You wouldn't do that."

"I might! First I will cry for the vision. Any Lakota,
man or woman, can cry for the vision from Wakan Tanka.
It's one of the seven sacred rites. Then I will know what
to do with you."

Van Vliet furtively eyed his holstered revolver lying not
far away. The boy would loose an arrow if Van Vliet dove

for it. He eyed the youth intently, finding no lack of determination in his countenance.

Then, swiftly, Watching Owl snatched the belt and withdrew the revolver, checking the loads in the cylinder and examining the nipples to see if they were capped. Satisfied, she cocked the weapon and aimed it at Van Vliet. The black bore seemed enormous, and sweat broke from him.

"Madam, I meant no harm—" he croaked.

"Ah! No harm! What if I went to where you live? What if I dug up the grave of your woman? What if I robbed it of her dress and shoes? What if I took her skull to my people so they could measure it to find out how inferior *wasicu* are? Tell me how you'd feel!"

Van Vliet smiled. "You'd do me a favor! Unfortunately, she's still alive."

She stared, the sour joke eluding her. "Is it so?" she asked at last. "More and more I despise my father's people. Then tell me this: what if we went to the place your father's buried and ripped open his grave? You have great stones upon them. Maybe we would steal the stones and no one would know who was buried there. No one would come and honor that place or remember your father. That's what you do to us! Maybe we would put your stones and your skulls in our sacred places, and show your father's clothing and shoes to others."

"Why don't you put that revolver down and we'll talk."

"No! Maybe I will kill you." She raised it to eye level and aimed it squarely at his face. A cold terror struck him like an icy anvil. "You steal from the grandfathers and grandmothers. You steal from little children, their toys and dolls. You steal the holy things of Ota Kte!"

"I'll put them back."

"No, I will. Your evil hands will not touch the *wotawes*."

He saw opportunity in that, thin and distant but at least some faint hope. "Go do it then. I'll wait. I want to talk."

"Ah! You think you'll escape. No. Lie down on your front. Your stomach!"

He hesitated, dreading a bullet to his skull.

"Do it!" She aimed the revolver again.

He eased himself to the grass. It had grown dusky and he could barely see her or the boy.

She spoke to the boy in harsh sibilants, warning him of something. The boy lowered his bow and then Van Vliet felt his ankles being handled, something being drawn tight.

"Now your hands. Put your wrists together!"

He valued his life too much to throw it away. She hadn't, after all, resolved to kill him. The bindings hurt. The ground under him felt hard.

He heard nothing for a long while, but knew the boy stood above him, ready to kill. Then he heard a faint, sad, woman's song from out in the blackness, as soft and desolate as an owl's voice. It took a long time, and his discomfort mounted.

He didn't hear her return, and didn't know she had returned until she said something to the boy.

"Now I will begin *Hanblecheyapi*. There is no *wicasa wakan*, holy man, to help me, and I cannot do the *Inipi*, the purification, and there is no pipe and no one to salute the six directions. But even so, Wakan Tanka hears his daughters in a time of need. We Lakota are a respectful people. We honor the spirits; why is that not true of white men? You all dishonor your religion. You are strange, thinking you have the true and only religion—and then you ignore it."

She vanished into the night. The boy stood over Van Vliet like a boulder in the darkness, starlight glinting on the Colt revolver. Van Vliet heard a distant crooning, soft in the warm night, ebbing and flowing like wind from a bellows, the language ancient and primal, as haunting as the plainsong he'd once heard sung in a cathedral.

He thought it might last for a little while, and tried to doze. But he couldn't. The woman's songs drifted to him but didn't lull him, for they contained his fate, perhaps his murder. So he lay bound upon Grandmother Earth, feeling the bite of her breast, his arms longing for release. And over him the whole while stood the silent youth.

He rolled to his side and alleviated the pain for a while, and then rolled to his other side, while the night ticked by as slowly as a cooling iron stove. It occurred to him that he would not know his fate until dawn. He finally dozed fretfully, nightmares of death cursing him every few moments. But he never really slept.

After eternities of blackness, dawn grayed the world and Watching Owl's songs ceased. His shoulders ached so much he was frantic with pain. He saw her gathering dry wood into a giant heap nearby, and suddenly he knew.

"Don't!" he cried, his voice the croaking of a toad. He sobbed, wrestling furiously at his bonds, frantic. "You mustn't!"

She approached him solemnly, no less beautiful for her long night and showing not the slightest sign of weariness after communing with all of creation. "When the eastern sky told me of the coming of sun, I saw before me sweet smoke carrying the possessions of the spirit people up to them, cleansed and sacred again."

"No! Those things are priceless!"

She smiled. "Yes, that is it exactly. They have no price."

He wrestled furiously with his bonds, flopping over Grandmother Earth like a fish out of water while the boy watched patiently, the revolver ready.

She struck steel to flint, dashing orange sparks into a nest of cottonwood fiber, and soon had a great fire sending prayers to the sky. Then she plucked treasure after treasure from the canvas-bound hoard and laid it on the fire, watching now and then as hot flames consumed wood, blackened leather, singed beads and burned quills, ate feathers, scorched bone, and lifted smoke skyward to the people on the pathways to the stars.

"I beg of you, stop! You're destroying the most beautiful creations of your people!"

"No," she whispered, "not destroying. Giving them back to their owners as I was instructed by Wakan Tanka."

He writhed against his bonds, finally loosening his ankle bindings. The boy saw it at once, but didn't stop Van Vliet, who stood up, his arms still bound behind him.

A great column of smoke rose against the dawning sun and drifted out to the star people. As he watched the flames consume his treasure, hot, unfamiliar tears leaked from his aching eyes.

"Madam, I'll give you anything—I'll give you anything—"

"Soon we will leave without taking anything of yours," she replied. "Wakan Tanka has given you your life and that is a great gift for one who has been scalped."

CHAPTER
50

Cyrus Billington Wood whipped his pickax into rock, broke loose a chunk, and kicked it out of the way. Then he peered, amazed, at what lay at the bottom of the little depression. Two ribs, thick white bands, curved through the mudstone matrix. Wood stepped back, mopped his wet face with his polka-dotted bandanna, and rejoiced. He could scarcely believe that it had come to this.

For more than two weeks he'd labored fiercely, driving his tired old body beyond its limits. The tone of his muscles had improved but he hadn't recovered much wind, and his flesh never stopped tormenting him. Even so, he'd learned to ignore pain no matter how fierce.

He'd learned how an old man could pace himself, banging with his pick and shovel until his lungs heaved like an accordion's bellows, then resting, not until the pain went away but until he'd recovered some wind. The sun penetrated that deep chasm only through the noon period, and he'd learned to quit then and take a welcome nap and return later for another assault on the tomb of the titanothere. Each night he collapsed into his bedroll and departed from the world, no longer tormented by the canvas cot. And more rapidly than he'd ever dreamed, he'd stripped away tons of overburden and sent it sailing down to the canyon floor in explosions of dust.

It was, he supposed, the labor of a madman—for there would be no way to lift the monster from its tomb and take it east. Crabtree had come each evening to mark the progress and mock, rarely saying a word but revealing his thoughts with a smirk that hinted he was observing a lunatic enterprise.

"We're all grave-robbers," Crab had pronounced one night. "Only Van Vliet robs the graves of aborigines."

But Cyrus Wood no longer cared. He continued his work for its own sake, finding a joy in doing something he'd never dreamed he could do. Each day's progress had not only excavated rock, but had excavated the overburden on his soul. A faint prickle of something new within him had finally turned into a flood tide of self-discovery.

He stared at his excavation, at its ten-foot rear wall cut deep into a sloping cliff, at its fifteen-foot breadth, at its floor, which lay inches above the slumbering monster. Had he done all that? He peered into the canyon floor at the rubble, amazed at the amount of it. He poked tenderly down around the exposed bones, with love in his gentle prying, and loosened more pieces until six or seven inches of the titanothere's ribs lay in sight. Now the work would slow down and he would be forced to chip away each chunk of mudstone as delicately as a jeweler repairing a watch.

But most of all he felt a wild unnameable joy, and knew it had less to do with the ribs below him than with the passage of his own character into a new world as strange as the one that opened to Columbus. He had come here as one sort of man, and would leave another sort. He knew that if he died now from the stress he put on his old body, he'd die fulfilled.

He set to work once again, cracking his pick sharply into the remaining tons of matrix. An hour later he exposed pelvic bone, and in the following minutes portions of tail and some lower vertebrae and part of a femur.

He heard the soft rattle of horses coming up the hot canyon and paused, wiping away rivers of sweat with his damp bandanna. Van Vliet at last, he thought. But when the first Indian pony rounded into view, burdened with an aborigine, his old heart clattered in his chest. He recognized Chief Little Thunder of the Brulés. Neither the chief nor the warriors crowding behind him wore paint or had their bows and arrows out of their quivers. Even so, Wood felt a small ripple of terror ride from his toes to his throat. His translator, Crowe, had been gone more and more, hunting game that seemed to have fled the country.

Wood lifted a welcoming hand and smiled as ingenuously as a puppy chewing on its first slipper. Little Thunder grunted his reply, his solemn face as blank as a student's slate in the morning.

"Well, gentlemen, I'm delighted you've come for a visit," Wood babbled.

No one replied. Instead, they crowded their ponies around the excavation, some of them even riding into the rubble to get closer, and studied his progress silently, sometimes exclaiming at the sheer size of the bones coming into view. Women too, Wood realized. Several Brulé women eased forward and studied this strange thing solemnly, their broad faces reflecting open curiosity.

Wood had scarcely seen Sioux women and found them comely, with wide faces, straight black hair rigorously parted and either loose or woven into two braids. They were lightly clad in loose dresses made of bright-hued trader's cloth. Only their small summer moccasins and belts were of leather. Even as Wood watched from his perch a few feet above them, more and more of Little Thunder's village crowded in, bright boys and girls, seamed old men, ancient women, stern warriors, smiling wives, a few pregnant and many with children by the hand. But no horses bearing travois or lodgepoles.

Wood realized the village was passing through, probably along the White River, and had detoured here to see the strange sight of the white men digging ancient bones. He felt helpless, unable to talk to them. But still, Toothache would help. He knew now that she understood English even if she didn't speak it. Somehow they'd all get along. Not a one of his visitors ventured to touch the fossil and he remembered that these ancient beasts were taboo—according to the belief of these people, driven underground in ancient days by the lightning bolts of an angry Wakan Tanka.

"Well, let's have tea," he croaked, scrambling down. He worried that his pick and shovel might be stolen, but resolved not to show his concern or the slightest lack of courtesy, and left them lying up there while he skidded down to the canyon floor and walked determinedly upslope to the camp.

They swarmed before and behind him as he trudged into the slump, and spread through the odd green park halfway up the Badlands wall. The young men and warriors beelined toward Miss Huxtable's Clydesdales, he noted; obviously word of their amazing size had traveled among these people. He wished she were here to defend them; it made him uneasy to think that the last of their horses might be snatched away by people who had no sense of property.

Others, especially the old men and women, headed straight to the two scaffolds bearing the collection that these Brulés had taken from Archimedes Van Vliet. They gathered silently around the posts and squinted upward at the mountain of things that he'd stripped from the graves of their wives and husbands, parents, grandparents, and children. Wood suddenly felt relief that Van Vliet had decamped.

Still others, the young women and children mostly, flocked toward the tents, finding Toothache there, hugging her, chattering happily, catching up on events, and no doubt gossiping slyly about the ways of the strange white men. Yet others who did not know Toothache gathered around Gracie, examining her as if she were a prize mule. One young warrior seemed especially interested in her, poking and probing and walking imperiously around her as if he were examining a warhorse.

"Tut, tut, tut," said Mrs. Rumley, placing a sprig of sage between the pages of her book.

"You never seen the likes o' me, I imagine," Gracie said, not unkindly, but flushed and unhappy with all the attention from the blank-faced Brulés. "Well, I never seen the likes o' you." She stopped her scrubbing of Dr. Crabtree's white trousers and shirts and stood, like a trapped animal, letting the children edge closer to her, touch her warm brown flesh, examine her work-hardened hands. Crabtree, like Miss Huxtable, was far away and no doubt unaware of the visitors.

"Can you serve them tea, Miss Gracie?" Wood asked.

"I don't have water."

Children swarmed like packs of dogs, poking into the shelters, the cases of staples, Wood's own field chest, and everywhere they went they plucked up what they could: pencils, paper, a coal-oil lamp, a shirt, spoons, candles, his shaving mug and folding razor and strop, and even his New Testament.

"Stop!" he cried, but they didn't grasp the word. Even so, he saw nothing being taken. The children studied each strange item and then returned it. They invaded Miss Huxtable's tent and held up skirts and pens and tins of biscuits. He finally realized he was seeing not theft but curiosity. He turned to find a large band of warriors coming toward him, leading the haltered pair of taffy-colored Clydesdales. At the same time the Brulé women clotted around Gracie, almost making a prisoner of her, while the giant Brulé warrior poked and probed until her eyes filled with fear.

"Stop them!" Wood cried to Toothache.

Crowe's squaw squinted at him. "Trade," she muttered.

Trade! Even as he peered around, he saw where this would lead. Chief Little Thunder had settled down in a shaded area. The warriors were bringing up the Clydesdales. Others had gathered a band of thirty or forty little Indian ponies—no doubt the coin of this transaction.

But Gracie's plight astonished Professor Wood even more. The throng, led by the giant warrior, was driving Gracie to the trading area. *That one wanted Gracie.* They all understood she was a white man's slave and thus something they could trade for. They wanted the beautiful, rippling, powerful Clydesdales and they wanted Gracie. And they were expecting Wood to do the bargaining.

The very realization drained Professor Wood of courage like a hemorrhage. He didn't own the Clydesdales. He didn't own Gracie. He didn't even know how to say no in the Lakota tongue.

"No trade!" he croaked at Toothache.

But she beamed evilly, and trotted toward the circle under the cottonwood tree, waiting to see the fun.

CHAPTER 51

Gracie grasped at once that the powerful Sioux warrior wanted her. He poked and probed as if she were a mule. She peered fearfully into his rawboned face, the expressionless eyes she could not read, the puckers of war radiating ridged flesh like starlight across his ribs and back. He looked cruel, but so did they all.

What did he want of her, this one? A drudge slave? A wife? Was her blackness unique? Would she be some sort of prize, to be displayed like coup feathers? She dreaded only marriage. She'd reached middle age a virgin and no longer wished for any liaison with any male. Even a black male, at this point in her narrow life, didn't interest her. But she feared the warrior had just that in mind—and that she'd have no choice at all.

Then something gave way in her, slowly and terribly, like a dam breaking and letting a cascade loose. She wanted to be free of Crabtree. She wanted these bronzed people who chattered about her to sweep her away, away, away from every white man—even those like Wood who saw her as an oppressed and miserable human being. It came to her as an epiphany: she could be free. Not only free, but maybe someone of importance among these people.

"Whoa, now, you little rascals, quit lifting my skirts!" she bawled at some imps who were determined to see if she was black all over. "All right, mister, let's go see whether you can trade me for something. But I warn you, my price is high. I'm worth a lot of your horses! You buy me, and you're buying costly goods!"

She let the swarm carry her to the trading circle, where Wood stood, unable to stem this sudden turn of events. She saw the Clydesdales, powerful and proud, held by some warriors who wanted to trade for them. She and the Clydesdales! Things these Brulé Lakota had never seen and wanted badly.

"I don't own these draft horses and I won't trade. You'll have to await their mistress," Wood babbled, but no one paid the slightest attention.

Gracie eyed the prize horses, each a giant that weighed twice as much as an Indian pony, and realized that they'd command a huge price if Wood was smart enough to demand it. But Professor Wood wasn't smart. He'd be even less smart about Gracie, missing the possibility of her freedom in spite of his abolitionist soul. His moral indignation would blind him, so she'd have to do it herself.

She peered about, looking for Toothache. She and the Brulé woman had learned to communicate during several weeks of sharing the camp drudgery. It had been a strange lingua franca of English words, Sioux words, and simple sign language she'd picked up from the Indian. She wanted Toothache to translate, or at least convey her meaning, because she would have lots to say. But the slim Brulé woman had found old friends, and was chattering with them.

"I say, I won't trade. We'll await the owners!" cried Professor Wood.

"We will trade," said a Brulé man in English. "You are the chief."

Gracie peered at this one, and decided he was a breed. He had green eyes and some freckles but the rest of him seemed all Sioux. She barged toward him, carrying the throng with her the way a shark brings pilot fish. He seemed to be a headman of some sort, judging from the deference of those around him and his own granitic dignity.

"You speak English?"

He nodded, surveying her.

"You translate for me. I got things to say."

He didn't nod.

Wood intervened. "My good man, if you'll tell your people kindly to await the owners, I'll send someone. It's not within my power to trade their, ah—" he peered at Gracie, embarrassed—"property."

"Little Thunder will say," the headman replied. "Where is Crowe?"

"Hunting."

"He is with the *wasicu* woman. We will send runners to them and to the man who wears white."

Gracie didn't want that at all. "You listen to me. If you want me, you better start trading, because my master, he don't trade for me, not even for lots of ponies."

The headman turned to consult the chief, who glanced at Gracie and the Clydesdales and said something to the headman.

"We will trade," the headman told Wood.

"You tell 'em, you want me, I cost a lot of horses. I bring mighty good luck to the village that's got me. I got big secrets from across the big waters. I make the lions roar. I make the plants grow. I put the bad eye on some enemy and he falls dead. I make your arrows go true. I make the buffalo come. You'll never starve. I make the rain fall and the snow stop. You want me, you gotta pay fifty horses. One horse, ten horse, I ain't goin'. Twenty horse, I make your village sick. I make your horses starve and the grasses stop growin'. I tell Wakan Tanka you're no good. I make the tobacco in your pipes go bad. You want me, and you pay the price to them white men, and your Brulé village, it'll be the best in war, the healthiest and richest you ever see.'' She jabbed a finger into his umber chest for emphasis. ''Fifty ponies. I'm worth more'n that even. You tell that to the one that's eyeing me like I'm some old mule.''

She stopped, stood triumphantly, sweating freely as the headman translated her every word. No longer did the Brulés laugh and crowd close and touch her. One by one they slid back, curious and half afraid, and she glared ferociously at them, letting them know that she commanded powers and principalities and kingdoms beyond their knowing. She smiled suddenly, letting her even white teeth show. She'd be traded. Slave she might be to them, but mistress too, the black queen of the Brulés.

''Oh, balderdash,'' muttered Wood.

The headman droned on, speaking directly to Chief Little Thunder while the great men of the band crowded around, eyeing her furtively, and finally debating. Fifty horses. She knew they were chewing on that—a huge price to pay for a slave. She exulted, eyed her purchaser with a malign smile, and waited.

Which is when Crabtree trotted down the slope, catching their attention as he made his way into the flat and toward them.

''Ah, Crab, just in time!'' cried Wood.

But Gracie saw freedom and empire slide away—unless the Brulés wanted her anyway. She could only stand and hope and wish she could command half the powers she claimed to command. She'd make Crabtree fall dead if she could.

CHAPTER
52

Leather and bone didn't burn easily so Watching Owl added dead cottonwood to the terrible fire that slowly ate up a treasure of Sioux artifacts. Sometimes the foul smoke from the burning cloth and hide twisted over Van Vliet, bathing him in the ruins of his dreams. He had inched himself upright against a willow trunk, his tormented motion followed by the bore of his own Navy revolver in the patient hand of Makes Coyote Bark. Van Vliet felt as if his shoulders had been torn off by the relentless bonds that pinioned his wrists behind his back.

Sometimes Watching Owl sang in a strange, quiet monotone, songs to her gods or to the spirits of her departed people. For her, this fiery passage of the work of so many loving hands had mystical meaning, as sacred as a communion wafer on the tongue of a white person. He grasped that, and forced himself to hold his peace. If he fought her he might endanger his life again.

It took her much of the morning to burn the treasures of the dead, but she plied her task serenely. But at last, around noon, the treasure of the Sioux had been reduced to black and gray ash.

"Will you release me now?"

"No."

"I'm thirsty. My shoulders hurt."

"It is good that they hurt."

She held a buffalo-bull-scrotum water bag over his mouth and squeezed in some tepid water. He lost some as it dribbled down his stubbled chin, but licked in the rest.

"You promised to let me go."

"My word is good. Is your word good?"

"Madam—I promise—"

"If I cut the thongs, do you agree to stay until I let you go?"

"I'll do anything you ask."

"I hold you to your word. And if you don't keep your word, your God eats you. And Makes Coyote Bark shoots you."

She cut his bonds. He pulled his tormented arms around and rubbed his wrists, the pain of movement shooting fire-arrows up his muscles.

"I wish to ask questions. You answer."

He nodded, wondering what was to come.

"My father was a *wasicu*. I know of the great cities of your people, and the farms where food is grown. I have never seen these things. Why do white men not respect the Lakota religion?"

"Why—we have our own. We have been taught it's the one true faith."

"That is not a good answer." She waited, but he had nothing to say. "You've opened the graves of the grand-fathers and grandmothers and taken the things they need to travel along the path to the stars. You had no respect."

"But madam, Watching Owl, I treasured these beyond words. Your people are artists. Your people dyed the quills and inserted them into the leather in beautiful patterns.

Beaded shirts and moccasins in ways that delight the eye. Fashioned bows that are supple and powerful, treated leather until it felt like velvet—''

''But not for you.''

''For your people. The things you've destroyed—they could have been taken east and placed inside glass cases where they'd last forever. There for generations to see and admire. Why, a hundred years from now, two hundred years, people would come to these things—and admire the imagination of the Sioux.''

''Why do white men think they should put the Lakota in museums?''

''I don't follow you.''

''Us. Soon you overrun us. Everywhere you swarm over our land. Someday you put us in glass cages too. The ones who make pictures of us take the image and show our images to one another—and we starve and be forgotten.''

''But it's the best way—we're, ah, an advanced civilization; we have a knowledge, an understanding—''

''Yes, that is so. My people do not have these things. But I am not talking about that. I talk about what is sacred. You do not honor what is sacred. What would you think if my people went east to your big villages and dug up your dead and stole things? What would you think if we walked into your big stone churches and desecrated the sacred meal my father told me of—the broken body of your Teacher? You would hate that! But you don't think of my people when you come and tear open our graves and spill the bones of the grandfathers.''

He wanted to tell her that his people contained within their civilization all the force of progress and all the wisdom of the past and all its art and beauty and science, from Socrates to Shakespeare, from Aristotle to Isaac Newton, from Da Vinci to Rembrandt . . . and that made it different. This was all about a sublime civilization capturing the best of an inferior one before it was forever lost.

"You have nothing to say," she said. "It is proudness. You are proud. Your people are better than mine."

"But you Lakota think you are better than other Plains tribes."

"We are. It is plain we are."

"Well, then!"

"We do not rob the graves of the other Peoples."

"Only to preserve the best!"

"I don't think so. I think these things would make you a great man among your people—you never thought of the Lakota when you took those things."

Her observation struck him with the force of truth about himself. He nodded, acknowledging it.

"Ah, you see. But you do not see us as the people of Wakan Tanka. He is the same as your God, the one above. You call him false and our sacred songs superstition, and you take our bread and wine from our grandfathers."

A great weariness slid over him. Her logic seemed impeccable to her, and he could not persuade her otherwise unless he took her east, to see with her own eyes cities and cathedrals and museums, or libraries of precious books such as dictionaries that defined every word of a people's tongue; or galleries of sublime art, or stately colleges filled with students learning about chemistry and physics and rhetoric and natural science and manufacturing and architecture and geography and theology and classical history and navigation. And all of it organized to permit people to pursue their own destinies, free from the oppression of tyrants.

If she had never seen these wondrous things, how could he convey to her that the most magnificent civilization in the history of the world was destined to overwhelm her aboriginal one, and would do it more humanely than some enemy tribe like the Pawnee or Crows, bent on slaughtering every Lakota man, woman, and child? Her neolithic people, after all, lacked metal; lacked the wheel; lacked a written language. The sooner they were absorbed into the great edifice of European culture and life, the better it would be for them.

"Wakan Tanka smiles upon all of creation, not just the Lakota. Does your God smile upon the Lakota?"

"I am weary, madam. I didn't sleep for fear of my life. You've ruined a treasure. Now I trust your son will lower that revolver and you'll be on your way. I'll grieve what you've done."

"That is what lies between us. I have only given back to the spirits of the grandfathers and grandmothers what was their own. I will let you go now if your word is good."

He gazed up at her. She radiated beauty even though she'd shorn half her hair in mourning.

"You must give me your word. You take nothing more from the grandfathers and grandmothers."

"No, I'll not give you that word. I intend to collect what I can. That's why I'm here."

She studied him a long while. "Well, that's plain. Very well. I let you go anyway. But I warn you. If any Lakota finds you with the sacred things, he kill you. Already you are known to my people, the Sichangus; but you are known also to the Oglala, the Minniconjou, and even the Oohenonpa—the Two Kettles. You are known; you are watched. You die if you are foolish." She waited, as grave as a minister at a funeral.

"I will do what I must," he said, knowing he could not help himself even in the jaws of death.

CHAPTER
53

J. Roderick Crabtree saw at once that the aborigines wished to trade. They'd gathered Miss Huxtable's draft horses and intended to have them. He hurried across the slump, dodging junipers, and burst upon the happy brown throng under the cottonwood tree. He elbowed his way into the center where poor Wood quaked and Gracie stood as immovable as an Egyptian pyramid. Crabtree knew he'd have to take over: Wood, straight out of the nunnery of Harvard, wouldn't know barter from blasphemy.

"What's this, Cyrus?"

"Why, Crab, they're set upon taking the Clydesdales and Miss Gracie."

"Gracie?" He scowled at her. "They want you?"

"Not if I can help it, master."

"What do they want for you?"

"Not enough. I don't want no heathen owning me."

"Many ponies," said a young headman in English. "This one"—he pointed at a stocky, rawboned warrior who radiated malign power—"he offers many ponies for her."

"I'm worth two hundred ponies, and I ain't going."

"Be quiet." He scowled back at her. Such talk deserved the lash.

"Crab—you wouldn't!"

"She's an old mule."

"But, master, I've been with you long as I remember, almost. I wash your clothes, keep your house, feed you meals, listen to your jokes—you're not gonna go hand me to some bunch o' mean heathen wild brown savages."

Wood bristled at the thought. "Of course not, Miss Gracie. It's—unthinkable."

That annoyed Crabtree. "It's perfectly thinkable. These Sioux know more about bondage than the whole faculty of Harvard, Wood. She's a drudge. I can replace her with a hundred more drudges. Get younger ones too, work harder, do more, less uppity and insolent than this one."

"Master, I'm sorry I ever got uppity; I just don't want—"

"Quiet! You've no say in it."

"You wouldn't!" cried Wood. "It's beastly!"

But Crabtree turned to the translator. "How many horses?"

The headman discussed the question with the calm, imperious buyer, who discussed it with a group of other warriors endlessly. Then at last the headman turned back to Crabtree. *"Weekchimnah."* He held up ten fingers.

"Ten horses for a human being!" cried Wood. "Crab—this is frightful."

Crabtree stared at Wood. "It's my property. That happens to be enough horses to draw a wagon and pull eight travois—enough for my giant boar and maybe even most of your precious titanothere, Professor Wood."

"But she's—she's one of us. Born to our world. It'd be unspeakably cruel—"

"I can't stand the thought, master. I'm too old. That red savage, he might make me a wife."

"That'd be entertaining," Crabtree retorted.

Gracie sulked. "I'm worth more. You make it fifty horses, and all broke to pull a travois. You get them to throw in the travois and them surcingles and halters and lines. You maybe get them to leave a boy here to herd all them ponies and break them to harness. I'm worth it. I'm worth more'n that. You got no one to wash your britches white."

Crabtree turned to the headman. "Twenty. Big and well broke. With travois. And a herding boy for the summer." He raised his hands twice, splaying out the fingers.

"You'll be sorry," Gracie muttered.

"On the contrary. You're lazy and insolent and it's time to trade you for some fossils. As long as Van Vliet ran off with the last of our drays, I'll trade you or anything else for something to get us out of here. One more word and you'll taste the whip."

"Then I be damaged goods."

That was true. He turned to the headman. "Why does this man want the woman? What's she worth?"

"She's *wakan*, holy. She make him powerful, great chief, a great *wicasa*. He want her plenty much."

That delighted Crabtree. The mighty red warrior and his holy woman, mincing about the Sioux nation like Punch and Judy. "Well? Tell him twenty big ones—I get to choose—and the travois. Forget the herding boy. I don't want any dirty—"

Another of those endless consultations ensued, while Crabtree waited impatiently. At last the headman turned to him. "He got to trade ponies with his—ah, *Akicíta* brothers. The chief, Little Thunder, he gives two just to get the *wakan* woman in the village."

"Well, I haven't all day."

The headman listened to the bargaining and finally

turned to Crabtree. "He is Eagle Shield, a Pipe Owner, a *Wakinkuza*, and Shirt Wearer. He says yes, and his word is worth much, as true as the sun. You are honored to trade with such a great one. The horses—they're down near the river with the herding boys. We go down now and you pick. He tells you which are strong and well."

"I'm a doctor."

The headman stared at him uncomprehending.

"I'll tell him what horse is healthy." He had no doubt that the aborigines would try to fob off a bad lot, with cracked hoofs, galled withers, and all the rest. Little did they know how well any Southern gentleman knew horses. He turned to Gracie. "Get your stuff."

She raced off with unseemly haste for an old waddling woman, and it struck him that maybe she liked this idea more than she was letting on. "Stop," he yelled. She halted. "Maybe I won't."

She looked at him blankly, the slightly crestfallen expression slowly becoming a hard glare.

"Do you want to stay with me?"

"I ain't supposed to say."

"That's right. I make the decisions. You're going. I need the horses. One black mule for twenty horses."

She sighed soulfully. "It'll be awful hard, master."

"That's too bad, isn't it? Get your truck."

She lumbered off, and he followed the throng of Brulés down the path, toward the horse herd far below.

"They're taking the Clydesdales!" Wood cried.

"I can't help that. The bluestocking's not here to defend them, and that lazy guide isn't either."

Wood stared at the culprits, two youths as skinny as rails, and dashed after them. "Here now!" he cried. He plowed right in and snatched the halter ropes from the boys. Wood turned, astonished, to discover he controlled the Clydesdales and not a Sioux objected. Some laughed.

"There, you've done it," Crabtree said. "They weren't serious. They're boys."

Professor Wood looked so astonished at what he'd done that it delighted Crabtree. Obviously bewildered, Wood led the Clydesdales back toward the pond and held them with surly defiance until the last of the village was plunging down the trail.

Crabtree scrambled toward the lower meadow, planning to do some sharp horse trading. Some useful horses for a worn-out, insolent, mean, miserable old black woman, he thought. He'd buy some young, shapely high-yellow honeysuckle next time; he wished he'd thought of it years ago.

CHAPTER
54

G racie exulted. She filled her flour sack with her spare shift, her hairbrush, some darned stockings, some slippers that fit around her bunions, needles and thread, and a few rags. All she possessed. Then she hurried down the path, surrounded by wild brown savages, as wild and brown as her bursting heart. She'd fooled the master. If she had shown the slightest eagerness he would have kept her. Even now, she had to be careful. Not until he'd picked his horses and her new people had ridden away with her could she relax.

Around her the Brulé women crowded shyly, as curious as blue jays. Children peered fearfully into her sweating face. They'd all heard the bargaining. They all thought she was *wakan*, holy, endowed with magical powers. A frown from her might turn them into stone. She didn't smile; not now. Not while the dapper doctor in snowy white could snatch her back. Later, she'd smile. Oh, she would smile.

Oddly, she felt a certain sadness. She knew she'd miss the devil doctor who'd owned and abused her for so long.

They'd been comfortable with each other for more years
than she could remember, a familiarity that no longer required words. She met his demands automatically, with
nothing being said for days on end, and he in turn had
rarely badgered her.

She felt fear too. The one who would soon possess her
had a cruel eye and calculating gaze; raw power in the
muscles of his youthful body. He would be about twenty
years younger than she. She didn't really know her future
among these wild people but she sensed it would be better
than her past. Toothache had conveyed that much. The
slaves of the Plains tribes soon became part of the family
and members of the captor tribes. She itched to kick Crabtree in the shins after this was done; just one final satis-
fying boot that would raise a welt on his flour-paste flesh.
But she knew she had to be smarter than that. Her new
master would be watching her, looking for something to
be mean about.

At the village horse herd a covey of youths, eager to
participate in the great trade, fanned out to halter Eagle
Shield's ponies and the ones he'd swiftly collected from
others. The doctor waited in the hot sun, eyeing the restless pony herd as the bronze boys filtered through it. Eagle
Shield stood beside him, a pillar of iron, his eye quick and
his long stares toward Gracie almost wilting in their intensity.

It didn't take the master long. One by one the horses
were presented to him. He walked around them as masters
did at the slave market of Charleston, sometimes lifting a
hoof or peering into a pried-open mouth to study teeth
and learn age. Many of the ponies bore the sweat marks and
chafing of travois. These were older ones, subdued and
potbellied and weary, unlike the fiery young warhorses
and buffalo-running horses.

Sometimes, with a motion of the hand, he directed a
boy to lead a horse in a circle, stop it or back it, and

watched to see whether the animal balked or limped or
fought. He chose some of the hammerheaded slope-
shouldered little things, rejected some, nodding or shaking his head in gestures known to all mankind. Gracie
watched fearfully, wondering whether the master would
ever satisfy himself with these ugly little horses. But he
did. In an hour Crabtree had twenty serviceable animals
and five rickety travois, hastily emptied of their loads by
squaws.

He smiled. "She's all yours," he said, patting Gracie
on the rear with a familiarity he had never shown before.

Eagle Shield nodded and motioned to Gracie. Suddenly
it all seemed bad, and fear laced through her. But she
trudged toward him, while his wife and daughters ringed
around her, poking and probing and examining as if she
were a prize nanny goat.

Crabtree never said good-bye, never even turned to wave
or even to insult her one last time with his cocked eyebrow
and sardonic jokes. Instead, he turned his back, ran a
picket line through the halters of several of the ponies and
another through more halters. Twenty unruly horses would
be more than one man could cope with, she thought, hoping they'd all run away.

She saw Rufus Crowe riding through the throng, his
gold-rimmed glasses perched low on his sunburned nose.
He greeted his adopted people in their tongue. The British
lady walked beside him, her mouth looking as if she were
sucking a lemon. Crowe paused at the center, saw Gracie
standing beside Eagle Shield, and saw Crabtree organizing
his horses. Crowe lifted his hat, grasping at once what had
transpired, and settled the hat back on his sweating forehead.

"Miss Gracie!" said Candace Huxtable. "What is
this?"

Crowe answered her. "There's been a trade. Doctor
Crabtree's gotten horses, Miss Huxtable. My friend, the

Wakinkuza, there, has a new member of his family. He's a Pipe Owner, big man.''

Candace looked stunned. ''Oh! You can't do that! You can't sell a human being to another! To—to—'' She bit her tongue.

Gracie wisely kept quiet, fearing it'd all come undone.

''An old mule for twenty ponies,'' Crabtree said. He paused, plucked a slim Havana from his shirt pocket, and lit it with a lucifer. ''Horses and travois for our fossils and duds. Got rid of one fossil and I'll get a young wench when I get back. Miss Huxtable, you may wash my clothes. Be sure to get them white.''

''You—are a beast.''

Crabtree grinned, his resinous eyes glowing with his private pleasures. ''You're wearing cotton picked and ginned by slaves in the American South and woven into muslin in your English mills. It came cheaper because of our slaves. If slavery offends you, take the dress off and stand nakedly upon your morals.''

She reddened.

''Crowe,'' he continued. ''You'll be responsible for these horses. There's not much grass at our camp so you'll have to picket them down here and keep them safe from the wild men. You'll break four or so to harness in our remaining weeks. And contrive packsaddles just in case we have trouble with travois.''

''I imagine,'' the guide said. He wasn't paying attention to Crabtree.

''You imagine! Those are instructions, Crowe.''

''I'm not your slave, sir.''

Crabtree's lips lifted slightly, the faintest trace of amusement mixed with mockery, and he flicked ash from his stogie.

Rufus Crowe dismounted and handed his reins to an eager fat boy who hung close. He pushed through the silent crowds, smiling and patting his friends and neighbors, until he reached Gracie.

"Come here for a private word, Miss Gracie." Eagle Shield eyed Crowe dourly but let him guide Gracie out of earshot of Crabtree.

"You're gonna be happy if you relax some and get to know them as good folks. They're not like white masters. You're going to have some bad moments, I imagine, but things'll get better when you learn their words."

She felt flustered. "Mister Crowe, I made them think I got powers I ain't got. I wanted to be traded so bad, I made up stuff. They think that I'm *wakan* and I'm bringing good times with me. You gotta help me."

Rufus Crowe stared, and slowly a delicious smile filtered across his pink face. Then he wrapped his arms around Gracie. "You're *wakan*, all right, Miss Gracie. You just tell 'em so, and believe it yourself. Or I'll tell 'em."

His hug felt good. She'd scarcely been hugged all of her long life, and never by a white man. "Oh, Mister Crowe," she said, the tears welling again.

"I'll be seeing you, I imagine. These are my people. I'm adopted. That one over there, Catches the Hawk, he made me his son in a *hunka* ceremony. I promise, Miss Gracie, you're going to have happy times."

She found herself weeping hotly. "Oh, Mister Crowe, I'll never see you again."

She felt his gentle hands tug her free so he could look into her blurry eyes. "This here's your beginning, Miss Gracie. You're gonna be like White Buffalo Woman to them—she's a powerful one of their spirits they all respect."

But even as she clung to him, she heard the village police, one of the warrior brotherhoods, summon the village to its journey. Eagle Shield's women pulled her away, and soon she found herself trudging beside them, her life and fortune in their hands, and nothing but a few rags between her and the elements. It was no good to cry. She wiped her soft eyes, and measured her gait to the sharp-boned woman beside her. All around her, women trudged and chattered, ponies and dogs dragged travois bowed under terrible loads, infants rode on their mothers' backs in cradleboards or sometimes just wrapped in shawls, dogs rocketed through the chaos, upsetting their travois, and on the flanks, wiry warriors rode solemnly, their thin wall the only protection the village knew.

Gracie pointed at a horse. "What's that?" she asked in English.

The woman beside her picked up the question at once. "Shoong-TON-kah," she replied.

Gracie pointed to her own nose.

"POH-gay."

Gracie pointed toward a little cottonwood.

"WAH-hon-chon."

Gracie didn't know whether that meant cottonwood or tree. But she knew she'd learn. And that's how the rest of her day went, even as everything she'd known from childhood faded behind her. She also learned the name of her companion: Zintkaziwin.

They stopped well west of the Badlands on the White River, with the indigo wall of the Black Hills looming higher in the twilight dusk. Her feet hurt almost as much as when she'd trudged westward from Fort Pierre. She wished they'd give her a horse; then her thighs could hurt instead of her feet.

She watched the surly-looking headman who had translated for them come toward her, followed by Eagle Shield and a dozen other subchiefs and shamans of the Brulés.

The translator addressed her. "Make the buffalo come."

She eyed them sternly. "I want good moccasins, a blanket, and a horse and saddle. Then we'll see."

CHAPTER
55

One by one, as August stretched into September, the oreodont sites that Candace had staked out for excavation yielded to her deft pick and chisel. Only that first skeleton had been whole. The rest lacked major skeletal components, particularly legs and tails. One's skull had been crushed—a condition she considered extremely valuable because it would give her some clues about what sorts of predators had feasted on the populations of the herbivorous little oreodonts. Ribs were often lacking too, because the rib cages had been torn apart by the carnivores.

But that was all priceless information. She kept a sharp lookout for coprolites, that would give her more knowledge of what had attacked the oreodonts. The dung of the carnivores, rich in lime from the animal bones they'd crunched and swallowed, often survived as coprolites, but only rarely did the vegetable dung of the herbivores become fossilized. She knew only that some carnivore with powerful canines had crushed that skull at the third site. In addition to the five sites that Crowe had found, she'd discovered six more in branches of her canyon. She'd grown confident and skilled, and some of the fossils took only a day or two to extract. She collected the skull and neck vertebrae of a dog-sized early horse she recognized as a *miohippus*, and a skull and mandible of a saber-toothed cat. The latter lay in channel sandstone not ten feet from one of her oreodonts, and she prized it for that. It would help her understand what preyed on oreodonts, and how oreodonts evaded the predators.

She tackled the last site with all that experience behind her, swiftly deciding how much of the fossil lay buried and how much she was likely to find. This skull, which lay partly exposed, looked different from the rest, with bony corrugations down its nose. It had unusual color, too, an odd blue-green. She'd often rejoiced because each of her sites had been located in different strata, separated by millions of years; an ideal circumstance for her work on adaptation and specialization. Now she was tackling the uppermost, or most recent, and perhaps the final stratum to contain oreodont fossils before something terrible extinguished them from the face of the earth.

This oreodont seemed so different from the lower ones that at first she doubted that it belonged to the same genus. It was tucked in the highest nodular layer with channel sandstone mixed into the mudstone, probably the same stratum being worked by Dr. Crabtree several canyons away. Just above lay a thick stratum of ash, probably from Yellowstone volcanoes. Perhaps that giant pig had been the fierce predator that had extinguished the oreodonts, or perhaps the volcanoes had destroyed them. She suspected the volcanic ash had buried their forage and them forever.

A half mile away, Crabtree had freed his monster, cleaned it, and examined the surrounding area minutely for missing bones and clues about vegetation and other life. After that he had unearthed most of a weird-looking protoceras, and now was hunting other bizarre fossils. He collected only monsters, he'd said one night. He enjoyed monsters, he'd explained, because they made God perverse. He was going to present a gallery of monsters to the local rector, "for the glory of God."

Let him have his vicious pig, she thought. It suited him. Gracie's departure had left a strange melancholy in Candace, and a curious hole in the camp, as if some vital and acerbic force had spent itself. Crabtree had worked industriously, mostly by himself, as cheerful and sardonic as ever, performing his own chores with just as much industry as he'd extracted from Gracie.

Candace settled into her work, this time at a difficult site requiring her to stand on a crude ladder to chip away at a fossil halfway up a heavily eroded slope. The angle of the gulch didn't help either: murderous sun sucked at her strength almost all day long, and she had to walk a quarter of a mile to find a shaded resting place. She'd grown bronzed and hard, and she'd lost weight because of the poor diet and ceaseless toil. Her ragged work dresses hung in bags over her bony frame, and she supposed her womanliness had vanished altogether.

Which saddened her. She'd never thought about her form and its attractions until this trip, when suddenly Rufus Crowe had pierced through the walls and veils and armor of her life. Over and over, these quiet days and weeks, her mind slipped away from the bone and rock of her contention to the shaded gully where she and Rufus had clung to each other for a beautiful trembling moment. She hadn't imagined in her prior years that such sweetness could exist; it had flooded over her unexpected, like a tidal wave, carrying all her resistance before it. His smooth flesh and soft frontier slur and stocky body had been deceptive. He wasn't soft; his flesh and muscle felt as hard as iron, and the force of his passion was volcanic, sweeping her upward into a heaven she'd never dreamed of.

In the ensuing days she'd relived that moment over and

over, and still it haunted her. She'd stopped him and then sobbed, broken, unable to endure the things that tore at her—the wild pleasure of his arms; the impossibility of it all; her chosen path in science, for which she had vowed to sacrifice all else, including her woman's yearnings.

She had wept that afternoon, feeling tears rivering down her cheeks, feeling helpless to stem her passion. Then she'd felt his hand about her shoulders, comforting her.

She'd stopped her weeping, suddenly embarrassed that she'd lost the cool English reserve that had been bred into her. She'd hastily drawn herself up and crawled to the canyon wall and sat there, so ashamed of herself she couldn't look at him. She'd made a vulgar display. That, more than anything else, dismayed her. She'd slid a finger over her cheeks, vanquishing wet tears while she recovered composure.

"There now," she had said. "That business is behind me. Tell me, Mister Crowe, about Toothache." She'd smiled at him, almost triumphantly.

"I should've told you about Toothache long ago, Miss Huxtable," her guide had replied. "I took her in because the Brulés can be cruel to a woman like her. She'd been cast out of the lodges of four warriors—she'd excited them to anger, it seemed. Her parents wouldn't take her; no one in her clan would help her. It became a hard case, and the ruling elders, the *wicasas*, were discussing what to do— mostly send her to another band, which is what they do when they've got a bad case. But I stepped in, having lost a wife recently, and I said I'd try. She's been good to me."

"But what did she do?"

The guide had sighed. "I think she wanted to be a friend."

She had waited, puzzled, until Crowe had begun a long explanation. The Sioux, he'd told her, didn't permit true friendship of men and women, even man and wife. Well before adolescence, boys played only with boys, and girls

only with girls. After marriage, the sharp division continued, along with real male hostility to women. The marital
act, Crowe had explained softly, was called counting coup
by the men. A vast body of tribal tradition and religious
belief had forever separated the sexes. Toothache had never
been able to live that way. And didn't have to in the lodge
of a white man. She and Crowe had been boon compan-
ions from the beginning. The elders didn't interfere after
that.

"Well, then," Candace had said too brightly. "I'm glad
we—that we didn't muss it up. I'm sure you're perfectly
suited for each other."

But even as she'd said it, she'd known that all this about
Toothache and Crowe's marriage, and becoming an adul-
teress, was not the real reason she'd squirmed free from
him just when her body had come alive to his. The abyss
she'd felt herself falling into had nothing to do with Toothache; it had to do with suitability, with returning to England with her reputation intact, her maidenhood secure,
and no chance of an unwanted child. It wasn't *proper*!

"I wish it were that simple. I'm fond of her. We're
friends, which is more than my other Brulé wives were.
But, Miss Huxtable, I love you."

"Well, you mustn't. You jolly well know it. Be a good
fellow now."

He had stood, slowly, and peered out into the white heat
of the far wall of the gully. "I always knew it," he'd said,
and stepped into the blinding light.

He didn't visit her again. After that, Rufus Crowe had
acquired new burdens. The grass around their camp had
vanished, and her Clydesdales as well as those twenty ponies had to be picketed far away in the claws of the Badlands, and watered at the White River once a day. Crowe
had to train several of them to accept harness and discipline. He hunted game through the dawns and dusk. And
even when he did have a little time, he didn't come to her

canyon. He avoided her in the evenings around the camp-grounds.

Each day, when the sun threatened to murder her, she retreated to a cool hollow in a cliff wall and relived the brief, futile moment of her surrender, longing for what she had forbidden herself. It never went away, not even when she was working.

But she knew it could not be. The ending of all this was clear. She could support him in England, but he'd be like a caged eagle there, drooping desolately, far away from the Western skies where he had soared and pounced and glided to his wild nest each night. No. She could not imagine introducing Rufus Crowe to her proper family; sending him to a formal banquet of the Royal Society; even calling at the homes of the Cambridge faculty for tea. No. They'd gaze at this wild man, be tediously polite, and privately sneer. She knew as certainly as the sun set in the west how it would be.

She was doomed to live east of Eden.

CHAPTER 56

For two days Archimedes Van Vliet sucked whiskey mixed with White River water and sulked. He neglected his draft horses even though they whinnied at him and pawed holes in the clay. Finally they yanked up their picket pins and watered at the river. He let them wander, grazing where they would. He didn't care about their fate. Sometimes he spotted them, other times he didn't, but he never stirred.

The whiskey slid down tepid and bitter, taking the edge off his temper even while driving him to the depths of despair. A summer lost. Prizes beyond imagining. The loss of a *wicasa* shirt, the only one he'd ever come across, beautiful and rare and important. The *Wicasa Itacans*, or Shirt Wearers, were the highest executives of the Sioux people, and the shirts they received upon their investiture to high office were among the most exquisite created by the Sioux. The one he'd found upon a desiccated old man followed the traditional scheme: bold blue on its upper half, bright yellow on its lower half, the colors representing two of the great Controllers, Sky and Rock. It was fringed with black hair locks, each lock representing the people of the tribe to whom the *wicasas* were responsible. As far as he knew, no other such shirt had fallen into the hands of a collector or museums.

Now it was ash. He sighed, unable to cope with a sadness that sometimes brought him to fits of weeping. He decided to solace himself again—the pain was biting his chest this morning—and lumbered off to his cask.

Which was empty. Disbelieving, he lifted and shook it, and finally got half a measure by tilting it and shaking the last drop of amber whiskey loose from its porous staves. All gone. It shattered him. He'd carefully provided ample whiskey for the summer by calculating his maximum daily needs and adding a large reserve. Where had it gone? Someone had been stealing it! But he knew no one had; he'd drunk the entire thirty-gallon cask himself. It shocked him to his bones. Weeks left, and no whiskey. He didn't know how he'd manage. Unless, of course, he drove to Fort Pierre.

To think the thought was to decide to do it. New Fort Pierre lay more than a hundred miles away, but with an almost empty wagon he might manage it in six days. Even the six-day dry seemed unbearable to him but he had no choice. They wouldn't miss him at the Badlands; he'd be back well before it was time to depart for Fort Union. Still, doubts plagued him. What if the traders at Pierre had none? Or refused to sell to him? Spirits were, after all, illegal in Indian country. What if he lacked the means to purchase a cask? What if they rationed what little they had? He dismissed that. The traders rationed whiskey in the winter and spring, but not so soon after their summer resupply.

The emergency cleared his mind better than coffee ever could. He walked and stretched, then dug into his duffel to see about cash. He'd brought little, not expecting to use any during a long summer far from any purveyor. He dug to the bottom of the trunk and slid a thin slat sideways and found what he desperately wanted to find: a twenty-dollar gold piece. Enough? He didn't know. He hefted its cool, authoritative weight and slid it into his pocket. Then he stalked into the burial grounds to find his drifting horses; he itched to be off.

He didn't find the horses at first, but followed what seemed to be fresh spoor that took him westward. He came upon the pair in a little dip, where they were cropping lush bottom grass. He caught the more tractable one, and let the other follow him back to his camp. Trembling, he bridled them, dropped the collars over their necks, and buckled on the surcingles and breeching. He backed each one toward the doubletree and hooked the tugs. He loaded his gear, clambered to the seat, snapped the lines over the rumps of his drays, and set off at a smart trot.

The effects of two days of heavy drinking, lack of food, and brutal heat struck him that afternoon but he never slowed down. He rocked and swayed nauseously on his wagon seat, while the fresh horses whipped the almost empty wagon eastward.

The second day a party of Sioux stopped him. They rode single file out of an obscure draw and blocked his path. He counted seven, none of them showing signs of hostility. He tugged at his lines until his wagon creaked to a halt, and stared, not recognizing any of them. He didn't know what band these belonged to but supposed them to be Brulés because this was their country.

One unsmiling warrior kicked his pony close and examined the bed of the wagon, seeing only Van Vliet's personal things rattling around within. Leisurely the warrior rode back to the rest to consult with them, and after that several more undertook the same inspection, eyeing the trunk darkly but not asking that it be opened.

"Do any of you speak English? I'm off to Pierre for supplies. I'm with the party guided by Crowe."

They stared blankly at him, apprehending nothing. Then, upon a nod from the headman, they trotted off as silently as they had come. Van Vliet pulled out his bandanna and mopped his face. Watching Owl had warned him: word of his collecting had traveled from band to band and most of the Sioux nation knew of it. This bunch had simply policed him. He hadn't the slightest doubt that if his wagon had been full of Sioux artifacts he would now be dead or dying, and everything in his wagon would have been confiscated.

He continued unmolested to the Missouri, drove by the ruins of old Fort Pierre and followed a deep trace northward through tortuous country until he clattered down a sharp slope and beheld the new trading post squatting not far from the wide river. That was the afternoon of the sixth day, as he calculated, and his horses seemed almost as fresh as when he'd started. After another hour of downhill travel, in which his wagon pressed into the horses' breeching, he reached a dusty flat where the small stockaded post baked in the August sun. Even as he tugged the lines of his drays, men erupted from within and hoorawed him happily.

"Ah, *monsieur*, welcome," cried a barrel-shaped one who wore a broad-brimmed beaver-felt hat. "It is Jean Picotte you address, and you are the doctor of science, Van Vliet, *oui*?"

Startled, Van Vliet nodded. How word got around the wilds, he thought. His name and description had preceded him.

"It is that you need something, *oui*? Step down and we will wet your parched throat."

He followed Picotte into a small trading house of thick cottonwood logs weathered gray. Behind the trading counter hung a delightful array of goods manufactured for the Indian trade: steel traps, boxes of awls, bolts of bright trade cloth, hatchets, Wilson knives, sturdy blankets with points, or bars, delineating their weight, kettles, skeins of beads, sacks of green coffee beans, sugar, and more, all dazzling and redolent.

"I know what for you come, *monsieur*," Picotte said, steering Van Vliet through the trading room into private quarters at the rear.

That struck Van Vliet as odd, since he hadn't revealed his purposes to a soul. Picotte motioned him to sit in a homemade chair crafted of cottonwood and rawhide. The trader reached for a cut-glass decanter, pulled the glass stopper, and poured a quarter inch of the clear liquid into a tin camp cup.

"It will clear the dust," Picotte said, waiting cheerfully.

Van Vliet lifted the mess cup and swallowed, and felt lava burn a track along his tongue and scrape flesh off his throat. He wheezed, then sputtered.

"Ah, it is strong, *non*?"

Van Vliet dabbed at moist eyes with his bandanna, and agreed. "I prefer corn spirits," he muttered.

That produced a Gallic shrug. "I am sorry, *mon ami*. We have none of that. And this is water, you understan', oui? We have no spirits here."

"What is—that stuff?"

"Ah, it is the essence, the heart and soul, the elixir, of trade whiskey, Doctor Van Vliet. It's two-hundred-proof grain spirits."

"Two hundred? You mean pure?"

"*Exactement*. Mix it this way: one part spirits, five or six or seven parts river water, some red pepper and some black chewing tobacco, and maybe black molasses or Jamaica ginger for flavor. Stir it gently and sip it carefully, very carefully. Ah, it is, as you say, water of the fire."

Van Vliet mopped up tears. "How much?" he muttered, as he shoved his cup forward for more.

"One dollar the cup."

"A dollar a cup!"

The trader shrugged. "It comes a long way, almost never on the boats but on the humble backs of mules. It comes in tin flasks, eh? It makes trouble, eh? Our license . . ."

"But a dollar a cup!"

"It is that for everyone, for red man and white. It is the price required by old Pierre Chouteau himself. Remember, s'il vous plaît, one cup properly cut makes a quart or two—or even three."

"I'll take twenty cups. In a jug," Van Vliet muttered. "And if you'll take a draft on my New York account, I'll buy a gallon more. It's steep but you're the only store in town."

"Bien, bien. Ah, non, no draft, no gallon. We never have enough for our thirsty customers, you see? Then we get no robes."

Van Vliet produced his gold coin and Picotte bit it.

"How do you know so much about me, Monsieur Picotte?"

The trader shrugged. "Our fine customers, they gossip, mon ami. They know all there is to know about you. Each day my dear friends the Brulés and Two Kettles and Minniconjous come in, petit parties, sometimes whole villages. Always they have news. Big news, little news. News of white men digging up the bones of monsters and ah, opening scaffolds. The Sioux have a thousand eyes and ten thousand ears and mouths full of gossip. And a trader, he gets all of this news. Now, if you had come to me with a wagon full of precious things from the burial scaffolds, wanting us to store them—Ah, mon ami, I would have to say non to the fine Yankee scientist. It would make my good customers unhappy. And we would lose their trade and I, ah, I would no longer be employed by my dear cousin Pierre. We never make the Lakota unhappy.'' He stared directly into Van Vliet's eyes. ''And, *mon ami*, you should not either. If you persist, it could make you dead.''

CHAPTER
57

B y the beginning of September Candace had what she needed: eleven oreodont fossils, ranging from thirty percent to ninety percent complete, most from different strata. She could study their variations at leisure back in England. She still had some rock samples to collect, some drawings to do and journals to write. She would also hunt for other fossils in the same strata as a means of correlating geological periods and learning more about climate and conditions at each site. But the last of the fossils lay in a heap, ready to be tucked into her wagon.

She knew she could do that herself, using a horse and a packsaddle, but she had other things in mind. That cool twilight she caught up with Rufus.

"Mister Crowe, could you help me bring the last fossil in?"

"I imagine. I'll come over in the morning."

She felt the emotional neutrality of his words, and feared she'd lost her only friend in camp.

She awaited him at the site all that next overcast morning, growing more and more miserable as she sketched and wrote a site description. But at last he rode up her canyon, tugging a packhorse behind. He surveyed the pile of oreodont bones and silently loaded them into the panniers, packing them carefully. She watched, grieving at his silence.

At last he finished and buckled the flaps of the panniers.

"I'll meet you at your wagon."

"Mister Crowe—Rufus—would you come to our little hollow and talk for a while?"

"I don't think the sun's oppressing me."

"It's a place where we were friends."

"Miss Huxtable—it's a place where I got into trouble."

"Please—call me Candace."

"We could talk here if that suits you." But she read uncertainty in him, and knew he'd come.

She smiled and walked down the main canyon to the little branch where the hollow lay hidden, a place familiar and dear to her, like her own bedroom in England. As fast as she thought that, she wished she hadn't made that analogy. He followed on foot, leading his horses, saying nothing, taciturn in the cool cloudiness.

She settled against the wall as she always had. He tethered the horses and joined her, keeping a scrupulous distance.

"I'll always treasure your friendship, Rufus. I hope I'm your friend."

"I'm sorry, Miss Huxtable—"

"I'm Candace. And don't be. What happened was very beautiful to me, and gave me a glimpse . . . of things I haven't ever known. It wasn't just you, you know. If there's blame—which there isn't—I'm the one who should bear it. I invited what happened."

"It's hard to call you Candace. I'm just a border man, and you're the upper crust of England."

"There are no distinctions here, Rufus. And it's the

other way around: the others have patronized me but you don't. You've taught me things, shown me how to look at my own work with new eyes. For the others, I'm Cecil's little girl.''

Crowe chuckled softly, and something eased between them.

''One of the most precious things I'll take back with me is the memory of all our talks out here, hiding from that sun. I want things to be like that again. When I leave you at Fort Union, I want to be secure in your friendship, as you are in mine. And the other blasted business forgotten.''

''I can't forget, Miss Huxtable.''

She smiled. ''I can't either. Every day I relive those moments. I glimpsed paradise. I wept because of the choices I've made, and all the rules that've been bred into me—the English are terribly proper, you know. Always proper.''

He didn't smile but he didn't seem angry either. He just listened, cautiously, emboldening her to continue.

''An Englishwoman lives with a thousand Mrs. Rumley rules. I never knew how many until I wanted to break them. Keep a stiff upper lip. Don't be vulgar. Never lose your temper. Don't be a scold. Never whine. Don't ever talk about certain things. Never cause a scandal. Honor manhood. Make our homes our little nests for our husbands. Be content. Don't try to educate yourself because you haven't the brains or temperament. Sew and darn and cook and wash and bring some little tykes into the world. Rufus, the only time it all vanished was when—you held me.''

''I'm sorry, Miss Huxtable—''

''Don't be. I wanted your advances more than anything in the world. This is a perfectly free place, right here. I'm thousands of miles from gossips and snoops, and I was mad with need, and reckless as a magpie. But I couldn't. I'm the prisoner of my upbringing, as we all are.

"Still, Rufus, it's not silly rules that govern me. It's more, you know. Our bodies are holy, and the temples of God—that's what we learned on Sundays from all those dreary homilies of the Right Reverend Willowby. Everything beautiful and good depends on the undistracted life of the mind and spirit. I'm whole only if I subdue the creature, my body, and enter into my life of mind. I made my choices long ago. I'd never marry. I'd never become— intimate with a man. Knowledge is sacred—science, rational organization of facts, hypotheses, all these things leading to truth. I couldn't—I couldn't just . . . surrender to lusts."

"I admire your discipline, Miss—Candace. I don't have it."

"Yes, you do, Rufus. If I hadn't invited—"

"Miss Huxtable, I love my little Toothache, but I can't talk to her about science or fossils or Owen or Darwin or heaven and earth or creation. I talk to her about meat and clothes. We gossip about village people. But I need your talk like a man dyin' of thirst. I can't be all Sioux. I'm hungry for my own world. You're the only woman I ever really talked with. I guess I lost my senses. You're going home to England, and there's no place for some old border ruffian there. I always knew that."

She slipped her hand into his. "Am I forgiven?"

The question obviously startled him. "If you'll forgive me for wanting you still."

CHAPTER
58

The titanothere lay clean and bare and brown in the bright September sun. Its rib cage had been flattened and some of it lost, but most of the ribs lay in disarray near the vertebrae. They were all free of their matrix rock. The pronged skull and mandible had been undercut so that they could be lifted away. Portions of the tail and the right rear leg and foot were missing, perhaps dragged off by predators before riverbed silt had quietly covered the bones and sealed the rest of the fossil for millions of years. The complex vertebrae lay uncleaned, with mudstone filling every hollow in them—a delicate task best done on a workbench in the East. The inside of the skull remained uncleaned.

Professor Wood still had crucially important work to do: detailed sketches of the site and each bone, and endless measuring. If he rushed, he could probably finish before they had to leave. The days had grown shorter, robbing him of work time. But they had grown noticeably cooler, which made the digging easier. His old body had never stopped hurting and he'd never gotten much wind, but he'd grown strong and lean. The soft sausages of muscle in his arms and legs and shoulders had firmed. In fact he felt twenty years younger.

He stood in the early twilight admiring his summer's work, still astonished that he'd achieved it with his own muscle and sweat. The feat had transformed him. He discovered a pride within himself that had lain dormant. For once he'd done something heroic and impossible, and above all, something grand.

But he could no longer delay confronting the terrible question that he'd pushed aside day after day. Could he take it east? Would this summer's labor be for naught? Sometimes Crabtree had meandered by, the faint mockery always in his face as he watched Wood gouge his bones free. Crabtree had finished his summer's work, transported his bones by packhorse down to the camp, cleaned them, and neatly packed them in the remaining wagon, eating up all the space in it. In recent days Crabtree had been out locating new sites for some future trip, or helping the guide turn the mustangs into draft and packhorses.

It irked Wood that all those mustangs belonged to the doctor.

"Don't worry, Wood," Crabtree had told him. "I've saved some packhorses for our personal gear. I'll get your stuff up to Fort Union."

Wood still hoped that Van Vliet would show up with the other wagon and team, but as the days fled by with no sign of the ethnologist, Wood had despaired. Van Vliet had probably stuffed the wagon with his booty and made for Fort Pierre with no thought of returning. It galled Wood. This outland, so far from the courtesies of civilization, had stripped the man of decency.

In the dusk Wood made his way up to camp and clambered into the tent, where Crabtree sat cross-legged, entering something in his journal with a stubby pencil.

"It's about my fossil, Doctor," Wood began awkwardly.

"Oh, that. You'll have to rebury it, Wood."

"You have a lot of horses and packs."

"Not enough for a titanothere. We'll need spares, you know. Horses gall up, get lame. No, Wood. It's a disappointment, I'm sure, but it can't be helped. You knew that when you began."

"I didn't know it. We had two wagons and two teams."

"I wish I could help you, my friend, but you see how it is."

"I've freed the greatest fossil ever found here! Maybe the greatest ever found in North America except for the Haddonfield dinosaur!"

"We can hope that Van Vliet returns with an empty wagon."

"He's gone. Perhaps you could help me find a wagon. You've time. Could you ride to Pierre, or even Fort Union?"

"Have you the means, Wood?"

"I'll find the means!" He wasn't sure of that. His small stipend from Harvard wouldn't permit the hire of a wagon and team. "You have the horses and a saddle; you would do the expedition a great service. We can't spare Crowe, but you're free now."

Crabtree shook his head, and that seemed to be the end of it. And the end of Wood's dreams.

Bitterly Wood fled into the dusk. He debated trying Miss Huxtable, whose oreodont fossils did not entirely fill her wagon, and decided against it. He wondered about using some travois, but didn't want to entrust the great bones to the jarring of those crude devices.

Painfully he made his way through a nippy dusk to his dig and sat there among his treasured friends the bones, laying a hand on a femur. He would have to make his measurements and then cover the site with the rubble he'd chipped loose all summer. He couldn't leave the bones to crack and die with every sun and rain and frost. He'd failed after all. He was just a gray old Harvard don on the fringes of natural science, doomed to obscurity.

"It's a blasted pity," said Miss Huxtable.

He turned sharply to find her settling herself beside him.

"Do you suppose we blighters could do something about it, Professor? I have a bit I could spend, if it came to that. I couldn't help but hear your little chat with the old boy."

"Miss Huxtable—"

"It's been a whole summer. You might venture to call me by my given name."

"Candace," he said, feeling an awful lump collect in his throat. "I can't ask you to help. I haven't—" He couldn't say the rest: he hadn't been a bit kind to her the entire time.

"Oh, hush! I've a bit of a plan. Do you think we could make a quick trip to Pierre and back before we all leave here?"

"Not in a week. It'd take two or three trips, you know. There must be tons of bones. I can't even lift a rib."

"Well, where can we get help?"

"Miss Huxtable—Candace—I've scarcely the means—"

"I have. Can we hire a cartman somewhere? At a post?"

"You'd have to ask Mister Crowe. But I don't expect—"

"Well I'll engage a bloke if I can. We'll get them. It'd be a blooming scandal to leave them here."

He stared at the ground, not wanting her to see what lay in his face.

"Professor Wood—I wish to repay you."

"Repay?"

"You were an inspiration to me. Whenever I got tired or hot, or felt like taking a nap—why, I thought of you. I thought, his every move hurts. His muscles torture him. His lungs ache. His bones cry. But he doesn't give up. He digs and chips while his bones hurt and his head hammers and his blisters break and bleed. Well! You've been my inspiration! I'm young and I was doing less! For weeks, for fortnights, you've fought the blasted mountain. Even when Doctor Van Vliet vanished with the other wagon— your only hope of transportation—you never faltered, you never quit. You worked all the harder, an act of faith. Well, I think faith should be rewarded."

"Oh, Miss—Candace. That was for me." It became important to him that she understand. He had done it for himself; because the work was transforming him.

"Of course you did it for you. But all of science bene- fits. I don't suppose Richard Owen writes his papers for the glory of Charles Darwin. Maybe you dreamed of writ- ing a celebrated paper. Hearing the applause at a banquet. Seeing this blooming thing all wired together and lumber- ing like some child's nightmare through an exhibition hall. Of course you did. Thank heaven we have dreams, Pro- fessor Wood. I've my own potty little one, you know. It's humbler than yours. I just want to be esteemed as a natural scientist—something no woman's achieved. I do it for my- self!"

But Cyrus Billington Wood didn't hear the last. He'd been blinking and blinking back the wetness welling up, and finally lost the battle. He stood before his titanothere streaming hot tears that slid down his ruddy cheeks and into his beard. Yes! If he'd truly, truly been an inspiration to someone else on this cold earth, he thought, then the summer wasn't lost. God willing, maybe he could inspire a few more undergraduates—as he'd inspired the young woman.

Miss Huxtable was hugging him and weeping too.

CHAPTER
59

G racie felt like a queen. Swiftly they brought a blanket to her, blue and thick, to shrug off the morning chills. And then a potbellied little pony with a woman's saddle on it, cantle and pommel rising much higher than on a white man's saddle. Zintkaziwin eyed Gracie's feet and soon returned with several pairs of quilled moccasins. One pair fit splendidly, and it became Gracie's.

They stood around her, waiting for her to make the buffalo come. She peered at one and then another and found none would meet her gaze. She supposed these Brulés were insincere because they wouldn't look her in the eye. But she remembered that Toothache had always averted her gaze, never openly looking at Gracie. She decided she would look them directly in the eye, and it would give her power over them.

She addressed the dour translator. "Tonight I will ask the buffalo to come, and in the morning I'll tell you where."

The women scarcely unpacked anything, and Gracie realized that she'd get little to eat this night. She saw no cookfires. Zintkaziwin had opened a single parfleche and extracted something that looked like sausage. Gracie knew it was pemmican, the trail food that consisted of shredded meat, fat, and berries, usually chokecherry, mashed together into compact lumps and often stored in buffalo gut. She knew she wouldn't eat a hot meal until the Brulés made a camp.

She sat down and waited. They made her do no work. Zintkaziwin doled out the trail food and then some robes for her family. If this was slavery, it beat the white men's variety, she thought happily. But she was *wakan*. Maybe they treated other prisoners badly. She'd heard enough tales to believe it.

An evening chill slid into camp on freshets of air. Summer was dying. Gracie pulled her new blanket about her and sat, watching the camp quiet as dusk deepened. The racket of horses and dogs and wheeling flocks of children faded, and as the stars popped into the indigo sky and a blue glow lingered over the looming darkness of the Black Hills to the northwest, the band of road-weary Brulés slid into silence. Not a lodge had been erected, and the poles and covers rested exactly where they'd been separated from the burdened horses. These brown people lived and worked and played and warred and loved in sunlight and rain and snow and wind and under stars.

She saw Eagle Shield studying her, as if he wanted to warn her about something. He didn't grasp that on this very day she'd been freed from a life sentence for the criminal act of being African. She smiled at him, hoping the warmth of it would scatter his gloom, but it didn't. He squinted, and then settled down, his hand on the haft of his belt-sheathed knife.

Off to the west, along the river, *Akicita* brothers night-herded the ponies, ghosting back and forth to keep a thousand nervous horses pinned to the river, and also to keep night raiders, the hated Crows or Assiniboin, from robbing the village of its wealth and transportation. Gracie felt instantly at home, as if this sort of living close to nature touched something in her roots. The soft tendrils of cold air carried the scents of people and dogs and horses.

When darkness narrowed her vision, she would clamber up to the top of the nearby bluff and commune with whatever spirits in the universe governed the fates of mortals. She either had to produce buffalo or a splendid excuse if she wished to retain her exalted status as a *wakan* woman. She would stretch this charade as long as she could, because Rufus Crowe had said she should. It pleased her. She'd taken girlish delight in having her requests swiftly met. The blanket solaced her aching bones.

When she judged that she was alone, she arose, drew her blue blanket close, and headed for the bluffs, faint in starlight. But she'd scarcely gone ten paces when Eagle Shield sprang up behind her and followed, his buffalo robe clutched around him. She paused. She'd learned more Sioux words than she could remember that day from Zintkaziwin, but they'd fled her mind. Even so, she knew the one she needed.

"Wakan," she said, and beckoned him to follow, which he did at a distance. It amused her; he wouldn't let his prize slave out of his sight.

She clambered up the steep slope, feeling the thinness of the moccasins they'd given her. At the head of the bluff she peered down upon the sleeping assemblage and could see almost nothing—except for her owner gliding up the trail. She settled herself into the grass, worrying about rattlers, and waited. He appeared back a way, leaving her to her communing with the buffalo she'd promised them.

She had no settled religion. The master had believed in nothing. Maybe he was right: no lightning dashed him; no disease rotted him, as was the lot of any blasphemer.

She remembered the backwoods gatherings of the slaves of her girlhood, the meetings in firelit glades far from the eyes of the masters. She remembered one from her childhood. An almost naked man had cut the throat of a chicken, and while it flapped and bled he had swept around a circle, spilling blood on each of them. Chicken blood had dripped on the back of her hand, glistening bright red, and she'd studied it, wondering about its powers and properties. They'd chanted and beat sticks on hollow logs and made throbbing magic and gone home before dawn, the masters all unaware.

Her first master had made her—made them all—listen to a sweating white Baptist preacher, who told them about a loving God and a forgiving Jesus and lots of strange stories. She had liked that better, but it didn't mean a thing. What could it mean to anyone who didn't own himself? To husband and wife who could be pulled apart? To children who might be ripped from their parents any time?

The preacher man had told them about the Golden Rule. It was the most important law of life. He'd whipped open his Bible and read: *Whatsoever ye would that men should do to you, do ye even so to them: for this is the law and the prophets.* She thought of it and laughed. And ached. She thought of all the white men listening in their pews to the Golden Rule at a thousand, thousand sabbaths; all of them stone-deaf, leaving their churches without heeding it. She thought of this great law of life brought to her by the white men, and sacred to the white men—and the prison of her life, and the whipping and torture of her people. She wept, great tears welling out of her. She wept for all her lost years, for her ruined life. She wept until she had wrung every tear out of her there was to wring. She wept because no one had ever treated her as he would wish to be treated himself. She sobbed through the night until she had bled away every hurt. A calm stole through her, and then she sat quietly.

In these past weeks she'd come to like Sioux religion most of all. She'd picked up the essentials from Toothache, jabbering in the queer little language they'd invented. Above, governing all, was the great spirit, Wakan Tanka. But everywhere were lesser gods, subordinate, kindred, associated. They included stars and buffalo, Iktomi the Trickster, Iya the chief of evil, Waziya the old man and his wife, Wakanaka the witch, and their daughter, Anog-Ite the Double-faced Woman. And more, so many that they all confused her. And all the lesser spirits that lived in animals and rocks and trees, and became the controllers and advisers of the people.

"Come, Buffalo," she whispered in each of the directions, hoping her gravelly old voice would magically be confided to the winds of night. "I need you. These sweet people need you. Come, help a poor old woman enjoy the rest of her few years. Come free a old woman that's brown like yourself."

She waited, hearing nothing on the breeze. "If you don't come, tell me where to go. I don't like to walk but I got a horse and I'll tell the old men where to go."

Not an inkling of a buffalo loomed in her mind. She waited a long time, feeling the chill sneak under her blanket. She ignored that. When had an old slave ever been comfortable, or slept in feather beds, or owned enough clothing and shoes? That was for soft people. She decided to try Wakan Tanka, the invisible great one, pretty much like the old-man God of the white men.

"You got some big old buffalo for an old woman? You care about some old slave makin' big lies to these here Brulés to get along a little better? I bet not. Some old woman sayin' she's some kind o' witch—that don't cut ice with you. You likely to get mad as a mean dog and make me tell that Eagle Shield I'm just a old mule, like Crabtree says, just fit for harness and work all day until I roll over and die and they stuff me into some old tree. But I thought I'd ask it anyhow, seein' as how they tell me you love all your children.''

She hadn't heard that of Wakan Tanka, but that old Baptist Sweet Jesus preacher that sweated his shirt wet down in Georgia, he'd said it like he believed it. She'd been eleven then, and giggled into her mouth when he'd preached, and grinned furtively at the other barefoot skinny girls in flour-sack dresses and string belts beside her.

She was getting tired of all this stuff, and decided she'd made her plea to whichever gods and devils ruled out here, and that was that. And that new master, Eagle Shield, he'd watched the whole thing like some wolf licking his chops just beyond her vision. At least he'd tell the rest of them redskins she'd been out making medicine in the night.

She lumbered down the slippery slope, stumbled through camp to the place beside the cottonwood where Zintkaziwin dozed in a grimy red blanket, and settled down nearby. She knew Eagle Shield had shadowed her back to camp, and it amused her. He faded into the grass near his sidestepping pony, and she smelled fresh manure. She settled onto earth as hard as a skillet, and tried to sleep. Maybe someday she could wangle some sort of buffalo-hair pad to solace her worn body.

The next cold dawn she awakened to shouts. Everywhere happy warriors were collecting their bow cases and quivers and dashing out to their horses. A great silent herd of the dark monarchs of the prairies had drifted into the bottoms a mile or two away, and were mowing the tall grasses like scythes.

CHAPTER
60

Archimedes Van Vliet dawdled around Fort Pierre for a fortnight, hoping to extract information about other burial grounds he might pillage. But the wily Picotte knew what Van Vliet wanted and kept mum. Van Vliet found personal items in his kit to trade for grain spirits, and kept himself well lubricated the whole while. A silver and abalone-shell hand mirror and brush and comb netted him enough firewater for a week. The post's buffalo meals came free, as they usually did to passing white men. Van Vliet enjoyed the comforts of the post, tables and chairs, and above all a life without the hazards of the wilds.

He corralled the busy Picotte one day after supper, when the trader was enjoying a pipe.

"My friend, how do I get artifacts from the Sioux?"

Jean Picotte eyed him and shrugged. "You do not get them by burrowing like a coyote into burial scaffolds, *mon ami*. It isn't polite. The Sioux are polite people."

"That doesn't answer my question."

Picotte shrugged and puffed. "You trade. In your fine

wagon you have a trunk of gewgaws and trading goods, *non*? You could go to any village—offer awls and knives and yards of cloth for shields and shirts and moccasins.''

''I could. I might get a few things. There'd be lots of things I couldn't get. Anything involving personal medicine. A shield with a warrior's medicine painted on it. A medicine bundle. The only things I could get are things they'd make just for me. You know that.''

''Ah, yes, I know that. Your scalp, what's left of it, knows that too.''

The mention of that bare patch of bone set it to aching again. He wondered how Picotte knew. He always kept his slouch hat clamped tight. ''You get all the news, Picotte.''

''All. I can tell you things you don't know. Professor Wood, he has excavated his beast.''

''Wood? Impossible. Who helped him?''

Picotte shrugged. ''It is more comforting to you to disbelieve, *mon ami*. I will say—in all simplicity—the Sioux know everything. If you take those artifacts on the scaffolds—the ones you snatched from the burial ground—they will know it. You would not be very wise to take them, *mon ami*.''

''Well, Picotte, I'll do it anyway.''

Picotte puffed and said nothing, the coals in his clay pipe crackling as he drew smoke. ''Forgive me, Doctor Van Vliet. You are the type that prefers to hunt for pirate's treasure, gold doubloons buried somewhere, than to get rich by boring means. Am I not correct?''

''Not correct. I'm a man with lusts. There must be medicine bundles and sacred shirts in my collection or I've failed.''

''*Non*, *non*, you are a treasure-hunter. If some Lakota woman sells you a sacred shirt, even one worn by her late husband, my friend, you don't value it so much as one you dig out of a scaffold. *Oui*? *Oui*.''

''No, it's lust. I must have whatever I want. Whatever

I can't have. I must have the greatest collection of Plains Indian artifacts ever seen. Enough to endow ten museums. And if any escapes me, I'll come out here and snatch that too. Call it greed. I'm the world's greediest mortal.''

"It's an abstraction, Doctor. Lust, greed or treasure-hunting, it's all the same. For you, it's better than trading for what you want. I have to think about the people I trade with or I lose them. You don't have to think about anyone. Temperamentally, you are a fortune-hunter.''

"Picotte, what's the rarest thing about Indians?''

"A bald one.''

"What else?''

"A left-handed Indian.''

"I'll find both, take them east, pickle them, and stuff them under glass, like Jeremy Bentham sitting in his glass wicket in the British Museum. Where do I get one or the other?''

Picotte laughed uneasily. "You make the point, *mon ami*.''

"Ah, Picotte. Now you know what mania is. I'm not the captain of my ship. That bit of scalp I lost—it's nothing. I'll risk the rest of it. Where are some burial grounds? On the Cheyenne River? There must be a dozen within reach.''

Picotte knocked the dottle from his pipe and tucked it into his pocket. "Van Vliet, at least spare the lives of your colleagues.''

The next morning Van Vliet tossed his gear into the Murphy wagon and harnessed the team while Picotte and the traders watched solemnly. Van Vliet headed out the Cheyenne River trace, which would take him in round-about fashion to the Badlands—and probably past several Lakota burial sites. He reckoned that if he wasted no time he'd be able to collect from two or three and arrive at the Badlands before his colleagues pulled out.

The trace running west from Pierre took him up enor-

mous slopes and plunged him into deep sloughs, wearying
the horses even though they pulled an empty wagon. For
long stretches he drove between vast slopes that hid the
surrounding terrain from him. But he knew that this rough
road would cut a corner and bring him to the Cheyenne
River in several days. From there it would follow the south
bank clear to the Black Hills.

He saw no river that day or the next, but late in the third
he topped a long ridge and beheld the Cheyenne, a woolly
green thread in the brown plaid of the plains. He let the
drays blow, and then eased the wagon down the endless
grade toward the Eden awaiting him, visions of burial
grounds on knolls near trees inflaming his mind.

He had not reached the river bottoms before a party of
Sioux materialized out of nowhere. They filed out of a
giant coulee and blocked his path. He pulled up hesitantly
and waited at some distance, knowing it would be fool-
hardy to reach for his Sharps. They weren't painted and
didn't seem bent on war, but neither did these warriors
give ground. They weren't Sioux he'd seen at Fort Pierre.
They wore much the same attire as the Brulés, but this far
north they might be Minniconjou. He spotted a war leader
among them, thick-lipped and imperious, with two notched
eagle feathers. And a *wicasa*, wearing the yellow and blue
shirt of high office. Sioux, then. Whatever the case, they
seemed to know him, and Van Vliet realized that every
band among the Lakota Tetons knew all about him.

The war leader motioned him to turn around.

"Do you speak English?" Van Vliet asked.

None responded. The war leader's finger described a
half-circle. Van Vliet eyed the terrain and hoped he could
manage a tight loop on the steep slope. They were turning
him back. Peacefully. Apparently the mantle of Crowe's
protection still wrapped him. Oddly, he felt no fear. He
had become fatalistic, knowing he was helpless to control
his greed and unable to influence these aborigines whose

tongue he couldn't speak. What could a red-nosed sot do but let it all play out?

He turned the wagon slowly, feeling the wheels shuddering and squeaking through the sharp turn, and the team reacting nervously to the aborigines. But he got his rig straightened out, his back prickling with the anticipation of an arrow. But instead the Sioux men walked serenely behind him as if they were driving a bull calf to market. He pretended they didn't exist and weren't shadowing him. He rested his horses periodically, watered them at seeps in that dry country back from the Missouri, poured himself some pure spirits from the jug and cut them with a niggardly dose of alkali water—which yielded an awful drink but an effective jolt.

That night he camped on a grassy flat by a spring, unharnessed and picketed the horses, built a small fire, and made tea. He didn't feel like eating, and food might numb the effect of the spirit-water, which buoyed him back toward Pierre. The Sioux stayed out of sight but he knew he could scarcely walk to the edge of the circle of light made by his innocent fire without their knowing all about it.

Nothing happened. At dawn no birds trilled, and he knew the Sioux lurked. He harnessed the nervous horses and drove them eastward again, into the sawteeth of the Missouri drainage, and fumbled his way back to Fort Pierre. Somewhere along the way the Sioux had turned off. He'd sensed it though he couldn't see it. They'd herded him back and vanished.

"Ah, *mon ami*, why is it that you've returned? As if I don't know, eh? You'd better head out the White River. Look at you, unpunctured except for a *petit* bit of flesh off the skull."

"Friendly bunch. I didn't catch their names."

"Oh, that was young Gall, *Pizi*, a Minniconjou making

a name for himself. You are lucky the *wicasa* was with him, *mon ami*."

Van Vliet wondered how the trader knew. Some sort of aboriginal telegraph, perhaps. It didn't matter. He reached for the jug. He would head out the Fort Laramie trail in the morning, back to the Badlands camp, his estranged colleagues, and the great scaffolds there.

CHAPTER
61

Professor Wood worked and grieved. He measured the titanothere as best he could. He ran his tape down the spinal column and recorded the result. He measured the powerful mandible and teeth. He surveyed the maxilla and zygomatic bone and almost brainless skull. He measured ribs and femurs and fibula and tibia. He got the circumference of a femur at the widest and narrowest points of the diaphysis, or shaft. But there were bones he didn't recognize lying everywhere, and all he could do was sketch them carefully. He lacked a proper background in comparative anatomy and would need help back east.

The others had finished and were waiting for him. Crabtree had packed his bones carefully in dried grasses and burlap bags. Miss Huxtable had long since stowed her oreodont fossils in her bright wagon, each in a bag with cushioning grass. Crowe had finished his training of the Sioux horses and now had several broken to harness and the rest broken to pack.

Miss Huxtable had scrubbed a summer's grime out of

her dresses and had mended them, and now roved the Badlands with a hatchet and stakes, marking fossil sites for the next expedition. She looked for all the world like a proper Englishwoman, except for those goggles. Mrs. Rumley had finished six books and seven uplifting Methodist pamphlets that warned against the temptations of hard drink, dancing, coffee, and cards. And Crabtree had emerged in spanking white again, even though no Gracie was washing his duds, and strolled about like a Carolina gentleman on an afternoon's lark.

They wanted to leave. Crabtree stopped at the titanothere frequently to frown at Cyrus Wood as he sketched and measured. But it was still a week shy of the mid-September date they'd set for their departure and their long trip north to Fort Union past several other fossil sites they wished to examine en route. They were scheduled to store their collections in the fur company's keelboat at the junction of the Missouri and Yellowstone no later than October 15, and arrive in St. Louis just ahead of cold weather.

A desperation had built in Wood. He couldn't take his brute with him unless Miss Huxtable came up with something, and now they wanted him to abandon his measuring and sketching too.

"How long'll it take, Cyrus? We ought to be off," Crabtree announced as he stared up at the busy professor.

Cyrus Wood wouldn't be intimidated. "As long as it takes to measure this fine fossil properly. To do a proper study. You profess to be a scientist," he added.

"We could save a week—take our time on the way to Fort Union."

Wood straightened up, relieving the ache in his back, and replied, feeling testy. "I have my duty to science and paleontology. In fact I could use your counsel. I have bones here I can't identify—especially in the feet. But I have a week and I'll take the time. As long as I lack wagons and horses, I'll do what I can—and all I can. I'm sure you understand. When I'm done sketching and measuring, I intend to cover this over to the depth of a foot. It'd be criminal to let it lie exposed.''

Crabtree smiled, the mockery visible in his resinous eyes. ''Anything to get going. I can do your distinguished work for your distinguished paper if it gets us off faster. The grass is gone; we're picketing horses a mile away. Everyone else is ready to go. And here you are. I tell you what, my distinguished colleague; I'll make you famous.''

With that he fetched his sketchpad, pen, and a stoppered bottle of India ink, settled himself above the site, and drew a dazzling, detailed overview of the entire fossil, bone by bone, carefully shaded with an engraver's skill. Then he drew the major bones one by one until they sprang from his paper as if they'd been caught by a daguerrotypist.

Then he unraveled mysteries for the Harvard professor: ''These are probably phalanges and metatarsals, but they don't resemble ours. Here's a cuboid, I suppose, and that's a navicular. This spur is really a calcaneus. They aren't so different from human feet, but shaped oddly. This beast had three toes—let's see now, if we can get some idea . . .''

Wood recorded as fast as Crabtree played with the bones, knowing that Crabtree was toying with him like a cardsharp at euchre. Wood realized that the man was simply speeding things along and enjoying his superiority as an anatomist. The papers grew until they formed an impressive sheaf, dotted with sketches and measurements. In two intensive days, Wood and Crabtree had numbered and plumbed every bone, sketched them from several angles, and even compiled a list of those probably missing from the site, washed or dragged away in some unfathomably distant past. Wood stared at the brilliantly rendered ink sketches, drawn by a man who understood bones and their functions. It amazed him. Carefully he wrapped the sketches in oilcloth and then in a leather portfolio. Having extracted all they could, they shoveled the mudstone rubble that Wood had so painfully chipped away only weeks before, and at last the fossil lay buried in its grave once again. They would leave at dawn.

That chilly night, under flinty stars, Wood trotted down the familiar path to his titanothere and climbed up on the shelf he'd gouged from rock, covered now with a foot of clay. There he tried to say good-bye to his ancient friend, and couldn't. During the hot summer days of his labor, he'd come somehow to know the creature, to feel the power of its stride, to know the terror it evoked in smaller creatures, and to grasp its own dread of packs of carnivores. This had been an old titanothere, Crabtree had told him; the sutures of its skull were firmly welded together; the fibrocartilage cushioning the joints had long gone, with wear showing. The epiphysis, or end, of the long bones showed abrasion. The old beast had lived and fought and aged and died. Wood felt a special kinship for the monster, knowing how his own bones rattled and snapped, uncushioned by the cartilage of infancy and youth.

"Well, old fellow. I'd like to see you all wired together and thundering through the Museum of Natural History. I ought to name you something, but I'm not a sentimental type. Maybe Archimedes. Archimedes the Titanothere. I'd like to show my colleagues your bones rather than sketches. I'd like them to try to lift just one rib or a vertebra, or wrestle with your femur. But it can't be. I don't suppose I'll ever get here again to disturb your sleep, but some younger chap might. I'm in your debt, you know. You challenged me and exposed my weakness, and I almost—almost didn't—'' Oddly, he found himself blinking back tears again, not of sadness but of joy. He knew what he'd achieved that summer; he knew he'd moved a mountain. He knew a miracle of faith had visited him; that he would return to brown old Harvard a better mortal than when he'd left; that in failure he'd grown. In the end, he'd been too small for the task. Crabtree had rescued him, shown him how the parts fit together, named what Wood couldn't name, determined the beast's age. Even so, even so . . . Cyrus Wood knew this summer had been precious, this moment of his life his proudest hour.

He sensed someone coming, and made out Miss Huxtable in a blue wrapper and flapping slippers, shuffling down the path. Swiftly he dabbed away the salty wetness from the baggy pouches under his eyes, and coughed ceremoniously. She saw him up there and wordlessly climbed the little ladder and settled herself beside him, as intimately as a spouse.

"I had to say good-bye too," she said. "I'll miss the blasted thing. He's a jolly beast, isn't he?"

"Miss Huxtable, it's a bit chilly, isn't it?"

"Oh, Cyrus. I'm going to call you Cyrus even if you think I'm impudent. You may call me what you will behind my back, but to my ruddy face I'm Candace. Cyrus, I've been having a bit of a chat with our good guide—and I've made him an offer. He's accepted—if you approve. I've brought the pureblood Clydesdales all the way from England because they'll fetch a price here. And the wagon. I planned to sell it in St. Louis. Instead, I've worked a bargain with Mister Crowe."

"Yes, yes, that's fine. He's a good chap."

"He'll have my wagon and Clydesdales in exchange for some work."

"Well, fair enough."

"He's agreed to return here after we've left, and dig up this beast we're sitting on, and carry it to Fort Pierre. It'll take two trips. He says his lady isn't very keen—"

"Dig this up? No, unthinkable!"

"Oh, it's all arranged. He'll dig this up and carry it to Pierre this fall and have it shipped south on the next keelboat."

"But—he doesn't know a tad. He'll leave half the bones. He'll toss them all into the wagon. He'll throw them into a boat. He's just a mountain chap married to an aborigine. No—"

"I must say, you've a peculiar way of thanking me."

"But it's unthinkable! This is my beast!"

She laughed.

"I don't know what you're cackling about. This is certainly upsetting." He supposed he'd have to express some sort of gratitude, though he didn't feel a smidgen of it. He knew it had been an awful mistake to let her tag along on this expedition. Awful! She said nothing while he stewed a while, trying to find ways to stop this madness.

"Well, I'll stop the bloody thing in its tracks if you want. Rufus Crowe's a fine amateur paleontologist. He gets a bundle of papers each spring on the riverboat. He's been shipping bones to the Smithsonian for years. He's helped me when he could, and he's as gifted as any trained scientist on a site. Why—as long as you're abandoning this thing, I'll have him ship it to me."

"But you can't! He's mine!"

She laughed, her voice a cascading melody in the darkness. "You might thank me when you get around to it, Cyrus."

"I don't know how to be so beholden," he whispered, choking back the titanothere that was his pride.

CHAPTER
62

They shadowed Van Vliet as he rattled along the Laramie road. He knew they were close even though he rarely saw them. He'd grown fatalistic about it: he could no more save his life than he could stop sucking spirits. But when he passed the pillaged burial ground on the White River, he sensed they'd finally abandoned him. Gall and his Minniconjou brothers would let him open no more graves, but would let him return to his colleagues.

He reached the Badlands seven days after leaving Fort Pierre the second time. He saw none of his colleagues, but of course he wouldn't; they'd be finishing up their digs back in the claws of mudstone somewhere. He steered the eager drays up the shadowed canyon and discovered no other wagons there. That didn't strike him as odd: they'd no doubt moved to some other little slump, using the Huxtable Clydesdales to draw both wagons. But Wood's titanothere site did seem odd. A great deal of overburden had been chopped away, leaving a bench now covered with loose clay. If Wood had gotten the beast out—which Van

Vliet doubted—there'd be little rubble and some holes where the bones had been.

Van Vliet parked the wagon in the welcome shade and hiked up the worn path to the slump, only to find silence. Not even a magpie stirred. The grass had been mowed short, and the pond had gone dry—which explained everything. He headed anxiously toward the two scaffolds, his pulse lifting as he approached them. He couldn't really see what lay above his head, but through the cracks between the poles he knew that their burden remained untouched. Intoxication flooded him, more profound than any induced by spirits.

And no one here to object! He hiked toward the campsite under the cottonwoods, finding it abandoned. But a small rock cairn commanded his attention. He found a sheet of foolscap pinioned under the top slab of rock, and extracted it.

It was a penciled note: "Van Vliet. We left this morning, September 8, for Fort Union, supposing that you have abandoned us. Wood."

"Not very friendly, Cyrus," Van Vliet said, amused. September 8 was yesterday; they were less than two days ahead. He could catch up to them if he pressed. Both wagons had vanished, which meant that somehow they'd gotten draft horses. He wondered how that had happened.

He squinted at the crags of rock towering above, wishing he knew whether the aborigines were watching him. Dark wasn't far away. He could wait. He prowled the abandoned camp looking for the hides and pelts of the animals Crowe had shot for meat, and found nothing. That disappointed him. He needed them to fool the Sioux. He had planned to heap them on the scaffolds after he'd removed the artifacts, along with sticks and a few rocks and a shirt or two out of his trunk. From a distance they'd look like the real thing.

He itched to begin, but this time prudence triumphed

over greed, and he settled patiently into the worn clay
where the tent had stood, and waited. For once not even
pure grain spirits tempted him, though it made him uneasy
that they rested out of sight in his wagon. Then, unable to
sit still while such a prize slumbered close by, he hiked
up the trail blazed by Crabtree until he'd gained the heights
above the slump and could peer down through the lavender
twilight. From that elevation he could see the scaffolds and
the artifacts heaped on them. His collection!

While he still had light he studied the neighboring cliffs
ruthlessly, looking for an observer. He saw nothing; not
even a feather poking above a crumbling mountain of
mudstone. Alone! In the last light he stumbled down Crabtree's path to the scaffolds, irritated by a band of blue still
lingering in the northwest.

He'd waited long enough. At the scaffolds he began
loosening the posts, working up a sweat as he labored. At
last he pushed a post wide, and the scaffold sagged. A few
moments later the male artifacts thumped to the ground.
Excited, he lifted a war shirt, remembering it; and grabbed
a feathered lance, hefting its finely polished shaft.

It took an hour to cart the entire contents of the two
scaffolds down to his wagon, and another hour to load
them all with loving attention to their safety. He rejoiced
in the starlight as his hands caressed one piece after another, old friends he knew by touch. Then he rode out of
the Badlands, guided by a quarter moon, eager to get as
far away as he could. He couldn't make out the wheel
tracks of the others but he knew that the path went west
along the White River. He drove deep into the night, with
the moonlit wall of the Badlands solemn and menacing on
his right. The horses picked up the Laramie road and stuck
to it. When he reached a motte of cottonwoods, shimmering silver in the soft light, he stopped. He must not abuse
his horses; not now, with a treasure snugged under the
wagon sheet. He picketed his drays on good grass and

settled into the roots of a great tree, his rifle across his lap, ready for war to the death.

The tree roots cradled him, and he settled into them, admiring the soft glow of moonlight spilling from the sagging sheet over his wagon. His riches lay there, blindingly beautiful, exotic, as rare as a cargo of spices and silk from the Indies, as exquisite as a gallery of Rembrandts. Each piece had belonged to a Sioux man or woman or child, and if Sioux legends were true, a hundred *nagi*, or spirits, prowled here, protecting their possessions.

"Ah! You've given up your possessions to the best museums! They'll be admired forever!"

They didn't answer but he knew they had been listening, all those phantasms dancing on the ether. How could they be irate? He was paying them honor. He listened closely, wanting to hear their babble, or the neighing of their war ponies, or feel the brush of their spirit flight across his arms or cheeks. But he discerned nothing and felt cheated. The evening would be magical if he could commune with all those owners. He wanted to believe all their legends. He wanted all the medicine in their bundles to be real. He wanted to be accompanied by a thousand Sioux spirits marching in a phalanx beside his wagon, guarding it with their spirit bows and spirit arrows.

The draft horses stirred restlessly, turned on the ends of their picket lines and faced something. One snorted. Van Vliet studied the pale phosphorescent flat and saw nothing. Maybe the horses had spotted the savage spirits. He peered about, feeling excluded from a Sioux universe of spirits and controllers because his roots were European. He had seen or felt nothing in the burial ground, even though the *nagi* haunted such places. No ghosts. Wearily, he slid into oblivion, enjoying the sleep of the unrighteous.

In the morning he picked up the trail of his colleagues: two wagons and numerous unshod horses. The latter made him uneasy. Was a party of Sioux escorting them to Fort Union? Some of Crowe's people? He didn't and couldn't know, so he simply followed the fresh trail. It turned out of the White River bottoms and struck northwest across a vast and lonely sea of weaving brown grasses. He imagined he was crossing an ocean. He saw no life, not even a crow, and heard only the low moan of a stiff wind as he plodded forward, the Badlands still looming on his right. Soon, he knew, he'd pass the last of the eroded escarpment and pierce into a rough plain Crowe had called Buffalo Gap. There the giant herds swept north or south between the Badlands and the Black Hills. It had always been a favorite hunting ground of the Sioux, in the very shadow of their sacred Black Hills.

Beneath him, the clear tracks of iron tires stretched ahead. He would catch up. The air seemed so transparent he thought he might see the wagon twenty miles ahead, but he saw nothing, even from a low prominence. His aloneness lay heavy on him: it was as if red men and white had declined his company, and abandoned him to wander an empty universe in eternal punishment. He wondered whether he'd died, and this snail-paced plod across an empty land might be some clever god's version of hell.

At last light he halted at a grudging seep, and found that the alkali water mixed better with pure grain spirits than the white water did. The horses hated it. He arose long before dawn, harnessed the two drays, and headed west again, guided by a retreating slice of moon. He hoped to catch them at the Cheyenne River. He knew he was gaining on them. His load would be lighter than their rock and bone. He drove that whole day across a shadow-dappled prairie, with great black anvils of cloud swinging angrily over him. But it didn't rain. A grand sense of doom built in him, as grand as this giant land he crawled over like an ant marching down a railroad track. He would live, he would die. An aborigine might believe his fate lay in a sacred bundle of claws, feathers, bone, or pebbles he suspended from his chest; some white man might imagine his fate lay in his supplications to the unseen God. But Archimedes Van Vliet never imagined his fate was governed by anything he did or said or believed.

CHAPTER
63

Crowe's adopted people called it Good River because its water ran sweet, but white trappers had long since labeled it Cheyenne. It drained much of the Black Hills, flowing northward and then east to debouch in the Missouri above Fort Pierre. Under sandy alluvial soil ran good sedimentary beds, often exposed, and of interest to paleontologists. Professor Wood determined to stop there to survey the strata and fossil-date it if they could. That suited Rufus Crowe fine; they were early, and an exploration of potential fossil sites from the Badlands to Fort Union had been planned from the beginning. Their route would take them around the northern cusp of the Black Hills, past the monolith of Bear Butte, sacred to both Cheyenne and Sioux, north to the Beautiful Fork of the Cheyenne that French trappers had called Belle Fourché, and then up the Little Missouri to the northernmost reaches of the Yellowstone.

They crossed the twenty-yard river easily on a hard bottom, the waters at a seasonal low. Even the unruly packhorses didn't fight the passage, though most of them paused midstream to lap up the sweet water. Crowe chose a campsite close to the western bluffs in good cured grass dotted with cottonwood. Vestiges of Sioux encampments remained in the area.

"It's paradise, Rufus," said Candace.

"I imagine it's an improvement on the Badlands."

"There's not a lot of exposed rock here but maybe we can date it. John Evans came through here a decade ago. Meek and Hayden did all the stratigraphy for the whole area five years ago, but there's more to be done. Professor Wood and Doctor Crabtree are going downstream. I thought I'd go up. Would you join me?"

The invitation delighted him. He had planned to hunt but would put it off until dusk, when he had a better chance. "I couldn't think of anything nicer."

And he couldn't. She might be wedded to science, but that didn't damp the love that welled up in him, or the joy he experienced in her magical presence. Now that the expedition was nearing its end he stole moments and shorted his duties just to be with her. Time ran like a herd of antelope, and he had no way to slow it. She'd soon be gone forever, and she'd forget him once she returned to bright, comfortable England. So he loved and grieved, and stole moments, and left too many camp duties to his amiable Toothache, who didn't seem to mind.

Candace wore her battered straw hat and her green goggles, and carried her shoulder bag chocked with fossil-collecting things. He could never see her eyes through those green lenses, and didn't know when she was looking at him. It put him at a disadvantage. Once in a while his gaze raked her lithe and lovely figure, and that usually brought a pursing to her lips, a faint affectionate smile. They both understood their mutual desire, and the impossibility, and the need never to talk of such things.

She could have asked anything of him and it would have

been his joy to do it. When she'd asked about hauling the titanothere to Fort Pierre, he had tried to turn down her gift of the wagon and the great Clydesdales. That equipment would make him rich among the Sioux, though wealth wasn't what he'd come west to find. He'd come west to escape into a new world. He would gladly gather the titanothere bones and haul them to Fort Pierre simply because she wanted him to.

Always, when she'd sensed the terrible yearning in him, she'd turned to science, the safe quarter of their friendship. And that's what she did now. Hunger and heat and sheer desire radiated from him and he couldn't help it. He wanted to enfold her in his arms and carry her into a bed of grass this sterling afternoon, with its playful breezes and puffball clouds scudding across a boundless heaven.

"Do you think we'll ever know?" she asked. "How old all this is? How it got here? Whether we're creatures devised in the mind of God, or the result of some endless transmutations over unimaginable eons, wrought by nature itself?"

"Or both. I imagine someone making a universe is in no hurry—at least by our notions of time."

She smiled. "I won't know in my lifetime. Neither will you. I wish we could meet here—right here—a hundred years from now. Maybe we'd know . . . It'd be fun to see you in a hundred years, Rufus."

"Miss Huxtable—every day you're away will be a hundred years for me."

"Please, Rufus."

He watched while she studied sandstone strata, poking occasionally with the pick end of her hammer, seeing things he hadn't been trained to see.

"Miss Huxtable. Pretty soon you're going back to England. Clear across an ocean. You're going to settle down in Cambridge and pick bones and forget about me. I'm hoping you'll write—I'd like to keep in touch."

She paused and lifted her green goggles to her forehead. Her gaze lay upon him, unblinking. "Rufus, I won't forget. I'll write you if you have an address. I'll write each winter, and my letter will come up on the riverboat in the spring. And I'll look for yours. I want you to send me fossils. I'll want to know exactly how you're doing. And how these people—your Sioux—are surviving. I fear for them."

"I'd like that," he said, feeling suddenly miserable. "I'll write. I love you."

"Rufus," she replied softly. "Please don't."

They walked back in silence, both of them withdrawn. He hurt. His amateur science had been a bridge to her, but that had been the only bridge. When she boarded the keelboat at Fort Union it would be like a funeral for him, a funeral of love for a woman he could never possess. He fought back the desolation that threatened to engulf him.

They reached camp when the sun lay flat in the west, its rays illumining the sheets of three wagons. They stared, unwilling to believe the testimony of their eyes. But there it was—the other Murphy wagon. And standing beside it was Archimedes Van Vliet in animated conversation with Wood and Crabtree.

"It's him! The man's found us! Oh, blast!"

Dread filled Crowe. For weeks the absence of Van Vliet had been a blessing. They had all been safer in his absence. They'd worked in peace for weeks, without the stern visits of outraged Sioux to remind them that they were in this country on sufferance.

"Ah, Crowe, I found you."

Crowe nodded. "You have the other wagon."

"I must say I was puzzled about your horses. Ponies for Gracie! Now there's a good yarn to spread around Brooklyn. You must have thought I'd abandoned you."

Crowe nodded.

"Well, my friend, I didn't. And your worst nightmares

have come true. I have the whole collection in there. Every last item off the scaffolds. Professor Wood here thinks I ought to abandon it for the good of the party. But I won't, you know. You can deal with the red devils, Crowe.''

''I don't really think I can, Doctor Van Vliet. I can't spare your lives now.''

CHAPTER
64

Professor Wood knew it would be up to him. He commanded this expedition and his word would be final. The guide's chill warning had shot terror through him. But perhaps Crowe had exaggerated. Crowe's loyalties lay, after all, with his adopted people.

Wood clambered into the Murphy wagon to see for himself. The artifacts had been carefully bundled in Van Vliet's tent canvas, except for lances, war clubs, axes, and shields, which had been bound and tied. Some large parfleches lined the sides of the wagon. He backed out, uncertain about what to do.

"Doctor Crabtree, have you an opinion?"

"Risk is amusing."

"That is not helpful."

"I've got my loot and Van Vliet has his. The Sioux haven't liked it, but neither have they scalped and killed him."

"Oh, they've done both," said Van Vliet cheerfully.

"I wonder about that," said Crowe.

"Mister Crowe, Doctor Van Vliet has traveled for some two thousand miles to engage in research. He's accumulated priceless artifacts that will tell ethnologists a great deal about the lives of these nomadic aborigines. They've been perfectly courteous about it, though of course they don't approve of his methods of collecting. I must say, given your status in the tribe, your ability to smooth things over—"

"I can't guarantee a thing. I'd like to leave these items on scaffolds right here—before the trouble comes."

"I think I'm going to overrule you, Mister Crowe. We'll proceed. If we do run into trouble, I'll ask that you negotiate. If Doctor Van Vliet has to surrender them, we will, of course. But I see no reason to abandon priceless material, not after such a long trip to collect these very things."

"You're jeopardizing lives, Professor Wood."

"Oh, forget it," said Van Vliet. "Unless you plan to take my collection from me by force, I'm keeping it."

"He feels deeply about it, Mister Crowe."

"I imagine the Sioux do too. Doctor Van Vliet, you've been away from us for some little while. I'd like to hear about your adventures."

"Oh, I was scalped and buried, and went to Fort Pierre for supplies."

"I imagine that's more accurate than these folks know. I know what *I* know." He turned to Wood. "I know your colleague has barely escaped with his life. The Sioux are a people that see outsiders as enemies. Even me, if I seem to be helping their enemies. They don't sit down and negotiate when they're mad; they come at you. I'm saying now, get those possessions up on scaffolds or it'll be too late."

"Please do!" said Miss Huxtable.

Wood punished her with a small frown. "Mister Crowe, we have no need for melodramatics. The aborigines know we're scientists peacefully adding to the world of knowl-edge. I am forced to direct you to carry on.''

He hated to seem so overbearing, so nasty and unaca-demic. But all Crowe had to do, if the Sioux objected, was tell them Van Vliet would comply.

''Is that your considered decision, sir?''

''It is. Carry on.''

''I'm afraid I must resign, sir.''

''Resign? You've contracted to guide us. You can't sim-ply leave us here, unable to find our way out or talk to the aborigines. No, I forbid it. In the most unequivocal terms, I must say, sir.''

''If you want me to guide, put the artifacts up on scaf-folds.''

''We won't abide a broken contract, Mister Crowe. You'll not abandon us here. We'll do what we must.''

A great indignation built up in Wood. Oh, the unrelia-bility of servants!

''Rufus, will you abandon me? Us?'' asked the British woman.

''Miss Huxtable,'' he muttered, and seemed to want to say more. A great sadness infiltrated his face. He peered at her solemnly, and at her bright wagon, and at the sky. ''You're not part of this expedition. Perhaps you should turn around and head for Fort Pierre.''

''No. We'll stay together.''

A great change seemed to flow through the guide, so great it puzzled Wood. ''Very well, Miss Huxtable. I'll share your fate. If you weren't here, I'd resign from the service of these gentlemen. I imagine we'll all be resign-ing from our situations, and plumb soon.''

''Oh, blast, you're making me the guilty party.''

The guide said nothing, simply staring softly at her, like a tradesman before a queen. It seemed perfectly obvious to Wood: the rustic had become infatuated with the woman.

She ignored him and turned away, the corners of her mouth drawn down. Crowe turned to Toothache and began some long and earnest discourse in her aboriginal tongue. The squaw glanced sharply at Van Vliet, and reached out to touch Crowe's cheek.

Van Vliet drank heavily that night from a jug he'd acquired somewhere, probably at a trading post. The wagon full of contraband sagged heavily beside him, dark as a curse. Wood felt that something ineffable had happened in camp. Darkness loomed not just out beyond the fire, but within the circle. Miss Huxtable withdrew into her tent.

But nothing happened. The dawn broke sweetly, with the raucous cries of magpies shattering the peace. No terrible horde of savages appeared. Wood had spent a restless night, his doubts crowding him. But in the morning he set them aside, feeling that he'd made the best decision he could.

They drove northwest along a fork of the Cheyenne that Crowe called the Rapid, the blue bulk of the Black Hills looming ever larger. They traversed broken plains but saw no one. Van Vliet, always the expert, said that they were leaving the customary grounds of the Brulés and entering country claimed by the Oglala, great friends of the traders and soldiers at Fort Laramie. They could relax soon. But Wood doubted that any Sioux were great friends of the whites now that General Harney had cut his swath through them.

They camped in a barren bottom close to the layered hills off to the west. Crowe's woman rode off some way, and returned with a heap of sticks for the fires bundled over the rump of her pony. An eerie tension pervaded the camp, and only Van Vliet seemed cheerful. They found little exposed rock to study, and gave up fossil-hunting at dusk. Miss Huxtable didn't venture out at all, but clung close to the camp, looking pale and distraught. Wood wondered again what lay between her and the guide. Sentimentality, he supposed.

That evening Van Vliet brought his bedroll into the common tent as he had the night before, but this night Crabtree had a coal-oil lantern flaming while he wrote an entry in his journal. Van Vliet undid his boots and tossed his slouch hat to the earth.

"Well," exclaimed Crabtree, "you weren't joking."

Wood peered up from his blankets and found Crabtree staring at something, something about Van Vliet that drew his gaze.

"A warrior got me. It's about three inches, and it still hurts. But the flesh around the edge has ridged up and healed. You know of some cure?"

Wood twisted until he could get a look, and found himself staring at a bluish circle of living bone on the back of Van Vliet's head. Scalped! Horrified, the professor studied the wound, his mind crawling with questions.

Crabtree plucked up the lantern and examined the naked bone carefully. "It won't grow over, you know. You'll have a headache the rest of your life. It'll get dry as the Sahara. You'll have to keep your fingers out of it."

"Is there some salve or something?"

"I've no idea. Scalpings are outside of my experience. You might keep lard or butter on it so it doesn't dry out. I might be able to draw the edges together with silk thread and see if it closes a little. And a hat—always a hat. Keep the weather off."

"I've my scalp. Could you sew it on?" Van Vliet tossed a curled brown thing at the doctor, who caught it and examined it.

"It's, ah, rather well cured, I'd say. Hard as rock. Good for shoe leather, maybe. No, Van Vliet. Maybe we can devise a soft doeskin skullcap and suture it down." He smiled, malevolently. "I don't suppose this has anything to do with robbing burial scaffolds."

"Oh, I suppose. I was minding my business when some chaps showed up and objected. They performed their surgery and sewed me in and buried me on some old boy's scaffold, using about three buffaloes' worth of rawhide thong—but I wriggled out. A thunderstorm saved me. Water from Wakan Tanka to loosen bindings and fill my mouth. It's too bad it didn't rain whiskey—I had a mean thirst. Sioux gods must not like Sioux warriors. Wait until they see me alive. The whole Lakota nation'll turn tail and run."

"Out of professional curiosity, what did they use?"

"Just a belt knife."

"Very professional, Van Vliet. Too bad they didn't trephine you. Your overstuffed head needs a drain. I've a saw in my surgery. We can release enough spirits to run a lantern."

"I couldn't do a thing, not with those mean-eyed devils pointing arrows at my tender middle. I told them to stop the heathen nonsense—that I was honoring the old grandfathers, snatching their stuff for posterity. But their aboriginal minds didn't grasp my thoughts. Anything for science, eh, Doc?"

The unalterable decision of expedition leader Cyrus Billington Wood was suddenly unfixed. He ran an aged hand tenderly over his virgin skull. "Doctor Van Vliet," he snapped. "At the first opportunity tomorrow, we're going to put your collection on a scaffold. For the safety of us all. I didn't know of this, and you didn't tell us. It changes everything."

"Oh, now, Wood," said Crabtree, "you haven't enough hair on the back of your noggin to make a decent scalp."

CHAPTER
65

Coping with all of Crabtree's packhorses and improvised packsaddles, as well as Crabtree's half-trained draft horses, had become formidable work that consumed Rufus Crowe's mornings and evenings. Miss Huxtable had usually harnessed, unharnessed, watered and picketed her own, but the rest of the horses had been left in his charge. The horse care, along with the guiding and hunting, had become burdensome. But this morning he felt far more burdened by his sense of doom. He would try to save Miss Huxtable; he doubted he could do anything for the rest.

In the nippy dawn he slid cold bits into the mouths of the reluctant drays while Miss Huxtable did the same. She was having her usual struggle with one of the Clydesdales, which refused the bit and bobbed its head around while she muttered polite imprecations. He had often thought to help her, but something always stayed the impulse.

It surprised him to discover Professor Wood up and dressed and trudging toward him through dew-laden shortgrass.

"A private word, if I may, Mister Crowe," he said, eyeing Candace.

"It's an awkward moment, sir."

"It can't wait."

Sighing, Crowe buckled the halter on the dray he was bridling, and picketed it once again. Candace watched silently, but asked no questions. Wood tugged at Crowe's sleeve, leading him out of earshot.

"I say, Crowe, I learned some things last night that give me alarm. Doctor Van Vliet was ritually scalped and bundled onto a burial scaffold while he was collecting back there. I've known the aborigines are quite testy about it, but I didn't realize it'd gone to such lengths."

Crowe listened solemnly to what Wood had learned about Van Vliet's tribulations.

"I imagine there's a lot more you don't know. We're always under scrutiny, you know. We're hostile strangers in the heart of their country. How did he spend all that time—did he say?"

"He's been to Fort Pierre and stayed quite a while. I know that."

"Picotte would have warned him. I'm sure of it."

"Well, you know the savages and I don't. What'll they do? Will they hold us all guilty? Does Doctor Van Vliet's collecting threaten us? I must know at once!"

Rufus Crowe wished he knew the answer to that. His Teton Sioux were a loose federation of council fires, and each band had its own autonomous chief and Shirt Wearers, or governing council.

"I imagine each band'll think differently."

"That's no help at all. What would be prudent? Let me put it that way."

"I think you know."

"Of course I know. But I'm outvoted. Of the three principals, I'm the only one—"

"You're the leader."

"Of course, of course, but we follow republican forms and I can't just overrule—"

"This isn't the academy, and we're not in civilization, Professor. Your life, Miss Huxtable's life, the lives of the rest . . ."

"You think they'd massacre us all even if we're not all guilty, then."

"You've got to understand that for the Lakota, other people are the enemies. Anyone who's not one of the People's an enemy, even if he's temporarily a friend or ally. I'm even an enemy of a sort. These things hinge on their feeling. They're calm and collected most always—except when they're berserk. Blood pounds in 'em and words don't reach 'em."

"It's coming to that?"

"I don't know. All it takes is one strong medicine man with an itch. We're fooling with bad things here—the bones of monsters they dread. Evil monsters Wakan Tanka drove into the earth. It's not just Van Vliet. I'd say Van Vliet's just a lightning rod drawing sparks."

"We're doomed—unless you can talk the Sioux out of it."

"Professor, when they've got their blood up, I look wrong to them. I got the wrong face and flesh. Like you. If I was among 'em with my woman, I'd be all right. But not here, guiding you. I'd be the first they'd go after."

"Why didn't you tell us?"

A disgust ran through Crowe, and he didn't think the question was worth answering.

"I can't persuade Van Vliet," Wood muttered. "He'll resist, and Crabtree'll side with him. Have you any suggestions?"

"Divide up."

"We couldn't do that! I'm responsible—"

But Crowe didn't listen. He walked back to the horses

and began bridling them again. Wood stood still, looking affronted.

"May I ask what that was about?" Candace asked. She held the reins of the bridled Clydesdales.

"It seems Doctor Van Vliet's been in trouble. He's been ritually scalped and buried."

"Oh! That's awful! Are we in trouble?"

Her gaze riveted him, and he loved her inexpressibly. "Miss Huxtable—Candace—I want you to do something and trust in me. I want you to turn your outfit around and go back the way you came. Back past the Badlands to the Fort Pierre road. I want you to go *now*. It's dangerous, I'll say that. But not as dangerous as staying here with us. Do it!"

"You're serious," she said. "Oh, blast."

"Do it. Believe me, you must. Now!"

"What will happen here?"

"I don't know."

"What will happen to you?"

"I don't know that either."

"And Professor Wood? And Doctor Crabtree?"

Crowe shrugged. "You rile up the Sioux and it's not in their ways to be particular. We all look alike to them."

"But surely they know we're not robbing graves."

"We're digging up bones of ancient beasts that were condemned by Wakan Tanka."

"I see." She looked drawn, her face pinched. "I don't know what to do."

"Go! Now! They'll find you, but you're women. They won't harm you and Missus Rumley."

"Van Vliet won't abandon his—collection?"

"No, and it's probably too late anyway."

"You make it sound—deadly."

He ached to see her turn around and flee while she could, but he knew he could only urge so much before he irritated her.

"Blast!"

He turned to his harnessing, throwing a collar over an Indian pony broken to harness, but his mind slid ahead to the time when their course would take them close to Bear Butte, Mato Paha to the Sioux: the sacred mountain of the Cheyenne and Sioux alike. His route would take them to Bear Butte Creek and beyond, to the Belle Fourché. Close to that brooding monolith where the gods lived. Close to the most sacred place of the Cheyenne, the Sioux, and the Arapaho too, eerie and foreboding and beautiful and mysterious. He wondered if the ethnologist, Van Vliet, had any inkling of what lay ahead.

CHAPTER
66

Everything Professor Wood had learned from Crowe goaded him to act while he could. He approached the tent where Van Vliet and Crabtree were stirring.

"Doctor Van Vliet, I've been consulting with Mister Crowe. I'm afraid I must direct that you leave the artifacts here. They're imperiling our lives."

Van Vliet grinned as he laced a boot. "Throw out my summer's work, eh? I'll do it if you and Crabtree and the British biddy toss out your fossils and notes and journals too."

"That's not a professional response, Doctor Van Vliet."

"No, but it's amusing."

"You worry too much, Wood," said Crabtree.

"Our guide informs me that the aborigines don't make distinctions between individuals in a party of alien people. If one alien is guilty of some infraction, the whole group is. They have strong racial feelings."

"He's right, old boy. We're all guilty as sin."

Van Vliet was toying with him.

Wood drew himself up. His tone had to convey proper authority. "Doctor Van Vliet, I am going to direct our guide to drive the wagon with your collection in it to the top of that mound, there. It'll be visible for miles—a beacon in fact. I'll have him remove your personal things, and we'll leave the rest, wagon and all. I gather that the Sioux prefer to bury on a hilltop site, and the wagon will do nicely as a scaffold. The message to the aborigines will be clear—and we'll be safe. I'm sorry."

"Oh, now, Wood, don't be an old fogey," said Crabtree. "If there's trouble, we'll surrender the loot—and if not, we'll proceed. If there's trouble I've got a lot of ponies to trade—buy our way out. And Van Vliet's still got a trunk full of trade gewgaws."

"I am thinking about the women in our midst."

Crabtree laughed cynically. "So am I."

"Look, old boy," said Van Vliet. "You're voted down, two to one. And secondly, I still have some collecting to do. I'll need that wagon and some packhorses. Just ahead is the sacred mountain of the Sioux, Bear Butte. It's an old volcanic laccolith north of the Black Hills. Sort of a Mount Olympus to them. All sorts of spirits live there. There's a medicine path to the summit. It'll be lined with hundreds of priceless medicine bundles and prayer shawls and totems—the best stuff yet, from the standpoint of my discipline. There's good stuff up there, old boy. I'll learn more about their religion than anyone alive."

A cold dread slid through Wood. "Good lord in heaven. Surely you're not going to rob their church too."

"Oh, you're a born fussbudget. Look, Wood, you're a Harvard don. You've hardly been out of Boston. The world's not such a bad place, you know. I know something about aborigines. I've an advanced degree in the field. I'm telling you, they accept payment for grievances. A few of Crabtree's ponies change hands and the whole lot'll be smiling and clapping our backs and sitting down for a smoke.''

Wood pondered matters. ''We have an irreconcilable division. I suppose we could divide up. You two go ahead to Fort Union in one wagon. I'll take the other and head east to Fort Pierre and wait for the boat. You'll have Crabtree's spare packhorses for your collecting. The guide and Miss Huxtable can do as they choose.''

''Sorry, old boy, I'm keeping my wagon.''

''It's not yours—it's the expedition's wagon, Doctor Van Vliet.''

''It's mine now, old boy.''

Mutiny among scholars! It astounded Cyrus Wood. He'd barely heard of such a thing. Crabtree smiled malevolently. Van Vliet looked innocent, his gaze obscure and cheery.

Professor Wood knew he had no means to enforce his edict. Being the leader of the expedition meant nothing without the consent of the others. He sighed, defeated. They were right: a life in the warrens of cold buildings on the Charles River hadn't equipped him for any of this.

''Very well, then,'' he said sadly.

He made his resolute way back to the horses and Rufus Crowe and Miss Huxtable, his mind forming sentences and sentiments. She had her horses harnessed and hitched. He was buckling harness on one of the expedition drays.

''Mister Crowe, I shall be going on with the others.'' He paused, waiting for the objection, but none came. ''One thing I've resolved to do is release you from service, with of course no prejudice. You've done a fine job; quite a splendid help always.''

''I'm afraid I'm confused, sir.''

''For your own safety, I'm releasing you. I can't ask you to proceed. We'll manage to find our way to Fort Union from maps. And hunt a little. Both of my colleagues are quite the experts, you know.''

Crowe stopped harnessing and stood, waiting for more.

"I can't say that I came well equipped to command the expedition—surely you'll understand that one doesn't acquire a habit of command in the groves of academe." He smiled deprecatingly. "And I must say, I've made things a bit tricky—for both of you. My apologies. In my defense I'll say I did what seemed best."

"I'm getting more confused by the minute, Professor."

Wood smiled softly. "I've been usurped. My authority, you know. They won't ditch the collection that endangers us. And they wouldn't hear of dividing up. I proposed to take a wagon and go to Fort Pierre, but they'd have none of it. I meant to include you—and your party, Miss Huxtable. It seemed safest. But of course they told me I'm imagining dangers that don't really exist."

"You have no need to apologize, Professor," said Miss Huxtable.

"Why, I'm touched, Miss. But I'll go with them now and urge you to get away, flee to safety. I—I don't suppose I'll ever see Boston again. My bones'll bleach on these Western prairies somewhere near here. But, you know, it's not such a great tragedy. I discovered here that it isn't digging up monsters that wins respect, it's what one makes of it. The meaning one extracts from it. Theoretical paleontology is what counts. Figuring out the pedigrees, how the beast lived, what its enemies were, what killed it, where it fits in the chain of life—you know. Things beyond the addled mind of an elderly taxonomist."

They said nothing, each listening to him intently. He enjoyed that. For the smallest moment he felt as if he were back in a lecture hall.

"But this was all worthwhile, you know. If my fate looks dark, don't cry for me. I've a duty now, and not one I regret. I'll go with the chaps and we'll see what happens. They'll visit Bear Butte ahead. Our friend Doctor Van Vliet fairly seethes with eagerness." He smiled gently at them both. "You go now, sir. And don't weep for a happy old drudge."

"Doctor Van Vliet's going to visit the sacred mountain?"

"Oh yes. He plans to stuff his wagon with it all."

"That's like cleaning out a cathedral. Like tearing away icons and crosses and images of saints and the Virgin."

"It's all for ethnology, you know. The sum of knowledge grows so swiftly in these times." He smiled. "At least that's what our Doctor Van Vliet says."

Crowe peered into the glowing eastern skies, as if hunting for something in them. "I've got a duty too, sir. I have to go and keep them from it—with your permission. I'll need to resort to certain measures."

"No, no, you're under no obligation, Mister Crowe."

"Not to you, sir."

"Well, to your Sioux friends, then. I can't stop you. I've learned in the past few hours that I cannot command the tides."

A long, awkward pause ensued.

"Miss Huxtable," the guide said, "I want you to leave now. I think you'll make it—maybe with a few scrapes along the way. You're no threat to them, and they'll admire your courage."

She smiled and slid her goggles over her eyes. "I'll bring up the rear—as usual," she said.

CHAPTER
67

Rapid Creek drove like an arrow into the heart of the Black Hills. The guide took them up it, and each hour the dark mass of the hills loomed higher and more forbidding, the ponderosa pines on its slopes giving it a gloomy aspect.

But it was Paradise for the Sioux, and Candace knew that her party was knocking on the gates of heaven. She rode grimly and so did Wood. Only Van Vliet and Crabtree, who shared a wagon seat, seemed to be enjoying themselves.

For the Sioux the great uplift, rising three or four thousand feet about the Plains, had become a refuge and fortress. They called it Paha Sapa, Hills of Black. Around the great oval, stretching a hundred twenty miles north and south, stood a ridge, or hogback, composed of sandstone and limestone lifted from the level of the prairies by the batholith within. There, a vast distance from the Rockies to the west, rose an upland teeming with game and water and wood. The Sioux wintered around its feet on timbered and sheltered creeks. But they rarely ventured into the sacred uplands, and then mostly for religious ceremonies. For them the place bristled with the *wakan* of thunder and lightning, and frightful mystery.

As the party approached the eastern wall, Candace found herself feeling things that transcended her senses. Something mysterious and solemn radiated from the mountains, something that whispered to her of holiness. She wondered if all the gods and spirits that crowded this place would permit them passage, or whether each rotation of the iron tires was turning them all toward their doom. Whatever her fate, she felt as helpless as a baby, unable to turn back, afraid to ride ahead, the tension within her tying her into knots.

Her fate rested in the hands of others. She surveyed in her mind each of those with whom she rode: the deceptively bland guide with his shrewd untutored mind; Wood, a man discovering himself here, an iron puritan who kept growing upon her; Van Vliet, the root of the terror that lay within her, out of control; and Crabtree, the bright sardonic cynic, almost as fatalistic and reckless as Van Vliet.

Odd, she thought, that she had never wondered about the character of those who would form the expedition. It had never occurred to her in safe Cambridge. But here she was, where the weaknesses she'd never bothered to investigate could kill her.

Late that day Crowe turned his pony in beside her as she drove. "I'm wondering how you're bearing it," he said.

"Have I a choice?"

"I'm thinking they might let us pass—if we just keep on going and don't stop anywhere"—he emphasized the *anywhere*—"to be picking up stuff. They might be glad to get shut of us."

"Perhaps they've lost us, Mister Crowe. We haven't seen a one."

He laughed shortly. "I assure you—they're watching every move we make. I see what you don't."

"Such as?"

"Oh, thin columns of smoke at dawn before the wind whips up. Movement on ridges. Signs along the trail—this is an old travois trail, you know, right smack dab in the belly of the Lakota country. Pebble on a log back there. Broken arrow."

That chilled her. "You mean they're all about us, unseen?"

"Oh, I see 'em."

"What do you make of it, Mister Crowe?"

"If they see me hustling you out, fast as we can get, I think we may have safe passage."

"Oh, I hope!"

He eyed her with regret in his face. "Tomorrow we'll be at the feet of Bear Butte. I'll need to keep us going, never stop. We'll push across Bear Butte Creek—a tricky ford—and strike for the Belle Fourché, and maybe we'll make it."

"It comes to that?"

"It does."

"What'll you do if they want to explore the sacred mountain?"

"It takes some doing to hold a firearm on my employers."

"What'll happen if you can't?"

Something private slid over his face. "I guess we'll have to see, won't we?"

He started to ride ahead.

"Mister Crowe?"

He waited for her to draw up.

"How can I help?"

"It's not a woman's task."

"Oh, blast! If my life's in danger it's my task!"

"I imagine you'll think of something. Just don't let Van Vliet near you."

"Why not?"

"He and Doctor Crabtree understand my weaknesses." He didn't wait for her response, but urged his pony toward the head of the column again.

They rattled through a day of eerie quiet, except for the cawing of excited crows. The whole country had become surpassingly beautiful as it lay beneath a clean blue sky, the dry grasses hip-high in places and golden, swaying in the soft September zephyrs. Rapid Creek had swung north, and now they rode with heaven on the left and hell on the right—and the stark purple cone of Bear Butte dead ahead. She saw it first from a rise, and then it disappeared, only to spring upon her suddenly an hour later, larger and more beautiful but still twenty miles off.

Ahead of her Van Vliet and Crabtree had engaged in animated conversation, their exultation conveyed by their babble. She wished desperately she could persuade them of their folly, drive off their horses, spike their wheels—anything.

Rufus Crowe took them up a long swale that led to a low hump of prairie and down a gentle grade to another creek that laced between banks wooded with bur oak, green ash, and box elder, as well as willow and cottonwoods in great profusion. This was Elk Creek, he told them, a favorite resort of the Sioux. Indeed, signs of encampment could be found everywhere, especially hacked limbs and well-grazed grasses. They followed its south bluff the whole afternoon, drawing ever closer to the brooding Bear Butte, and didn't stop until dusk.

"I wish to call a meeting," Crowe announced, after they'd stopped the wagons and picketed the horses. "Now, before supper."

He waited patiently for them all. Van Vliet and Crabtree

seemed to be in no hurry, and Candace knew their delays were deliberate.

"We're alive," said Crowe. "That's more than I expected. We're being watched—every step of the way—by Brulés and Oglala and maybe others. Minniconjou, Hunkpapa, Sans Arcs. The whole Lakota nation. Missus Crowe and I've seen signs of it. And messages from our friends. I think we have passage through to Fort Union if we keep going. They're glad to be shut of us. Tomorrow we'll drive past their church. Mato Paha. Bear Butte. Call it their Mount Olympus or their St. Peter's—it's a sacred place for the Lakota, and even more for the Cheyenne. I'm going to ask you for your own sakes not to stop. If you stop, I can guarantee you one thing: you'll never get going again."

"We'll take your learned opinion under consideration, Mister Crowe," said Crabtree. "Doctor Van Vliet, here, has already been scalped, and he says it's an exhilarating experience, something to tell his grandchildren about."

"We've a trunkload of traders' toys, old boy. Give them hand mirrors and they'll preen," said Van Vliet. Candace noticed he was drinking again.

"Mister Crowe, there's a bit of scientific history of which you're no doubt well aware," said Crabtree. "A few years ago Doctor Ferdinand V. Hayden climbed Bear Butte. He was the first white man to do so. He wandered through here for months, collecting fossils, quite unmolested. He's very much alive, and on the Raynolds Expedition this very hour, collecting fossils as always. Oh, it's true the Warren Expedition had a little trouble two years ago—it wasn't long after Harney'd whipped the Brulés. Chief Bear's Rib himself saw to their safety."

"I don't recollect that the Warren Expedition was collecting the property of the *nagi*," Crowe muttered.

"Sorry, old boy. By tomorrow night my wagon'll contain more *wakan* medicine than any ten bands of Sioux could divide among 'em. Crowe, by tomorrow night if any Sioux looks at my wagon too long, he'll be turned into a pillar of salt.''

Professor Wood listened solemnly, his leadership usurped.

Candace saw at once how the meeting was going. The guide broke off without further comment, and walked out into an indigo twilight looking grim. The matter had gone beyond words.

CHAPTER
68

Bear Butte mesmerized Archimedes Van Vliet. It loomed higher and higher as they toiled northwest, fording several branches of Bear Butte Creek. It stood isolated from the Black Hills, an upwelling of ancient magma shaped like an inverted teacup, with a ragged dike of dark igneous rock projecting off to the east. It erupted out of the prairie, leaving only a few pockets of pine around its base. Its slate-gray middle heights lacked any vegetation, and were composed of smooth talus. A cap of scraggly pines topped the laccolith.

He thought that was all there was to see, but as the somber mountain grew through the afternoon, he discovered an amazing additional feature: a pair of giant claws stretching down the south facade, turning the butte into a headless Sphinx. These sent a thrill of delight through him: ah, what the aboriginal imagination could do with that! The holy trail to the top, he knew, wound along that eastern slope, hemmed in by the ragged dike. Ah, it was going to be fun!

Crabtree sat beside him, having turned his wagon over to old Wood, who seemed unusually eager to drive it—no doubt to steer it as far from Mato Paha as the guide directed. It seemed an unusually solemn party crawling across the toes of the gods this sunny day. Miss Huxtable had refused even to say good morning, and had glared at the pair of them. Crowe had slid into a wary alertness, his gaze never straying far from the Murphy wagon carrying Van Vliet's contraband. His squaw had ridden ahead, unwilling even to be close to the pair of them.

Crabtree observed it all with vast amusement, puffing on one Havana after another as he rocked on the seat in his white finery and planter's hat.

"Do you suppose Crowe's right—about being watched?" the doctor asked.

"No doubt about it. We're crawling through their bowels."

"What do you think of his notion that they'll let us through if we keep going?"

Van Vliet shrugged. "Probably true."

"He looks ready to point that Sharps in our direction." The doctor puffed cheerfully.

"Well, we'll be a pair of angels, won't we?"

They both laughed.

"You'll be wheezing before you reach the top, Van Vliet. I'll make it even if you don't. I intend to tell the rector in Charleston that I sat directly upon a dozen heathen gods. For once he'll approve of me."

"I don't care about the summit. Just help me with the medicine bundles and totems. Some are large—an armload."

"I might offend a spirit, Van Vliet; I could never do that."

Van Vliet knew *he* could. He'd offended a thousand and had lost only three inches of scalp for it. "Crab, it's the Cheyenne you'd have to worry about. This is where Sweet

Medicine received the Four Sacred Arrows. This is their place. The Sioux—their legends don't really incorporate Bear Butte very much, even if Crowe seems to think they do.''

"Are you bolstering your nerve or do you really know something that Crowe doesn't?'' Crabtree was studying him with those mocking, resinous eyes.

"Bolstering my nerve.''

They chuckled.

Twilight caught them southeast of Bear Butte. Crowe made camp on a nameless branch that curled around the south facade of the sacred mountain. His pinched gaze followed Van Vliet and Crabtree as they unharnessed their wagon and picketed the drays. A preternatural quiet lay over the whole outfit that evening as they all went about their tasks. The angry mountain blotted out the northern sky, but the night seemed serene.

A gibbous moon catapulted out of the east, shedding melancholy light upon the slumbering prairies. Crabtree erected their tent and Van Vliet made a noisy ceremony of his evening toilet. Not a word had been uttered; supper that night consisted of cold slices of venison wolfed down in bleak haste. Crowe's suspicion lay like a blanket over them, and Candace Huxtable's disapproval stabbed like icicles. As for old Wood, who could tell what whirled behind his mask?

Around midnight Crabtree poked him. Van Vliet laced his boots swiftly and the pair slid into the whitewashed night. It all turned out to be easier than they had imagined. They threw halters, blankets, and packsaddles onto two of Crabtree's calmest ponies and led them north toward the sacred mountain. No one awakened. They'd feared Crowe most of all, but the guide hadn't stirred.

They led the ponies up a gentle grassy slope and found a footpath in the dim light. It took them into a little gulch with water trickling down it, and up onto an eerie flat that lay as quiet and mysterious as a lost continent. Black rock beetled over them, compressing their world as they walked. They plunged into ponderosa forest, dappled with stern light from the cold moon. If they pushed a thousand spirits before them, neither sensed it.

"As long as we're crashing the party, you'd better introduce me to our hosts," said Crabtree. His low voice seemed unusually loud.

"It's a big party and we won't meet them all," Van Vliet said.

"Well, I'll settle for some divine beauty."

"That'd be White Buffalo Maiden, the Beautiful One, who is really the Goddess Whope visiting the earth. She came to instruct the Lakota in their religion, in the homage they pay to the Great Mystery, Wakan Tanka. She gave them their seven sacred rites, and instructed them in the care and protection of their women. She's the protector of chastity."

"Try another," muttered Crabtree.

Van Vliet stopped to catch his breath. His pony began to graze. He studied the web of dark limbs closely, hunting for dangling medicine bundles, amulets, anything. But he saw only boughs. Where were all the supplications to the controllers and the gods?

Crabtree stopped beside him. "Who else'll I meet up there?"

"Oh, let's see, the superior gods—Inyan the Rock, Maka the Earth, Skan the Sky, and Wi the Sun." He felt uneasy describing all this to Crabtree because it sounded like sacrilege. "There's some mean ones up there. Iktomi the Trickster, Waziya the Old Man, Wakanaka the Witch, his wife; and Anog-Ite, Double-faced Woman. That's all I'm going to tell you. Just don't dance with Anog-Ite. I've got to hunt for the goods around here. Leave your pony; I may want it."

"Do the aborigines really believe these spirits are up there? Is it Mount Olympus?"

"No, I don't suppose. It's a place where a Sioux can climb up and plead with them, or give thanks. The spirits live in some stupendous, mysterious universe filled with terrible forces such as thunder and lightning."

The doctor, his white clothes radiating eerie light, began padding upward and rounded a bend. Suddenly Van Vliet stood alone, with only the light of a flirtatious moon for a friend. A small cloud slid across it, leaving him blinded by blackness for a moment.

Van Vliet untied one of the ponies and walked upslope, pausing every little way to hunt for artifacts. Now and then he emerged from the trees onto a barren place, the talus naked and dark. But he found nothing. Perplexed, he pushed higher, climbing a natural stair, his pony restless behind him. From some points he could peer up the wall of rock to the stars beyond, some infinite distance away.

He hunted along the trail, poking under dark trees, hastening over barren spots, but saw no gifts or offerings of any sort. For some reason he couldn't fathom, it pleased him, and he realized that he didn't really want to steal these things. His own scruples surprised him. He'd come here charged with lust to possess; now he stood here drained of it and content with what he had. The contentment seemed a novelty.

What was this strange holy mountain doing to him? He drew the pony to him and stroked its neck under its mane. The pony lowered its head and butted him gently. He wondered if he could live the rest of his life in this sort of liberty. He couldn't remember when he'd been free of the need for a drink. He could barely imagine not lusting for glory, for fame, for everything his heart demanded. It might be a lovely world and a lovely life. Maybe the sacred mountain would release him from his Babylonian captivity.

He found an overlook and settled to the rock there, watching small clouds tag the white moon. A peace such as he'd never known stole through him. He wondered if Lakota spirits were toying with him, and decided that they weren't. They'd be tormenting him, not freeing him. But what of the Great Mystery, Wakan Tanka, that Deity of the Tetons which came closest to God, the unknown power overarching the mysterious universe? He didn't know. He knew only that some profound spiritual force rising from the bowels of the rock, or descending from some stronghold of the sky, had brought him a moment of joy and gratitude. For this moment, at least, he was the slave of no lust. He was the captain of his soul. He didn't know who or what to thank.

CHAPTER 69

J. Roderick Crabtree made his way to the summit, having no trouble finding the well-worn path in the bleached light. It amused him to climb to the lair of the gods, and perch upon its crest like Zeus. The path spiraled around the slopes and ended at the domed peak, a place of lightning-blasted pines and shattered basalt. A stiff westerly breeze sluiced warmth from him but he ignored the chill. Not every man got to enter heaven and leave again. He paced the dome, peering over the moonwashed plains below.

He sat on a convenient ledge to hold court. Religion and superstition would be in the dock, and he'd be the judge. The thought delighted him. The indictment would be the perversion of Truth. He peered about him, looking for gods and spirits and found none.

"Now's your chance!" he cried, but no spirits materialized. He beheld only the moonswept Plains, rock, and wind. "If you exist, scalp me!"

He felt no tug upon his black hair, no incision of the scalping knife. He laughed.

"You're all guilty of fostering Superstition, and I condemn you to vanish from the mind of man. Off to the museums with you for the next ten thousand years."

He enjoyed that. He pulled a cigar from a canister in the breast pocket of his white linen suitcoat, and a lucifer from his hip pocket, and set the cigar aflame. The breeze whipped the smoke away.

He sat upon a rock overlooking a material universe devoid of design, the happenstance of random accidents over inconceivable eons of time, the laws of chemistry and physics playing out to form simple life, and ultimately complex life. Rarely had he felt so intoxicated with insight. His mind had turned as keen as a scalpel, slicing through to the only reality.

The real question was God. Paleontology had already begun to split asunder over that, and the split would deepen swiftly, especially since Charles Darwin and Alfred Russel Wallace had published simultaneous papers about the mechanisms of natural selection. Were all the creatures of the earth the product of a Divine Mind, producing archetypes and variations of the archetypes, or were they the result of happenstance, the survival and adaptation of those mutants better able to perpetuate themselves?

God, he thought, must have been a blunderer, considering all the blind alleys his work had led to: bizarre monsters; extinct species like Owen's dinosaurs or the beasts that lay in the wagon, other species unchanged since their first fossil records in Paleozoic rock, maybe even retrograde species working from the complex to the primitive.

Ah, how comfortable were the timid with a world governed by a benevolent Mind. Back in Charleston he could barely grasp it because man's design lay at every hand. But here—here!—the universe stood naked and undisturbed, except for a few aborigines, and the truth of creation slapped him with awesome force. He was strong because he had no illusions or delusions; truth would always be strength.

"Well, my friends, I find you guilty. Court adjourned." He regretted he had taken no prisoners.

The breeze kept eroding his comfort, and he decided to meander down. He reminded himself to tell Van Vliet that he'd seen no gods or demigods, and if one had presented itself, he would have caught it and stuffed it into his cigar tin for study under a microscope.

He doffed his planter's hat. "It's all been divine," he said. "You're sterling company—but a bit taciturn. Especially you, White Buffalo Maiden. I'd hoped to make your acquaintance. I admire beautiful women. If you ever want me, I'm at your service."

He puffed happily, the tip of his cheroot crackling and orange beyond his nose, and found the trail downward. He paused at its head, waiting for Wakan Tanka's lightning bolts, but none descended. After that he strolled downward, and discovered Van Vliet halfway down, peering dreamily over a moonswept panorama.

"Well, Van Vliet, I've been communing with divinity. Have you got your loot?"

"There is none."

"Of course there's some. Let's look for it. We've got some time."

"What'd you find up there?"

"I found nothing, Van Vliet. Here now, get that other nag and we'll go dig it all up. The medicine stuff's around here somewhere."

"Leave it alone, Crab."

"Ah! I perceive the meat in your skull has grown tender. No doubt because of the hole in your scalp."

"Let's go on back. I'm tired."

"Did you have a transcendent religious experience?

Hear voices? Maybe it was White Buffalo Maiden instructing you in chastity.''

''For a few minutes I didn't need anything. I owned myself.''

''Well, I don't know any ascetic divinities. You'll have to introduce me.''

Van Vliet didn't reply.

They left the holy mountain with empty panniers on their ponies, having found not so much as a medicine bundle dangling from a branch, and cut along a grassy flat hemmed by its great dark walls. They headed for their camp but were stopped suddenly by a dozen Indians rising out of the shadows with lances and drawn bows in hand.

The first arrow struck Van Vliet in the middle, catapulting him backward.

''I'm dead,'' he gasped.

The second arrow pierced Crabtree's right lung, rocking him back. His lungs quit drawing. His heart flailed wildly, driving blood up into his throat as he toppled. Another arrow seared through his belly, piercing his stomach and kidney before erupting through his back. It hurt. He couldn't breathe.

Something dark loomed over Crabtree and lifted his head by the hair. It hurt. He felt the bite of a knife cutting over his ear. He couldn't breathe.

Oh God, he thought as a cloud slid over the moon.

CHAPTER
70

Wood knew his colleagues had slipped out early in the night. He'd always been a fitful sleeper, never accustoming himself to the rigors of camp life. He had awakened and found them gone. He had known where they were going and had expected them to return by dawn. Now, with light piercing through the tan duck cloth, he knew they hadn't returned. He lay in his warm blankets, not wanting this day to proceed. Outside, the rhythms of nature seemed wrong. Too silent. Perhaps this September day he would die.

He sat up and pulled on his stockings. He laced his boots, scratched his great beard where it itched under his chin, and stepped into the gray light. Forty or fifty Teton Sioux men sat quietly beyond the wagons, many of them wrapped in trade blankets to ward off the sharp chill. They had obviously been waiting for him. Terror climbed swiftly up his throat, though he saw no weapons in hand, no war paint. He spotted Crowe sitting among them and Tooth-ache just behind, outside the circle.

He peered about, wanting to find Van Vliet and Crabtree. Perhaps the pair remained on the sacred mountain and these Tetons had come to protest. He hoped it would be no worse than that. Miss Huxtable had not yet arisen—at least he didn't see her, either.

"Professor," said Crowe, summoning him.

Wood walked warily to the council in the meadow just beyond the wagons. He knew at once these were great men of the Sioux, though they weren't decorated in any particular way. Beyond, in the morning mists, warriors held a large number of horses. Much to his astonishment he discovered Gracie sitting quietly just outside the circle, wrapped in a blanket like the rest.

She returned his gaze, looking somehow like a noblewoman at a funeral. Her blanket had fallen loose, revealing a snowy doeskin dress exquisitely quilled across its ample bodice. She wore high moccasins lined with rabbit fur. She looked like a queen, like Indian royalty, pampered and privileged and savoring every moment of it, power and pleasure lighting her eyes.

In spite of the peaceful tableau before him, Wood fought back terror..Something awful had happened. Gracie didn't smile. Neither did Rufus Crowe, who seemed subdued.

"Professor Wood, these here are some leaders of the Teton Sioux. Some chiefs and the *Wicasa Wakan*—the shamans, or Dreamers. Over there's Bear's Rib of the Oglala. You know Little Thunder of the Brulés. That one is Pizi, Gall, of the Hunkpapa. The next two are Tashunkopipape, Man Afraid of His Horses, and his son, Young Man Afraid of His Horses, of the Oglala. The next is Mahpialuta, Red Cloud, of the Bad Faces band of the Oglala. You've met Tatanka Yotanka, Sitting Bull. The young man next to him you've met—he's Short Bull. And also the young gentleman here, Sinte Galeska, Spotted Tail, of the Brulés. Beside him is American Horse of the Oglala. This is, in

short, an important council of the Teton Sioux nation. They
invite you to sit.''

It wasn't an invitation. Shakily, aching for a cup of coffee, Professor Wood settled to the cold earth. The sun
burned a hole in the northeastern horizon, turning the eastern facade of Mato Paha into fire. Wood waited. Bad, bad,
bad things were coming. No one produced a peace pipe.

Young Short Bull arose and cast aside his blanket. He
faced the sun, letting its orange light bathe his bare chest
and arms, and then he sang, while the rest listened solemnly.

Softly, Crowe translated.

> The blessings of Wakan Tanka are on the people;
> The sun warms us and grows the grass.
> My people are thankful!
> All the creatures on earth are thankful!

The young shaman recited the same prayer facing south,
then west, and last north, even as the sacred mountain
gathered the light into its bosom and glowed like a pyre.
It seemed a lovely prayer, celebrating the sun. Wood
sensed the reverence, sensed the spiritual nature of these
people, and the holiness of this moment. And yet he
squirmed with questions—and dread. Where were Van
Vliet and Crabtree?

He spotted Miss Huxtable peering from her tent in dishabille, looking alarmed. She vanished. Then, about when
the young shaman's prayer had ended, she emerged,
dressed, with a shawl wrapped tightly about her. She
walked slowly toward the circle, as if forcing her feet to
propel her, and edged quietly around the periphery, settling at last beside Toothache. Questions lit her eyes. She
caught Wood's glance, wanting explanations, but Wood
shook his head gently.

The sun-prayer done, the shaman settled himself within

the circle once again. These Sioux were more quiet than a convocation of cardinals. Or maybe a tribunal of hanging judges.

Little Thunder arose, dropped his blanket to the earth, and faced Wood. No chief among the Tetons had more reason to despise white men. He wore his hair in cloth-wrapped braids that whipped and bounced as he spoke.

Quietly, Rufus Crowe translated.

"He says they've always welcomed the *wasicu*—the white man—because he brought good things to trade with them. In the winters they opened their lodges to the trappers, and gave them their daughters. But the white man is not content to trade or be friends . . . He wants their land and game. He scorns the beliefs of the People. The Wasp, General Harney, he springs like a thousand wolves at dawn and kills women and children, and then makes a treaty with them, telling them they must not strike back, and must open their lands to more white men . . ."

Wood listened thoughtfully, knowing that Indian oratory would require that the whole case be made, point by point. Little Thunder's eyes snapped; his lips compressed in bitterness. Quietly, Crowe followed, his soft voice meliorating the harsh messages from the Brulé leader.

"Even so, they opened their lands to the great wise men, the learned old men, the readers of the books, knowing that all would be well, for their own adopted brother, and their own Dreamer—ah, myself—would guide you and see to it that you followed their customs. They opened their lands to you, the learned ones, to see for yourselves the terrible bones in the rocks of the Badlands. Some didn't like it that you would dig up the bones of the monsters that Wakan Tanka drove into the ground. But their brother, ah—Rufus Crowe—thought it'd bring them no harm."

Little Thunder paused, and then his voice turned low and biting, the outrage in it cleaving air like steam from an engine.

"He says the one that wished to examine the people, to talk with the old men and watch the women work and see how they live and how they govern themselves—this one surprised them. This one came to their burial grounds and robbed the dead, the *nagi*, of their possessions. They couldn't imagine such a thing. They would not let him have such things—but they would not punish him either. They warned him. They took the things away. They warned him again. Some of their people warned him. The trader, Picotte, at Fort Pierre, warned him. The guide—he means me—warned him. But he took the sacred possessions of the *nagi* anyway. And all he met warned him he must not climb the sacred mountain. It would mean his death."

Little Thunder stopped, letting that sink in. Then he began again, his voice staccato and his words tumbling out, his thoughts erupting from some fiery furnace within.

"He says this became a great matter for the Teton Lakota. He sent runners summoning the chiefs and headmen and the shamans. They knew that when you left their land you would go to Fort Union—and pass by the sacred mountain. They smoked and prayed to Wakan Tanka—and some of them wanted to kill you all. Others said that would only bring the blue-shirt soldiers down upon them, and their women and children would suffer . . . In his band lived Buffalo Woman, ah, Gracie—She Who Makes the Buffalo Come, and they asked her if you would leave quietly or if you would climb the sacred mountain. But she would not tell them."

Little Thunder glared disdainfully at the white men, and Crowe paused too. The indictment was almost complete. Wood knew for a surety what would be said next. "In the night they slipped away—the robber Van Vliet and the white-coat Crabtree, who traded Buffalo Woman to them for ponies. They watched them; they slid along silently and Crabtree and Van Vliet didn't see them. The white men climbed the mountain looking for more sacred things to take, knowing the penalty. They came down the mountain without any. They died.''

Little Thunder drew back an imaginary arrow in an imaginary bow; his muscles flexed and bulged, his fingers released the arrow, but his body remained rigid. Then, slowly, he returned from the remembered moment, and sat down.

Dead. It had all been building to this, but the word struck hard. J. Roderick Crabtree and Archimedes Van Vliet, dead. Two fine scholars dead, killed by the aborigines. Good men dead, both of them better scientists than he'd ever be. What a horror to carry out to the waiting world. And there he sat among the savages who did it. Dread and loathing seized him. Let their savage race die away; let them become as extinct as his titanothere. He glared at them, seeing not mortals but brutes.

Candace froze, her face a ruin, and then sobbed, as great convulsions of sorrow racked her. She snuffled back the wetness that slid down her cheeks, and rocked quietly, moaning to herself. Wood sternly refused to cry. Dead. Warned and warned and warned, and now dead. A desolation pooled in him. His colleagues cold and senseless and mute, the work of lifetimes spilled out of their minds even as their blood spilled from their bodies.

Little Thunder produced a japanned canister that contained Crabtree's cigars, and handed it to Crowe. Then he handed Crowe a Barlow knife that had belonged to Van Vliet, the very knife that had sawed open scores of burial bundles and cut loose a treasure. Crowe and the chief talked briefly in Sioux.

''He says that's all that was found on either one. We'll not see the remains. They can't lie within sight of Mato Paha. They've been taken far away where no white man'll ever see them, to lie with the under-earth spirits and demons.''

''Is there no other proof? What am I to tell—''

Little Thunder seemed to grasp the English. He beckoned to one of the warriors standing out among the horses. The man led two familiar horses forward, each bearing crudely made panniers on a packsaddle. Crabtree's. Proof of guilt, proof of death.

"I suppose they took those up there to fetch the holy things, Professor Wood."

Cyrus Wood nodded, suddenly too weary to think. He felt old. Bitter toward Crabtree and Van Vliet; bitter toward their murderers. The rising sun sent shafts into the flat, driving off the chill. The holy mountain lost its fiery glow and assumed its daylight colors, slate gray and dark green. It would have been an ordinary day.

"Very well. What is to be our fate? Are we next?"

The guide consulted again, and eventually had an answer. "He says they're keeping the possessions of the *nagi*, the spirits of the dead. They'll keep that wagon too, and drive the entire lot back to the burial grounds on the White River. Give them back to their owners. You and Miss Huxtable and Missus Rumley are free to leave if you leave at once and don't waste time. I'll be taking you. Toothache, she'll come along and help us. I'm to deliver you to the factor there at the post, Robert Meldrum, and tell the story exactly as it happened, and ask Meldrum not to bring down the blue-shirts. They see this as entirely justifiable and want the facts presented that way. I do too."

"What about Van Vliet's private possessions?"

Crowe smiled slowly. "I'll ask."

In short order, warriors lifted Van Vliet's trunks out of the wagon and deposited them before Wood. Chief Little Thunder watched, a sardonic lift to his lips, his thoughts transparent.

Wood sighed, feeling like a drowning man gulping air. Then, inspired, he addressed Little Thunder. "Mister Crowe, tell him we'll use some of Crabtree's ponies to

carry Van Vliet's things—but the free ones . . . I'll give
to the Brulés. With my apologies.''

"I suppose that's a good thing to do.''

"I'd like to conduct a small service for the departed. I
can't bear to leave this place without one.''

"Professor, the one thing any Plains Indian understands
about white men is religion. Any minister, any blackrobe,
as they call priests, travels through here with their blessing. Father de Smet did, all of his life. You conduct your
funeral, and I'll promise that every one will understand
and respect it.''

"A funeral for an atheist and an apostate,'' said Miss
Huxtable, coming out of some sort of trance.

"Miss Huxtable, the mercies of God are beyond mortal
understanding. I will commend two distinguished American scientists to His care, and we—you and Mrs. Rumley
and I—shall pay our respects.''

CHAPTER
71

Cyrus Billington Wood was an impressive sight, Candace thought. He wore a black clawhammer coat, the packing creases still showing; his great gray beard made a woolly apron over his white shirt. Gold pince-nez perched on his bony nose, enabling him to read passages from the King James in his hand. This was not the man who had debarked at Fort Pierre three months ago. That man had possessed dignity but not strength. This man had both, and more: a charity of soul that pleased her.

His impromptu oration dwelled on each of the dead, finding no fault in men who had either laughed at him or defied him. Rufus Crowe was translating again, this time turning English into Sioux for the benefit of the chiefs and shamans who stood quietly by.

Gracie, looking solemn, stood close, nodding with the flow of words rising from some mystic fountain in the professor. Great tears slid down Gracie's brown cheeks, tears for her tormentor. Was there something about Crabtree that Candace didn't grasp? Wood was dwelling not on

Crabtree's private temperament, but upon the man's great contributions to science; not upon a slaveholder's debasement of another mortal, but upon Crabtree's grandeur of mind and keen intellect.

How beautiful Gracie looked in her finery. But the sorrows of her life still etched her solemn face; the sorrows of life denied and stunted and wounded. What on earth had she become to these people, that she should attend high councils? And why, oh why, were tears steadily welling from her soft brown eyes as Cyrus Wood commended the souls of J. Roderick Crabtree and Archimedes Van Vliet to the Almighty?

Candace marveled, and wondered how Crowe could translate these things to the Sioux chiefs, who listened attentively, glancing occasionally at Wood. But the guide seemed up to the occasion and never at a loss for the Siouan expressions.

Wood turned at last to the promises of life hereafter, perhaps for the sake of the handful who could grasp his words. He opened his Bible to a place where a purple ribbon divided the pages: ''I know that my redeemer liveth, and that he shall stand at the latter day upon the earth: And though, after my skin, worms destroy this body, yet in my flesh shall I see God.'' And then he found another verse: ''Behold, I show you a mystery,'' he read. ''We shall not all sleep, but we shall all be changed, in a moment, in the twinkling of an eye, at the last trump.''

This man of science had no trouble at all reconciling his faith and his learning. Wood concluded with a prayer, his words echoing through the quiet like the last note of taps from a bugle. The day had barely begun and yet it seemed as long as a week.

She waited for Gracie to rub away her tears, then approached.

''Miss Gracie, it's so good to see you.''

''Miss Huxtable, you got to let me pull myself together.

That old devil, he was all I ever knowed. From the time I was a girl to just a few days ago.''

"You cared for him, then.''

"I hated his old dear heart.''

"You've wept for him.''

"Miss Huxtable—you don't understand. He was all I had.''

Dimly Candace did understand. We come to love the devil we know. "And now?'' she asked softly.

Gracie smiled suddenly, sunlight blossoming across her oaken face. "I'm still a slave. But a boss queen slave,'' she said. "They call me Buffalo Woman. They say I look like an old buffalo, with my brown skin and this hair, and this nose and eyes. I think big old buffalo are the ugliest things walkin' the earth.'' She smiled. "I never was pretty nohow.''

"They honor you for that?''

"Oh, they's more. They think I'm *wakan*, I got powers. Mister Crowe, he tells me to let 'em think that. They tell me, Make the buffalo come, and I went up on a hill and I called the buffalo, and next morning they all came. After that—anything I wanted. I tell 'em, dress me up fine and get me warm blankets and a good horse.'' She laughed, pleased with her new status.

"You sound happy. But you're still a slave?''

"Oh, I'm in bondage, all right. They got me. But no slave of the white men ever got what I got. Oh, Miss Huxtable, I miss a lot of things, like a house and a place to set down. There isn't a chair in the village. This here's hard on a old woman. Them skin lodges—when winter comes, I'm gonna be so cold I don't feel my toes no more.''

"Do they make you work?''

"Oh, yes, every old person works. It take a heap of it to keep a village going. But they give me easy stuff because I get so stiff, especially in the cold. I sew and mind the fires, and watch the boys and girls.''

"Would you like your freedom?" Impulsively, Candace thought she might purchase it somehow.

Gracie didn't hesitate. "Oh, no, Miss. You leave me be! They take care of me. Where would an old woman like me go? With the master dead and all? I like these people. I'm gettin' to speak a little Sioux and I tell big old stories to the babies. I'll be all right if it don't get too cold.''

Around her, this impromptu council of the Teton Sioux nation was breaking up. Wood was solemnly giving horses to Little Thunder. Toothache was breaking camp.

A sudden sadness leapt up in Candace. "I . . . don't suppose I'll ever see you again, Miss Gracie.''

"Oh, don't . . .''

"I'm going to leave my address with you. If you're ever in trouble, write—ah, have someone write me. Please!''

"What do you care for some old black woman?" Gracie's voice crackled with some submerged hatred.

"I care! I always did! I love you!''

"Well, mercy sakes, you're a strange one. You got no sense. You git now. You go home to England.''

They hugged, and Candace turned away to conceal her tears. "Oh, blast!" she muttered.

Behind her, Gracie scowled, her head high and the corners of her lips low.

CHAPTER 72

Venerable Fort Union shimmered across the Missouri, its ancient cottonwood palisades bleached by the harsh sun. It stood in an arid country of red and yellow rock not half so attractive as what they had passed through. On the far shore boatmen, alerted by Rufus Crowe's shots, were loosening the keelboat. They would pole across the great green river and board the wagons and horses and people who waited on the south shore, burdened with fossils and news.

The Smithsonian party, or what was left of it, had struck northward from Bear Butte through verdant and hilly country drained by the Belle Fourché, to the Little Missouri. They had crossed sweeping plains, worked around badlands, and reached the mysterious Yellowstone, rising in legendary mountains far to the southwest. They had followed the Yellowstone to its confluence with the Missouri, where the famous old post stood.

Rufus Crowe, true to his word, had not let them stop to collect fossils, thus aborting what had been planned for the last leg of the journey. Even so, he hadn't objected to evening strolls, or marking sites, if it could be done without delaying their passage through the tribal homeland of his people. That had yielded a number of sites, each carefully recorded. Crowe had told them that they were watched; but never were they harassed. None of them felt like doing much. Miss Huxtable had turned silent and solemn. Her flesh seemed pale beneath the summer's tan. Her gaze often lifted to horizons.

The keelboat pleased Professor Wood's knowing New England eye. The approaching one looked to be about sixty or seventy feet long, with a beam of sixteen or eighteen feet, and a decked hold perhaps four feet deep. A cabin rose in its center, with foot passage to either side. As the boat closed, the sound of spoken French arrived with it. The man operating the sweep rudder seemed to be in command. *"A bas les perches,"* he said, and the voyageurs on both sides lowered their long poles, which had a socket that fitted into their armpits, and walked aft, pushing the vessel forward. *"Levez les perches,"* he cried, and the men lifted the poles and trotted forward to the bow as the boat's momentum slowed.

"Ah, welcome," cried the bilingual steersman. *"Messieurs et . . . "* They were gaping at Miss Huxtable as if she were an apparition.

The steersman brought the boat almost to shore, and the swarthy voyageurs leaped into the water to anchor it. It took them little time to position a wide stage to the abrupt bank, and urge the nervous horses, unhitched from the wagons, aboard. Then with brute strength and an odd Gallic merriment, they pushed and dragged the heavy wagons up the stage and onto the deck, maneuvered them, and chocked them there. Candace Huxtable never escaped their attention all the while.

An hour later they stood on the left bank beneath the brooding brow of the old post, and Professor Wood beheld the seat of a great American empire, the American Fur Company, chartered in 1808 by John Jacob Astor and continued by the Chouteaus of St. Louis. The strategic fortress looked seedy now, with the beaver trade long gone and the buffalo-robe trade in decline.

A burly man pushed through a throng of engagés and Indians to greet them. "Ah, Meldrum here. You're early! We were looking for you in a week or so!" He spotted Candace. "Now, bless me, this must be Miss Huxtable. The *Spread Eagle* brought us that bit of news last June!"

"Professor, please introduce us. This man's too familiar with strange women," said Mrs. Rumley.

Wood made the introductions as Robert Meldrum surveyed the women with keen interest. "You've been a long time in the field, my ladies. I fathom that you'd like the comforts of a hot bath and a spot of tea, eh? We've some fair Assiniboin ladies here"—he waved at several tall, pretty Indian women decked out in crinolines and hoop-skirts—"to help you settle in."

Mrs. Rumley pursed her lips.

"Why, look at those Clydesdales. That's a sight for this bairn. I haven't seen the like since I boarded the clipper at Aberdeen," he said, watching Rufus Crowe lead them down the wobbling stage to the bank. "And a bonny pair, too. Nothing like them in all the Northwest. Whose are they?"

"Mine, Mister Meldrum. And shortly, Mister Crowe's."

"Yours? Yours now? Well of course. You're the Cambridge lass. Well, we'll keep them for a time, though hay's scarce. Say, Professor Wood, where're the rest, eh? Coming along in a few days, I suppose."

"No, Mister Meldrum. They're dead."

Robert Meldrum's face turned bleak. "I think you'll want to tell me, eh? I've a decanter of scotch in the cottage."

"I'd like Mister Crowe to join us, sir."

"Yes, of course, of course. My old dear Rufus."

Around them swarmed a motley crowd of breeds, French engagés, Indians of all sorts and descriptions, and sweating clerks in black frock coats. Meldrum corralled Crowe and led his guests through the huge double gates and into a crowded yard, toward a shake-roofed mansion that looked as if it had been transported whole from St. Louis. Within was a wallpapered parlor, as well furnished as any in the East. The kings of the upper Missouri lived well indeed. Wordlessly, Meldrum dashed whiskey into tumblers and added water.

"Dead, you say? *Dead?*"

"Killed by the Sioux at Bear Butte almost three weeks ago."

"The War Department will want to know of it. The pesky Sioux again. Have the bloody Brulés forgotten Harney already?"

"I want to talk about that, Mister Meldrum."

"Mister Crowe, they're your people and you'll defend them. Perhaps I should hear Professor Wood first, eh?"

Wood obliged. He saw no reason to conceal the conduct of Archimedes Van Vliet. He described the scaffold-robbing. He described the warnings of the Brulés, and the trader, Picotte, at Fort Pierre. He described Rufus Crowe's warnings about the safety of the entire party, and finally Wood's own flat prohibition when they reached Bear Butte. He told about the moonlight trip up the mountain and down, as described by the Sioux, and the punishments that followed. And finally the impromptu council of the Sioux nation, attended by several of their great chiefs, and the indictment of Little Thunder.

"Mister Meldrum," said Crowe, "my people charged me with telling the whole story on their behalf, but Professor Wood has done it. I have nothing to add."

Meldrum stared out the window thoughtfully. Wood

knew that he was the real government here; the fur company, not the United States Army, ruled the Northwest. If he lifted his hand, the Army would act; if he didn't, the commissioner of Indian affairs would probably accept Meldrum's judgment.

"Tell me about Miss Huxtable," Meldrum said.

"Why, sir, she's a proper Englishwoman, daughter of a distinguished naturalist. She's a bit of a bluestocking, and I'll tell you I was dead set against her. I did all I could to discourage her attachment to this expedition. But she's comported herself with dignity, and her research is invaluable—a contribution."

"Would you have behaved any differently if the women weren't present?"

"I confess I would have worried less about Van Vliet's collecting. It was all for the sake of his ethnology, you know."

"Mister Meldrum, I warned Doctor Van Vliet right sharply that he was endangering the women," Crowe said.

"So, actually, the presence of the women made you more cautious. Without them, you might have gone along with Van Vliet's reckless conduct."

Wood felt chagrined. "I fear that is so, sir."

"Perhaps their presence saved your lives."

"I hadn't thought of it that way."

"I'm seeing it that way, Professor Wood. Your colleague stabbed at the heart of their religion. And perhaps you did too, digging up those fossils. Now tell me about Doctor Crabtree. What did he do to deserve this fate, eh?"

"He climbed the holy mountain, sir. Perhaps to mock the gods. He had that in him."

Meldrum stared into the yard again, and downed the last of his scotch. "I traded with the Crows for years, you know. Up the Yellowstone. If there's one thing a man learns fast, it's to respect the beliefs of the Plains Indians.

Everything they do is governed by their beliefs, their spirits, their myths, their dreams. It sounds to me like the Sioux were patient, even under the worst sort of provocations. Do you see it that way?"

"I do. I've no complaint against them."

"Professor Wood, how would you like all this to be made known to the world, eh?"

"I wouldn't. I'm not one for falsehoods, and I'm not one for provoking a national outrage and starting a war against people defending their holy place. I grieve them, sir—two men of outstanding merit in their field. And the country will too."

"Gentlemen, I'll draft a report to the commissioner of Indian affairs in St. Louis, and ask you to read it and attach your corrections and observations. It'll go down the river on the keelboat with you. It'll be confidential. How you deal with the public will be up to you, but I'd just as soon the government smoothed over this business, and the War Department kept out of it."

"Sir, I can't conceal the truth from the Smithsonian, or our colleagues."

"I don't expect you to, Professor. Do your duty. Mine is to prevent another war. And—I might say—make the whole area safe for further exploration, mapping, geological studies, and of course your paleontological work. Are we of the same mind?"

"I'm grateful, sir. Your discretion will bless my people," Crowe said.

"I have no love of your Sioux, Rufus. No tribe's more relentless and ruthless. The poor Crows have been driven out of their homelands because of the Sioux. And the Pawnee and Assiniboin. Show me a Sioux warrior and I'll show you a man who knows no mercy."

"I understand that, Mister Meldrum—and I'm able to add some small caution to their councils."

Meldrum smiled. "You hold the tail of the tiger, Rufus"

CHAPTER
73

After the incredible luxury of a hot bath, Candace selected a bottle-green velveteen from the bottom of her trunk, just the dress to ward off the sharp chill of the October evening. In spite of all the excitement and comfort of the old fur post, with its bevy of Assiniboin servants, she felt a certain melancholia—the English Disease, she thought wryly. Had the American wilds witched her so much? The thought of leaving on the keelboat in the morning mists cut keenly through her euphoria. It pleased her to be here, and safe, and in possession of a great treasure that would cast light on aching questions. The Duke of Wellington had put it so well: Nothing except a battle lost can be half so melancholy as a battle won.

She found Rufus Crowe waiting for her out in the crowded yard, and together, as if by prearrangement—though no word had been spoken of it—they strolled past the redolent warehouse sheltering heaps of baled buffalo robes, past the smithy and kitchen and engagés' barracks, past the trading room bright with blankets and hatchets, knives and awls, out through the great worn gates sagging on their iron hinges, and into the lavender twilight.

"They close the gates at dusk, but I imagine they'll let us in," he said. "You can always get them to open if you're a white man."

"Are you sure? Are we safe?"

"I'm sure. This here is neutral ground. These are old enemies—Blackfeet, River Crows, Assiniboin, Cree, northern Sioux—getting along because the company won't trade if they cause trouble anywhere close to the post."

She clutched a white crocheted shawl to her, uncertain of that. She'd seen death only weeks before, and it had stamped her perception of this harsh land and its aborigines forever.

As if to compound her worries, a crowd of Indians of all sorts, solemn children, curious women, bold warriors, trailed along, studying the white woman, something they'd never seen before.

"Will they—bother us?"

"Curious is all. I've seen a white woman only once or twice all the years I've been on the borders. They've likely seen none at all."

On their left, ten or fifteen feet below, the mysterious Missouri hurried along on its way across the continent. The northern evening had a pleasant aspect, open and clear, with the first star—a yellow planet—looming in the shaded lavender of the afterglow. She sucked in the dry air, and didn't want to leave. It intoxicated her, this wild place, the tang of sagebrush on the curling night breeze, the silvery ripple of the cottonwood leaves. The bitter-sweetness of the moment tore at her heart.

She found his rough hand and held it tight. He turned to her, and she saw the ache in his eyes.

"Miss Huxtable," he said shyly, "did you find what you came for?"

"Oh, yes! Eleven oreodonts! Most of them unknown

species. I'll have so much to do. They'll all be shipped to the Woodwardian Museum at Cambridge. My father's friend Adam Sedgwick'll help me clean and analyze them. And then the writing begins.''

''Did you expect more?''

''No, Mister Crowe. I expected less. I didn't know whether I could do it. But I did! I think only two or three are alike. The rest, oh, the rest, Mister Crowe, will help us understand specialization. Why, one even had claws! One is almost five feet long. And I've collected enough material—it'll be a book before I'm done.''

''I'd like to see it—when it's published.''

''Of course I'll send it.''

''You're going to name all the new ones?''

''Yes, that's my privilege.'' She turned to him, smiling. ''I don't remember the Latin word for crows—*corvidae*, maybe—but I'll find out.''

He said nothing. He seemed, actually, to be brimming with some awful sadness. And somehow they had to say good-bye.

''And how was your summer, Mister Crowe?''

''I'm sorry I didn't bring you all here safely. I failed. Those deaths'll eat on me. I could've done more.''

''I think we're each responsible for ourselves. You warned them. Others warned them. The choice was theirs, not yours.''

''Reason never laid bad feeling to rest. Miss Huxtable.''

''What'll you do next?''

''I'll go get Professor Wood's titanothere and haul it over to Fort Pierre and get it crated up. Then—I'm hoping to be of use to other expeditions. If none come along, I'm thinking to go dig by myself. I could dig them up and ship them back, and maybe some of them back there—Doctor Leidy, for example—might pay a bit. I'd like to dig up every fossil in the Badlands. I'd like to find a dinosaur.

This Missouri River country right around here—it's Cretaceous rock. I've learned to tell. I check the fossils.

"I'd like to be the Fossil Man. I'd like to ship a hundred oreodonts to Cambridge, England, Woodwardian Museum, care of Miss Huxtable. I'd like to run twenty titanotheres into the Harvard Yard and park them in front of the professor's office. I'll be the Bone Man. I know what to look for, how to dig, and how to map the strata and other fossils in it. I'll put those Clydesdales and that wagon into the service of every paleontologist east of here. I'll keep six gross of ammonites on my shelf; two pecks of turtles, three for a dollar. Dinosaurs a hundred dollars plus shipping."

He was laughing softly, but she discovered tears on his cheeks.

"Mister Crowe! Don't joke! Would you do that?"

"For you I would, Miss Huxtable."

"Would you *really* do that?"

"Yes, for as long as you want. As long as you care. Forever, if that means just one letter a year from you on the steamboat. For as long as I have breath and strength to dig. For as long as you remember me."

She stopped him, and pulled him into her arms. "I won't forget you, Rufus Crowe. Not ever."

He drew her to him, his arms enfolding her, his hands saying tender things.

"I love you, Miss Huxtable."

"I love you, Mister Crowe."

"I imagine we're both married—to something or someone."

"Yes, I am. And I think you are too."

"Would you—may I kiss you good-bye?"

She smiled.

He kissed her on her lips, and it was very hard to let go.